RISE
THE
MOON

RISE THE MOON

A NOVEL

JACOB KOCKEN

Copyright © 2024 Jacob Kocken

Printed in the United States of America.

ISBN: 979-8-218-45790-7

All rights reserved.

This is a work of fiction. Names, characters, businesses, places, events, and incidents are either the products of the author's imagination or used in a fictitious manner. Any resemblance to actual persons, living or dead, or actual events is purely coincidental.

To my parents Ronald and Tammy Kocken
who decided to undertake the impossible
task of raising children.

RISE
THE
MOON

Claude

IN A SMALL, MOUNTAINSIDE CABIN deep in the Sierra Nevada, the woman discovered pain. It was long into the night, but the darkness of wild Californian forests could not shroud from her the tearing flesh which flickered in the firelight of a dozen candles. She was giving birth, and her husband heard the ordeal through the walls while he put their first-born down to rest in the adjoining room. This labor had been hard and quite unlike anything she had experienced before. It had come on sudden and awful. Her husband had paused with curious awe and almost failed to fetch the midwife in time; it was an arduous climb down and back up the mountain. But help was recruited for this second birth in the form of old friends, a mother and father in their own right, intimate with the miracle. And now, as screams pierced the timber, the man was grateful he was not alone.

When the older daughter was secured in bed, the man returned to find a second one screeching through her first breath. The infant's cry was harsh, but when she was placed in her mother's trembling arms, that terror did diminish.

The man spent a good hour admiring the child. This father, Claude Pollard, had a lazy eye that always looked a touch inward at his nose. It was blurry with close-up things, so Claude spent the whole time here with one eye closed, watching his baby with the good one. Strings of black hair already covered her head, making the porcelain, heart-shaped face more radiant still. She was just as an infant is supposed to be.

Before long, the sky was breaking orange. The man left his sleeping girls and came into the communal part of the little house. The midwife sat there talking with her own husband. Her name was

RISE THE MOON

Willa, and lines of toil rimmed the old woman's eyes. Another observer may have found them lost among the crow's feet in much the same way as an elephant's sagacious expression blends into the webs that crease the face of any wise beast. Claude saw clear as day those marks of exhaustion even through her usual aged wrinkles. The same was true of the midwife's husband whose veins still pulsed beneath jowly skin, sagging with age over taut muscles and touched with a permanent red glow from a long life of midday sun. They were the senior, though they referred often to Claude with patronal deference.

"Jasper," said the new father. "To the valley."

Two axes hung on the wall near the front door. The men took up their tools, leaving the wall bare except for the hooks and one lonely rifle. The two friends marched down the mountainside drive to a plateau where a forest of sugar pines rose so high they seemed to puncture the heavens.

"How's the baby?"

"She's healthy," said Claude. "All's well and level." The relief on his friend's face was plain.

"Mhm. Good. That's just fine then. Did you name her?"

"Anna Lee."

They reached a small clearing in the woods. Several trees had already been felled and their pieces squared in the midst of the valley to form the beginnings of a small log chapel. The man picked out another trunk, the tallest in sight and remarkably slender for its stature, and the two of them set to bringing it down.

"Your wife," said Jasper. "She's alright?" His axehead split the bark of the tree. It cracked again and bent as the steel was retracted, sticking out like a splintered bone until Claude's axe came swinging from the other side, gouging again and bursting the loose pieces from the body.

"She felt this one, Jasper. That's for sure."

"It's better that way. Things are only worth the price you pay for them."

"Don't disgrace on Nancy for going easy. She is a gift from the Lord."

"And this new one?"

"A gift," Claude declared. "I feel the same blessing today as

JACOB KOCKEN

when Nana was born."

"Does that mean you'll uproot again? Move to a taller mountain and take the rites a second time?"

Claude shook his head. "I moved here to give up a life of sin. In the eyes of the Lord, fulfillment of one true thing is as good as infinite. It's the truth of heart that makes the difference, not the echo of repetition. That's why Christ had only to be hung up once for every sin of every soul on Earth."

Jasper gave him a weathered, thin-lipped smile. "They're talking down there already. Your chapel should fill the moment the capstone steadies. But I'll say again, Claude. It seems to me the Lord has touched you as you say. He's touched you, but it's with His closed hand, and I don't know that any man is wise enough to divine these things. Omen or auspice, I think signs are for getting our attention and attention only. Just to say that whatever comes after is of importance and you better take heed. That's my piece."

"I know your piece, Jasper. But the Lord has consumed me. I love my girls. That is divination."

Something snapped in the woods then, and the two men caught sight of a figure coming their way. The night was at an end, but a blue-grey shadow still covered every peak and valley here. Claude Pollard faced his companion with a look of inquiry. Jasper shook his head one curt, decisive time.

The one coming through the forest was a stranger. He was dressed in grime from a long day's walk, and when he saw that they stood there his feet began to stumble. He came at a near run, stopping just several feet before the two of them.

"Is one of you Father Pollard?" The man's voice was hoarse and dry.

Claude stepped forward. He asked the man what he wanted.

"My wife is sick," he said. When he spoke the last word his voice broke, and it was clear the weariness of his constitution was due in no part to the physical demands of his journey. "She's been failing, and nothing works. It's been a month, Father. She's turned gray. But I know Randy Simmons. I know him, and I know his wife. I know them both, and he told me what you did. I saw what happened to her, and now she's walking all on her own. He told me to come. Randy Simmons, Father. I know, Father. I know."

RISE THE MOON

Claude came to the man and laid a hand on his shoulder, telling him to hush. Then he pointed toward the four walls of the unfinished chapel.

"Can you bring her up the mountain?" he asked. The man nodded feverishly. "Bring her here tomorrow at this time and lay her on the ground inside those walls. Then you must walk back down to the base of the mountain alone, and when you return it will be done. But I cannot have you there. Understand?"

The man nodded, his hopeful countenance rising.

"Say it," said Claude. "You'll take yourself back down the mountain. You won't be there." The hope in the man's expression fell partially into consternation. His attention flicked to the pastor's drifting lazy eye. But he waited only a beat.

"I promise," he said. "I'll leave her in your privacy. I'll walk back down the mountain."

"An hour should be long enough," said Claude. "Bring her."

"Yes, Father," said the man. "Yes, Father." He affirmed his understanding once again as he stumbled, running back in the direction he'd come. Each one of his heavy, desperate steps struck the ground with audible force. Twigs and acorns popped underfoot until the man had covered some hundred yards and disappeared beneath the mountain slope. Claude turned back to Jasper who stood there solemn.

"You disagree with that?"

"I don't like all of it."

"Would you send him away?" asked Claude.

"No."

They chopped in silence for some time, Claude on the live tree and Jasper on other raw, fallen logs. At long last, a great crown of light lashed up off the eastern horizon as the ever-seeing Cyclops rose. The breaking morning was a bright, hot red that bled over the cool blue mountain shadows, blending earth and heavens on the horizon. Claude followed the long line of this mixture as far as he could see, silently awed by how it somehow touched at once every point of the great circle all around him. Claude pitied himself as he did each morning that amidst the ubiquitous majesty his gaze could only light on one point at a time. First one mountain peak, then another, then a wavering tree, and finally the sun directly who scolded

JACOB KOCKEN

him, the brazen voyeur. What might he gain, Claude wondered, if permitted to view it all at once, God's blueprinted plan? But try in vain it only hurt his head.

"A man so holy he even crosses his eyes," said Jasper, mimicking the face of his teacher with converging pupils. Claude smiled. His right eye straightened out while the lazy left one remained askew. Then the two went back to work for several quiet minutes.

Sweat was prickling on all the sides of Claude's head when he saw his friend moving into the forest. His eye was trained on the ground some ways away. When Jasper came to where he'd been looking his figure stooped down at the knees. He came back up holding something, and when he returned to the clearing Claude saw it for a stone big and round as a bowling ball that he carried in one hand.

"Your daughter loves their shine," said Jasper. "I expect the new one will too. Birthday present?"

Claude smiled. "Let's keep it for the chapel. We'll take the girls out to find their own some day. It's more magical that way." Jasper nodded and dropped his treasure into the dirt. He took up his axe again and struck hard with whetted steel. There was a dull crack from beneath the singing axe head. Jasper's boot kicked at the broken stone. The two halves unfurled, showing pointed shards of amethyst gleaming in the dawn, a thousand geometric ridges rising and falling like little lilac Sinais.

"Very good," said Claude.

Jasper marched both pieces over to the unfinished building. He laid them down amongst a collection of others against the inside wall. Then he returned to his axe, and the two went on chopping.

Suddenly, there was a profound crack that moved the ground, and Jasper dropped his task to watch the wavering pine. Claude had tried to cut it toward the clearing, but the weight of the trunk decided otherwise and tipped down sidelong into the forest. They braced for a crash, but the tree was stopped halfway down, wedged in the crook of another's sturdy branch.

"Damn," said Jasper. "There goes an hour's sweat. Unless you chop through it halfway up it won't roll out. That catch is clean."

But Claude did not respond. He seemed struck by swelling emotion. His eyes moved back and forth over the half-fallen tree.

RISE THE MOON

He put a hand up before him as if measuring something in the distance. Then he retreated into the clearing. When he was fifty yards back he turned and faced the site again.

"What is it?" asked Jasper when he came out to where his friend stood looking with an angled neck. The preacher's good eye was trained on the half-fallen tree while his lazy one was stuck on the vertical. Claude raised his finger and traced the dimensions of the cross. The aim of the ascending sun neared this axis and paused on its march to seem hanging by its most prominent rays as they stretched out here and there toward the beam. And then, unseen before as it was outshined by its fraternal twin, Claude made out distinctly the pale, dampened majesty of the moon encroaching on the blazing solar edge. These eyes of God moved imperceptible as the hour hand until each had half of the other in its possession, the fire relinquishing some of its heat and the quiet lunar rock wakening with redness like long-slept sclera.

"Another sign from the heavens," said Claude. "Think it's just for my baby?" Jasper did not answer but looked with awe upon the scene. "If only I'd had the faith when Nancy was born, perhaps I'd have looked up to see that token. And look at this." He gestured to the pine they'd toppled. "The two tallest trees on the whole line and they catch each other just like that. You might be able to see it from the base of the mountain. Every church needs a crucifix at the head, Jasper. That's another touch of the Lord. Isn't it beautiful? When I die, Jasper, I want to be buried at the base of those trees."

Sweat dripped down Claude's face from chopping. The axe had remained in his hand, but he dropped it now. The razor's edge cut into the earth and the handle stuck up like an empty signpost beside their assemblage of chapel logs. Jasper pulled his gaze from the celestial dance and looked long at the face of his young friend. The dark hairs on that chin glowed gold and showed clear as the forest pines whose bark marked lines of providential plans in cuneiform scribble.

"The hands of God light heavy on you, Claude. I said I don't like it all, but when the angels arraign me and mine, we won't be surprised to hear that Claude Pollard is still on Earth and probably won't ever die."

1.
Ira

IT WAS A SUNDAY AT the end of summer; the humid, dull kind of day in the shadow of something large, the kind that tends to slip the grip of history. In this momentous wake, Ira and Furke sat on the latter's living room carpet stacking houses of cards and watching them fall whenever one of the countless, heavy bags of luggage shook the floorboards from the next room over.

Furke, whom Ira had befriended so early in life that their origin together was lost in a receding tide, had a gangly body and a wide-mouthed, froggish face that along with his arms and legs was heavily dappled in red-brown freckles. Furke's teeth were crooked. He was being raised by a single mother, and there were more urgent things to claim their funds than braces and retainers. As a result, he had developed a tendency not to smile in public, and despite a later outgoing and gregarious disposition was generally snubbed by those with immaculate reputations, relegating him to the class of children known for carrying cigarettes and spending all their extra time at school in detention. This prejudice against him was not entirely without cause. A strong curiosity tended to take him into places unknown, and because the uncouth gets hidden away, Furke was often found feeling out the darker corners of the world. On the other hand, he was not exclusively interested in the crude and base. In addition to his habits of smoking and trespassing, Furke did have fascinations of a nobler sort. Such things however, pale in scandalous comparison to the trouble he caused, and in consequence, were not the kinds of things people remembered.

RISE THE MOON

Furke was quite different in these aspects from Ira who was known to most everyone as a kind and quiet lad. He was of average height and, taking after his father Saul, was regarded as handsome enough. The father and son looked almost entirely alike except for the large, perking ears of his mother's side as well as her rich chestnut hair which grew ambitiously and flowed always down below Ira's shoulders. All the women in that line, and now one of the men, had the same glossy, angelic follicles.

Because they shared so few aspects of character it was clear to everyone that what Furke and Ira each admired was truly the other's personal soul and not simply the reflection of one's own thoughts and interests which indeed forms a great portion of society. Between them was a bond unique and familial that no triviality could sunder.

They were in the midst of a conversation. Talk had been dour lately for several reasons. Ira had the five of clubs in his hand and he looked at its face instead of his friend's as he spoke. He worked to make his posture nonchalant, and in doing so leaned into his tower of cards which fell and in turn collapsed the project of the other architect.

"Sorry," said Ira.

"It's alright. Stop apologizing so much," said Furke. "So, what does your old man do all day?"

"I don't know," said Ira. "Not a lot. Mom says he's finding himself."

"He could be a baseball coach again," said Furke. "Fall is coming, and you still can't throw a curveball."

"Yeah," said Ira. "But baseball only lasts a few months."

"I always thought he was a mope to tell the truth," said Furke.

"It used to be like anger. About the hotel and how stupid the bosses were. He did their jobs back before we moved. So, he should be in charge, you know?"

"That's why they fired him?"

Ira shrugged. "But now he's not angry. It's something else."

"Fired." Furke was musing. "You need money for food. And property taxes."

"My mom still works."

"That's right, your mom's a dentist."

JACOB KOCKEN

"She's a dental assistant."
"How much do they make?"
"I don't know."
"Less than the dentist?"
"Probably."
"Still," said Furke, "thank God she has a job."

Ira's budding tower of cards fell again, and as the clubs and diamonds fluttered down, he took to his feet. "I need to use the bathroom," he said. Ira turned the corner into the hallway where he passed by the bedroom of Furke's sister, Bella. Her back was to the open doorway. She was methodically pulling clothes out of the closet and shutting them into luggage bags on the bed which was now only a bare mattress, blanket, and one pink pillow. There was a second girl in the room, Connie, Bella's friend. They worked together packing Bella's things and speaking in rapid, girlish conversation. Ira kept walking and entered the bathroom one door further down.

He stood there looking at himself in the mirror. The thin wisps of hair on his chin and upper lip had condensed over the previous months to the point of visibility. Individually, they were almost transparent, and only when the light hit the right angle did they show with any conviction. His face was still red with sunburn. Just days beforehand, he and Furke had spent the end of their vacation down at Duval Park jumping into the lake from the tall outcroppings on the western shore. Within the limits of a bike's ride, yet sufficiently far out amongst the forests, the cornfields, the town penitentiary, and other suburban afterthoughts, the nooks of the wild park had become a precious place of their own. But even under the intermittent shade of friendly trees, the sun had pierced down from Heaven hot and sharp as the devil's fork. The skin all across his face and torso was still painfully tight. Ira splashed half a hand of cool water from the sink to his forehead, becoming more conscious of those lingering effects under the sudden, quenching relief.

Ira moved his chin up and down, looking sidelong at the mirror and petting his whiskers between thumb and forefinger. He had worn his best shirt today; the checkered crimson one with a collar that people said made his eyes glow, made him look quite the

RISE THE MOON

young man. Then Ira turned to the wall that divided him from Bella's bedroom and leaned against it, pressing his ear to the paint. He could hear their voices. The words were muffled and indistinguishable, but Ira stayed leaning there until things went quiet.

Four years older than the boys, Bella had once upon a time been a friend. The three of them played for years like timeless, androgynous cherubim. But as childhood graduated to adolescence, the girl drifted. She did not turn mean or frigid, only missing. At first, Ira's longing was only for the friend he'd lost. Now, as he passed an age of change himself, the girl came to occupy a different place, and every interaction stirred his blood.

Once, when they were young, before it could mean anything at all, she kissed him. They'd been on her bed; just sitting there talking make believe. He'd told Furke about it. Then the two of them didn't speak for several days. He understood something of it now, but back then they were kids. All Ira had known then was that there was something exciting, that adults kissed and that it must mean something important.

Now, separated from that room by a bathroom wall, Ira pulled his ear from the plaster and examined the mirror a final time before relieving himself. He flushed the toilet twice and washed his hands till they were pink with rubbing. When he stepped out into the hallway there were Bella and Connie each with two cases of luggage.

"Ira," Bella said, smiling. For a moment, it brought back a roundness of chipmunk cheeks before sharpening again into a face much like her mother's.

He waved.

"Carry this to the garage for me?" She set the two heavy cases down on the hallway floor. Then she turned away and reappeared a second later holding a cardboard box taped all the way around in two cross strips. Her friend looked Ira straight in the eyes with a smirk and he blushed. She was a tall girl whose gaze had to follow the downward slope of her nose to find him. She had curling blond hair and a shapely waist accentuated by the way she stood with one hip habitually cocked. She greeted Ira in an easy silken voice and led the way swaying through the hall. Bella followed after, and Ira picked up the bags, trailing both girls out to the garage. "Oh, you are so helpful," said Bella. She wore a pink cotton shirt that stopped only most of the way down her waist. The thin strap of a bra rose in outline across her back. She had black jeans that flared a bit at the bottom. The back pockets were a trapezoidal pair of dark sunglasses, shielding some invisible eyes that caught him staring. "That's what I love about you, Ira. I wish all my brother's friends were like you."

The night was humid; so much so that little teardrops condensed on everything solid as if the very earth of the town were mourning. One could almost see steam rising form the concrete sidewalks. Though it was late into summer, these last few days of August had been the hottest of the year. The evil temperatures had come unpredicted and went on unrelenting for several days.

The garage smelled of wet concrete and Bella's cherry blossom perfume. Her belongings lined the whole wall, and Ira dropped what he carried right there among the rest. Bella opened the trunk of their family station wagon, and the three of them began loading.

"Are you nervous for college?" said Ira.

"You kidding? I've wanted out of this house for years," said Bella.

Connie stacked one of the dozens of bags and boxes as far up toward the middle seat as her long arms could reach. "After this past week everyone else in town should be getting far, far away too." Ira's gaze flicked down the dark roadway. So did Bella's.

"Let's not talk about that," she said. "I don't want to talk about that."

Ira nodded. "College," he said, taking up another bag.

"I met my roommate over orientation," said Bella. "She's nice. Plus, Elliot will be there. We're even in the same dorm building. Isn't that crazy? Everybody says the first week is just a big party. Elliot got a twelve-foot beer bong."

"Cool," said Ira.

"He'll be there?" said Connie. "I thought he was going to jail."

"No, no, no," said Bella. "He only sat in jail for a night. He got out the next day." Her lips tried to hold back a smile at Ira's wide, inquiring eyes. "Elliot got in a fight last week at Brett Tilman's party. He was drunk and that asshole Chandler Gevas insulted him."

"I thought Chandler insulted you," said Connie.

"Well." Bella gave the lightest touch to her chest with all five

RISE THE MOON

fingers. Her eyes rolled back and there was a dreamy smugness in her smile. "He won't anymore." Connie giggled with her as Ira lifted the heaviest bag from the floor to the trunk. It was full of books and heavy enough that he began to sweat.

"So, yes," Bella went on. "Elliot will be there. And we're only in class like three hours a day. They don't babysit like high school."

"Are you coming back for Thanksgiving?"

"Who knows," said Bella. "Elliot says he wants to come back before winter and jump the gorge with his car. Can you imagine? Jumping the gorge?" The green in her eyes seemed to glow, and everywhere Ira looked the world was filled with her hue.

"Are you hearing this, Ira?" said Connie. She reached out and grabbed his shoulder as he leaned by her to load another box. It was a quick touch, and before Ira could even move his head to see the hand on him it was pressing back into her lap, covered securely by its mate. "Jumping the gorge? That's insane."

"Elliot's insane," said Bella.

"Isn't that illegal?"

"Probably. My criminal will have to spend another night in the slammer." Bella tucked her fingers into the pockets of her night-black jeans. She sighed with mock exasperation and the girls had another short fit of laughter.

Ira loaded the final bags, and as he stood back to close the trunk door Bella's hand glided into his cascading chestnut hair. She rubbed his head softly and gave a little pat. "Ugh, I just love you," she said. Ira's head began to rush. He could not find anything to say.

"That's all then?" said Connie. Bella confirmed that everything was packed, and the two girls embraced. "Come back soon, Bell. I'll be bored as hell at Tech." Then the tall blond girl trotted out to a car parked along the curb. She blew a friendly kiss to Bella then another to Ira, and with a delicate wave of the fingers she was driving off down the road, her taillights lit like little red embers.

Ira was still standing under the light of the porch watching the lights blink around a turn in the distance when Bella left for the front porch. On her way into the house she turned back. "Ira." He jumped as if awakened from sleep by the quick stab of a razor's point. "Shave the peach fuzz." One hand brushed her upper lip. "You're such a nice boy, and it looks dirty." Then her footsteps

JACOB KOCKEN

sounded in the hall as the door swung closed behind her. Ira raised his finger to his own lip where it was scratched weakly by little stray hairs.

As Ira returned to the living room, he noticed the additional voice of Furke's mother. "It's not polite, Furke. Not polite at all."

"I was only asking," Furke was saying. "And his mom works too. But what would we do if you got fired? Why doesn't Bella have a job?"

"She was busy getting scholarships, dear. You're about that age now yourself."

Ira turned the corner into the living room where their eyes went to him.

"Ira dear," said Ms. Kepling. "Were you helping Bella load things? You didn't have to do all that. Very kind. Very good. That's why we love you." She smiled down fondly. She had an attractive smile Ira thought. Her lips were still pink and full. He watched them as she spoke. Then he caught himself and shut his eyes. Heat started to rise on his face as she spoke to him again. "Need anything? I'm going to bed. It's a long drive to Kent State, and we'd better be up early." Ira shook his head. "Do you want the air mattress out?"

"The couch is fine," he said. Ira opened his eyes again to find her bent over searching beneath the coffee table's lid for a blanket. He shut his eyes a second time.

Ms. Kepling then handed a fleece to Ira and left them for the kitchen. Only then did he notice the ambient sound of the microwave. It cut off, and beeped loudly twice before Ms. Kepling opened and shut the door. She reentered the living room with a glass of milk.

"Just like your mother does," she said to Ira. He took the glass she handed him. It was warm, and the soft dairy scent eased through the room.

"Thank you," said Ira.

Ms. Kepling smiled and tousled his hair before heading down the hallway toward her bedroom. The woman's head poked past Bella's open door. A moment later, the girl's bedroom light flicked off. The hallway light followed suit, and the bright, irregular flashing of television news projected itself on every wall.

"They're going to put him to death," said Furke. He took his

RISE THE MOON

hands momentarily away from a growing tower of cards to gesture at the screen. The scratch of static touched the picture, and Furke ran to fix the antennae.

"Yeah?"

"If anyone deserves it, right?" It was always the same picture they showed of Yokoven; under custody but still in his own clothes, matted strands of sunshine yellow hair falling over part of his florid face. The rest of it closely followed the form of his skull, as if he'd worn the same old hat for years on end. Ira, like everyone else for one reason or another, was privately captivated. There were marks on his face; ugly ones like old pocks that didn't heal. The soft eyes of the killer were looking down, hiding a peculiar aspect. The lips hung open slightly showing no tension. Instead, there appeared an expression of indifference, or rather, resignation. It chilled Ira, and he looked out the living room window, his eyes flashing again into the darkness down both ends of the street.

"All those stories people told about the woods when we were kids;" said Furke, "makes me think the werewolves might be real too."

"Think so?" said Ira.

"All I'm saying is if you get so scared you piss our couch I won't blame you." Furke smiled ear to ear. "Like in the graveyard." He laughed aloud and flicked a card through the air, striking Ira on the shoulder.

"I did not," said Ira smiling softly. He whipped the jack of clubs right back.

"Did too. Even Bella remembers," said Furke. Ira went a bit red. He remembered that Halloween. It was perhaps his last memory of the three of them, before things really changed. They'd gone to visit the ghost of Daniel Pert, a young arsonist whose habit had perished him under the weight of a barn's fallen loft. Ira's parents had gifted him a video recorder that summer, and the three children snuck off to catch his soul on tape. Furke wondered aloud how he might look; whether his ghost would show the agony of death or whether the next world was more merciful. Some people said they saw his body at the funeral, touched by fire so that it still glowed with pain beneath the coroner's make-up. Others said the parents had purchased a casket only out of tradition. The true details were

JACOB KOCKEN

lost on young Ira, but he remembered how the story had gripped people. It had gripped Bella. She hadn't known the boy though he was just a few years her senior. Whether it was the particulars of Daniel Pert or just the awakening such things have on young, unexpecting minds, she was different afterward. All of them were. That jolt of tragedy alerted Ira to the presence of many changing things; both the sudden kind that strike like lightning and the subtleties that only announce themselves upon contemplation. It seemed like a holiday trick to Ira; how her face under the moonless graveyard sky had looked so grown. They had been running. The groundskeeper had seen them and howled in pursuit. Furke being even at that age the tallest of the three necessarily caught the guard's attention and led the chase while Ira and Bella tucked away to safety. The excitement of fear had taken Ira, and as he and Bella lay side by side against a broad tombstone shield, he felt that he'd wet himself. That was something for toddlers; something Ira hadn't done in years. Bella noticed. Her mouth had dropped open and Ira's mind raced for an excuse. His face had gone all ripe. When her laughter peeled out Ira would have traded places with the man who lay facing him from below. But she'd tried to soften her ridicule. It was a joke, Ira only half realized, when she said she'd done it too; that the scare was enough to make anyone do it. Ira laughed nervously. He touched the spot on his pants. And whether it was under some incredulous spell at her words or a joke of his own or something else altogether, he'd touched hers too. Her face went grave and the laughing stopped. 'I didn't,' he'd said immediately. Both hands froze at his sides. The October wind bit. Her stern and distant expression only faced the graveyard sky. She'd stood up and said they'd ought to find Furke, but Ira lay still on the ground, stuck in his act. Bella had looked down on him, her face framed by the stars. 'That's not good Ira.' Her mouth pursed and frowned. 'I didn't,' he'd said again. Then he began suddenly to cry. The tears dribbled down to the grass where his forehead rested. After a minute, Bella's touch returned. She remained silent, but she'd kissed the top of his head and brought him to his feet. It was there that he realized she no longer resembled the picture in his head. When he called her by name it didn't seem to fit. Her features, blurred by tombstone shadows as they trespassed the grounds, disappeared. She moved with

23

RISE THE MOON

an ethereal, womanly grace, and Ira, lost in visceral wonder, chased every twitch and turn of her silhouette. He had looked down at his video camera and couldn't help but wonder if he had any better chance of catching her than the haunt they'd come to see.

"I'll miss her," said Ira.

"Okay," said Furke.

"Are you going with to drop her off tomorrow?"

"Yeah. I think Mom's afraid that if I'm not there she'll get some empty nest syndrome. It'd be a ten-hour drive with just her since Bella's riding with—"

"Yeah."

"The asshat."

"Yeah," said Ira.

Furke's tower was leaning. He tapped some of the top cards lightly but overcorrected, and once again they came to litter the floor.

"Well, I'm going to bed too," said Furke. He took up the remote and pointed it toward the screen. "You want company?" The man's mug shot was up again.

"No," said Ira. The screen went black, and Furke was gone.

Ira curled up on the couch. His mind raced, and for a long time he lay thinking. At first, it was the image of Yokoven that occupied his mind. But as he settled toward sleep, his thoughts were gradually roped back. The scent of Bella's things was on him. With his hand up beside him on the pillow, Ira could smell the cherry blossom from her luggage, and he stared down the hall toward her room. In the darkness, his vision blurred. Shades of lingering light danced on the walls, and the edges of things blended. To Ira's troubled mind, it reared the memory of a grainy black and white security tape.

He'd heard Bella telling everyone the previous winter; her friends, Furke, and even her parents, how a boy at her high school had totaled his car doing donuts in the school parking lot. How he had been caught on tape, and his parents were forced to pay the damage. How someone, perhaps the boy himself, had gotten hold of the tape, and soon it floated from one screen to another, the old jalopy drifting gleefully through three inches of pure white snow and the control slipping away from the driver with a sort of young and romantic freedom as he slammed into the base of a pole. That post, bearing a sign with the Graumont High logo, came tumbling down over the roof of the car. The climax of destructive action was capped by the grainy image of a boy who climbed out of the car and threw his shoulders back in laughter. It was the laughter in particular that gained him fame. Bella's tone dripped with particular excitement when she talked of this dangerous young man, Elliot. And then when his birthday rolled around in spring, the boy's parents woke him up to a brand new Corvette, blue with a white stripe and a powerful V8 engine.

From the couch, Ira's eyes kept searching through the dark to Bella's door. His shoulder blades shifted back and forth against the fabric, inching his body to and fro like a restless worm. There was a toil inside him, and he flipped from back to stomach. The cushion pressed into his cheek and nostril, filling him with old, reminiscent smells. Chief among them was the cherry blossom.

Ira, even though there was no one around to see, feigned a large yawn. He stretched and undulated with the movement of his breath. The thin cotton blanket slipped off from over his torso, and in the dark, Ira hastened to replace it. The cushions of the couch, long sat on, were worn down to their fibers on each end. The middle seat retained some of its original shapely spring. With all the lights off, the sofa, brown during the day, was void of color, black as the jeans Bella had been wearing. Ira heaved a breath and lost himself for a moment. Then his eyes flicked down the hall. Had he heard someone, or was it only his own movement? He froze and peered into the black hallway tunnel. He was met with silence for a long minute until the frustrated waiting collapsed on him, and Ira sprung up from the couch. The blanket stayed wrapped around his shoulders, all around him so his form was flat until he reached the hallway.

Bella's door was shut, but not all the way. A sliver of space revealed the room in small slices. Like everywhere else in the house, the lights inside were out. Only a bit of moon was there, creeping through the window to show the shapes of things. Ira pressed his face to the jamb, one eye penetrating. There was no definition on the face. It could have been anyone at all lying there at rest. Her curves were only faintly discernible as they rose and fell with the easy rhythm of sleep. Up and down. In and out. All beneath the

RISE THE MOON

lightest satin cover. The scent hidden among the fabrics of the sofa was strong now, womanish and floral, emanating from the slit between door and frame.

Ira turned swiftly. He dropped his shroud, and the blanket fell into a trailing clump of cotton at the base of the next door down the hall. Ira was careful to make no noise as he closed himself inside the bathroom. When he pushed his finger down into the handle's button lock it clicked, a sound usually subdued by the most ambient goings on of a house. But through Ira's caution it made a snap like black powder. He waited in vain for two things; either footsteps toward him on investigation, or else for the little erect hairs down his body to lose their excitement. As neither came, Ira hung his head chin to chest. He crossed the little room that way, avoiding any glance at the mirror even dark as it was, and sat himself down on the porcelain. His mouth was opened wide. He tried to breath slow and steady and quiet. The light remained off.

2.
Miriam

WHEN MIRIAM FOSTER WOKE UP that Monday morning her husband was staring at her. Saul's eyes were clear of any morning bleariness, but the blanket was still up around his chest. He lay on his side with his neck bent sharply against the bulk of two pillows.

"It's eight o'clock. You better hurry," he said. But Miriam could see the alarm clock numbers on their shared nightstand. It was only seven thirty-four. So she nestled back into the mattress and found his body with her leg. She moved closer, resting her head on Saul's arm. When she caught the unnatural scent of his skin her eyes opened, and her head tilted up. She touched his cheek, and finding it shaven smooth, traveled up to the hair on the side of his head where her fingers came away damp and warm.

"Did you take a shower?"

"Yeah," said Saul.

"And then came back to bed?"

He shrugged at her intonation. They were quiet for a moment before Saul spoke again.

"Bedalaus is hiring in accounting. It's not even an accounting job really; more administration. I'd sort of be my old boss." Miriam nodded slowly. Her gaze lowered from his eyes to his arm on which she tenderly pressed her cheek. She traced the bicep with her finger. Much of his definition had been lost to early middle age, but the muscles twitched beneath her tickling touch, and Miriam smiled to herself. She used protruding knuckles to caress him. The hand that dragged there across her husband's arm had been locked that way

RISE THE MOON

long ago. An accident as a child left it always curled in. It did not look deformed at a glance. Only by noticing Miriam's movements, such as the crooked way she held a pen or her habit of propping objects between her waist and forearm did people discern her mild disability. Without these observations, Miriam simply appeared to be a woman with a habit of clutching.

"Don't you want to work for a different company now?" she said.

"It was just a thought," said Saul.

"Sorry if I was rude about it. Last night I mean." Her husband's hand flapped casually as if shooing off a fly.

When the real eight o'clock arrived Miriam rose. She cleaned herself up and got her things ready for work. When she came downstairs, Saul was at the table waiting for toast to pop up. He looked at her expectantly then back to the toaster.

"That funeral is today," said Miriam. Saul was sucking on his lip. He turned to her again and nodded. "I'm going to go. It's at six, so I'll just head there right after work. Did you plan on going?"

"Give them my regards," said Saul restlessly. "But all that kneeling. And the things they recite; I don't know the words."

"Okay," said Miriam. She kissed him on the cheek, and he smiled as she left the house. The day moved slowly. People were quiet down at the dentist's office where Miriam worked. It was as though a great cloud covered the city. Miriam passed her shift with an eye always on the time as the hour fell to the bottom of the clock. Eventually, it came, and Miriam drove down to the oldest part of town where a line of civilians seemed to keep the great oaken doors of St. Francis church perpetually open. The lot was already full, so Miriam parked along the curb to join this woeful procession.

The summer air was humid even in the church. Tears mingled with sweat on the faces around her as people moved in slow file from the foyer to the sanctuary. One place where moisture was not in abundance was the piscina. The great marble pool set at the entryway had once been overflowing, a constant fountain whose lower lip caught the falling current and recycled the holy water back through the bowl. Some weeks ago the plumbing failed, and parishioners had gone without their ceremonious, baptismal washings. Father David had taken to filling an old bucket from the office

JACOB KOCKEN

sink, blessing it, and pouring the sanctified contents into that barren basin. Compared to the original form, it was a measly puddle, one that must be replenished each week as it leaked slowly past the rubber wine stopper jammed into its center pipe; once a flume, now a drain. As Miriam passed it, she dipped her bad hand into this vessel, the one whose fingers continually clutched the palm, and made the sign of the cross with bony knuckle joints.

The line moved forward at an erratic pace. Some took several minutes to cry with the parents; others moved on with nothing more than a conciliatory nod or pat on the arm. Miriam could see them standing up at the front of the church. She had made their acquaintance briefly before, here in St. Francis. Before Communion she had shaken their hands in these pews. Gillian, the mother, had been pregnant then. Today, they looked different, sallow and weary. Gillian's face was tear-stained, and she turned away from the people intermittently to compose herself. A dark, netted veil dropped from the rim of her hat. Her wet eyes and full pearl necklace were the only glimmering things against her black dress, black coat, hat, and shoes. The father did not cry, but also did not speak.

"I have a child as well. A son," Miriam said when she came to face the parents. "I'm so sorry. It's inexpressible." She opened her locked fist as much as possible to press Gillian's hand with both of her own. The grieving mother pressed back. The tips of the other woman's fingers were yellowed from a habit of smoking. She smelled strongly of cigarettes and was shaking with a desperate need.

Perhaps everyone in the growing crowd had a child at home. That was why Miriam had come. For as much sorrow as she felt through these two broken parents, the news of the last several days had struck in her an equal amount of fear. She had her own son. She had her own perfect little child who no one should want to hurt. He was a gentleman, unspoiled by idle sin and evil brooding. Yet, here was an innocent, attacked in the night just four blocks down from where she lived. As Miriam passed the grieving couple, she encountered the casket. The top was closed and sealed. It was no more than two feet in length.

The daily paper had contained the story of the murder two mornings after it occurred. The print was mercifully plain and fac-

RISE THE MOON

tual, though the facts alone were sufficient for imagination. For a day and a half, the news traveled only on ear-prickling whispers. They said she was asleep. That it was the middle of the night. People reminded each other how easily windows slide in the summer when you're used to letting the breeze roll in. She was the first thing he found inside. 'That's why we sleep on the second floor,' said some. It said little in the paper about the man himself except his name; Gordan Yokoven. Yet, everyone seemed to know he was sitting in her room when the police came; that a neighbor had been awake and witnessed the entry, but in fear did nothing aside from call the cops. It was also rumored, and later confirmed, that beside her in the crib they found an egg. The man had kept several chickens and a cock whose crow echoed retrospectively in everyone's mind. He'd brought it and placed it there beside her body; brown, round, and freshly lain.

This time yesterday Miriam had been caught by the arm as she strode past a neighboring house. Dale Hawkins, an old, retired librarian who spent his days resting bad knees and sipping sweet tea on the porch expressed a horrible shame at having let it happen. He had seen some son of a bitch out walking too slow down sidewalks, he said, and vanishing again toward that forest across the bridge. And didn't everyone know what horrible things isolation cooks up in the brain? 'I wish you'd said something too,' Miriam had told him. 'She might still be alive.' He had stared at her with an awful inquiry after these words. She had seen the expression turn towards her several times before. Even her husband showed it to her now and then when they talked of hard things. It was one of surprise and, Miriam felt, cautious accusation. Life became that way after the death of her mother two years back, and perhaps people saw in Miriam the ghost that had taken the other woman's mind. That is what Miriam suspected when they looked at her so; even though in reality it was an altogether different sort of spirit that Miriam was possessed of. She always contented herself to repeat her words before dismissing the looker, and so she had done with Dale Hawkins.

There was the old man now, across the pews. He appeared more solitary, more solemn. His eyes were ringed with brooding, and his jaw was hopelessly clenched. It was the expression worn by many

JACOB KOCKEN

in attendance. The tension on every block of the town had risen. Miriam herself thought about it every night when her son turned out the bedroom light. She'd even hidden a butcher's knife in the top drawer of her nightstand, and she, like many others, went about now in dread of every pitter patter in the house.

In another pew, she saw the sheriff. He was dressed in uniform, a badge on his chest. Everyone had seen him on the news letting loose the few details fit for the public. He had spoken little of the criminal except to say that even had he not given a formal confession upon arrest, the contents of the man's household would have been evidence enough to convict. At the time, the sheriff was hounded for more from reporters and civilians alike. Here, under the arches of St. Francis, he sat shoulder to shoulder with other mourners, each confined to their own silent thoughts and prayers.

There was a spot in the corner where small pews and old chairs turned obliquely and nestled into short, stinted rows. The pew Miriam took had been there for nearly a century. The wood had turned pale and porous. Termite tunnels ran its surface. Now and then, small children found some interest in moving their little fingers through the insects' work. But children seldom found themselves here. Children come with parents, and these smaller corner sections were populated most usually by the lonesome.

Miriam took the pew furthest back, nearly against the wall. She sat alone beneath stained glass windows. The mosaic saints were alive now, bursting with the strong setting of the summer sun and set to die again when night came. Below each window there burned a redolent, lavender candle. The scent brought Miriam back to younger years where she used to sit beside her mother. 'Eyes see the present and mind sees the future, but your nose sees the past,' Emily had said. 'And everything about a church is old. That's why they wave the censer, to send you back to where Jesus stands at the beginning of time. It helps unravel things to a clear view. The world is a terrible knot that no one can find the ends to. That's why things happen over and over again; because if the world weren't all knotted up it wouldn't find us always picking the same dead-end strings. But that's why they light the candles and wave the censer; to bring you back.'

Constructed more than a hundred and sixty years before, St.

RISE THE MOON

Francis was the oldest building in Graumont. Small stone statues depicting Stations of the Cross were fixed to the walls. Beside Miriam was the Savior falling for the first time. He was on one knee. His brow was against the earth, and the mocking crown of thorns pressed into His flesh. The sculptor had spared no horrible detail in the marble. By His side stood a Roman in soldier's garb holding a spear at the Lord. His head was thrown back in delight. Miriam ran a finger along His skin below the cross beam. Even in humiliation, with His back bent and His face in the mud, He felt strong.

Miriam solemnly considered the permanence of the marble. A moment of history captured forever in the minds of everyone ever since. He would outlast the rock itself too. When time whittled the most durable things down into dust He would still be there lying face first on the ground in the minds of everyone who knew.

Her reverie was broken when a dark grey suit strode up beside her, and Miriam beheld an unexpected face.

"Dad?"

"Can an old man have a seat?"

Miriam pursed her lips. She did not immediately move. Her late mother had been the religious one, and in the two years since her death, Miriam had never encountered her father amongst the pews, had never encountered him at all, in fact. He was a heavy man, defined by corpulence as far back as Miriam could remember. His face was tired. The old black jacket he wore was one he used to teach in long ago. Now, to Miriam it was almost strange seeing it draped over his shoulder and not in a heap on the floor. It provided a frame of contrast from which the pinkness of his cheeks and nose stood out clearly.

She shuffled over and her father took the end of the pew. The old wood creaked beneath his weight. Miriam's spine stiffened then relaxed again as she became conscious of another scent. It was faint and fresh as that of an orange peel and would have gone unnoticed but for the long-harbored and now nearly forgotten comfort it invoked in Miriam. It was her mother's old habit to leave the peels lying about wherever she'd eaten. Oranges didn't go rotten like other fruit. They got stiff and shriveled but always gave something pleasant to the nose.

"You're not so old," she said. Her father froze for just an instant

JACOB KOCKEN

at the sound of her voice. His eyes shot sidelong as though someone had whispered over his shoulder.

"These bones disagree," said Frank. He exhaled hard, running a hand through his hair. It was gray now and much thinner than since Miriam had seen him last. He'd always had a bald patch at the back, but it was now overtaking him. He seemed to guess her thought. "I'm thinking of just shaving all this. Nature's decided. And age does run down some people faster than others."

Miriam looked up at the little casket then back to her father. His face surprised her. The man she'd known once was in there somewhere between the wrinkles and bristling eyebrows. He was even fatter now. His face seemed widened like his stomach. It made his nose look small as if drawn by a poor artist. The old jacket was clinging tightly at his wrists and shoulders. She'd set herself away from him for two years, and even before that they'd only spoken by phone for a long time. Perhaps the rasp in his voice had been shaded or cleaned up by the receiver. Now, in person, his throat shook like a junked-up engine.

"The whole town's here," said her father. "Where's Saul? Where's little Ira?"

"He slept at a friend's last night. Thank God. I didn't want him to come. And you know Saul. So I came here straight from work. I mean, he would've come in to shake their hands and say nice things."

"But he wouldn't kneel down in a church," said Frank. Miriam shrugged and nodded.

"Same old. How's the boy doing?"

"He starts school tomorrow."

"How old is he now? Is it high school?"

"Yes," said Miriam. "He'll be a freshman."

"Does he still have the hair? Like yours?"

"He still keeps it long."

"Isn't that something," said Frank. "I keep a picture up by the door from when he was a toddler. One you sent us from California. It hangs right next to one of Emily. You can hardly tell you three—"

"Saul's in a bit of a transition," said Miriam. She shut her eyes, avoiding her father's gaze. She could hear him choke back his sentence as she cut him off. Then they lingered for a moment in

33

RISE THE MOON

mournful silence.

"Fired?" asked Frank. Miriam, over the course of their absence, had lost touch with how perceptive her father was capable of being. There must have been a look of surprise on her face for he went on explaining, "The way you said it, *transition*, that's how people said it when the school boxed me out too. Your husband, is he on his feet?"

Miriam gave a shrug and looked back up at the congregation. "He's been a bit down, acting strange. I think he's stifled. He loved working at the hotel back in California. Directing a whole branch agreed with his personality or something. He never really bounced back from the new position after we moved. I want him to find something fulfilling. He used to be so ambitious."

"That's the first thing I thought when you two came home. Ambitious. He had that tone about his business that kills conversation. Because you knew there's no saying anything against him. He was going where he was going and that was it."

"He followed me all the way to Wisconsin."

"Your mother changed me too. There's always one woman."

Miriam looked down at her hands on the pew. She shut her eyes a second time. For a moment, the air inside the church seemed to compress as if the walls were moving in. The shuffling steps of the mourners dragged on in a white noise of static echo. The discomfort showed on her pursed lips..

"Sorry to bring it up," said her father. "Should I move?" He took his coat up from the seat.

"No," said Miriam, reviving again and touching his arm momentarily. Frank laid the coat back out and settled into his seat again. "How are you?"

"I've been seeing Grandma most days. She's getting worse, but you wouldn't know it by talking to her. And she tries to keep me in check." He laughed, but Miriam didn't. "I'm doing fine, really."

The long line of consoling parishioners came eventually to an end, and the parents of the deceased child collapsed into a front pew. The thump of the mother's bones against the wooden-backed seat quieted the hall. And then another scent rose up that wrinkled Miriam's nose. A thin, dark train of smoke was leaking up from out of the foremost pew. The grieving mother held a cigarette to her

JACOB KOCKEN

lips as her head lolled forward and back. The soft, orange ember called all eyes to her until the priest arrived to commence the Mass.

From up upon a lonely balcony where the choir would have sung on a happier day, soft organ music began to flow over the people. A short processional of priest and deacon followed, moving through the pew sections up to the front of the church. When they took their places before the congregation the music came to an end. The already somber room turned entirely silent again. Father David spoke from the lectern.

"I'd like to thank everyone for coming. I seldom see pews so full." There was a solemn pause. The priest wore his regular Sunday garments. He was a young man for the profession, about Miriam's age with a gentle disposition that she found inviting. His features were boyish ones that sat behind a pair of thin glasses.

"I baptized Sophia Joy right here. Eleven days ago. She was asleep, but her eyes shot wide open when the water washed away the only sin she ever had. She cried so loud I can still hear the echo." The priest paused again. He paced slowly from one end of the dais to the other. His head hung and his hands twirled in absent motion as if caught in some invisible web. Then he turned on his heel and paced back the other way, now and then lifting his head to speak before resigning again to a slow walk.

Up in the heavens above, the laden clouds had begun to roll in. Most of the skylight windows had gone dark around the rafters. Colors in the stained-glass saints diminished, and the crowd fell under the penumbra of the dying day. The only beams of brightness that escaped the overcast sky came in through the northernmost skylight where the lectern stood below. Father David shone even more brightly in his white robes by contrast, and Miriam watched with a beseeching eye. Save the mother and father, there was no countenance more sorrowful than the priest's as he shuffled around looking for words. At length, he spoke.

"Now, that untarnished soul looks down on us as we celebrate her life. In these cases, I find it most consoling to know that God welcomes those into His kingdom when they are ready. She didn't get a chance to show it in this world, but her soul must have been ahead of the curve. Just a month and a half old, but we could see and hear her personality already shining through. She would have

RISE THE MOON

been a beacon for God's Grace in this community. When I showed her the flame of the Holy Spirit burning on a candle she smiled. Toothless." He took a few moments to clear his throat. There was something in there, holding on to him. When he did resume speaking the gravel in his voice was not gone. In all the time Miriam had spent listening to David, he had seldom seemed so troubled. "She was a perfectly innocent soul. It truly is one of the joys of my vocation—the privilege to witness the human spirit at such a moment."

The force of his words trailed off, and again there was hollow silence. It stretched on, and some of the faces in the pews regarded each other.

"She. . ." Father David began. He adjusted the glasses on his face, pulling them off to wipe the fog away with his liturgical robe. "We. . ." The priest trailed into silence. "We all. . ." The dais floorboards flexed and creaked as Father David turned his slow gait back and forth. The deacon shifted in his seat.

"In your faces today it's hard not to see her; to see the child you once were. We are reminded that life is a gift. And we are reminded how strange it is for that gift to be received or revoked. So many days pass by without a moment's thought of why it's us living out God's gift and not someone else. What role might I fulfill that might not be better accomplished by another? You who've been here for a decade or an hour will know I'm a flawed man. Perhaps the world could be a much better place if it were inhabited by a better priest. So when a new child comes through those doors I am emboldened with hope for what they might become. And the sense of death is so much greater compounded both by the loss of what was and of what could have been.

"It is natural to question, 'why?' Why does God see fit to take life in such a way? We're told He has a plan we cannot comprehend; too big, too deep, too complex to fit into the narrow scope of our understanding. It is therefore tempting to say no. 'No, a God who steals the life of a child so young she had not yet the opportunity to understand her mother's words, that God cannot have a plan, and if He does it cannot be a good one.'"

A third time now, the hall fell quiet, and the priest paced the floor. His hands clasped and unclasped, grabbing at thin air. He stood with his back to the congregation. The silence stretched on

JACOB KOCKEN

for a long time. Miriam heard her father exhale sharply. He gave a cockeyed gesture in the direction of their shepherd. Miriam turned away from him, stone-faced.

Father David still stood inverted. His shoulders slumped and his head bobbed slightly as if he was in conversation with some invisible spirit. People shifted all around, their narrow eyes turning to one another. Whispers rose up, raining heavy on the holy man's head. He seemed almost to start again. With a half turn and a broken word he caught up the hope of the congregation before it slipped once again through his teeth.

There was a creaking sound as the deacon rose from his chair. The priest motioned at him again, but he did not return to the seat. He caught the priest around the shoulder and the two communed in tones below the crowd's rustling. Then there could be heard the rhythmic stride of a woman's shoes. Those steps came down Miriam's isle to show a face she'd recognized only as one of many that regularly appeared here. Soon the doors were swinging back on their hinges as the woman exited the sanctuary. A black suit shot up several rows down and began to follow in her wake. The next words spoken aloud came from the pulpit, but they were not from the mouth of Father David.

"We cannot dampen the hurt, brothers and sisters," said the deacon. "I can only believe it is through trusting in Him and moving on with our sufferings upon our backs that we get a glimpse—and allow others a glimpse at His eternal designs. They seem unfair, arbitrary, meaningless sufferings. And there is no darker travail than the meaningless." While the assistant addressed them, the priest had paced toward the far wall beside the dais. One hand pressed the face of the building while the other rubbed the temples of his bowed head. An alabaster archway leading toward his private corridor stretched over top, dressing his robes with a deep grey shadow. He hunched there, and the deacon went on.

"What we have before us now is a challenge. Where do we go? What can we think now, knowing so intimately the evil this world contains? How to move on? Brothers and sisters, don't let the burden be meaningless. Don't let the day turn to darkness. May we move on but never away. Keep her in your hearts. Let her life fill you with light. Rejoice when you see the morning star rise and

RISE THE MOON

know that Heaven's fire scorches sin and chases darkness off the ends of the Earth because she looks down on you. She shines on the world. Let the infant laughter resound so that it might break apart the Devil's idle toying. Love her and be righteous in her name, and by rebounding it tenfold you taunt the one who took her goodness from us. Love your friends and family and neighbors with the love you feel for this baby girl. Through our love, her soul smothers the evil that took her."

There was a long minute of silent communal prayer. Miriam could feel the close heat of her father's body as well as his gaze moving between her and his own thoughts. She turned away and closed her eyes. Miriam thought of her son and husband. But most of all, especially now amongst the fragrance of peeled oranges, she dwelled on her late mother, Emily, whose mind had drifted away from the woman they all knew. And when Miriam prayed, she prayed that God knew that woman as her daughter did and that the right woman was up there in Heaven while all the rest were just demons of the Earth's confounding.

There was a reading from the scripture, and the Lord's Prayer was said. Then they all knelt and the music began once again. Two young boys dressed in white like little priests came marching down the aisle baring a full cup and dish for the holy sacrament. They placed each atop the altar, bowed, and stepped away. During the procession of this ceremony, the deacon had retaken his chair at the right hand of the presider's, while the leader, who seemed to have gathered himself again, accepted the gifts at the altar.

With the Body and the Blood awaiting their blessing, Father David took up the censer. It dangled on a golden chain. The smell of incense flowed. He rocked the censer back and forth at each corner of the table. Then he faced the congregation and swung it their way several times. Thin white smoke leaked out the sides and broke like fog in the wind over the heads of the people. The cloud was inescapable. Miriam looked at the candles on the wall and her mother returned. 'That's why they wave the censer, to send you back to where Jesus stands at the beginning of time. Because if the world weren't all knotted up it wouldn't find us always picking the same dead-end strings.'

Father David's voice dragged in song beneath each note of the

JACOB KOCKEN

organ, intoning a distant consecration of bread and wine. The congregation stood and filed one pew at a time down to the altar. Father David stood with the dish of hosts just feet from the little casket. At the back of the building, Miriam watched the people from her knees. Their figures bowed to the Body and Blood, but their faces lingered on the little brown box.

The line carried on and Miriam followed her father into the aisle. From the back, his hair seemed even thinner, the wrinkles on his neck deep and wandering like cracks in the concrete. His portly body swayed back and forth with small processional steps, and Miriam felt a very sudden and private panic at the thought of having to catch him. On the tail of her panic came an anger that threatened to overtake her had she not so immediately encountered the Body of Christ. Miriam bowed and held her hands out to the priest. "Amen," she said and ate. She stepped aside to take the chalice and waited. The organ turned soft, and between its notes of praise she could hear her father's breath against the cup. Then Frank turned and circled back toward the pews.

"The Blood of Christ," said the deacon.

"Amen," said Miriam. The acrid scent of cheap cigarettes accompanied the taste of wine in her mouth. Behind her, the murdered girl's mother still sat smoking. There was a scattered pile of four snuffed tobacco butts sitting on the pew between the two parents.

Miriam was the last of the congregation, and by the time she knelt again, the music was ending and Father David was returning from the tabernacle. Everyone stood as Father David addressed them a final time. An announcement was made that anyone who wanted to honor Sophia with the lighting of a memorial candle need only stop in at the adjoining chapel. While the priest spoke, Miriam's eyes turned again to her father. His tongue licked slowly out over his lips. His body swayed slightly in and out of a beam of stained glass. Colored light reflected off his eyes like little waves before the tide. Again, his tongue traced the line of his lips, top and bottom. Then he turned, and she knew he'd seen her looking.

"Your grandfather used to shoot whiskey at breakfast. He called it his medicine," he said to her. "One's my limit, and some days it's none. But one's the limit. Even if it's just a sip and despite the transformation." Miriam nodded at his words though their power of

RISE THE MOON

persuasion was left somewhere far in the past.

Then the priest's words ended, and the people stirred. The family of the child and the rest of the funeral party was the first to file out. Four men took up the palls on the casket and marched solemnly outside where the hearse was waiting.

"I knew him, you know," said Frank. Miriam followed his eyes to the open church doors where the family was loading up.

"The father?"

Frank shook his head. "Yokoven. He was a student of mine at the university." He stared long at the great entryway of St. Francis. The little brown box was descending a short set of stairs to the road. It might have been bright with summer sun outside but for the black vehicle that waited there to steal the daughter away, a pinpoint on the Earth which seemed to collapse the light forever.

Then Frank stood and shuffled out from their corner pew. He was looking down at himself, fiddling with a button on the breast of his jacket. "It was good to see you here, Mimi." In the trail of his leaving, Miriam's nose caught the memory of orange peels again. It found her with longing, then sadness. She rose and followed her father into the delicate outdoor breeze. She neglected on her way out to dip her hand into the baptismal fount.

Frank in all his keen perception must have discerned the sound of her feet across the parking lot's blacktop. But when he spun her way, Miriam diverged. A hollow guilt was revived when she turned her back. Miriam let it ring. Sins committed were solid as the stone that made her fallen Christ, solid as the iron palls that bore the babe. With such awful things drumming in her head, Miriam wished now to cleave to something better. He was calling her name, weak and anxious. But she walked on, leaving her father standing in the shadow of the steeple; Miriam wanted only to return home and love her son.

3.
Ira

IRA WOKE IN A SWEAT with an itch crawling over his body and a sharp pain on his forehead. The armrest of the Keplings' couch had become just too narrow for his growing body, requiring him to sleep with his knees tucked up between his gut and the back cushion. He could remember back a decade ago when the Keplings first bought it. Sleeping foot to face with Furke on this same spot was among his earliest memories. Now, the fabric was pilling with overuse, and this once cozy nest had, over the last several hours, caused him a great deal of discomfort.

It was nine in the morning. Ira wiped a sheen of grease from his face. The rising sun trained down through the living room windows, and when he threw off the blanket the smell of him hung in the air. He blinked hard, and in the blur he saw Bella passing through the hall.

"Up, up." Furke was there, standing at the foot of the sofa. His wrist flicked back and forth as he slung playing cards at the boy on the couch. Then one of them struck Ira's face, reproducing the sharp pain that had woken him. "We're off to Kent." Again, Bella walked past in the hallway. She wore a peach-colored top that stopped before her shoulders and a denim skirt. Her step was an eager bounce.

"He's here now!" she was saying. Her voice was loud and urgent. "He's ready!"

Then she flew into the room holding a pair of red Chucks and sat down on the sofa. Her full weight came down on Ira's knees,

RISE THE MOON

though she seemed not to notice. Ira sat motionless as she pulled on the shoes and brought her feet up on the edge of the couch to tie them. Her legs were a milky tan from the long summer. He could feel the heat from her skin pulsing.

"Calm down," Furke said to his sister. "You're going to see the asshat every day."

"Why can't you be nice like Ira?" Bella smiled sidelong. She pinched a lock of his long hair and spun it between her fingers. "That's the difference with you. He goes to church. You should tag along next time, and maybe it'll shape you up."

"You don't go to church either."

"That's because I'm going to study Buddhism at college. And besides, regular people don't go to church. There's just two kinds of people that do; the really good ones like Ira who want to stay good and the really bad ones like you who need fixing. And they'll have a whirl of a time trying to straighten you, won't they?"

"I'm a Goddamned saint compared to you."

"Remember how you stole Mr. Penner's lawnmower when you were five?" Bella said to her brother. "You stole it for no reason except to enjoy stealing, and that's why kids don't like you, and that's why Mom is always sad. She has to spend all her time keeping you in line."

"I didn't steal it just to steal it," said Furke.

"Then why did you?"

"I don't know. I was five. Who even cares?"

"Mr. Penner cares, doesn't he? Mom cares."

"Shut up, Bella."

There was a knock at the door, and Bella hopped up from the couch. To Ira's great surprise, she bent at the waist and kissed him. Not on the mouth but on the forehead. He sat stunned. The air felt cool where her lips left their little mark. She looked at him still huddled there on the couch. "Such a handsome boy too; without all those peck marks you have, Furke. Good looking and nice? Why, you deserve the world. Don't you, Ira? Doesn't he, Furke? Yes, that's right, you'll get any girl you choose once you catch her attention. That's it, and you've got everything else. So handsome. So nice."

Then she was up and at the door. The room lit up with sunlight

JACOB KOCKEN

as the boy was let inside. Elliot wore thick army boots that pounded the floorboards indiscriminate of gait. He was a natural six foot three, and the boots made him tower even higher. He cast a long shadow that outstripped the floor and crawled up the wall before the door was shut, blocking the sun behind him. Bella squealed and jumped his way. She collided with Elliot chest to chest, and he caught her as if she were a plush toy. Their eyelids closed, and their mouths locked around each other's for several long seconds.

Suddenly, a pattern of white and red cross sections flew through the air, striking Elliot on the side of the neck. "Save it," said Furke as the four of diamonds fluttered down.

Elliot lowered Bella to her feet and calmly bent over to pick up the fallen card. He flipped it around in his hand several times before his fist closed tight. The edges folded in, and the whole card collapsed into a tight paper ball. Then Elliot's arm cranked back and slung forward like a pitcher. The fastball hit Furke in the forehead and added one more red mark to his freckled face.

"Watch out kid," said Elliot. "Didn't you hear what happened to Chandler Gevas?"

"I heard he kicked your ass."

"You're talking to the wrong people." Elliot left Bella behind him and stalked over to where Furke was standing. "See, Chandler didn't have much respect for people. That was his mistake. And some people only learn when the truth gets shoved in their face." The older boy's big palm swiped at the deck of cards Furke was holding, spilling them all over the room. Then in one quick motion, he swung behind Furke and wove his arms around Furke's, locking his vice grip hands behind the younger boy's neck.

"Hey," Furke yelled out. His lanky arms flailed toward the ceiling, and he tried to kick back like a mule. Elliot leaned forward, doubling Furke over and stretching his arms toward the floor.

"I'll let you go when you pick up your mess," said Elliot.

"You're breaking my arm," hollered Furke.

"Pick it up. There's an ace right in front of you. Pick it up."

Just then, Ms. Kepling came in from down the hall and pried the two apart. "Elliot you let go of him, now," she said. "You're too big to pick on a freshman in high school. And Furke, don't even say it. If I know you, I know you did something to deserve it."

RISE THE MOON

Elliot relinquished the hold and stood back with his arms still flexing. "I was just giving him a hug good-bye Ms. K."

"Well, good riddance to this," said Furke's mother. "Out to the car with you before it starts up again." Elliot strutted out the door, his big boots whomping left and right.

"Bye-bye, Ira," said Bella. She gave him a little wave and chased after Elliot.

Ira's farewell was breathless. When he stood up and faced the window he saw the two of them. She and the boy were traipsing across the lawn toward a blue Corvette.

"Ready, Furke?" Ms. Kepling asked.

"Yeah," he said. Ira went with him to the front door where they put on their shoes and walked outside into the morning brightness. The family's station wagon sparked up and hummed as Furke slipped into the back seat. "See you at school," he called out the window. But Ira was watching the Corvette. Its engine roared. Bella and Elliot shot out loud and fast as a bullet. One moment she was at rest against the curb and the next she was halfway to Kent, her eyes trained on that reckless boy.

The station wagon pulled out to follow, and only after both were out of sight did Ira turn to start the mile and a half walk back home. His steps were slow and somber as he rounded the corner onto Lennox Avenue, a long blacktop road which cut through the whole width of the suburbs.

Graumont, like most of the Midwest, was once a farming town. Now the land had turned to concrete except for green squares of lawn and a notable apple orchard at the far north end of Lennox whose product had become the pride of the people. The real vestige of the old environment lay over the bridge in Old Graumont on the other side of the town's natural barrier. This borderline came in the form of a once deep and narrow river used to irrigate the land. Torrents of the past had carved a gorge between the two sides of town, though, over the decades, the river separating east and west had all but dried up. There was now only a trickling creek whose water dribbled from one plain of barren dirt to the next. The hole in the ground descended thirty feet at its deepest, and nearly the same across. Down in its trenches, the rocks were colored with spray paint as, like a condemned building, it had long been taken over by

JACOB KOCKEN

young men and women with nothing to do but run free and exercise their harmless, youthful debauchery.

The land to the east of the river had failed one spring some years back, sending the farmers elsewhere. As the population rose, the land east of the bridge stayed abandoned and grew over in patches of long wild grass. A single road disappeared quickly from the bridge into a forest of pine and cedar. The houses behind this wooden veil were sparse and dilapidated, and anyone living there now was a recluse whether by choice or consequence, for the people of Graumont generally disregarded the old side of town. The tax dollars did not go there nor did anyone on a pleasant stroll. If the bridge that connected these municipal sisters fell spontaneously to pieces, it may have taken a year or more for anyone from the new side to notice.

Ira now shuffled beside this bridge, clouded with dejection. He looked out to that line of trees where he knew the killer had come from. He could smell the old growth of forest even from where he stood now. But it was not the scent of pine that lingered in Ira's nose. Rather, it was that of cherry blossom.

He approached the gorge. It was a steep drop into the chasm on both sides, but here and there the crumbling rocks jutted in and out of the wall. One of these sites made an irregular staircase which Ira dropped himself onto. Now and then one of the boulders rocked beneath his weight as he descended thirty feet into the rift. Down at the bottom, the trickling water was shallow enough to walk through without soaking the shoes. He splashed over it toward the underside of the bride. Beneath its shade was the bulk of the graffiti; crude drawings of animals, symbols, and human anatomy. It was an adolescent kaleidoscope. *I love you Dean Bettis*, was written through an old, fading sketch of a person surrounded by multicolored spheres. *Jennifer is a slut*, was stark and black in spray paint across several older, layered images; a tall man, a woman, and a baby. *When life gives you lemons, fuck them.* This was written as if an epitaph below a stick woman smoking a cigarette. All around her were people on fire.

Ira stepped on something as he walked along and read. He bent down to find a scuffed-up sharpie marker, undoubtedly forgotten by some recent vandal. He uncapped it and the smell of ink entered

RISE THE MOON

him. The tip was mashed but not dry. Its lines were only slightly faded as Ira ran it along what open space he could find on the bumpy rock wall. *Bella,* he began, those letters inadvertently crossing over the outline of a large breasted woman.

He couldn't get her out of his head. Her laugh, her scent, the way she looked at the boy as he revved his engine. And at the same time, the particulars of her were already fading. Much as how she had once changed from childhood friend to a figure secluded and alluring, she now receded further, and in this abandonment his longing intensified. Whatever it was it tightened Ira up. He was all on edge. A lonely desire stirred in the pit of his chest and like hunger, it drove him.

Ira replayed the last moments of her flight. Boxes. Black pants. Cherry blossom perfume. He could hear the haunting of her words. 'Elliot wants to come back before winter and jump the gorge with his car. Can you imagine? Jumping the gorge?'

Ira looked out at the expanse beneath the bridge. His heart began to pound, and in a moment his feet were tearing over craggy steps and down the sidewalk as fast as a blue Corvette.

He turned off Lennox, leaving the gorge, the bridge, and the forest behind him. He cut through neighboring yards, and with a heaving chest came hustling up to his own house. The garage was open. His father's Chevy Cavalier sat lonely and unused in the second stall as it had for many days now. Ira's gaze caught the blue handles of his bike buried in the storage stall. It too had a white stripe down the middle.

Ira entered the house. His feet wheeled through the hall and clambered upstairs to his room. The lights were off, and the walls were quiet. Ira shot to the floor, grabbing the old video camera from beneath his bed. He turned it on and started recording. Full battery.

Then a deep silence imbued the house. It caught Ira's ear when the shower across the hall suddenly stopped and sent its white noise dripping steadily down the bathtub drain. Crouching there at the foot of his mattress with the camera on reel, he heard the twisting of a knob.

Directly across the hall, the bathroom door swung smoothly open. With a towel to wrap her hair but nothing at all around her wet and gleaming body, out stepped a strange and beautiful woman. There was no spark of recognition in her face as Ira gaped up at her from the floor of his bedroom. She walked with light, unhurried steps through a cloud of rolling steam and into the hall. Ira stood frozen on his knees. Her backside was lithe and supple, and the structure around her shoulders stood out like a prowling cat. She moved with that feline grace until she was out of sight down the hall.

Ira's heart sank to his gut. Her bare body still floated before him wherever he looked. He felt compelled in two opposite directions: to run from the house unseen and also to follow.

He crept out into the hallway. It was empty. Wet footprints darkened the carpet. Murmured tones came from the only lighted room in the house. If they were words, they could not be understood, and they drew his curiosity up to the threshold of his parents' bedroom. As he crept, he kept looking down at the wet footprints she left. His own shoes beside them dwarfed their size, beginning already to evaporate into nothing. The door stood a quarter open, holding back the full scene of the room like a crescent moon.

In that sliver, he saw the end of the king bed. Over the edge hung four naked feet. One set of toes pointed down while the other set looked up toward the ceiling. Behind the door, Ira placed his eye just above the hinge and saw from a different angle. Upon the bed lay his father, Saul. He was unclothed. The hair on his chest was bared out and the cheek of the catlike woman nuzzled against it like a pillow. Saul lay there with his eyes closed. His fingers followed the curious shoulder line of the creature on top of him. They rested with a lazy pat on the small of her back. She was having her way.

Ira's fingers dug so hard into the wall that his pinky nail split and pressed fresh blood on the plaster. Then Ira moved on instinct alone, raising the camera. Its screen caught how they moved against each other; every undulation a little byte of memory. Ira's fist clenched the camera in petrified wonder. Never again would it be used. It became a holy of holies, a sacred keeper of what could never be confronted or forgotten. A terrible lump rose in his throat until it burst and let a piteous whine from trembling lips.

Like a rat caught in the middle of a room, Saul popped up, alert on the bed. Ira removed himself from the rolling screen and met his father's eyes. Without a moment's hesitation, Ira turned and

RISE THE MOON

ran. He bounded through the hall, down the stairs, and out into the garage. Saul's voice boomed through the walls calling his son's name. Ira's feet were numb against the floorboards. His mind was in a frenzy.

In the garage, he pushed through brambles of boxes, Christmas decorations, and tools over to where his bike leaned against the far wall. A porcelain statue of Mary among a Nativity set toppled over. The Virgin's body split in two, starting at the ruination of her face where she first struck the concrete floor. The crash sung out, and Ira glanced at the Mother with a broken heart.

He pushed through more debris until he reached the handle of his bike and wrenched it out just as Saul's bare chest leaned into the garage. He was calling, waving and keeping his body tucked behind the door. A curious crimson streak was smeared across his chest. Blood ran out from one of the sweeping hands. The boy, stumbling out of the driveway, pedaled as hard as he could down the blacktop.

Humid summer air closed in around Ira as he sped through suburban streets. Cold and warm sweat mixed on his skin and soaked into his cotton spun t-shirt. The bike handles twisted dangerously under a clammy hand. He used only one to steer as the other clutched the camera close to his chest, documenting his hard breath and hot tears in every passing scene.

He hit Lennox Street, just a hundred yards from the bridge, from the gorge. The pavement flashed by in the space of a breath. A call came out from the belly of the earth, and Ira steered into the grass. There was a slight slope from the road to the precipice. He was picking up speed but no longer cared for the glory, for the girl.

The east and west sides of Graumont came together for a moment as he rumbled toward the gap. Then they stretched out again, gaping and void, and Ira was in the air.

And when the bike frame collided with the gorge's eastern barrier it sent Ira spilling over the front end. He clutched at the dirt wall. His teeth broke against the railing between his handlebars, and twenty feet below, sitting crumpled up at the bottom of the cavern, his throat was filled with the taste of blood. Instinct to break the fall had extended one of his arms. As his body came crashing down, impact bent it like the slender spokes on his mangled tire.

JACOB KOCKEN

He wailed in wretched agony, in pain and despair. The walls of the gorge loomed above, hiding him in shadow. The little stream of water at the base trickled red. He felt his bad arm with his good one. An unnatural angle shot off above the wrist. The skin was puffed up, hot and tight to bursting.

Ira's fingers slipped over his writhing body, wet with water and blood. He would not look. All he could see through the pools in his eyes were the bright rays of sunlight, shining iridescent in the bright blue sky. Only the walls of the gorge would come into periphery as his tears and heavy breathing rocked him. When he shifted too far one way or the other his arm swelled with pain, the blood inside rushing from one side of the break to the other. Again and again, Ira bawled at the sun.

And then that sun turned black. There shot a flash of dark rays over his vision. They disappeared as fast as they'd come. Then again, those strings of shadow returned. This time, instead of evaporating, they swayed back to their source. Above him there knelt a woman; her head surrounded by a habit of flowing black hair. Her shoulders were wrapped in perfect white, and her eyes were so dark there seemed little distinction between iris and pupil. They shimmered as she bent to him. The woman said something, and though he understood the words, they mystified him. He lay there on the muddy riverbed immobilized. Slipping underneath his shirt, her hand felt from his stomach up to his chest. Her fingers were soft, yet Ira let out another cry of pain when they clutched down into his skin. With her left arm, she seized his right where it had snapped and swollen. Then she whispered. Her lips were up close to him, moving slowly between his ear and cheek. Her breath landed on and in him, and it was wet and cool, a mountain waterfall. Then the coolness turned to ice, and her words froze in crystals upon his flesh. In his twisting, writhing contortions, he struck out at her. His hand never made it to her face. His blood felt stopped with chill. Then things went white. Ira was in a blizzard, and the snow packed around him with a heavy embrace. The cold went straight through his body, numbing every nerve.

4.
Anna Lee

DECEMBER 13TH
The mountains still hang at the end of the world like a shadow. Mom says we're too far away from home and whatever I'm seeing is an illusion. But I can still see our mountains down at the end of everything. When the clouds go low some of the peaks disappear, but then the storm passes by and the sky turns blue again, and I can still see them looming way back there. And no matter how they shift and blur I can always feel which one Dad is on. When I come back I know where to find him. Beneath the sugar pines. He could point up to the tops of those trees and tell you every bird that flew by. He especially loved the scrub jays. The first time he took us out with his gun he said he'd never shoot a scrub jay for anything in the world. And I don't believe he would because he wasn't so happy to shoot anything at all even if it was food. In the winter, the blacktail deer eats the lichen on the trees, and when it warms up it eats blackberries. Dad said things like that whenever he brought something home because don't you think you ought to know who gave you their life? He only shot once not for food. It was the first time he took us out with his gun. He made me hold Nancy's hand the whole time because the trees are thick, and it's hard to find your way. Her blouse hangs from her shoulders to her knees like a big white tent. She cries like a baby when they try to put her in real clothes. So she wears the same thing all the time. They don't wash it, of course. It's just white and draped over her, catching in the wind and the branches as we walk. She made noise at all the birds

JACOB KOCKEN

and squirrels and scared everything away. 'Papa, Papa,' over and over, the only word she knows. Dad wrapped his arm around her and calmed her down. Only he could. We got to one of his trees, and he showed us how he sat. He had a hundred trees just like an animal that lived there. I wanted to see more so we moved on, and I was the first one to notice a little fawn moving in from behind the brush. It walked like Nancy. Like it was just learning everything. We all stopped and watched it search through the grass with its nose. Then Dad pointed away and whispered to look. I thought it was a dog, and Dad said coyotes are dogs but not the kind you pet. It looked right at us. Dad said to stand up tall and raise our hands, and I had to raise Nancy's hand too because she doesn't understand. Dad said that usually scares them off, but this one kept walking with its head down right toward the deer. I started to cry. Nancy copied me and started to cry too, and I squeezed her hand hard when Dad's gun clicked. He raised it to his shoulder, shut his lazy eye, and aimed. Then there was the loudest sound I ever heard. I let go of Nancy's hand to cover my ears. The fawn and coyote ran off. So did Nancy. She screamed and ran and fell to the ground somewhere in the forest having one of her fits. 'Papa, Papa!' Nancy's shrieks are fast and sharp like a razor blade. Dad left the gun and went to where she'd run off and dropped to the ground. We didn't see what happened to the fawn. I like to think some buck came around with strong antlers and led it off somewhere safe. We never did see what really happened though. Dad came back with Nancy in his arms. He set her down on the ground and picked up his gun and told me to hold her hand. I am sick and tired of holding her hand. I feel now like she did then when she screamed, 'Papa, Papa.' Mom looks tired too. She tells us we need to sleep, but whenever I wake up no matter where we are she's always stirring. We slept at a motel again, and I woke up in bed with Nancy, and Mom wasn't there. The heater in the room was bad or broken, and it was cold outside the covers. I got goose bumps when I slipped out of the bed to look. She wasn't in the bathroom either. Then her voice came through the thin walls, and I opened the door, and she was out in the hallway talking on the phone again. When she saw me her face said to go back to sleep, but I couldn't. I got back in bed and just laid there awake. Nancy had

RISE THE MOON

her whole body, even her head under the covers, and she wrapped her arms around me. Part of me wanted to whack her away. But I could feel her heartbeat against my back and that babbling in her mouth. I think she was asleep. Sometimes you can't tell. I can't even tell right now as I look back at her sitting there blocking the view of the mountains. Sometimes I just hate her.

5.
Saul

BLOOD WAS RUNNING DOWN SAUL Foster's wrist. The moment he'd seen his son he was overcome by a terrible reality. He had popped out of bed immediately, leaving the naked woman behind. He dressed only to decency and rushed after the boy. But Ira was gone. He had called out to him in the garage just as the boy mounted his bike, but he did not turn back. In the rush of it all, in his panic and regret, Saul had not even noticed the pain. Only when he had come back upstairs to where the woman stood clumsily hooking her bra did he notice the cut across the palm of his hand. She pointed to the one nightstand beside the bed which long ago had broken at the edge and bared a sharp wooden stretch of several inches. In his haste, he must have slid across it, for the mahogany too was coated with blood.

Everything in the house felt far away. Saul's bloody hands groped about for something to hold on to before coming back only to themselves. He sank to his knees and from there he melted onto his backside. His gloomy, simian figure leaned there in the corner between his bed and nightstand. The strength in his legs was gone. He could not move. For weeks he'd done nothing at all but lay at home for lack of a motivating thought, and now he sat almost naked, paralyzed by the sight of his own disheveled bed and the young pink-haired woman dressing frantically by the opposite wall. She spoke to him through her shirt, but the words died somewhere in the eternal void between Saul and everything else. The chandelier above shone down a harsh and abrasive light, each one of its crystal bulbs refracting radiance into confusion. He covered

RISE THE MOON

himself with his limbs.

Everywhere he looked the light was too strong for his eyes. This chandelier he had lived beneath for a decade now felt somehow unbearable, glaring. Only a night ago, he'd sat here with his wife under the same fixture, and its glow was dim. He was lying on the bed as he had been most of the day wallowing in the thought that there was nothing to do. She had gone to see the priest after work again, and Saul had eaten alone. The phone was ringing.

"Your dad called earlier, Miriam," Saul had told her. "It's probably him again." She was at her closet facing away and didn't stir at his voice. "Mimi?"

The ringing cut out and Miriam turned around. Her arms were crossed. Her bad hand hung idle while the other was up in her hair twisting it around her fingers. "Did our son bring a toothbrush to the Kepling's?" she asked. His wife was chewing gum again. The habit bothered Saul. It was not the sound; her mouth stayed sewed shut as she chewed. Rather, it was that her disposition reliably turned quiet, inward, and closed-off whenever the scent of spearmint accompanied her. That was what bothered Saul. The habit had begun two years ago when her mother died. Grief did things to people; Saul knew that, so he paid no mind at first. He figured it would go away. But the event seemed to hit her in a particular way. Even her voice had changed a bit he thought.

"I think he brought one."

Miriam came to the side of the bed and looked for a moment as if she would sit, crawl under the covers, and sleep. Above her head was a crucifix. The blood and anguish on the man's face and hands curdled Saul's stomach. It had hung over his wife's side of the bed for two years now. Her bowed head was always glancing at it. Miriam turned away again, pacing back to the closet with her hair in her hand.

"Did you see that priest?"

"Yes," she said. "David is quite good. He always remembers when it's time to change Mom's candle. He takes special care; wise for his age too. He's quite wonderful. I'll see him again tomorrow."

"Mm. I picked up when your dad called before."

"He's in a bad habit of not brushing right now."

"He called to see if you'd go visit your grandma with him."

JACOB KOCKEN

"Is there a good way to trick a kid into brushing?" she said.

"Mimi."

"Saul, it's fine."

"He sounded good."

"He can," she said.

"The first time I met your mom she said if you want to know what Frank is thinking you have to watch his body because he gets as confused by what he says as you do."

"Yes, that was one of her lines."

Miriam opened the window and stood there looking out. It was early in the night, and the first stars were blinking. A warm summer breeze drifted in. It blew the strands of hair right out of her grip. Saul watched her stand there for several minutes. A bundle of clouds rolled in across the moon, and the distant lunar reflection cast them as dark and shifting tea leaves on the sky.

"Can you see her up there?" said Saul. Miriam exhaled a long breath of spearmint and closed the window.

"You know that apartment complex going up over by the lake?" she said. "There's a banner on the gate that says they're hiring."

"If it's a project underway then they're not hiring for anything important," said Saul. He waited there on the bed, but his wife passed him by once again and made for the doorway.

Saul could hear the spinning fan in the bathroom down the hall as he got up and put on his shoes. That white noise droned on and on and crept inside his head, whirling in his ears even after its source cut out. When Miriam returned her face was damp, and her makeup was gone. Saul sat on the edge of the bed tying his laces and trying to shake the droning sound away.

"It might be good for you to do something physical," Miriam was saying.

"And just keep sliding down the ladder?"

"Hard work is satisfying. The harder the better."

"I could be a stooge on the Alaskan oil rigs."

"Would you find it fulfilling?"

"More fulfilling than sitting around here all day? It's hard to say."

"Well then," said Miriam, "why don't you go to Alaska and try it out?"

55

RISE THE MOON

"Sure." Saul gave her a flat look, and she returned it, so he stood from the bed and found his keys on the nightstand.

Outside, the full darkness of the night had set in. The air was warm and thick, holding back a rain that had not come all summer. Saul dropped in behind the wheel of his car and pulled away from the house. A droning sound still moved all about him with the static in the car radio and the rolling tires beneath. There was a bar not far from their house, but he drove further into town to a place called the Yellow Jacket, just a few blocks from his former employer, the Bedalaus Hotel.

The tavern smelled like cigarettes. The lights had a soft, warm glow to them, and as he sat, Saul contemplated his low reflection in the bar mirror. The scrag of an idle beard shaped the sides of his face. He could smell the effusion of body grease on his fingers as he patted down the hair. But beneath that was a strong, attractive jaw line that was emblematic of his entire aspect. Though he was generally thought of as handsome, it was in a sort of brutish way that mainly inspired the baser carnality of others. He was, as some said, quite attractive for a night. Indeed, much of Saul's younger life was filled with flings that confused him deeply. With regularity, women, often strangers, would practically throw themselves down at his feet with their infatuation. He could still hear some of their words, their compliments and exhortations, ringing in his head from decades past with a constant sort of renewal. Few days passed, in fact, where Saul did not at some point muse on one of those doting lovers, imagining their wide-eyed expressions and feeling their breath light upon his face in reverie. He would smile to himself and let the thought run away just as their original forms once had. Indeed, not until he met Miriam did Saul have so much as a second date with a woman. It had been a fact he was keenly aware of, and when Miriam appeared to be sticking around he jumped on the opportunity to see what it was to share in something greater. They married, and he loved her though even she was not entirely immune to the waning that seemed to possess them all.

Saul ordered a rail vodka.

"Two olives," he said. "Don't touch them with your fingers. Two different ones. With the pimento. Damn it. They ought to be given with the pimento. That's the best way. That's how it's done."

JACOB KOCKEN

He saw the bartender's annoyance but paid no mind and handed him a twenty with a flick of the wrist.

"Straight Fleischmann's," barked a man two barstools down from Saul. "You've either spent a chunk of time in Russia or in Hell, eh?" The man had a thick head of salt and pepper hair with the beard to match. His eyes were small and of a similar black and white complexion while his chest and shoulders were broad and bulking, the mass of muscles breeching through sleeves and collar even onto his face. He was dressed pristinely well in white button down and slacks. A shimmer was on the toe of his shoes even in the low light of the bar. The chair between them was draped by the man's suit coat, a sterling bronze to match his pants. And on top of this there sat a white leather Brexley hat embroidered at one end with the small black letters, *B. Nabers.* He raised a glass of his own which threw the peaty scent of neat scotch rolling through the air. "What do you do son?"

Saul stuck his nose into his tub glass, hoping to avoid the man's attention. But when he came back up for air the beady, Rottweiler eyes were still trained in his direction. "I'm in hotels," said Saul.

"Which ones?" The man's voice was loud and sonorous. It sounded as if each of his lungs were bellows, firing gusts to feed a foundry's furnace.

"Never mind," said Saul. "You probably haven't heard of it."

"Which ones?" the man insisted. "I travel for work. I travel a lot. More than you might imagine when you hear my line of work. But I know hotels. I travel, I'm telling you."

"Bedalaus."

"Bedalaus?" said the man incredulously. He seemed if possible to be getting louder. "Well of course I know them. There's one right here in town, not five blocks away. I have to pass it on my way here. Big lights on the top, ivy vines on the east side. Everybody knows that building. I remember watching them put it up. There used to be an orphanage there, did you know that? Well, the land must've been meant for boarding. Ha! One type of guest then another; from babies and brats to businessmen."

"And you?" asked Saul.

"Agricultural science."

"Does that make you a farmer or an egghead?"

RISE THE MOON

"Ha!" The man's empty glass came crashing to the bar top with a clank that made Saul jump. His canines gleamed as he flashed Saul a rakish smile. "Get this man a second," he called to the bartender. "On me. But pour something nice. Glenmorangie. No, wait. The Brocken Bow. Yes, two of those." The new glasses were filled with smooth amber and set before each of them. "Women and scotch; try them all. If some are especially to taste, keep them around the house. You like scotch?"

"Usually," said Saul. "I've never had this one."

"Little can wash your troubles better," said the big man. He gave a shrug and another toothy grin. "Well, of course there are other things. But go ahead now, try it out. Take a real draught though. Try to notice things. Saul took a good sip from the glass, letting the liquid run around to coat his teeth and tongue. "Well?"

"It's very good," said Saul.

"Damn straight!" the man nearly shouted. "But what do you taste? Specifics. Come on man, sink into your senses."

Saul licked his lips. "Smoky," he said. "But there's something sweet."

"Sweet how?"

"Vanilla?" Saul offered. "No. More like fruit."

"Which fruit?"

"Nothing citrus. It's not sharp or sour I mean."

"You're onto it," said the man. He swirled his own glass with great show from his long arms and with his nostrils took a deep inhalation off the surface. "Get the flavor in your nose too. Corner it." Saul took the direction and breathed the sweet spice into his head.

"Cherry?" said Saul. "Cherry blossom and some kind of toffee?"

"Can you tell the wood?"

"I don't eat wood often enough."

"But you've smelled it! Everyone knows the scent of a pine from a poplar."

"I'd just be guessing."

"Well, give it a guess."

Saul closed his eyes and took an exaggerated whiff. "Apple wood?"

Thunder cracked between them as the big man's palm slapped

JACOB KOCKEN

the bar. "By God, he got it! A great nose! You're a blood hound like me aren't you? What's your name, man?"

"Saul Foster."

The big man took a long sip from his glass, and the silence dropped like a cavern in the wake of his booming voice. Saul mirrored the action implicitly and saw in his periphery the beady eyes were appraising him.

"You look unhappy, Saul." The chair to Saul's right swiveled more to face him. The broad shoulders opened up, showing the front of the man's towering body. He must have been six and a half feet tall if Saul could judge by sitting. "But you're a smart man. What's there to bother a smart man? You've got a ring! You're a married man too. And you're in hotels. That's good business. I'll tell you this. I met a man last week who was really down on his luck. I can sniff it in you because my nose is refined, I'm a connoisseur, but anyone could smell this fellow. He had the stink all over him. I bought the man one drink, and he spilled his whole guts to me. Girlfriend left him, had no job at all, and a bad habit to boot. Gambling. That's how he lost it all. He put a bet on the Packers preseason game while we talked. Preseason! That man had it bad. You're not him, Saul. You ought to cheer up. Barman! Another for my friend and I." The glasses were filled again, and the big man went on. "Whatever it is, forget about it. Forget about it. Now, how about it, Saul? When I stay at Bedalaus next can I mention your name? Will I get a discount? Give me something."

Saul waved him off the idea. "I'm really trying to find something else actually."

"Is that so? The hotels don't suit you? Do they do something wrong? You've got to tell me if it's health code. I'm a frequenter I tell you!"

"No, no," said Saul. "It's a personal fit more than anything."

A giant paw came clapping down on Saul's back. "I sized you up right away, Saul! There's more going on in your brain than bedspreads and check out times. I can see it in your eyes. You've got a penetrating look. And an intuition!"

"Thank you," said Saul. The man beside him stepped down from his seat. His impressive frame blocked one of the hanging chandeliers and cast a shadow over Saul. The scent of their drink

RISE THE MOON

wafted off him as he reached out for his hat and coat and donned them with a grace surprising for his size. He stuck out a meaty hand for Saul to shake.

"I better be on my way before you have me drinking all night." He let go of Saul's hand and retrieved a small white card from an inside breast pocket of his suit coat. "I like you, Saul. Give me a holler if you want to get into the sciences. We can always use people of quality." He left a neat stack of bills beside his empty glass and addressed the bartender. "There's one more for Saul here in that pile. The rest is yours. Have a night!" The floorboards creaked behind Saul as the man walked toward the tavern door. Saul slipped the business card beneath his drink where the impromptu coaster went waterlogged, running the ink into illegible streaks of black.

The tall man walked with an easy saunter into the night. When the front door swung closed its little windows reflected a picture to Saul of the bartender pouring him a third glass of the smoothest scotch he'd ever had.

In the absence of the man's hulking body, the barroom space opened into a lighter, more fluid shape. The blues music streaming from each corner of the ceiling flowed with a more sonorous clarity into Saul's ears, reverberating softly off the oaken walls like the inside of an old guitar. Movement became more apparent. There were people all around. Those to his left were huddled at one rounded corner of the bar top dealing cards. A chorus of jeers erupted now and then from their little gambling circle. The blue-backed cards flashed across the table as comers and goers passed by them through the front door beyond which the black night flickered with the red glowings of taillights and smokers' cigarettes. The appearance of new faces came in a frequent but disjointed parade. Saul looked into the bar mirror with a distant glaze over his eyes as the people passed behind him. The haze of drink had begun to settle.

Then, while sipping his scotch, he caught the sound of familiar laughter down near the end of the bar. Her hair was bubblegum pink now, and it drew in all the bar lights with a smoldering vibrance. Darla changed her color every couple months, and the last time he'd seen her behind the reception desk she was as blonde as Pam Anderson.

She was in conversation with a woman in yellow. He ap-

JACOB KOCKEN

proached, and when she saw him standing there she sang his name aloud. *Mr. Foster* Darla called him.

"Where's your suit?" she asked touching a palm to his chest. The drink she held never moved more than a few inches from her face. There was lipstick on the glass. That glossy red color pressed from her mouth fashioned a clash of aesthetic with the bright pink hair above. Her eyeliner was sharp yet overdone. From the day he'd met her, Saul's opinion of Darla had remained constant. Though now in her twenties, she was well taken care of by her parents' money. This caused an inevitable yet comfortable boredom which she escaped by tiptoeing delinquency. Darla flirted with everyone. She was clumsy at it as it was not out of genuine interest in the men she met but rather out of that boredom and a desire to fish something interesting out of them. Even when taking a drink she kissed her glass with a forced sensuality rather than sip off the edge. One could almost see in her fluttering eyes how she watched others pay attention to, not what she did, but exactly how she went about such ordinary things. She was not difficult to see through, and Saul had for a long time played with her in much the same way.

"You look like a different man," said Darla.

"Same old Saul," he said.

"I've never seen Saul out at a bar before."

"You've never seen the real Saul." He sat down.

"I must not have," purred Darla. "If I'm not mistaken I just saw you talking with Brock Nabers. Is that why you left us at the hotel?"

"Who?"

"The man you were drinking with," said Darla. Her eyes dazzled with a knowing expression. "You don't know him?"

"Not outside of scotch. Do you?"

"I'll bet half the women in Graumont know him," she said with a cackle. "But he's important, Saul. He's rich, don't you know? He owns things. Businesses."

"I see," said Saul, flatly. "Well, there's things more important than career. What're you drinking?"

"Shots now," she said. The girl beside her whooped and burst into earsplitting laughter. This same woman flagged the bartender with a stack of one-dollar bills. The proprietor poured three little

RISE THE MOON

swigs of Jose Cuervo. Saul clinked glasses with the girls and tossed his head back. He sucked a hard breath through his teeth which lit fire to the lingering taste of cheap liquor.

"You forgot the salt," said Darla, licking the back of her hand like a cat. Saul began to wave off the idea, but she was quicker, and soon her wet, salty knuckles forced their way across his nose and chin and lips. The delight in this stunt overtook her with laughter. She could not conceal her teeth, big and white with a small lipstick stain on one incisor. "You got fired just to get away from me, huh?"

"What I'm getting away from is Greg, his stupid goatee, and the rest of the racket."

"We ought to run off to California and tell the big guys what a dope he is," said Darla. Then she took a worn-out slice of lime directly from her friend's mouth and spoke to the woman through its dying sting. "Saul was a manager in California. Their branch was right on the beach. Imagine that; getting away to live in the sand and sun. He teased me every day talking about it; the red carpets, the fancy bar, indoor and outdoor pools. Nothing like our dingy place. After all, a hotel ought to be lavish or what's the point? So, now that Greg has finally decided to spice up the place, Saul wanted to bring in the red carpets they used on the golden coast."

"That would be gorgeous," said the woman in yellow.

"Yes," said Darla. "They're going with hardwood floors, but the carpet options Saul picked out were really indeed very gorgeous. Far too expensive for Greg."

"Thirteen percent more than wood," said Saul.

"Thirteen. That's an unlucky number," said the other woman.

"Well, Saul's the unluckiest guy around," said Darla. "First of all, his wife is a nut; the religious kind who only talks about her problems to God. Then at Bedalaus they give him assignments that don't matter and fire him to cut the costs. That's why he spent his days at the desk talking to me instead. I'm his therapist."

"I never said my wife was a nut," said Saul. "She does buy the bullshit they sell at church. But so does most of the country."

"Nut. How often does she go? There's no service in the middle of the week, Saul. Just one lonely man in pretty white robes. A normal person would find that suspicious for one reason or another."

"Please."

JACOB KOCKEN

"You know," said Darla, "when I was a kid I went to Catholic school. The girls had to wear skirts every day. They forced us. It's repressive; makes you sort of bottle it all up under that little uniform. I used to fuck Don Parsons in the choir room during communion."

"Jesus, Darla."

"That's the class all these church schools don't mean to teach. Everybody learns how to hide it, but that don't mean anything's gone away. And you know, I heard that priest was married not long ago. I heard she left him, so he turned and wed the church." She sighed, twisting into a wry smile. "But there are some things Jesus just can't do for a man."

"Miriam would kill you if she heard all that," said Saul.

"She would kill her husband for agreeing." Saul gave a tacit shrug and nod. The bartender came by, and Darla signaled at the three of them. "Your turn to buy," she said. Saul acquiesced, and the bartender poured three more shots of tequila.

"Now," said Darla, "when you move back to California, take us with you because a girl needs a little adventure. I can't believe you let her drag you here in the first place."

"It was my idea," said Saul. "And besides, there was a lot of decadence there. Not the place to raise a kid."

"It's boredom that breeds decadence, darling, not excitement. Take a look at the kids who grow up here." She grabbed his shoulder and pushed her foot off the crossbeam of the barstool. Her body stood up and spun, and she sat down abruptly in his lap. Laughter poured from the mouths of both girls. Saul went red. He tried feebly to push her off, but she leaned into him.

Darla's friend stood to use the restroom. She stopped abruptly and turned back pointing at her wrist. "Time to get to Jenny's." Darla nodded.

"Too bad you can't come," she said. "Since you got a nonsuspicious wife to get back to." Her mouth was so close he could taste her swallowed Cuervo.

"Where are you going?"

"Party in Middleton. All night fun."

"I can't be gone all night."

"I know, darling," she said. "But you've been missing out." Her

RISE THE MOON

body wriggled, and she slid from his thigh down to solid ground. "One of these days you'll have to run all the way back to California to find me." Her friend emerged from the restroom and walked out the front door with a whirl of her arm. The pink haired girl shrugged at him and started after her.

"Darla," he said abruptly. Saul grabbed a napkin from a tray on the bar and scrawled his address. He told her to come by his house the next day around noon. And she did just that.

Now, Saul sank against the side of his bed with blood on his hands. The pink-haired woman was gone. For a moment, he harbored the hope it was all a guilty, ecstatic hallucination. But Darla had seen him too. "Was that your kid?" she'd kept saying over and over. She'd tried to whisper consolations while pulling a tight pair of jeans up to her hips, but he did not hear them. Her young skin that had once shone so beautifully in the bar light appeared now as a sallow, diaphanous drape, only a dressing for that barren frame. Then she left.

He sat now still half undressed on his bedroom floor consumed once again by that terrible feeling that there was nothing to do. The scent of his wife was all about the room; subtle but rising off their marital sheets to loom in the air above him. The droning noise had finally left his head, evicted by the pounding blood in his ears and the strain of the bright chandelier lights. Doing was of no consequence to him now. His future was comprised entirely of a long and dreadful wait. Two things caught him up there. First was a photo of their son on the far wall. He was an infant playing peek-a-boo. Adult hands framed his face from just after leaving his eyes, revealing the world again. His chin and cheeks were wrinkled with perfect laughter. Second was the man that hung above Miriam's side of the bed. Blood leaked over his face and palms too. The cross was soiled with it.

The carpet on which Saul sat, long shag and only two years old, was now imbued with the blood that kept running from his hand. He pressed one palm to the other to stop the bleeding. He squeezed them together so hard they might fuse under pressure. And with his hands folded like that, for the first time since he was a child, Saul prayed. It was a resentful and desperate prayer that broke his pride with all the force of his broken heart. He chewed and spit the

JACOB KOCKEN

words as they came into his mouth. He prayed for his troubles to be erased, to be taken away. And in his misery he wallowed. He prayed hard and long until the bleeding subsided. The carpet was colored with little rusty pools of red. He washed himself up, and when it was clean he saw the wound on his palm was raised in little tracks and fixed to scar no doubt. He wrapped it with gauze and went downstairs to wait. On the staircase wall, he found the print of his hand where he'd steadied his haste. The grooves of his flesh patterned in red, drying already against the white paint. Saul wetted his hand at the kitchen sink and returned to scrub the mark. Its color diluted to orange and teared down the face of the wall. When Saul wiped the belly of his shirt over the spot he found it come away merciful. He slunk over to the living room couch where he sat in silence. Time passed until the distant church bells chimed seven. Then his wife came home dressed in black.

6.
Saul

THE TIME BETWEEN THEIR BREATHS of conversation hung morose and empty before Saul like butcher shop carcasses. His every nerve was dread. He couldn't even respond when she said hello.

Miriam had left that morning as his wife but returned a dark and somber mourner. Her clothes were as black as her blurred mascara. When she came through the front door she walked right up to Saul and threw her arms around him. She did not sob, but her breath was deep and shaken. He could feel Miriam grabbing her bad hand with her good one to squeeze him tighter. Saul put his arms around her shoulders, but he was glared at by the laceration of his own hand and felt too weak to squeeze back. Then she let him go, taking the warmth of her body off his chest, and his breath collapsed like a swimmer in the ice.

"Is my baby home?" Her words sounded miserable and pleading, a tone Saul had hardly heard since the passing of her mother. Saul could only shake his head.

"She was such a little angel," said Miriam. "Did I tell you they baptized her two weeks ago? She wore the tiniest white dress that covered everything but her fingers and little bald head. How can people do these things? I want to see my baby." Miriam looked for a moment as if she would cry, and so Saul gathered her in his arms again, this time squeezing like he would never let her go.

"You will," he said. "You'll see him soon."

"Weren't the Keplings going to Ohio? Shouldn't they be gone? Shouldn't he have come home?" Miriam broke away from his embrace and went to the phone. He could hear the line ringing on the

JACOB KOCKEN

other end. It rang and rang in the silence until the automatic voice told Miriam no one was there. She set the phone down and wiped her face with her hand. "Oh my God," said Miriam. "Where is he?"

There was fear in her face. She stared down at the phone, and her fingers tapped on the marble countertop with fervent impatience. Even through Saul's panic, her maternal fear touched him. "It's okay, Mimi." Saul put his hand on her again. "He'll come any minute." Miriam's breath moved audibly through her nose.

"It's our son," she said more sternly. She faced him, but her eyes were back in memory, beginning to swim with tears from an old and poisoned well. "We are supposed to protect him. That's the order of things." She said it again, "The order of things, God damn it. Sweet baby. Good, sweet baby."

Saul took her into a third embrace before the trembling tears could fall. He said nothing at all, only felt the rise and fall of her slowly calming chest. When they disentangled Miriam nodded to him. Then she moved toward the pantry and began absently preparing food.

While Miriam made dinner, Saul made up his mind to walk around the block or down to the Keplings' in search of his son. He put on his shoes and came out through the garage where things were in a state of disarray. Down on the storage end, boxes were overturned, Christmas lights leaked out onto the concrete, and the Virgin Mary statue from the Nativity set Miriam's mother had gifted them was broken in a dozen pieces across the floor. He pushed the larger things back to where they belonged and took up a broom.

With a minute of sweeping, Saul had the Virgin's dust and fragments all in a pile. He was picking up the larger pieces of her torso and what was left of her radiant face when he heard the sound of creaking metal. It came undulating toward him from somewhere down the road. He looked up and saw the bike. Saul put his face against the ceramic saint and froze. It should have been cold or smooth on his skin, but all he felt was the dead pin needles of numbness.

Slithering closer, the sound danced a slow, elliptic taunt as he felt it enter the garage. Then the squeaking chain ceased, and he felt a wooden knock pounding at his back. There was Ira beside him. A video camera dangled nonchalantly in his hand.

RISE THE MOON

Saul's ears began to beat. His mouth went dry. The boy's hand was on him, eyes looking up to his father. Ira's lips were moving, but the words moved past Saul unnoticed. Then the hand came down and with a look of confusion Ira was walking away.

"Hold it," said Saul. He dropped the pieces of the Mother, and she shattered once again. He stumbled forward, catching hold of Ira's shirt. The cloth balled up inside his fist, and he pulled Ira face to face. "Don't say anything. It doesn't mean anything," he said. Saul spoke in whispers. "I am so sorry. So sorry! Leave it up to me. Now is not the time. It's my mistake. Let me fix it."

"Will you stop?" said Ira. There was anger or irritation in his voice.

"Please," said Saul. His grip tightened. "What do you want from me?"

"I want you to let go of my shirt." Ira twisted and Saul released him. "Why are you all crazy over it? You could've ripped my shirt. I love this shirt." And with that he turned and went indoors, leaving Saul still numb and trembling in the garage.

The sky turned orange with the setting sun. Saul stared at the closed door and knew deep in his stomach it would be locked if he tried to enter. He paced back and forth in the garage, and out down the road he saw the sun fleeing over the horizon. He thought perhaps to follow it; to run to the edge of the Earth away from all his trouble, to where doubt and sorrow did not hold a place of certainty. He ought to run away with Darla. She would go with him wherever until she got bored. He had a car. The keys were only up in the bedroom.

Like a thief in his own home, Saul crept inside. The television was on. The news story was always the same now. They were talking about the egg the man had brought. It had been fresh and spotless brown. He'd kept a dozen hens they said. The culprit's face was on the screen, and the air was filled with guilty conviction. Through the empty living room, Saul could see the kitchen where Miriam brought a steaming bowl over from the stove. The smell, to Saul, was one of burning. Ira was mulling about.

"Where have you been?" Miriam was saying. Saul saw her bend in and kiss their boy on the top of his head as she often did. The camera sat unattended atop the counter. The stairs were through the

JACOB KOCKEN

kitchen.

"Furke's house," Ira said. The kitchen lights were low, and now a red glow from outside colored everything. Since the moment of Ira's arrival, the sun had begun to hurry. Saul walked in the half cover of the dying light. He could not see Miriam now, but her feet shuffled on the wood floor by the dining table one room over. He tried to peek around the wall and saw the flash of her hair and clothes bustling.

"I guess we went down to the gorge," said the boy. His voice sounded tight.

"You know I don't like you playing down there," said Miriam. The ends of her words were still shaking with breathless relief. "For God's sake, baby. After what's just happened? You worried me sick. Sick. You can't be doing that to me. My goodness." Then there was the soft shuffling of clothes, and she smothered him in her embrace. Saul could see the little veins rising in her hands.

"Mama," came the muffled answer. "I'm sorry, Mama."

"Did you watch that Jezebella leave? Is she really gone now?"

"Yes."

"Thank Jesus," said Miriam. "She was getting real skimpy with those outfits. God save Ohio now. At least you don't have to deal with her anymore." She tousled Ira's hair and kissed the top of his head.

Saul waited and listened a final moment before stepping swiftly into the kitchen. From the corner of his eye, he saw his wife. Her eyes were closed. He walked as quickly and quietly as possible. On the fourth stair, he heard her voice.

"Saul, if you're going upstairs will you bring me a clean hand towel? Hallway closet."

He didn't even turn to face her. He simply climbed the stairs. Up in his bedroom, the lights stayed off. He could find his dresser in the dark, and the car keys were on top by his wallet. He took a small luggage bag from the closet and packed a couple extra sets of clothes; his toothbrush; his daily Allegra; essentials.

As he carried the bag out into the hallway, the clinking keys inside it cut the silence like bells. He shoved the bag into the back of the hallway closet, covering it beneath a stack of bath towels and extra linens. It was a temporary hiding spot. It wouldn't sit too

RISE THE MOON

long. From the top shelf, he took a clean hand towel for Miriam and walked solemnly back down stairs.

In the dining room, Ira was at the table fixing a plate.

"Did you get too much sun?" said Miriam to the boy.

"I feel great," said Ira. Miriam was sitting across from him. They were eating already. Her eyes met Saul there at the bottom of the stairs. The hand towel dangled out before him.

"On the drawer by the sink please," she said.

Saul tucked the towel into a drawer handle. He watched them eat for a while across the room. A spot at the table sat open between them. The kitchen light, like their bedroom chandelier, seemed to beam in concentration on his usual chair. For as long as he could, Saul kept himself in the recesses of the kitchen. Then eventually he made his slow way to where they sat and leaned against the back of his wife's chair. He stroked Miriam's shoulder. His lingering touch was delicate as if he were petting a wild fawn. In the living room, the television news spoke of the impending Yokoven trial.

"Furke says they're going to kill him," said Ira.

"Let's not talk about it at dinner," said Miriam. Saul slouched into his chair, his whole body going limp, waiting. There was an empty plate there for him. His wife had made spaghetti. She always put basil in the marinara because Saul had a special tongue for the accent it gave. She couldn't even taste it she'd said many times before. She couldn't even taste it, but she always put it in there for him. But today Saul did not reach for the serving fork. His stomach was a brick.

"It's what he deserves, right?" Ira spoke through his cornbread. "Isn't that what you said yesterday, Dad?"

"I suppose so," said Saul.

"I think I've had enough death for today," said Miriam. "And baby, no more being away so long without telling us. And don't be locking your bedroom door like you have been. What if something happens to you, and I need to get in? You don't need to be locking your door." She gathered her plate and glass. Her food was hardly touched, and it slid heavily into the garbage. Dishes clinked together in the sink. Then she was gone up the stairs.

Saul watched his son keenly while Ira's sole attention turned to food. He ate voraciously, lips smacking as though he was all alone.

JACOB KOCKEN

"Sometimes people make horrible mistakes, Ira."

"Like murder?"

Saul directed a solemn look over his shoulder toward the staircase. The dull creaking sound of his wife's climbing steps ceased at the top, and another level of lonesome silence enveloped Saul. "I don't know why Yokoven did what he did. But it's possible he feels like the worst man in the world. Not because he got caught." Saul watched his son intently. The fork in Ira's hand spun around in his noodles. He poured himself a second glass of milk. "He's destroyed his world," Saul went on quiet and hurried. "So that no one can live the same way anymore. Now they will live in pain, and so will he."

"So you don't think they should kill him?"

"I don't know maybe they should. But they should still know. Know that he's sorry. He realizes the pain he's causing. He didn't, but now he does. He wants it to stop."

"Did you know him?"

"You know I'm not talking about him, Ira." Saul's throat closed up. Finally, the boy put down his fork, and the two met eyes. "What you saw today." Saul tried to find more words, but thinking made him dizzy, so he put his head down and waited.

"Oh," said Ira. "Does it really matter, Dad? We'll get a new one just as good."

"What?"

"A new one. She might not even notice. Or maybe she'll like it better." Saul curled up over the table, splayed his hands over the wood, then leaned back and stood up straight again. He moved uncomfortably and looked at his son sidelong.

"What are you saying?"

"They have to sell Mary statues all over. I saw you broke the one Mom uses. It's not Christmas time yet, but they'll have them somewhere."

Saul stared blankly for a moment. His eyes were watering. He blinked, and when he opened his eyes the boy looked new. His skin was shining like an infant's. His long brown hair appeared soft and feathered. Saul squared up against the backrest of a chair. He searched the boy's face and found nothing but genial concern.

"Don't fuck with me." The words were curt and furtive. Ira continued to chew but looked taken aback. "Stop eating," said

RISE THE MOON

Saul. More still, the boy looked startled. His fork froze. "Are you being serious?"

"Why are you harassing me?" The two stared at the space between them. Saul said nothing. Soon enough Ira stood and departed, leaving behind his dirty plate as he was wont to do. His feet climbed the stairs with the slow and rhythmic tapping of a careless mind.

Saul found himself alone in the kitchen. Miriam was upstairs in the shower; he could hear the water running. He thought of Darla's wet figure. Little rivulets of water were streaming off her body and tickling his skin when he first heard his son and saw the little red light of the camera.

There it was sitting on the kitchen counter; just sitting there beside the dishes like it was waiting to be washed.

Saul wiped the sweat of his hands on his pants and opened the recorder. He flipped through the tapes. He watched the first couple seconds of each video, seeing when they were from. In red numbers, the date appeared at the bottom left corner of each. The first was from Ira's birthday two years ago only moments after unwrapping his gift. There were a dozen recordings of Ira and Furke playing games or talking with their faces pressed against the lens. The last was from four months prior; Ira some distance away with the camera propped up. He was trying to throw a curveball. Several extra balls were at his feet, and he threw them all in succession, each one firing toward the screen before falling away. Saul hit fast forward through the video. He watched it closely. Then it ended.

He tried to scroll further, but there were no more files. He watched the final video through once more, but again it ended there with Ira's mitt by the lens as he came away from the pitcher's mound. Saul closed the camera and stood there wondering to himself. The sound of running water from the shower upstairs stopped. He set the camera back on the counter and paced the empty kitchen. More movement came from upstairs; footsteps following his own, doors opening and closing.

Then he took up the camera in his hand again and climbed the stairs. Coming out from his bedroom for the open bath was his son. They met there in the hallway. Under the single ceiling light, Ira looked like one of those stained glass figures he knew from some-

JACOB KOCKEN

where in his memory.

"Your camera," said Saul. He held it out to the boy. A moment of recognition passed before Ira came forward.

"It's weird," he said. "I can't even think why I brought it to Furke's house." Then he smiled and took it. "Goodnight, Dad." He disappeared into his room where he began to rummage beneath the bed, returning the camera to its customary box.

Saul's eyes flicked between the two bedroom doors and the closet with his hidden bag. At the bottom of his vision, he saw footprints. The carpet was wet where Miriam had come out of the shower. Already the edges were turning light with dryness. He followed the footsteps with his own toward their bedroom. Saul cut the hallway light, and all was dark except for the crack beneath their door. He went there and pushed it open to find Miriam lying on the bed half dressed. She smiled at him tenderly, and he smiled back. Then Saul crawled onto the bed and met his wife with wild enthusiasm.

7.
Anna Lee

JANUARY 3RD

It is the third day at the apartment in the city. I don't like it here. It always smells like cars. There is no room inside for all three of us. Mom always wants the curtain closed, and since its only one room and the light is dim it's always twilight in here. There are no sugar pines or real trees at all except the lonely kind planted between the roads and sidewalks. Mom found a job at a supermarket, so now she'll be gone all the time. I want to go outside and explore, but Mom doesn't like it when Nancy is alone. I don't get the point anymore. She says next week I'll start school. I can't wait for that. I can't wait to be away. Nancy is rude. You can hardly believe she's older. If I'm reading a book or holding anything at all she takes it. She tries to take this notebook away all the time, but only when I'm holding it. Mom says I did that stuff when I was a toddler. It's like she can only see things other people see. Like everything she should think will be found in other people's thoughts. I remember once when I was little and she was sort of little too, me and her and Dad were out in the forest with Jasper. They were taking us hunting but not for animals. We went down to the plateau where the river runs to look for thunder eggs. Dad said Jasper knew where to find them because he studied rocks when he went to school and that when he took Jasper real hunting he would only stare at the ground and hunt for rocks instead. We walked along the river bank for a long time until the grass turned to sand and the river got wide and shallow. Dad went in first with his shoes off and his pants

JACOB KOCKEN

rolled up to the knees. He shut his lazy eye to search. Dad always did that when he was looking for things. Beneath the rushing water everything shimmers like treasure. Jasper found one first. I led Nancy over to see, but it wasn't pretty at all; just brown and round as the Earth. But it was light, like a bubble pretending to be a rock. Only after Jasper cracked it open on shore with another big stone did we see. Jasper said it was called a geode. I'd seen them before in Dad's chapel. This one was white, but there are purple ones too. Those are called amethyst. We hurried back into the water and picked up every rounded rock we could find. They're as big as your hands when they're good, or bigger. But the one I got was small. I found it in a shelf of big bank rocks where the crawfish like to hide. It was small enough to fit inside the palm of my hand but filled with shining white like diamonds. It split down the middle in two good halves. Jasper gave one piece to me and one to Nancy, but Nancy kept dropping hers and taking mine, and I got so angry I threw it at her, and the rock hit right in her stomach. Dad yelled at me, and I said what was the point, and he said it was his job to yell at me because bad things are bad to the people who do them and not just to who they are done. Then he picked up that rock and told me to carry it wherever I go to always remember. 'Look at this gem and tell me what you feel,' he said, and I told him I felt sad. 'That's what sin does,' he said. 'It turns everything grey. Hold on to this and work to love your sister. One day you will pull it from your pocket and find the beauty redoubled. It will tell you that you sinned once, but it will also be a sign that you have not done it again for so long, and that you and your sister are well. And then you will carry it out of happiness.' It is in my pocket right now. Now it's in my hand. The bottom of it is round and grey and smooth. The crystals are white, and they stick up from the middle of the rock like teeth. I threw them as hard as I could right at Nancy. I want to throw them again.

8.
Miriam

MIRIAM LIKED TO LAY CLOTHES out for her son. When he was a newborn she had to choose his outfit every day. Then he began to grow, and not only did she have to dress him, she had to buy new things every time the waists or shoulders got tight. And as a child continues growing steadily, Miriam became habituated to the task of dressing her boy. She got to play with colors and styles. He would stand as she held up shirts over his chest, peering over him at arm's length. Some outfits looked good with his hair pulled back; some with it down at his shoulders.

This morning, she'd woken as the sun broke. It provided an easy, natural light in through the windows as she tip-toed into her son's bedroom. He was asleep as usual at this time. His breath was soft and precious, and Miriam stood just inside the threshold for a minute watching him. Years ago she used to watch him sleep for hours; when he was young enough to doze in her arms. When she stood here, in line with the foot of his bed, the ends were partially blocked by the footboard, and Miriam could pretend he was still an infant in the crib who needed her to lift him out over the side rails.

Inside his dresser, Miriam flipped through piles of pants folded into perfect squares. There were dress shorts too which she thought about picking from. It was supposed to be hot again today. But when her fingers touched the green corduroys her mind was made up. There was a white and navy combo of shirt and jacket hanging in the closet that had caught her eye, and she laid the three pieces over the top of his dresser. For shoes, she went with white and took one of several pairs from his closet floor. It was the first day of high

JACOB KOCKEN

school. His outfit would be cute.

"Wake up, dear," she said back at his bedside. Miriam put a hand to his shoulder and rocked him easily back and forth until his chest swelled with the first morning breath and his eyes cracked grudgingly open. She lifted the blanket back, waking him up in full. "I'll make you breakfast before I take off." Her boy propped himself up on an elbow and yawned. She waited until he met her eyes and nodded.

"Thank you," he said.

She bent down and kissed the top of his head as he began to sit up. There was an empty glass on the bedside table. There was always a glass in the morning. Little white lines were visible where the dregs of milk had evaporated through the night. Miriam took this up, cradling it in her bad hand and left the room.

Downstairs, she began making buttermilk pancakes. Her baby liked blueberries in his. While the batter was being whipped, she heard him moving upstairs. The toilet flushed. The bathroom sink went on and off. A series of shuffling steps moved between there and his room. She timed her heating of the stovetop pan so that her son's breakfast would still be hot when he came bounding down the stairs.

He was dressed almost as she had planned. The corduroys fit perfectly. The navy jacket, however, was missing.

"That's just the undershirt, dear," said Miriam. "Did you see the other piece? I put it on the dresser too."

"It's too hot today."

"The material is light," she said. "Give it a try. You'll look so cute."

Her son turned back to the stairs and climbed. She had the pancakes out and steaming on a large serving plate when her son trod back into the room modeling now the full extent of her vision.

"See, doesn't it look nice?" she said.

"It looks nice."

Miriam brought him two of the pancakes right where he stood. They were drizzled lightly with maple syrup, and she cut them into small, regimented pieces with the edge of a fork.

"Blueberry," she said.

"Thanks Mom."

RISE THE MOON

Then Miriam stabbed one of the little squares and lifted it toward her son. "Taste," she said, holding the fork inches from his mouth.

"I can do it myself."

"Taste, darling. I made them with blueberries. Your favorite." She held the fork steady.

Her son opened his mouth, and she fed him. Then Miriam kissed the top of his head and set the plate down on the dining room table.

"I've got to be off to work," she said to her son.

"Alright."

"But this afternoon we're going to the zoo, so come right home after school."

"Can Furke come?"

"He could," said Miriam. "But I thought it could be just me and you. They'll be closing for the season soon. The lions will be stuck inside in a few weeks when autumn comes. Do you remember when you were little and saw the lions for the first time? Remember how it roared by the glass, and you hid behind your mama? But I held your hand, and then we looked at the lions for nearly an hour. I thought we could do that again. Wouldn't it be nice? To see the lions?"

Her son sat down in front of his breakfast. The fork began pecking at pieces of pancake. "Okay," he said.

"Good," said Miriam. "And you just saw Furke and that Jezebella yesterday, right? Okay, I've got to run." She hugged him from behind as he sat there in the chair. The warm smell of milk was all about him underneath that of maple syrup and pancakes. A final time, she kissed him on the top of his head and left out the front door.

9.
Saul

WHEN SAUL WOKE UP THE next morning, his wife was gone to work. Sunlight streamed in softly through the window. He rose naturally without an alarm or the lingering fog of sleep. The events of the day before swam through his head with the evanescence and profundity of a dream. He laughed in wonder until head and heart began to race. Then from another room he heard the wooden clap of cabinet doors swinging open and shut again. It dawned on him that it was Ira's first day of school. Saul hopped up, pulled on clothes with alacrity, and hustled downstairs to catch his son.

In the kitchen, the boy was pouring syrup onto a plate of blueberry pancakes. There were already bits of food clinging to the porcelain under swirls of maple syrup from the first helping. The boy was eating voraciously, filling an empty pit.

"Hey there," said Saul. Ira greeted him pleasantly. His shoes were already on, and his empty backpack sat leaning against one leg of his chair. "How are you feeling?"

"Great," said Ira.

"Good." The boy nodded. He shoveled another forkful to his mouth. "Big day isn't it?" said Saul.

Ira shrugged.

"Nervous?"

"No, I want to see Furke."

"You just saw him yesterday."

"There was something we were going to do yesterday. I can't think what it was."

"Oh?" For the first time since the night before, Saul felt a flash

RISE THE MOON

of anxious tension brush through him. Ira nodded as if to himself. The boy's eyes glazed over as he cut pancakes and thought.

"I woke up on his couch, and Bella was in the room, and we were all playing card games and stacking them. Then she was gone. Then me and Furke were in the house. I don't know. We were at the gorge. I was biking. It was down in the gorge. I think Furke left early. We don't usually bike down there. There's bad cracks all over. But it was getting dark, so I came home."

Saul simply shook his head. "Do you want a ride to school?"

"No, I'll bike." Ira tossed his empty plate in the sink and headed for the door. Saul sprang to catch him. He cinched a hand around each of his son's shoulders, and the boy looked at him with round, wide eyes.

"I love you," said Saul.

"Yeah," said Ira. "Love you too." Saul held him there for a while, searching the depths of the young pupils across from him. After a while, Ira blinked, and Saul saw himself on the ocular reflection as clear as looking in their bathroom mirror. He loosed his hands, and Ira threw not a second glance as he stepped out on his way to school. Through the living room window, Saul saw his son flip the kickstand and roll down the street. Now and then he dropped an arm to his side, sometimes both. He steered with the simple weight of his body and pedaled smoothly without a care in the world.

The hands on the hallway clock ticked audibly. Saul sat around in bliss until nine o'clock struck. This time just yesterday he'd been sitting in the kitchen with the paper waiting for Darla. She'd looked sort of horrible at the door, hung over and irritated. But inside she'd turned as bright and lovely as the night before. Saul put the thought out of his mind and sighed with great relief.

Up in his bedroom, the carpet on his side of the bed was still mottled with dried blood. In the strangeness of all that had happened, Saul had entirely forgotten this and, indeed, the cut across the palm of his hand as well. He tried removing the red spots with soap and water, but at best they smeared things, and the stain was only wider and more noticeable. It wouldn't do. Instead, Saul took a box cutter from the garage and slit the carpet at one corner of the room to get it started. Then he stooped and pulled up hard to snap

JACOB KOCKEN

the carpet from its fastenings. It took him what seemed like hours to pry the whole thing up. There was a bed to move and two dressers, a nightstand, and other heavy, boxy things. But in the end, Saul had stripped the room to satisfaction. He would replace the carpet with something lavish. He already knew what.

But that would come another day. For now, Saul moved to the hallway closet. Beneath the bath towels and linens, he found the bag he'd packed and took his keys. The rest he re-hid and drove downtown to the hotel where he used to work. Partway through the drive, just as he had turned off the highway and into the business district, the alarm in Saul's Cavalier began to sing. Several lights on the dash blinked in unison. It was not the first time this had happened. Invariably, sometime during a drive the machine would fall into such a fit. But Saul detected nothing in particular that was wrong. It still handled well, and so he simply got used to turning up the radio. Today, he didn't even need music to help him ignore the sounds. Today, he was consumed by something more important.

It was the first time he'd been to the Bedalus building since termination. Upon entering the parking lot, he drove in as close to the curb as possible, took his foot off the gas, and rolled along the big lobby windows. His head peered out the car door, and through a flashing window glare he saw a woman moving at the desk. Saul parked where he was sideways in a stall and went in.

Automatic glass doors opened at his presence. His vision swam with black shadows adjusting to the lower light and the great depth of the room. The lobby was capacious, long and wide with thick limestone pillars reaching for a sunlit dome three stories up. One of these high walls held a giant iron timekeeper, the hands spinning round a wheel of twenty-four roman numerals. It was noon. Again, Saul was bombarded by thoughts of the previous day, and how when the clock last showed this time the receptionist below it was in his bed.

Four corridors finished with cherry wood floors branched off from this central room. The cross section of those corridors harbored the front desk.

"Darla?" said Saul aloud. He approached with some enthusiasm. But the woman behind the desk was not who he sought. She was brunette, mousy, and looking at the computer screen with the

RISE THE MOON

expression of one who is lost.

"Hello," she said finally.

"Who are you?" said Saul.

"My name is Maria. Are you checking in?"

"Is Darla here?"

The girl stammered a bit. "I'm not supposed to give out room numbers."

"Not a guest," said Saul. "Darla. Is she here? Back there. Behind the desk." The woman looked slowly over each shoulder verifying that she was quite obviously alone. "She works here at this desk. Darla."

"I'm sorry sir; I don't know anyone with that name. Did you want me to call a manager down?"

"No, no," said Saul. He turned away with a growing excitement. As he walked back to his car, the feeling overtook him, and he laughed in delight and wonder at everything around him. He sparked the ignition and sped from the parking lot so fast he left a ghost of the tires behind.

Cruising down the roads, he only picked up speed; fifty-five in a thirty, hardly realizing it. Houses swung past in a blur of color. Saul was flying.

As he swung around the corner of Ballard Street, the strong sun struck his eyes and sent him squealing against the curb. For a moment, Saul could not see, and he slammed the brakes right there on the road. When the Cavalier came to a stop he sat there blinking away the floating print of the sun on his vision. The intensity of the light was gone, and when he looked up at where the sun should have been it was blocked by the towering steeple of St. Francis church.

Saul threw his car into park and ran up to the old building. It loomed like a great medieval castle with heavy stones and an ancient spirit.

The doors were open, but the halls were empty. "Hello," he called out. His voice and steps echoed loudly in the vacuous space between the stone walls. The arches were dark and hidden in their own shadowy drop. There was no electric buzz in the room. Light of all colors poured in through mosaic-bodied saints; half human, half heaven they seemed in their continually waning and waxing

JACOB KOCKEN

radiance. From long millennia the dead disciples stood firm in this spirit. Brighter light came through the latticed windows like the needled eaves of some old pine branch canopy. It produced an awful and captivating contrast of illumination and shadow.

Saul walked about, blinking hard and squinting to examine the empty sanctuary. Just passed the entryway doors he bumped into a great stone bowl. It was four or five feet in diameter with a thin puddle of water evaporating at the bottom. Saul ran a finger down the smooth rock face. He flicked the water with the tip of one finger before moving on toward the center of the building.

There was an earthy, wooden smell to the place. Dust floated in the air. He watched little particles fall continually through the sunbeams, and as he walked through them he could taste a material decay in his mouth. Saul found it unpleasant. He licked his lips and spat. Droplets of his distaste were left on the floor behind him.

There was a certain weight to the church. With its statues and icons, ancient things stuck firmly into the glass and bricks of St. Francis.

Saul passed by the long rows of pews and stepped up the dais to the altar. A long green cloth covered the great wooden table. Its legs were adorned with gold plated palmettes. Behind it, suspended high on the wall was the Savior crucified. His hands and feet bled small rivulets while His forehead poured unbridled. Blood. So much blood. It was gruesome. His mouth was crooked. His eyes looked to the sky clenched in pain and wide with horror all at once. The yet unrisen Son disturbed Saul's stomach.

"Hello?" said a voice. An inconspicuous door at the front of the hall was standing ajar. There in the threshold was a man dressed in plain clothes except for the religious black and white around his neck. He smiled when he saw Saul.

"Are you a priest?"

"I am. Are you looking for one?" His voice was low but agreeable. They met in the center of the great room.

"You don't know me," said Saul. "I've never really been here."

"The house of God is open to everyone." Dark black hair covered the head of the priest but was entirely absent from his face and neck. His stature was that of a growing boy, and his maturity showed rather in a certain patient demeanor. The priest extended

RISE THE MOON

his hand graciously. Saul took it and introduced himself as Miriam's husband.

"Ah, the man from California," said Father David.

"Yes," said Saul. "She talks about me?"

"Well, we've both discussed our families."

Saul regarded him quietly. The priest seemed to detect discomfort.

"I hear confessions every week, Saul. They don't leave me."

"Confessions. You heal people?"

"It's one of the sacraments; a sacred contract between man and God. I am only a conduit, the wire through which people express their souls. Authority lies above. Salvation and condemnation are out of my bounds. All I offer is all I have; prayer and contemplation."

"But God does respond? How do you know the judgment?"

"There's a private sense for some. I am in the dark." The priest was no longer looking at Saul. He didn't seem to be looking at anything in particular. All of a sudden, his body began to fidget, and he returned attention to Saul. "It's not always about sins though. Some people just need to talk. When Miriam first came to see me it was all about her mother; you can imagine. Maybe two years ago."

"Yes, that was horrible," said Saul. "She didn't say a word for weeks."

"She's found improvement."

"Mm."

"Death changes people. If nothing else, I'm glad it's brought Miriam to God. I hope happier circumstances have brought you here today." The priest stood with one hand clasped over the other at his waist. His kind expression was expectant.

Saul's lip quivered for a moment as he thought how he might express himself. "What do you know about miracles?" The young priest made no immediate response. His hands began to move, and he caught each of them with the other.

"It's a tricky thing. Anything to do with God seems twisted up in paradox. Why don't we sit down?" He motioned for Saul to follow him down the pews.

They came to the same door from which the priest had emerged. It was a hallway with white painted walls and fluorescent ceiling lights. Halfway down the hall they turned left into a small office lobby. The walls were bare except a lone black crucifix beside the door. There was a small card table with two angular wooden chairs in the corner.

"Is this part of the church?"

"The clerical side," said the priest.

"It's sort of plain."

"There's still a vestige of the ascetic in religious life. Down at the abbey our rooms are worse than this. And the food could be better." Father David sighed. "But what comforts should really concern us?"

"God prefers you to be poor?"

"Minimalism is a personal choice; to help cultivate a relationship with the more eternal things," said the priest. "As for preference, we're taught He loves all people the same." Father David was at the office counter filling a disposable cup with black coffee. He tapped his fingers against the Styrofoam and pursed his lips. "It's not a sin to have things of course, and it's not a virtue to suffer." He shrugged. "Perhaps it takes a certain relationship with suffering to appreciate the Lord's abundance. People tend to forget the inevitable need for Grace. Then when tragedy strikes they go eye to eye with their demons. That sudden fall lays one low. Coffee?" asked Father David. Saul shook his head.

"People in such desperation," said Saul, "are they more worthy of that Grace?"

"Worthy, no. I don't think so. Though perhaps there are some states of mind you have to earn."

Just then a woman walked through the room holding a folder in her arms. She smiled at the two of them and went for the coffee pot as well.

"Before it's gone," she said with a shrug.

Father David patted Saul on the arm. "My office is across the hall," he said. Saul followed the priest into an even smaller room. Hanging on the wall was a scene of someone preaching. It was the Christ frozen in gesticulation. His mouth was open, His long brown hair windswept. It was not a painting or a print. Rather, the image was spider-webbed with thin, interstitial shadows; a jigsaw, framed and hung upright.

RISE THE MOON

They took seats on either side of the desk. Father David took a minute to clear the table. There were newspapers; not whole bundles, just the back ends where the crosswords and Sudokus were printed. All were completed in blue pen without a mark of correction. As the puzzles were gathered up, they revealed a check marked pattern. Two-inch squares of light and dark brown stretched inlaid over the desk.

"Chess?"

"I was state champion in high school," said the priest.

"Hm," said Saul. "Who was that woman?"

The priest looked up over his glasses at the open door. "Cindy? She does book work for the church; finances, logistics."

"You have a secretary?"

"Yes."

"She's beautiful."

"Quite," said the priest. "You asked about miracles?"

"Will it stay between you and me?"

"If you wish."

Saul took a breath. "I have never really been involved with religion. I know my parents were atheists, and they died that way. We put them in the ground, and if you had asked me then I would have said that's the end of the story. But yesterday," Saul paused. The priest leaned forward in his chair. "Well, yesterday I prayed for the first time. I said a few desperate words, and something happened. I want to know your secrets."

"I try to be an open book. The truth sets us free after all."

"Not your secrets, sir."

"*David* is fine."

"What I want to know is how you get to be you. How you know what you know. About God and all that. The stuff that separates you from the crowd you preach to." Saul was sweating some. He wiped the back of his neck.

"Well Saul, it's a long road to priesthood. I do, however, believe I know what secrets you mean. I call them mysteries."

"Yes," said Saul. "I do mean something I can't quite put into words. I feel different ever since it happened. I feel closer to Him, to something great. I want to move in that direction, but I don't know where to start."

JACOB KOCKEN

"How did the Lord work?" asked the holy man.

"I cannot describe it."

"That is quite understandable."

"Other than to say He took away my sins."

"It is a remarkable feeling. As for what you can do, we have a program for those who've recently come to faith and are not yet part of the Church."

"What do I do?"

"It's composed mostly of meetings each week where we study scripture and discuss its relevance in our lives. Participants become closer to God and each other over about six months and prepare for the sacraments."

"Is there a streamline version?"

"I appreciate your enthusiasm," David chuckled. "The reason it's spread out is that there is a lot of material to work through, and even what we can present in six months is limited."

"Can you give me the material? I can go through it at my own pace."

"The other reason is the community. The Church is more than a system of belief. We must be in constant dialogue with each other in order to fully appreciate the Word. God's kingdom is, after all, not one of geographical constitution. God created the ends of the Earth, and He has always ruled them. People are a bit different. Through free will we have encountered sin, and so it is ourselves and each other we have to bring back to God. That is a task that cannot be done alone. That is the real task of the Church. We are a family. Unfortunately, we are all busy, and once a week is the most often people will reliably convene."

"Okay, I'll come to the meetings. But will you give me the material in advance anyhow?"

"I would never deny Christ to a man who asks."

10.
Ira

GRAUMONT HIGH SCHOOL WAS ONLY a mile or so from their house. Ira had woken that morning from such a deep and dreamless sleep that even now, biking his way to the first day of classes, he was hardly conscious of the progression of time. His mind flit constantly between inward reverie and the wonder of some familiar but heretofore unappreciated sight such as the red cardinal swooping overhead or the subtle change in the temperature of the air as the breeze danced across his skin. Now and then a somewhat nagging thought surfaced of Furke or Bella. He remembered suddenly what the girl had said about the nascent hair on his face; 'It looks dirty.' But these thoughts had few particulars and were, for the moment, pushed out of mind by the rhythmic hum of his tires as they rolled him a mile and a half to the school.

A path of slate grey bricks wound off the road and around the football team's practice field. He approached the school building from its back entrance. Idling buses could be seen around the corner with indistinct faces filing out one after another. With a few minutes to spare before the bell, some mulled about the sidewalks while the rest disappeared at the front of the building.

Ira fixed his bike into a rack beside an old equipment shack. As he dismounted, something slammed with a loud and hollow sound against the back of the shed. Several voices erupted at once. The words were indistinct and guttural.

He followed the sounds. Back behind the shed, three boys were tangled in a violent scrum. All six fists were flying. Furke was on the ground rolling in the morning dew and caught between two

JACOB KOCKEN

familiar redheaded rascals.

"Ira," yelled Furke from his back, "stab 'em!" Ira did not move, but the heftier of the Paulsen twins who had a knee on Furke's chest snapped up to his feet. His eyes trained warily on Ira through disheveled red hair. "Stab 'em!" yelled Furke again as he caught the other twin with an elbow to the ribs.

Ira's hand went to his empty pocket. He never carried a blade. He didn't even own one. Furke gave a good shove to the wheezing boy and scurried out of his grasp. He got up and came to Ira's side with his fists to his chin and dancing on the balls of his feet. "Try it, Paulsen," said Furke. "Try it, and Ira here will cut you to pieces."

Ira's face shot back and forth between Furke and the twins who were both standing now and eying Ira's pocket. "What's happening?" said Ira.

"Bobby owes me smokes," said Furke, "but he's a cheapskate."

"I ain't cheap," said Bobby, the larger of the twins. "It's Garret that owes you."

"I don't know what you're talking about," said the other one.

"You son of a bitch," said Bobby to his brother. "I'm not paying your bad bets."

"I didn't bet him. You did!"

"All I know is I'm getting cigarettes, or else Ira's carving you both like ham," said Furke. Ira's hand trembled, and he squeezed a tight fist in his pocket.

"Two shoes, you really got a knife?" asked Bobby.

"You'll get your answer in twenty seconds if you don't fork over my cigs," said Furke.

"Give 'em up, Garret," said Bobby.

"It wasn't my bet," said Garret.

"Who owes you, Furke?" asked Ira.

"Hell, I don't remember. I just know it was a Paulsen." Ira took a step, and the twins flinched.

"Half a pack each," said Ira.

"Ten seconds," said Furke. The brothers shook their heads and dug into their pockets, all the while surveying Ira and muttering words of disgust at each other. They stepped forward, each with a handful of cigarettes.

"Am I supposed to smoke 'em all right now?" said Furke.

RISE THE MOON

"Give me a box." Garret flipped over his empty pack. "Good, now Ira doesn't have to live in the slammer with the Yok on account of cutting both your necks."

"It's just the heat of the moment that got me twisted," said Bobby. "We know he's bluffing."

"He ain't," said Furke.

"Bet you one pack of cigarettes."

Furke looked over at Ira, offering the stage for an unlikely coincidence. But Ira only blushed and shook his head confirming suspicion all around.

"Yeah," said Furke. "If Ira owned a knife he'd have a haircut by now." He laughed and slapped Ira on the back before putting a cigarette to his lips. He lifted a flame as well, one that caught the attention of the three other boys.

"What's that?" said Garret.

Gleaming through Furke's fingers was a draped and hooded figure of silver chrome. Furke struck some mechanism on the back, and the little man's silver hands shot out a brilliant one-inch flame. It burned bright and orange before a veiled face. The glow of lit tobacco blinked on and off, and Furke exhaled a long stream of smoke. Each of the twins was trained on the lighter.

"The Necromancer," said Furke. "Fifty bucks at Hutchin's."

"Give it here," said Bobby. "I want to necrotize something."

"Did you hear me?" said Furke. "Fifty bucks. I'm not letting you touch it."

"Looks heavy," said Garret.

"Oh come on, at least necrotize me," said Bobby. He held out a cigarette. Furke obliged and sent up a flame for each of the twins. The three of them sat down on the grass, leaning against the back wall of the equipment shed. Each one of them was scuffled with mud. Furke had a bruise brimming out on his jaw, and he touched it now and then with the same fingers that held his cigarette. Ira stood beside them with both hands back in his pockets.

"Ira?" Furke extended the pack as he often did, and as always, Ira shook his head.

Furke turned to Bobby. "I heard Carla broke up with you."

"She's a bitch like the rest of 'em," said Bobby. Furke nodded.

"Yeah, the love of Ira's life just ran off to college."

JACOB KOCKEN

Garret looked up at Ira and chuckled. His laugh vibrated extra low with the weight of the smoke. "Keep dreaming."

"He had a better shot than you," said Furke. "Bella kissed him."

"Yeah, just like he was gonna stab me," said Bobby.

"He told me about it himself, right bud?" said Furke. Ira nodded. "You know Ira don't lie." Bobby squinted and took a slow drag. The thought squirmed around inside him.

"You slobbed her, angel hair?"

"Sort of," he said.

"Well Goddamn," said Bobby. "She coming back for Christmas?"

"Probably," said Furke.

"Should I get her something nice or is she giving it away?"

Furke notched the cigarette between his lips and swung a good fist into Bobby's stomach. The boy had a fit of coughing, and his own cigarette fell to the wet grass.

"I'm only playing," said Bobby.

"Keep her out of your dirty mouth."

"Take it out on the guy who's groping her, damn."

"Hit Ira?" said Furke. "You ever seen him fight, or lie, or cheat? He's the best kid this town ever raised. If Bell ends up with a guy like that it's for her own good. You two on the other hand. You're tragedies. Me and Ira have a bet on whether it's one or both of you flunks that gets held back again. I don't think the luck's on your side."

"Fuck you," said Bobby.

"They're not looking for perfection, the teachers," said Furke. "All you need is sixty percent and you pass. I mean damn, all you got to do is get close, and they won't hold you back. In math you don't even have to get the answers right. They give you credit just for showing half straight work. Like they figure even a fool glancing in the right direction should figure things out eventually. That's all they want is you looking in the right direction, but all you can do right is puff smoke."

Bobby looked away. The cigarette on his lips had burned down to the butt. He pressed the glowing end into the dirt. "Necrotized," he said.

The first school bell rang, and the boys stirred.

RISE THE MOON

"We're late," said Ira. Furke stood up and pressed the dying coal into the ground with his shoe. They walked around to the front of the building. The sidewalks were vacant. The twins dragged their feet and quickly fell behind.

"Want to come over after school?" asked Ira. "My mom wants to go to the zoo."

"Later maybe," said Furke. "I've got to get to Betty Blossom's before they close."

"The garden store?"

"There's a sign that says they're hiring. Five dollars an hour. I just spent everything I had on this Necromancer, and what if my mom gets fired, you know?"

The boys reached the back doors of the school and split off in separate directions. Ira navigated the halls looking for B109. The room he sought was at the end of the hall, and he ducked in just as the teacher was calling roll.

There was an open seat in the first column near the back that Ira slid into shortly before his name was called out.

"Here," he said. The teacher, Mr. Callan was an elderly man with short white hair. He squinted, even through his thick circular glasses, at Ira, taking in the new face. Then he nodded and made a mark on his clipboard for every student on the rolling list.

"Harrison Grant. Katie Jasbecki. Allison Loam. Devan Noble." Mr. Callan repeated his squint after each of these names, studying them. His mouth soundlessly formed the syllables of their names a second, private time. "Anna Lee Lac." A hand went up beside Ira.

He had never seen the girl before. She sat forward in her seat, leaning on both elbows with her spine erect like some meerkat sentinel peeking over the berm. She had long black hair and large, dark walnut eyes. "Bella?" The word jumped from his mouth. Her attention flicked toward him momentarily while Ira's head snapped away, his cheeks filling hot with blood. A vague intimation of the previous day touched him and disappeared in a moment. Ira stole another glance at the girl. There was a kind of vigilance about her face; stern, looking, protecting.

She had heard him he thought. The corner of his vision showed how she stared his way before drifting back, her face bent over something.

JACOB KOCKEN

There was a little green book on the desk before her. Its pages were blank as eggshells, and every now and then the soft sound of her scratching pen touched Ira's ears. No lesson or instruction had been uttered by the teacher, yet her hand scrawled until an entire page was impressed with ink. A syllabus was passed down the rows, and only then did she look up from her work.

The first school period moved forward in a haze of flitting attention as Ira came continually back to the stunning girl beside him. Her hair was dark, second only to her eyes; and both so pure.

Ira saw her again in chemistry and later still in history. At roll call, he too mouthed the syllables of her name; Anna Lee Lac. She stuck in his mind all day, and it was after the final bell had rung and the students were let back out into the world that Ira saw her leaving down the same slate brick sidewalk behind the school. She walked slow with a stiff, bent-over posture he found peculiar even from a distance. From the bike rack, he watched her go, and when she turned the corner it was clear to see the little green book held open over one hand while the other inscribed private words even as she walked.

11.
Saul

SAUL SAT ALONE IN HIS living room. His wife was upstairs cleaning.

In the beginning God created the heaven and the earth. It was the first biblical sentence Saul had ever read. Miriam kept the tome on a shelf in their living room. It had been given to her years ago by her mother, Emily, after being confirmed in the Church. Bound in soft brown leather, it was the weightiest book Saul had ever held. Its outside was thick and skin-like. On the inside cover, the gifter had written in tall black letters. *Keep it with you. Always.*

Saul read with the book either in his lap or resting on the coffee table, his neck craning overtop. This posture was due to the cut on his hand. It was still tender. He had unwrapped and rewrapped the gauze today and had been pleased with its progress in healing. Still, the book was heavy, and its modest pressure caused pain. So now, with a lamp at his side and the evening moonlight piercing the window behind him, Saul read the Good Book from a distance.

Father David had assigned a folder full of paper. It laid splayed open beside the Bible. Saul paged through the contents as soon as he'd gotten home. He read the prayers and creeds and set them in their own pile. He took out Miriam's Bible upon beginning the reader's guide. This guide was broken down by book and chapter with bullet points beneath. Saul moved through the chapters slowly, referencing the template at every paragraph. It spoke of God, and the order of things, and the nature of man. And when the third chapter came to a close it spoke of a curse pressed into the fabric of human life so enduring through the generations that it made Saul's

JACOB KOCKEN

lip curl and his eyebrows converge.

It was in this pondering moment that Miriam knocked on the door frame. Saul looked up to find her leaning against the wall with her long brown hair tied up in a bun.

"Reading?"

The question swirled around him. She was using that tone of voice she had that rung in your head over and over. Saul simply tilted the great Bible up to show the binding. She stared at him and the book for long a moment. A breathy sound escaped between her teeth. Spearmint. She shut her eyes and nodded. "That's good," she said.

She lingered for a moment, chewing. Then she was gone, and Saul put his mind back to the guide. This time he did not read long. He went back over the parts about the snake and the curse three or four times before gathering the papers together and closing them back inside their folder. Beneath the coffee table there was a stack of old newspapers and magazines still bound by their original folds, never having made it out to recycling. Saul threw his Church folder atop the pile and leaned back in his chair to think.

12.
Miriam

MIRIAM AND HER SON HAD gone to the zoo. They'd only spent an hour there total, moving quickly through the exhibits. She had tried to linger at most of the cages. She pointed out what the animals were doing and read the descriptive plaques. She read them out loud so her son could hear. But he was on the move. Even at the lions' pen he did not stop long to admire the majesty. She succeeded in making him hold her hand for a minute but no longer. She stopped to put a quarter in the feed dispenser when they neared the peacocks. Her palm was filled with dried corn, and when she looked up her son was halfway down the path to the reptile room. Then the circuit was completed, and they marched back out to the parking lot.

The rest of the evening passed quickly. She made dinner. Her son did homework from the first day of school. It was still relatively early when he announced he was going to bed.

"Just a minute, dear," said Miriam. "Let me fix things up."

Miriam cleaned the house every Tuesday night. This ritual had begun two years ago after her mother's sudden death. She found sponges and rags to be intimate tools. She knelt and scrubbed the floors with all her wiry strength, cleaning with a sort of sanctifying reverence. Not a spot was ever missed. Yet, every week there was more dirt, so Miriam never stopped scrubbing.

She always started with her son's bedroom. It never took long. Her son kept his unworn clothes folded in drawers or hanging in closets, made his bed every morning, refrained from eating outside the dining room, and always took his shoes off at the front door, so

JACOB KOCKEN

little dirt was ever tracked up here. Her son was a clean boy, and she loved him for it.

So, Miriam dusted the dresser top and wiped the window. She sprayed disinfectant on the door handle and reorganized the sporting paraphernalia that was piling at the bottom of the closet; his old aluminum Little League bat and the new one she'd gotten him for high school, his mitt, and a dozen balls whose stitches were outnumbered by grass stains. Sweeping his floor necessitated that she crouch all the way to the ground so her bristles could reach the far end of his bed against the wall. Miriam retracted herself out from the little cavern and brushed the meager mess into a dust pan. With nothing left to do, she went to tell her angel his space was ready for sleep.

"I'll meet you up there," she told her son. He nodded and climbed the stairs to his room while she went to the refrigerator and took out a gallon of whole milk. She poured a glassful and stuck it in the microwave just long enough to give it a human warmth. Its scent was soft and calm, and Miriam kept it to her nose as she moved through the house up to her son's bedroom.

He was just climbing under the covers when she entered to hand him the glass. His whole room smelled of that softness even when the glass left her proximity. She watched as he sipped, making sure the elixir got into her baby boy. He thanked her, and she bid him goodnight. With her son out for the night, Miriam went back to the task of cleaning where she moved on to her own bedroom.

Her husband Saul had ripped up their carpet. The damage had shaken her immediately when she'd first seen it all. It was not a thing he'd ever complained of, though now he insisted their old floor was no good. Underneath the old shag was just flat, motley grain plywood that was cold and rough on the sole. She did not like it.

When she took the sheets off the bed to wash, Miriam confirmed a lingering artificial scent on the fabric. She had a keen nose and had smelled it the night before as she slept.

In the bathroom, Miriam set a ring of bowl cleaner to work in the toilet. She scrubbed a transparent coat of grime from the sink, polishing the silver faucet and handles until they reflected the lights above them. Then while cleaning the shower, she pulled several

RISE THE MOON

long strands of pink hair from the base of the drain. The pieces came together in a moment. Saul had been acting strange. Her son had been gone.

    Miriam's eyelids fell, and she locked the bathroom door. The pink hair was twisting knots between her knuckles when she sat on the edge of the tub. She held it in the permanent grip of her bad hand, the one that had been malformed so long ago. Miriam went dizzy for a moment. There was a great lump swelling in her throat, and she clenched her teeth when the tears started to come. Hot water fell from her eyes, and she started the shower just to cover the noise. She sat there on the edge of the tub wringing the stuff in her hand. Her own hair fell into her face, sticking to the tear-stained cheeks until she tied it back behind her head. Steam filled the bathroom and fogged the mirror, and when Miriam finally wiped her eyes and left, the hallway air seemed so cold and dry that all the hairs on her body stood on end.

    She rolled what she'd found into a tiny ball in her palm. Her feet felt numb on the stairs as she descended. From her back pocket, Miriam took a pack of spearmint gum and started chewing two strips at once. She worked it forcefully between her teeth. From jaw down, her whole body was stiff. With night on its way, the house was quiet.

    At the bottom of the staircase, Miriam turned and found him sitting in the living room with a book on the coffee table. His eyes were on the page. She bit the inside of her bottom lip hard, and her knuckles went white squeezing the little knot of pink hair.

    Then she recognized the book. It was a gift from her mother. Miriam saw her own reflection in the window behind her husband. The long chestnut hair and the late woman swarmed her. The sense of betrayal redoubled, and there were the walls again. They descended on her, invisible, and the sound of her own heart echoed hard inside them. Creeping shadows painted her periphery with a pigment so black it sucked in the surrounding color. She saw only straight forward; at the window; at the book. The lump in her throat swelled again, and she swallowed all her words. Her tight fist locked. Her teeth loosed and clenched again, and the iron taste of blood leaked slowly over her tongue.

    She stood there for a minute entirely alone before he raised his

JACOB KOCKEN

head and took notice. His eyes lit up to greet her, but his lips never parted as if there was and never would be anything at all to say.

"Reading?" she said. The word touched her ear three times. He lifted the book and showed it to her. It was as though he raised it with both hands all the way up to Heaven, and its radiant gold letters pierced down through her from on high. She bowed her head in small redundant nods and left him to his penance.

Miriam quit the house and strode out to the sidewalk. The ball of pink hair moved from one hand to the other. She pulled on the strands and pressed them between her fingers as she walked. Under the darkness of night, she approached a house at random. It was two stories of brick and belonged to some neighbor she'd never met. Between the side of the house and the fence there was a large green garbage bin. She opened the lid and let the little ball of hair tumble through the cracks of her bad hand into the trash. The smell of rot filled her nose, and she spun away with tears in her eyes. *Reading? Reading?* The dead word consumed her solemn chamber. Miriam tossed her swimming head to the sky.

Stars were starting to blink into the night. There she was again. The vision of her mother broke clear in those distant lights. Such celestial eyes met her with the same sober plea they did all those years she was a child; all those nights when her father came home in a stupor. Why it should be so strong now, Miriam never could decipher. But there was no way around it. In the face of the stars above, she was a child again with her mother looking down; and those eyes pleading mercy on behalf of a sinful man.

The first time she saw her father incapacitated she was only old enough to recognize something was wrong and watch as her mother tried to daub the vomit from his shirt with a dishrag. As she grew, his habit stayed constant, and Miriam came to know two fathers; one attentive and loving, a caring husband to her mother and a well-regarded professor of rhetoric; the other, hardly a living man at all.

For several years she encountered her father with instinctual trust. She ran to him. He held her. They played games, and he taught her the rudiments of his courses. They lived and laughed beside one another in childish bliss. Many of her earliest memories were of her parents. They danced with each other. A gramophone played sweet

RISE THE MOON

music, and they danced. And every now and then, with Miriam's growing capacity to perceive and remember, she would notice that he was not himself; that he did not speak as a man ought; that his steps were as uncertain as his words. He was not a violent drinker but rather, an inert one, losing faculties of mind and body.

'Mama, Daddy had an accident.' 'Mimi, be a big girl and wash these clothes. Hold them here, yes, where it's dry. Do you remember how the machine works? Good. And then put it out of your mind. Are you perfect? No. God will handle him.'

The next day he'd leave the house with his head straight up on his shoulders, wearing a suit and tie and carrying a brief case filled with the world's most eloquent thoughts.

'Momma, Daddy fell! Daddy fell!' 'Remember the antiseptic I showed you? Bring it quick. The band-aids too. And then put it out of your mind. Are you perfect? No. God will handle him.'

Weeks would go by without incident, followed shortly by the same incapacity. She was ten when she came to realize he was doing it to himself; that his habits always preceded such episodes.

'It's that stuff that makes him dumb, right Mom?' 'Don't call your father dumb, Miriam. He teaches people how to think for Christ sake. Put that out of your mind. Are you perfect? No. God will handle him.'

But the older she got the more the uneasiness grew. Her mother began to frequent the doctor's office, though a diagnosis never leapt from anyone's lips. Nor did she yet fully grasp the practices of her father. An abstract sense of frailty came to hang about young Miriam like a fog.

As Miriam grew and developed such interests of her own as all adolescents do, she found herself in the unfortunate position of free mind and dependent body. She was not allowed nor yet able to inhabit a career that would set her up on her own two feet. Her housing, her meals, her comforts were all provided for. This teat she was forced to nurse, and even her extracurriculars were not entirely void of parental shadow. Twice each week, on Tuesdays and Thursdays, she needed either mother or father to shuttle her across town or state to the diamonds where her softball games were played. She'd been a Graumont Tiger for several years and may have walked if only it had not been so far, or biked if only a catch-

JACOB KOCKEN

er's gear was less cumbersome. Often her mother took her to such things, but she worked out of town now and then, and so, gone for days at a time, left every task to the professor. And while most of these proceedings went off without incident, she had long gained a wariness of social events either frequent or prolonged where her father's vice was wont to rear its head. The concession stand, for instance, sold beer. And while it was not unusual for any of the attendant dads to drink a brew or two over the course of nine hot summer innings, it was noticed by some, Miriam chief among them from her bullpen cage, how the level in Frank's bottles seemed to fall faster than average and his trips back to the stand made him seem as if he were pacing back and forth in ponderance over some terrible dilemma. The crashing of glass when he threw his successive bottles into the trash was a bell tower for Miriam, keeping time and striking every inning as the end of every game approached.

On one of these particular nights, when the final out yet needed recording, Miriam succeeded in distancing from her constant worry by making herself the hero of the game. With the lead of a single run, and a lady on second base, Miriam crouched behind the plate in her full catcher's pads and called for the pitch low and inside. As the wind up came she braced herself to block a bouncing ball, but to her surprise a sharp metal clink cut past her ear. The batter had swung low like a golfer, catching just the tangent of the ball and spinning it off toward third base. The defenders charged it, pitcher, catcher, and baseman, as the yellow ball spun along the white painted line, questioning whether to go fair or foul. Ellie, who played third base, left her post to try and make the throw to first. Alas, it was late and the runner from second moved easily forward, rounding toward home, bouncing on the balls of her feet. The infield hit should have stopped there. But the poor girl who played first, a young daisy named Allison Brown who was placed there by the coach because of her inability to throw was tricked by the eager look of the runner. She had an awkward hand, and while her glove was passable, the way her spindly limbs twisted as she tossed was pitied even by the opposition. The ball arced shortly up and down, landing only partway to the plate. She stood already in shame, her cap too big for her head and falling down to cover her face. It was Miriam who sprang into action, rushing from third base line to first.

101

RISE THE MOON

Her facemask fell as she sprinted and saw the tying run head for home. It was a race to the plate for equal competitors, one sliding, one diving with ball outstretched in her bare hand. The tag was made just before the score and the umpire's call set the Tiger's team to jumping. The win came, however, by sacrifice, as Miriam's tag was recorded on the runner's cleat whose metal teeth were sharp and ripped across the unprotected hand. By miracle or toughness, Miriam held on, closing the game, but the dirt turned red beneath her grip as she squeezed the ball in pain. Her coach came out to inspect, and after a moment of consoling, wrapped her wound in gauze and athletic tape. Though it stung, she could move her fingers fine and once again the people cheered. Never before had she felt so adored and gritted through the stings as the Tiger girls tapped gloves with the other team. After some final congratulations and even a proud pat from the impartial ump, Miriam returned to the bleachers to find her father dozing. He was slouched back against the seat behind him, taking up the space of two or three bodies as his natural girth combined with an unconscious sprawl. His legs splayed nonchalantly over the ground, and a dark blue bottle rested in the loose grip of his right hand. Miriam prodded him with her catcher's mask. At that moment, another one of the fathers called his name. 'Frank!' A group of them were standing with their girls, uneasy smiles on their faces. 'You've got a visitor.' A smattering of chuckles floated over them as Frank stirred. His bleary eyes came alive one at a time. When they came to focus on Miriam he squinted. The scoreboard in right field showed the story, and he sat up with a moan. 'We won,' he managed to say. 'Go Tigers. Go Tigers.' His moan continued and transformed into a yawn as he rose to his feet. There was a final knell of glass as he tossed his bottle into the trash. 'Take it easy Professor,' someone shouted. The two of them plodded across the grass to where their car was parked. Miriam felt her father's hand on her shoulder. It pushed downward in self-support as if her skeleton were a cane or railing. He stumbled twice on the uneven ground.

    Inside the car, he yawned again, blinking hard as he gripped the wheel. 'Did you see it?' asked Miriam. 'See it?' he repeated. 'The game.' 'Oh yes, honey. You know, you're really ripping into the ball these days. That line out you had in the second inning.

JACOB KOCKEN

I mean, you just smashed it. Bad luck the short stop was there. Just bad luck is all.' Miriam nodded silently and buckled herself in over all her gear. 'What happened there?' her father asked, one shy finger raising to indicate the tape around her right hand. 'Hurt it sliding,' she said. 'Happens,' said Frank. Her eyes began to fill with mist, and she put the facemask back on; as little a shield as it was. They sped over the downtown roads and turned off onto one of the old county highways. The radio music was low and nearly overrun by the shifting cobbles of the rural road. Miriam tried to keep her face pointed out the window to where the trees rushed by like a running river. Now and then the bumps in the ride rattled her bandaged hand. It stung anew and red streaks were beginning to show through the white tape. Then the trees, it seemed, grew larger. Their shadows loomed more powerfully over the car and the rumble under the tires changed from road to gravel. Miriam saw her father's grip slip from the wheel as she looked up in alarm. His eyes were closed, and his neck lolled back as if he were sitting in the bleachers again. Miriam's scream awoke him, but only in time to hit the brakes as they went skirting over the shoulder and into the shallow ditch. The car rocked like a dingy in storm and came to a sudden halt against the trunk of a young evergreen tree. Glass and wood shattered alike as the passenger side's fender caved in. Miriam, caught by her own gear as well as the car's belt and airbag, was saved the trauma to her head. Instinct, however, had thrust her injured hand out in front and something had cracked against the force of the crash. The bone throbbed relentlessly beneath the bandage and Miriam shrieked. The middle of her hand, up through every finger, was crushed with pain. Her arm seized up and the mist in her eyes gave way to full torrential tears. Her father jumped from his seat. He left the car and circled around to the passenger side. He opened Miriam's door and appraised her with terror. His nose was bleeding, and a bruise was already welling up around one of his eyes. 'What is it, Mimi?' he said. 'Are you hurt?' She bellowed in answer as he checked her head and neck, his fingers gliding softly underneath the facemask and trembling cautiously over tender vertebrae. 'My hand,' she cried. 'Baby, listen,' said Frank. He blinked several times as his head bobbed. His eyelids were pulled up by great concentration. 'Is your head hurt?' 'No.' 'What about

RISE THE MOON

your neck?' She bent it back and forth, testing, showing her range of motion. 'What about your back?' Does that hurt? Do your legs feel normal?' 'Yes,' Miriam said with a snivel. Everything else was in working order. But her hand beneath the bandages felt hot and bloating. The little bones crossed over each other in torture. Her father cradled her masked head. His breath was short. He caressed her hair lovingly. 'We ought to get away from here first thing,' he said. Frank shut her door and reentered the car on the other side. He turned the key and the engine choked itself to life. 'We're going?' said Miriam. 'Going home,' said Frank. He reversed away from the broken tree and sloped back up the ditch onto the old road. Two forest curtains hid them the whole way along the county highway until they turned off onto their own street. Frank parked their wreck inside the garage and shut the door. Inside the house, Miriam laid her arm gingerly on the dining table where Frank removed the tape with kitchen scissors. The cleat cuts were red and open, so Frank smeared them with disinfectant. The rest of the hand and wrist were swollen into the knuckles and fingers. 'Can you move it fine?' Miriam tried to stretch her thumb and pinky. They moved, but as the fingers separated the pain grew worse. 'It hurts,' she told him. 'But they do move? Can you do each one?' Miriam twitched her fingers in slow succession, contracting and expanding only slightly. 'Are we going to the hospital?' whimpered Miriam. Frank let out a long breath. He rubbed both palms over his face, momentarily masking the blood dripping over his mouth and the purple skin leaching toward his forehead. 'We can,' he said. But neither of them moved. Her father's mouth hung open a minute and Miriam waited for it to issue his hidden thoughts. 'We can go to the hospital. But if we do, I'll be in trouble, Mimi. I don't know what will happen. God, I don't know. Your mother will be so sad. So disappointed. I'll be in real trouble. People can go to jail even for accidents. I don't know what will happen. We can go to the hospital, Mimi. If you really think you need to go. I want what's best. But I don't know for sure how you're feeling. I'll leave it up to you. Take a minute. I'm going to wash this off,' he gestured at the drying blood from his nose. 'When I come back you tell me. Tell me if you really think you need to go to the hospital.' The four legs of Frank's chair scratched the floor as he stood up. He sauntered off toward the bathroom.

JACOB KOCKEN

Miriam stood alone for quite a while. She could hear the bathroom faucet running unobstructed. The door was shut. She tried to test her hand against tasks in the room, holding a fork, pressing buttons on the microwave, flipping the latch on the window above the sink. She could press only lightly in any direction before the pain surged. But as long as she kept her wrist and fingers still, curled in slightly, and free of impact, the discomfort waned into the tolerable. Then with her clumsy left hand only she opened a drawer of the living room's hutch. She sifted through a miscellaneous mess of crafts and trinkets and found a roll of thick white medical tape. Her bad elbow kept the cylinder in place against the dining table as she peeled up its adhesive edge with a bloody fingernail. She prayed it was not horribly broken as she began to wrap it. She prayed there was nothing really wrong as she tried to mimic the way her coach had coated every part of the palm. She prayed for herself and for her father who was still shut alone in the bathroom with the water running.

    As the days passed and Emily returned home from her trip, Miriam lived a silent life of left-handedness. When her mother asked what had happened to her arm, Miriam relayed the end of the softball game. Her teammates and coach corroborated the story. 'Woah, that win took a bigger toll on you than we thought,' they'd say. 'Miriam's not playing with an injury like that, is she?' 'Not today. No, Miriam will be out a while. Suzie will have to play catcher.' More than a month passed before Miriam took her wrappings off entirely. Still, there was pain when she squeezed the palm or stretched her fingers too wide. So, she refrained from its use as much as possible, keeping it huddled together before her stomach whenever she walked about. At length, Emily became concerned. 'How's it feel, darling? It doesn't look right.' Miriam was taken to the doctor where an x-ray showed three splintered metacarpals, bowed and fused together at inappropriate intervals. 'Your hamate and lunate look to have broken too,' said the doctor. 'Those ones here in the heel of your palm. See the ossification compared to this normal model? All of that's causing your ankylosis.' 'Can it be fixed?' 'I don't know," said the doctor. 'They're all significantly fused. I can refer you to a surgeon, but it would likely be extensive.' After a consultation they elected not to begin a foray into surgery.

RISE THE MOON

Miriam did not want the pain and was reluctant even to discuss it with her mother or the professionals. She resolved herself to learn to live limited.

One weekend during Miriam's sophomore year of high school her mother was out for an examination. Alone at home, Miriam and Frank sat down to play cribbage. Her father held the cards in his left hand and a mason jar of basement whiskey in his right. Miriam fit the cards into the cupped pocket of her bad hand; the fingers, being stuck in a clenched position were glad for such tasks of low dexterity.

'Bet you I win,' she'd said. 'What does my girl want to bet?' 'If I win you don't drink for a month.' 'Miriam, that is inappropriate. You're talking about an adult thing you don't understand.' 'Isn't it bad for you?' 'According to who, Miriam? Too much water can kill person, either by drowning or by diluting electrolyte balance. Should I stop drinking water too? But no, water is essential to the thriving of life. So, Miriam, we run into a problem. Too much water may be as bad as not enough. This suggests an optimal amount. What happens if my body is at that equilibrium, yet I have just eaten something with a terrible taste? Should I refrain from washing down the displeasing sensation because it will tip the scale however slightly toward hyperhydration? Doing so might even increase my life expectancy. But this is not how we live our lives. Optimizing long term health is only one good on a list of many desirable things. Don't agree? Implicitly, my dear, you do. Under what circumstances is it good for you to eat potato chips and ice cream? Your health never benefits. Yet you do these things; you celebrate these things. Strawberry ice cream in a fudge dipped waffle cone; I saw you eat that only last week. Not only did you volunteer to harm your health, but you also begged your mother and me to let you. Begged. You were on to something there. Your ice cream, it makes life nice, doesn't it? Also consider a situation in which you turn away from the ice cream stand with your health in mind, and in walking away you enter the street where you are hit by a truck. Now your goal has been thwarted anyway, and on top of everything you haven't even gotten your strawberry ice cream fudge-dipped waffle cone. An all-around loss. Now, of course I don't mean to suggest that you loiter beside the ice cream stand soaking up every ounce of momentary

JACOB KOCKEN

pleasure under the fear of random and imminent death. There is a balance we all must strike with regard to hedonism. And therein lies a human mystery. Because each one of us is endowed with different genes and dealt a separate set of circumstances in every moment, it is only the individual who knows in his or her own heart where this balance lies. Only the individual. We feel it in our conscience; we measure it with our rationale. Don't presume to do my measuring.' He picked up his playing cards and resumed a posture of relaxation. 'Now, we were playing a game. Let's have fun, huh?'

Even so, he did not drink for a while after that. For a moment, she thought she'd done it. They had two months before she saw her father zombified again.

'Mom, his words aren't making sense. It's freaking me out.'
'Humor him, darling. It makes sense to him. Put it out of your mind. Are you perfect? No. God will handle it.'

When Miriam was fifteen she asked her mother why he could never stick to quitting. Emily said he would, but people needed to come to Christ on their own before they can change. 'Your father is too sharp to think he has to listen to anyone but himself,' her mother had said. 'He doubles down on mistakes out of pride, but give him some time and Frank always comes around. Besides, our God is eternal. Let us not hurry Him.' Then she held Miriam close and ran a loving hand through her child's long chestnut hair. 'And after all, there's something to it when he talks about treasuring and enjoying our present while we can. You know I love you, yes Miriam? You know it? Even when I'm asleep; even when I'm gone. I will always love you. Please say you know it. Yes, good. He does too.'

Shortly thereafter Miriam had her sixteenth birthday. Her father had been sober for nearly a month. But the university's semester was coming to an end, and the stress had been showing on his face all week.

Friday night arrived, and eleven girls from Miriam's class had come over for a party. Emily had decorated the room with pink and white streamers. It was evening. Her mother was in the kitchen arranging snacks. Pizza was being delivered, and Frank was supposed to bring the cake on his way back from teaching. He was later than usual, but there was no rush. Miriam and her friends sat in the living room. Blankets and pillows covered the floor, and the

RISE THE MOON

girls were strewn about in a circle. There was a movie on making ambient noise amongst their scattered conversations.

A repeated metallic grinding interrupted them as the front door handle moved back and forth. Frank broke in and crumpled into his recliner beside the girls.

"Hello Mr. Garland," said Julie, Miriam's longest held friend. Perhaps to them he just looked tired. His tie was undone but still hanging low around his neck. His shirt was partially unbuttoned, and his glossy eyes fixed on the flashing television screen. He did not respond to Julie. She looked Miriam's way with a silent, inquisitive brow. His distant, unfriendly presence amongst them quieted all the girls.

On the movie screen an exchange of wit befitting a flick for teenage girls ensued, and Frank burst out in laughter. His cackling lasted a very long time.

"Funny show," he announced to no one in particular. His foot was waving unconsciously around and kicked a girl named Lucy in the back of the head. She turned around sharply. But he only sat there looking at nothing and swinging his lazy foot from side to side.

Lucy scooted herself forward with a mystified smile to the rest of the room. Some of the girls giggled. Some stared at Frank or Miriam while both the more shrewd and naïve types kept their eyes on the movie. The tension might have all blown over, forgotten in ambiguity; but her father reposed into the chair, closing his eyes and drifting far away from them. He emitted a long and sudden moan of relief. The smell was instantaneous with the sound. The forehead on every one of her friends wrinkled, and their necks turned to where a continuous stream of urine came dribbling off the leather seat and down his leg onto the hardwood. The girls sprang up. Exclamations of disgust and hilarity confounded them. They chopped their feet and held their own noses and each other's arms, backing away from the incontinent adult. A girl named Penny accidentally stepped in it. The splash set them all off again.

Miriam's eyes felt like hot springs. She took two steps toward him. The dark spot on his pants continued to spread while the chorus of confused laughter from her friends called Emily into the room. Her mother rushed over to Frank and threw a light blanket

JACOB KOCKEN

over his body. His head lolled back as if asleep though his flat, glassy eyes still panned the room like a distant mountain range.

Then the girls began to leave. There was a gagging sound from one of them as she went for the front door. The others followed, throwing looks of compassion or cruelty, but all of disbelief, directly at Miriam. Julie came last. The girl's head spun from Miriam to her stream of fleeing friends, to the man sitting catatonic in his piss, and back. Her palm came up to her forehead as if it had all spun her into dizziness. She said something hurriedly in farewell, avoiding Miriam's lost and broken expression as she slammed the door behind her. Out of the front window, the girls could still be seen convulsing and screeching disgust as they scattered into the falling night.

The living room was in hurried disarray. Miriam heard the sound of wooden cabinet doors swinging as her mother searched for a towel. Her father's eyes hung half open. His jaw dropped slack and his breath rattled. Miriam stared, but he would not look back. Then she flung the remote at his lifeless stomach. It clattered to the floor, and the television went silent. Frank's head popped up for a moment, searching. When his chin fell again to his chest, Miriam exploded. She screamed and hit. Her scrawny fists died in the bulk of his flesh as if she punched the unfeeling earth beneath her feet. She yelled at him, and she begged him. But when finally he looked in her direction the only thing she could see in his eyes was her own tearful reflection.

Her mother returned with an old bath towel to daub the chair and carpet.

"Run a shallow bath," said Emily, trying to lift Frank to his feet. Her mother had to say it again before Miriam knew the words were spoken to her.

"No," she said. "Let him sit in it."

"We don't let family *sit in it*. He changed your soiled clothes for years."

"I was a baby!"

"And right now, you're the parent," her mother said. The tone took Miriam aback; it was soft and almost imploring, the quality of voice words carry when they've harbored in the throat for some long, foreboden time. Miriam's own throat constricted, and

RISE THE MOON

she could feel the heat burning off her face. He was twice her size; more than twice her age. People called him Dr. and paid to hear him teach. Then the imploring command rang again, "Run a shallow bath."

Miriam obeyed, and in quiet obedience, her heart shifted. She filled the bathtub halfway with lukewarm water. Her mother entered soon after, supporting Frank's enormity with her shoulder. She had already undressed him. Miriam, at the sight of her father's body embraced anger rather than endure shame. His mouth tried to speak, but it produced only a dribbling, brackish filth.

While Emily scrubbed him down, Miriam closed herself in her bedroom. She locked the door, and with the lights already off, stumbled to bed. Her head was wrapped in the thick fabric of two blankets where she screamed into her mattress. Tears poured even while fury squeezed her eyes tight shut. She began in her frustration to sweat. Encased in her covers, the stale smell of body water turned rank, and she relived the horrible scene with redolent vividity. She reached out blindly, hoping in the depths of her heart, beyond any rationale, to meet the warm comfort of someone's touch. Finding only linen and the dead, wooden shape of bed posts, Miriam curled into a ball on her side, embracing her own knees and elbows.

As she caressed her body, rocking back and forth in the darkness, she found in the back of her head, a rhythm. It came faintly at first. Her ears pricked up at the sound, a distant, melancholy music. It faded slowly, and another distant but familiar rhythm filled the air.

Miriam arose, shedding the blankets from her face. At the front of her room, she undid the lock and poked her head into the light of the hallway. She peered down into the open space of the living room where the gramophone sung low. Beside the spinning record were two shapes that moved in consort. They leant together like two fallen trees and swung with the rise and fall of the music. Back and forth; back and forth. Her eyes, bleary from tears and darkness, struggled now and then to identify them separately. She knew the song too. The lyrics spoke of sadness and betrayal, and still they danced with tenderness. As this second song faded to an end, Miriam slammed her bedroom door once again.

Three dark weeks passed in circular fashion with Miriam play-

JACOB KOCKEN

ing the resentful mother to her father in his most unconscious times. If Emily asked, Miriam would assist in his care; otherwise she kept a distance, never engaging him with even a word. She adopted the dreadful certainty that while people grow in stature, they never really change, and that once a drum is struck it just keeps on pounding the same rhythm over and over, and that is the heartbeat of life.

Then one night when the house was quiet, Miriam drove west with everything she owned in the back of her car. She called her mother from Utah after several states were between them.

There had been no plan except to live for herself. The money she had could pay for gas and a few nights in a hotel once she hit the Pacific. In less than a week her stores were running scarce, so she took to sleeping in the back seat of her car. A bakery near the water hired her to run the register, and it was there that she met Saul. He was zoically handsome; he was ambitious; and he managed a hotel, taking care not only of himself but of three hundred guests at any moment. He became a regular customer, and one Saturday on her break he followed her out to the beach. When she told him how she lived, Saul put her up in the hotel he ran. He didn't let her spend a dime for a month, and soon enough she moved out of his hotel room and into his home. Saul's parents had passed away when he was young. He did not volunteer conversation of them, so when Miriam neglected stories of her own folks he did not pry. Two quick years later, she had a wedding ring and child.

The first time they put her baby boy in her arms she kissed the top of his little bald head over and over and would not let him go. He had the delicate aroma of warm milk, and she couldn't bear to stop holding him, kissing him, smelling his sweet little scent. And for a long time after, even into his adolescent years, Miriam would fix her son a glass of warm milk before bed just so she could sit beside him and breathe the same air she did when he was born.

With the birth of her son, Miriam's disposition lightened. She did not reconsider her convictions; everything that was tainted once was tainted still; sins were marked by heavy ink. Even Saul, the man she loved, had his flaws. But now there was a newer hope. Now, she could share in a right love; a pure love. When she put her baby down to rest at night he would fall asleep, and she would just stand there looking into the crib. On some occasions, he was even

RISE THE MOON

roused from the precious slumber as she took him back up into her arms, overcome with the need to feel the warmth of his body on her bosom.

Her whole time on the coast, Miriam did not see her parents. After moving in with Saul, there had been a permanent place to phone, and her mother rang three times a week.

"Did you pick a name?" Emily asked.

"Ira."

"Beautiful."

"He's the most precious thing," Miriam said.

"I am so very happy for you," said her mother. "We ought to come see him."

"How are you and Dad?"

"Just fine," said Emily. "He's in the other room. It's a boy, Frank. They named him... What was it, darling?"

"Ira."

"They named him Ira." The phone scratched and shuffled. "He's happy for you too. We really ought to come meet both your men. I'd like to fly out there tomorrow. I just can't wait to see you, and Saul, and Aaron."

"Ira."

"Ira, yes, that's it. Ira. Send us a picture of the angel, will you?" The thought to visit must have slipped Emily's mind. Years went by, and though the calls continued, her parents never came to California. Miriam never mentioned it directly. She made a habit, however, of doing as her mother had asked and mailing copies of her son's captured moments. They were frequent, especially at first with the myriad milestones of early life. Then when her baby was four years old he started school.

"We have to move," Miriam told her husband. Their coastal city was beautiful, but Miriam began to feel it was a place for tourists rather than families with its expensive beachside properties selling the lifestyle of extravagant parties and Hollywood hopefuls. She wanted a home with less transience; a place where her son could have friends to keep. It was a forty-five-minute drive to the preschool, and even there the people always seemed to be drifting.

At the same time, the Bedalaus hotel chain was expanding. Construction was started in several growing towns across the coun-

JACOB KOCKEN

try. When Saul told her the names of these cities and she heard her own Wisconsin home Miriam produced such a reaction that Saul seemed compelled to complete the circuit of his wife's travels. She had not meant in that moment to suggest moving back. But once her husband assumed she wanted to be with her family again, she felt a certain shame at telling him different. Over the next few weeks, Saul got himself transferred, and Miriam moved back to Graumont with her two boys from California.

Shortly after settling in, they dressed their little man in a white button-down shirt and went to visit Frank and Emily. The knock on the door was a surprise. Emily squealed at the sight of her grandson and invited them inside.

"Such a nice boy. Look at you all. You're back for good?" said her mother.

"It's a better place to raise children," Miriam said. The little boy was leaning against her leg. His hair already hung down past his ears.

"He looks kind of like a girl, huh?" said Frank.

"Well, he has mine and Mom's hair and likes it that way," said Miriam.

"Not an insult," said her father. Frank tousled the boy's head. "My favorite people keep that style." Out from Frank's back pocket, he pulled something wrapped in glistening sliver foil. He untucked the folded ends and produced a chocolate which her boy grabbed greedily. He smiled ear to ear while smashing the sweet between his teeth.

"Dad," Miriam said, swatting away a second silver ball. "We're about to eat real food."

"It's just a chocolate," said Frank. "Look how happy he is!" The toddler was indeed overflowing. His little cheeks bunched up so far toward his eyes he had to squint at the old man who knelt before him returning the expression out of unbridled joyful reflex.

"You'll ruin his appetite and tomorrow I'll be the one he's mad at when the hankering strikes."

"I just wanted to see him happy."

"You'll ruin him, Dad."

Frank acquiesced, popping the chocolate into his own mouth. He had another half dozen in the time it took for Emily to set the

RISE THE MOON

table causing his small talk to be marred by brown tinted teeth and smacking lips. Soon they sat down to dinner, each married couple on one side of the table and the budding child at the head.

"Now Saul," said Emily, "Miriam says you run hotels?"

"I was the general manager at Bedalaus on the coast. The branch here is a new foray for the company, and admittedly, I expected with the transfer I would have retained my old title, but they've got me doing something a bit different at the moment. No sweat. I climb ladders quick."

"Bedalaus," said Emily, "Isn't that the old children's center, Frank? The building your mother used to work in?"

"I believe so," said Frank.

"My last location was always near capacity," Saul went on. "I won director of the quarter three times in the last two years. It's all about first impression. When people are choosing a hotel, see, they pick on instincts. Few ever stay long enough to care about the intricacies. Every other night it's new faces, so you've got to master the image. A hotel has to inspire two things simultaneously; excitement and comfort. People need something interesting, something worth staying there for. At the same time, they have to have a place to let their guard down. Traveling is stressful. You've got to make sure they know Saul's got it covered." Miriam saw her father's interest drifting. Long years of drink may have stolen all inhibitions away, and he wore his thoughts quite plainly. Saul must have noticed too for he turned the conversation on Frank. "Miriam tells me you're a college teacher, yes?"

Frank sat up very straight and set his fork down on the placemat. He eyed his son-in-law. "I came into education to pursue the value of freedom. It all depends on your initial value, see? My parents signed away all their time and energy for a wage. I worked at the factory processing chicken bodies for three years after high school. Every Friday they'd hand me a check, and every day that wasn't Friday they'd leave us with a written slip of what we'd earned that day. It was done that way so that all we thought about was money. And for three years that goal was accomplished. Forty dollars at the end of the day. And all the good that money was supposed to do for me got left on the wayside because it was that money itself sitting on all my thoughts. God bless Emily who convinced me to go to

JACOB KOCKEN

college. Critical thinking. Argumentation. In just one semester I learned how to see the world at a more fundamental level; how to unscrew money from that grip it held on all my decisions. It was the wrong thing to focus on. That valuing of simple purchasing power was implanted in me by someone else. I didn't have the tools to choose a guiding value. That's what freedom is. Everything is bottom up. Find a thing to believe in, and let it guide you. Better to define that thing too narrow than too wide, or else you're bound to lose it in all the commotion. You can't let the lesser things, false gods they once called them, leverage you out of your deepest value; let them do that, and you've lost your soul. Freedom is that basic value. Freedom to live how you see fit."

"You teach philosophy then?"

"It was Rhetoric."

"Frank and the university decided to part ways this year," said Emily.

"Oh Dad, I had no idea."

"No pity please. A man has got to guard his principle."

"Faculty responsibilities were rising out of the classroom," said Emily. "Frank didn't like how it took him away from me."

"I wouldn't expect them to fire a long-standing member so swiftly," said Saul.

"And you thought you'd be directing this hotel. Nobody gets what they expect," said Frank. Miriam had turned red and looked at her mother with flat eyes. Emily understood and changed the topic.

"Will you come to Mass with us tomorrow?" For the full duration of their young marriage, Saul and Miriam had only spoken of religion a handful of times. Ritual and belief had stayed behind Miriam when she left, and Saul, a staunch atheist, had expressed desire early on not to be bothered with things so outside of his control as Jesus and fairies.

"Mass?" said Saul.

"It means church," Miriam told her husband.

"You're not a Catholic then, Saul?"

"I'm not even sure I am at this point, Mom," said Miriam. "The last church I've been to was here." Her mother's eyes widened as she looked over the three of them.

"I find religion a bit cold," said Saul. "Adam and Eve and all

RISE THE MOON

that."

"Cold?" Emily inquired. She looked worried.

"Not to put down. No, I mean, theology and all, it's a bit heady. Distant, I suppose. Cold."

"You couldn't be further from the truth," said Frank.

"Honey, be polite," said Emily.

"But he couldn't. Couldn't be further. From page one the Bible engages Man's carnality. It defines him. Yes, I really mean defines him by it. Adam, the forefather, the first thing created in God's own image and likeness, that's a word with meaning to it. *Adam*. This is literature for Heaven's sake. Everything is a double meaning, and the first name is a play on Hebrew words for flushing; *aw-dam*'; going rosy in the face. It's going red that makes a person special is what it means. When do we flush? Embarrassment. Anger. Sex. Passion. It's all carnality. That's the definition of Man. Beautiful, warm, and red as the sun on horizon. Saul couldn't be further from the truth."

"But Frank, dear, you hardly come to church either," Emily said.

"I've got my own thoughts about religion," said Frank, "but I wouldn't call it cold." Emily waved off the words that were about to come from her husband's mouth.

"So, Ira hasn't been baptized?" she said.

"He has not," said Miriam.

"Honey, it's a sacrament."

"I'm not sure about all that stuff, Mom."

"But it's his soul in question not yours," said her mother. "I had you baptized right away."

"I know you did."

"You could still get it done. We have a great new priest here; a young man hardly older than you. I know he'd love to do it."

"Can we talk about it another time?"

"Soon, I hope," said her mother. "If you do one thing for me the rest of your life I hope you'll have that child baptized. My one wish."

They let it drop. The toddler was squirming in his seat. The little plate of food they'd given him was picked clean. Emily rose, moving toward the pantry. "Dessert time for you. Want a cookie,

JACOB KOCKEN

Aaron?"

"His name is Ira," said Miriam.

"Oh goodness, of course it is. Ira, Ira."

"Goddamn it Mom, he's only been your grandson for four years."

"I know, I know. I'm so sorry, dear. I've been fuzzy lately, forgive me."

"It's not a lot to ask."

"I know, I know. Oh, please don't leave darling," said Emily. Her daughter had stood up and lifted the little boy from his chair. Dinner was done, and Miriam did not want to be there any longer. She gave a hasty farewell and said they'd come again soon before walking out the front door with her son in her arms and her husband in tow.

For several years thereafter, Miriam did not return to her parent's house. Her mother called frequently, but Miriam rarely answered. For all the physical proximity they now shared, it was as if they lived further away than even California had been. When Miriam did pick up the ringing phone they talked of the same old things. The conversation became increasingly circular near the end, and Miriam knew in the back of her head that something was very wrong. But then the receiver would be off, and her child would be asking for food, a bath, or a story. And she put everything else out of her mind.

Then one day, Miriam happened to see her mother again. It was mid-afternoon, and Miriam was coming home from work down the old county highway that connected downtown and suburb. Her son had a baseball game that night. It was the last of the season, and she hoped they'd let him pitch. She'd seen him working on his curve for months.

She was trailing another car when suddenly the leader's taillights burned red, and Miriam had to come to a screeching halt. Everything shifted forward in the car, and she nearly collided with the trunk of the other. She heard the driver in front of her yell something. It was a man's voice, and he was angry though he did not stick around long. A moment later, his engine roared. He was off down the road again, and in his place, having half-crossed the street, there stood a frail old woman inside a swirling cloud of dust.

RISE THE MOON

Miriam's heart was beating in her ears from the near accident. It redoubled when she realized her mother. Miriam parked and stepped out of the vehicle. The old woman was hunched at the neck, and her eyes were wide with fear and staring at the box of empty space from which the man had yelled a minute ago.

She reached Emily's side in a moment. Miriam slipped a cardigan from her shoulders. "Mom!" she called out several times before tying the long sleeves in a knot around Emily's waist. When the woman turned her head again she looked on her daughter with a stranger's gaze. They held there for a moment with Miriam asking questions and repeating her private, familial appellations. Slowly and surely Miriam saw recognition begin to fill the cavernous eyes. And then, as if she had stepped through some foggy ether and into the sun, Emily was herself again.

"Oh dear. We shouldn't stand like this; in the road," said Emily, only half alarmed. "We're not so close to home now, will you drive me?"

Indeed, Miriam took her mother home, nearly shaking with surprise, worry, and anger.

"What on Earth, Mom?"

"I just went for a walk." Emily's voice was hers, but it was far away, quiet as if the cords in her throat had been slackened. She kept looking around at the scene as they drove. Her eyes were wide but now with a shameful awe rather than the gaping wonder she'd had in the road.

"How long have you been out?"

"I don't know, Mimi."

When they arrived at the old family home, the man of the house was not there. Miriam came inside to see her mother to comfort.

Her parents' bedroom was on the second floor. A staircase set into the middle of the building rose in one direction before doubling back on its ascent and disappearing behind a wall. The stairwell wound three flights, giving the first floor a capacious fifteen-foot ceiling. Emily had only just crossed her fiftieth year, yet the plodding climb up the steps took all her breath. Miriam could not help but notice again how slight she was. Though never a large woman, everything about her mother had seemed to shrink. Emily lay down on the bed as soon as they reached it.

JACOB KOCKEN

"Do you need something to eat, Mom?"

Emily nodded and Miriam took to the kitchen downstairs. She was going to fix something easy, but the loaf of bread she found in the pantry was green with mold. There was only the one beside a stack of canned beans and soup. The fruit in the fridge was shriveled and giving off a stench that deadened that of the orange peels which once imbued the very wood of the walls.

Miriam microwaved one portion of the chicken noodle soup and brought it to her mother upstairs. She carried the bowl with her good left hand while keeping the spoon cool in her clenched right. The meal looked thin and watery, but the woman ate with visible desire. While Emily's meager victuals served her, Miriam turned out toward the tall glass pane windows that gave the master bedroom a view far beyond the front yard. She looked out down the winding street until it snaked behind a curtain of fir.

"Where is Dad?" she asked.

"Frank took a job at Harvey's, the gas station. He comes home around seven. Dear? Mimi? Could you grab me a glass of water?"

Miriam returned to the first floor a second time and filled a glass with cold water from the tap. When she handed it over to her mother she took in its place the empty soup bowl.

"Thank you," said Emily. "Thank you, darling. It's good to see you now. This house hasn't felt quite full in a while."

"It has been a long time," said Miriam.

"Your room is still like it was when you left, you know."

"I figured Dad would make an office."

"He doesn't teach anymore, dear."

Miriam nodded.

"You're not alright, are you, Mom?"

"I don't know, Mimi. Everyone gets old. But I don't feel myself sometimes. It's lots of the time. It's lots of the time."

"But the doctor," said Miriam. "Weren't you seeing a doctor? You talked about it."

"Yes. I'm seeing Dr. Andrews next month. They're going to look inside my head with new technology. It can see more than an x-ray. Then they'll know what's wrong, and they'll know what to do. Isn't that something?"

"A month?" said Miriam. "What about now? You're not taking

RISE THE MOON

care of yourself, Mom. Everything's rotten downstairs. All the food is bad. Where is Dad? Why isn't he here?"

"Frank works at the gas station now. Say, did you get your Aaron baptized yet?" Miriam's lip began to shake. There were no crow's feet or lines of age about her mother's face. It was, instead, in the space of breaths before speaking that senescence was reared. Miriam ignored the question.

"You know Palmette Place, Mom?"

"Honey."

"It's right on down by the lake in Duval Park. Less than a mile from here."

"It is close to the lake, dear. And close to the prison."

"Come on, Mom. You can't live this way. And the doctor will help you like you said. You can check out when you're better; when you're safe and not wandering in the road like a lost deer."

"Mimi, I have a home. I've lived here ever since Frank and I married, and this is my home."

"You shouldn't be alone."

Her mother was quiet for a moment. Miriam could see she was working something up in her throat, some words that didn't fit together right.

"Your room is just as you left it, Mimi."

Emily had been looking down at the bed but lifted her head slowly now. Her eyes were large and puppy-like. Miriam shook her head, slowly first, then with vigor. She set the empty soup bowl on the nightstand with a clatter. Then down below them on the first floor the front door opened. Miriam could hear her father's voice droning some broken melody and the steps of his feet on the stairs. She met him at the halfway point as he climbed. He nearly fell backward when he turned onto the second flight and saw her there. There was a brown bottle in his hand. It sloshed over the lip with his sudden movement. Already the air was putrid with the beer on his breath. Frank had had no time to catch her or question her or even say hello before she reached the landing and left the house behind her.

She drove home in a flash, and back where she belonged, Miriam found her son. She embraced him without a word. The hand she'd broken in the crash years ago ached with a phantom pain as she squeezed. He was older now and nearly as tall as her. She kissed the top of his head.

"Are you hungry, baby?" she asked him. "Do you want anything to eat?" Then she fixed dinner for him and Saul. At her son's baseball game she sat on the bleachers with her husband watching and cheering. Her baby did not pitch, but he had two hits and a stolen base which came after Saul, frustrated with his perceived incompetence of the coach, loosed himself from the stands and stuck his face into the metal fence near first base.

"Ira!" he'd called loud enough for all to hear. "There's two outs! You're running on every pitch." The coach shoed him away, but thirty seconds later a skipping fastball and catcher's bobble had their son sliding safely into second. Miriam dropped her popcorn to stand and applaud.

"You should be out there coaching," she said to her husband when he rejoined the rest of the fans. They had as warm and lovely an evening as she could remember. Two days later, a policeman's fist knocked hard on the door, waking them at sunrise. Emily was dead.

Another two years had passed since that day, and with the old woman looking down through some far away star, Miriam, empty-handed, reentered her home. Saul had not moved. His head still craned over the Bible splayed open on his lap. Where once, only a couple years beforehand she may have lain into her husband with all the vitriol betrayal can deserve, now she slunk through the house imbued with a dark, guilty shadow. When she passed by he didn't move a muscle. Nor did he come up to bed until long after she had turned out the lights and sent up a silent, sorrowful prayer to her mother.

13.
David

ON DAYS NOT MIRED BY obligation, those scattered times not filled by occasion of marriage, or death, or sacrament, Father David liked to walk down the Lake Duval trail where people were sparse. He had finished his morning puzzles quickly that day. It was a five-star Sudoku, as was the crossword, and David's aptitude for idle riddles had long been a point of pride. He had them all figured out. Over the last week he had come to wait upon such amusements as the paper with particular pining. Sorting numbers and letters occupied him. Most importantly, such activities provided answers; inconsequential placeholders soon dismissed to recycling, but answers, nonetheless. Upon completion of the final squares he was darkened, and with that laden heart he left his parsonage room and began driving for the lake.

He stopped for gas halfway there. Prices were down from the Labor Day spike and David filled his tank all the way to the top as if in case he had to drive somewhere far and nonstop. David hung up the hose, shut the gas cap, and headed for the building to pay the owner. As he reached the sidewalk curb before the entrance, one of the big glass doors swung open and a woman walked out. She wore an autumn jacket zipped up to the neck. Her head was hunched and turned back over her shoulder so that she almost collided with David at the threshold.

"Father," she said with wide eyes. Her startled face transformed to an enormous smile. Her arms crossed over her body, covering the front pockets of her jacket.

"Laverna," David said in return. "I trust you enjoyed vacation."

JACOB KOCKEN

The woman worked as secretary to the principal at Graumont High. She had been at the post so long that David had passed her every day at the front desk when he was a student there himself. Now, David was accustomed to seeing her on Sundays— she sat most usually in middling rows of the section of pews second to left from the lectern. The occasional appearance was also made on Wednesday evenings when she desired absolution. She had a habit of small sins. Lies and gossips, curious petty acts of shoplifting and embezzlement peppered her common life. She was a good-hearted woman. That had always been clear to David. The deepest part of her yearned for love and harmony. But now and again she became paradoxical, talking herself into crimes not of passion but perhaps of boredom.

"Oh yes," said Laverna. She went on speaking in a wandering staccato pattern. Her eyes darted back and forth between David, her car, and the building she'd just exited. "My husband and I spent a month at the cabin. Up near the Boundary Waters. It's the most peaceful thing. Sunrises over the lake. Sunsets. Eating fresh caught fish. A fire every night. It's so primal. It makes the whole Earth feel like home. The natural part at least. One hardly wants to come back. It's busy here. There's so much going on it scrambles a person's mind. Makes you antsy." She shifted a little and the sound of scrunching plastic leaked out from somewhere near. Laverna's cheeks and forehead went rosy. "I should get going," she said. "Busy day." The concrete clapped beneath her hurried feet as she moved past him.

"Laverna," said David. She froze all at once at the sound of her name. Just her eyes bent back toward where he'd called. "I hope to see you soon."

She let out a choppy breath as her mouth curled into a big smile again. "Of course," she said. Then Laverna pattered over to her car and slid inside. David saw the jacket zipper being undone through the window as she turned out of the gas station lot. But she was a good woman at heart. When she stood amongst the pews for hymns her song was filled with true longing and admiration of Christ. Mass was not a timestamp pattern in the monotonous clockwork of the week for Laverna. She was among the class whose belief was organic. He had seen her at retreats, under his very instruction fall-

RISE THE MOON

ing in love with Christ. They had sat in prayer and discussion and ritual song together laying bare the soul of Man. Many attended the event and all benefited somehow or another, but some touched depths that struck a rare divine resonance. So rich and immediate were Laverna's intimations of the truth that she, in moments of ecstasy, may have been confused with one of the heavenly chorus who never tires of singing praises though the notes stretch on for years and the verses eons. David knew this, and it saddened him.

At the gas station counter, David paid for his tank. His eye wandered up the back wall as the clerk made his change. There were the usual things; cigarettes and liquor, knickknacks, sunflower seeds and jerky. At the far end hung a set of fishing poles. Gold and silver hooks gleamed in packages below beside bobbers, sinkers, fake worms, and line with extra strength.

"Going for a fish?" asked the man behind the desk. He handed David three wrinkled bills, a quarter, and two pennies.

"Just going down to the lake," said David, shaking his head softly.

"That's just where the fish are," said the attendant. "You won't find 'em much place else. Those poles are on sale since summer's coming to an end. After this week, they won't be back up till spring. It's a good way to enjoy the last of the heat. Relaxing."

"Not today," said David. He thanked the man and headed back to his car. It wasn't long before the town fell back behind him and the road wound into the trees. Lake Duval opened to sight as he crested a small hill and drove into the park's dirt lot. He left his keys and wallet in the center console and struck out on the trailhead path.

With the lake on one hand, expanding its pure blue water into the even wider, more open, more fluid blue sky, all of which encouraged a free and wandering type of thought; with that in one direction and the forest paths on the other with the trees and bushes in summer thickness, secluding the walker and insulating him and those meandering thoughts from the rest of the world, it was a treasured place for private contemplation.

He chose a trail leading into the depths of the forest. The paths, formed by the continual trodding of wanderers throughout the years, wound with no structure save the whim of their first explorer.

JACOB KOCKEN

They crossed each other, stretched into the wilderness, and doubled back or simply ended at random. They were, after a time, formally mapped, and a sign at the trailhead disclosed a combined length of over twenty-two miles. This was a fact which David learned only sometime after his wife had left and he had begun to run. Especially in those early days, when the pain was fresh and consuming, David had come to the lake to run the length of the trail. Evie, his wife, had been pregnant. He'd been petrified when the news had come. That was somewhere more than a decade ago now. For a long time David had wished he could've gone back, that he could have received the moment with more happiness and grace. But he was a pup himself at the time. He had been twenty-one, she was twenty. They'd married in a childish passion that clouded every doubt from their minds, and only with the announcement of the baby did David begin to understand the gravity of his role. He'd had no real career and hardly any money. Evie was even less stable still. She was filled with a grave importance; that much was clear, yet his wife's dammed lips were keeping back a melancholy flood. For a while, though only privately, he'd hoped the pressure would overcome her too. He never suggested anything, of course. But he did go as far as to drop the name of a doctor now and then into conversation, one whose specialty was known but rarely printed in those days. After some weeks, a change came over David. It was less an inspiration than it was a decision. The child was coming, and he'd better be ready. He'd rented some books on the health and development of infant children. He'd talked with his own mother who related the joys and trials of rearing him and many of the lessons better heard than earned. He'd argued for a promotion at work and got it. Every laboring hour passed sweeter under the money's new purpose; a beautiful, hopeful life for his soon-to-be-born.

Then, after one of those days' long shifts, he returned to a house that was little more than a wooden box. The furniture was still there; things lay all about, but it was empty. A note on the countertop told it all. Evie had gone. She was very sure the child was not his. She felt terrible shame but did not want to resolve it. She did not want the child to know.

David had never seen or heard from her since. He'd been overwhelmed. And with no one in the house to speak his heart to, he

RISE THE MOON

ventured often to the seclusion of these woods at Duval Park. He found that running the trails, with its constant, painful labor, its physical demand, did something to suture a nearly infinite emotional abyss. It was out on the trail, with dry lungs and a pounding heart that David first felt the clarity that carried him into seminary school. He found after some months that the pain had become less acute but that a different longing had only doubled. He'd made a habit of future fantasy, imagining his child growing up under his strong hands and loving words. Sometimes he saw a boy, sometimes a girl. The constant thing in such visions was the warmth of pride he felt when the young one learned some new trick or called him Dad. The loss of his title as husband hurt, but the loss of his paternity carved him hollow. Without a woman around to reproduce the purpose, David joined the seminary where soon everyone would call him Father.

And now, having achieved the holy designation and yet having lost for a second time one whom he called his child, David returned to his place of serenity at Duval Park to walk and think.

Under the forest veil, with rodents and birds the only audience, David could mutter things as he tried to tease them out. The squirrels were not listening. The beetles could not be led astray. After near on a decade of vocation, David had hoped things would become easier. For a while, they were. Now, he was a novice again.

There was Confession tonight. Every sacrament was intimate, and for as many years as David had been a priest, performing the rites had been where he particularly felt his calling. If someone had come in the middle of the night rousing him from dreams with rocks against the window pane, David would have rolled happily from his covers to listen to their penitent pleas. Each of the seven had their sacredness, but it was Confession most of all that called forward the skills of the shepherd. Back on David's final day of seminary, Father Lelmond, his cherished mentor, had given an address on the subject. David remembered it well and wrote it out by hand some days after taking up the St. Francis post. He had long kept this paraphrased document hanging on the inside of his office door.

It is said in the scripture that Heaven will rejoice more for the one sinner who returns to righteousness than for the ninety-nine

JACOB KOCKEN

who never left. As with much of the Gospel, it is one thing to proclaim the proverb and another to cheer alongside those joyous angels. As a holy shepherd, your wayward flocks do not simply go lost in the wilderness. You will only learn through torturous particulars the harm your repentant child has done. The sins in themselves may be as abstract as the proverb. But in practice you will be acting in the service not only of your child but of your child's abuser. They are both God's fledglings. In these private meetings, you will learn the lives of your family in Christ. As Fathers, we have a wide responsibility. But a group is always made of individuals as secret and complex as the sea. Each and every soul has enough blood to fill your chalice a countless time. Platitudes do little help. Even the Gospel can seem cold and distant to a sinner who runs hot with shame, anger, or heartbreak. This is why the Church needs priests. You are not to be a mimic of the Word. You are to become a tool of impossible shape; a shepherd's staff whose foot is intimate understanding and whose hook is the warm hand of guidance. In this, you will be alone. Inside the confessional, your duty is to the pursuit of Grace; outside, it is to the harmony of your broken children. Such goals will never be in conflict, yet they will always be a twisted and sticky web, a knot that only your hands may free from tangle.

Of course, the particulars will be your own, and so I can only give one piece of advice: Do not make the mistake of choosing between right things. When offered either bread or water both necessities alone bring death. The problem lies inside the question. The singularity is so subtle everyone falls for it now and then. Of course, it is written that the serpent was the subtlest of beasts.

To accept our moniker is not to assume the wisdom of the Father but to play the role of the father to those who need it; to lead them forth in two ways at once; security and forgiveness. The end of time is foretold for the soul a bodily resurrection. One does not go without the other. As you become priests today, know that your responsibility is bound to the whole of Earth and to the whole of Heaven. It is an impossible task from which there is no escape.

David often thought of these words. In these intervening days since the girl's death, as they had not yielded anything he recognized as guidance, he had abandoned them to the waste basket and let them drift from mind just as he now drifted through the wilder-

RISE THE MOON

ness. So, he brooded.

Oh, Sophia Joy. He had known her parents. In high school, the father was one grade above him, the mother one grade below. Two weeks ago when he'd baptized their daughter they invited him with the rest of the family out to lunch. At the table, they'd asked him to say grace, and in such moments of love and community, in the smiles, held hands, and joyful infant laughter, he could find quite easily the words for a passionate prayer.

Oh Sophia. The words no longer sprung from his heart. He could not sleep at night. The light in his bedroom stayed bright at all hours as he reread Augustine, Aquinas, and Tillich. He circled in paradox at Kierkegaard's *Fear and Trembling* until visceral confusion crushed him. The book remained open, downturned on the bedside table for the last several days. And if his mind could not sort it out, perhaps his body would lead him to a place serene and scrutable.

But now as he walked even the once familiar paths lay before him shadowed and mixed. He'd tracked these acres a thousand times before, yet today more than once he stopped in his tracks unsure of where he headed and turned in a new mistaken direction. The light, the arrangement of trees, the stretching brambles, all appeared alien. Fear of having lost his way spurred him to hasten. Tracing the way back and forth over forking paths, he wandered on. The speed of his gait made him sweat. Soon he was running until the tree tops ahead dissolved into a small patch of clear blue sky. Protruding on that tranquil color was the tip of a brown brick turret. A watch tower. It belonged to the southern corner of the town penitentiary a mile or so further out. The rest of that bin for bad apples was hidden away behind the trees. He traveled away from its pointing like a distrusted compass needle and eventually found the open shoreline of Lake Duval.

The dense forest lay at his back. Calm water stretched out before him. There were no clouds in the sky, indeed nothing up there at all. Yielding to the beating sun, David undid the collar around his neck and the top buttons of his shirt. Still, the heat built up, and he shed the thing entirely. With the shirt draped through one hand and his collar in the other, the priest began to run half naked along the lake.

JACOB KOCKEN

It had been many months since David had come running. His throat was the first to go sore. Each inhale seemed to scrape the esophagus; the exhalation starved his lungs. But the echoing voice in his head quieted down. David picked up the pace and the burning spread from throat down through the rest of his body. He could feel it coming; the clarity, even though his vision blurred as his glasses bounced slightly on his nose. Distress slowly melted away. There was no room for thinking, only for heaving lungs and the rhythm of a war drum heart. Such pedestrian discomfort, arising immediate and somatic, demanded attention. It consumed him and he praised it. Sweat dribbled down his brow, and he used the shirt in his hand to clear himself.

Soon enough his legs reached their limit. He rounded an inlet bend and slowed to a walk. A sharp ache was in his ribs. Then he stopped altogether and bent over forward. For half a minute all he did was breathe. His head was down between spread knees, and the rushing blood made him swim.

At the far end of the trail, where it peeled back off into the forest, David sat down on a shoreside bench to watch the rippling water. He put his things on the seat beside him. His face went into his hands. He sat for several minutes until the sun's heat came through his hair. By now, his shoulders were pink and burning. His feet wriggled out of their shoes and socks. After a swing of the head, he undid his belt and the rest of his clothes dropped to the ground where little tufts of grass poked up through the sand. He entered the water slowly. Out before him, he watched the shimmering reflection of his body. The thought of being seen crossed his mind. With the events of last week the town was bound to keep a watchful eye. One could be arrested for public indecency, or at least find himself with a ticket or on the mouth of every gossip in town. It may be a more dignified retreat from duty than simple failure. It would excuse from the minds of his parishioners any more devastating or existential reasons. Where is Father David? Why has he not shown up for the service this Sunday? Has anyone checked his home? Do not worry dear faithful, he is only in jail.

He lay down in the lake, floating on his back. The cool water calmed him. Little undercurrent waves touched his backside. For a moment he felt secure, held up by the water in a place without

RISE THE MOON

gravity. The sun was directly above, and he had to shut his eyes. Fiery light shown even through his lids. Now and then he would twitch or open them a slit and feel the fire threaten to blind him. A sharp and flashing dot burnt itself onto his vision and remained there throughout his float. It danced. It shimmered white and orange and purple.

For a moment, here on the lake, away from it all, he felt free. But a free mind drifts, and all loose thoughts are pulled into orbit, washing eventually on the shore of the weightiest among them. And so the sounds of the shifting water, the fish, the grass, and the wind all twisted, bent, and whispered.

'Thoughts are not in themselves a sin, Gordan. Providence punishes what we do; that is judgment's domain. But such that arises within us lies on the heath. Neither Hell nor halo will claim you for musings. Rest assured there. Calm yourself. What is it you're thinking of?'

'Father, I fear your delineations grow narrow, and for that you miss how they echo hollow. A thought perhaps has immunity in itself, but it is not so isolated as you pretend. It springs from the void, planted in the mind invisibly, and by such a same kind of transmutation turns henceforth into crystal and weighs itself upon the world in physicality.'

'Have you never rejected a thought, Gordan? You'd be a madman. Never could you cease moving and cultivating these seeds if every thought were to come so quick to fruit.'

'What takes the dandelion a day takes the Douglas a decade.'

'Of course a thought may sit, Gordan. But you are the father of your brood. Can you not act opposite to your demon's wish, and by so doing transform the seed of one tree into the form of its better brother?'

'You must first believe the brother better. I see the future, Father, in all its modes and moods. I perceive every form by a holy human dream. But why choose one? What does it matter where we walk when suffering attaches like a shadow to the feet of every stride, lifting for the interval of a step but only for so long as gravity allows a man to fly? You will argue to me that one suffering is worse than another. Is one great horror meant to subtract that of a lesser? Is only the most persecuted among us ripe for pity? No. All have crossed that old threshold. And those who haven't will. Pain and shame are the axes that grip the revolving world. Hurled into them; hemmed-in in sin.'

'If indeed our Earth is locked by these foundations, then the key to loose them is in transcendent Heaven. Only, one needs to get there first, and Judgment falls harsh on those who quit their life. Is that what you've been thinking of Gordan?'

'Is it the death that is the sin, Father? God Himself foists death on us all by the tossing down to life. Is there any ladder back out? No. It is foisted on everyone, Father. Foisted.'

'Very well, and being foisted on us we must make the best of it by following God's Law like a north star to Heaven.'

'Forgive me if the Law, and indeed the Master Himself, falls under the same suspicion as Creation. Why believe in Him at all?'

'Better to live righteous only to suffer the empty hand of theism than shirk the Law to find a gaveled hand at death, yes?'

'Your wager is miscalculated, Father. It is not an even flip between God and void when each philosophy acts in exclusion. Even the pious play parlor games; roulette. Your cross is just one holy relic on the whirling wheel.'

'Are you an atheist, Gordan?'

'Not at all.'

'What breed of faithful can be so faithless?'

'These are my observations, Father. This is not a good place, this Earth, Father.'

'Blame not God.'

'Is neglect a sin, Father?'

'It can be.'

'Then who really is the Devil?'

'It is the human that strayed, Gordan; not the Lord.'

'How is it, Father?'

'It's a complicated subject. You might look to Ignatius.'

'Tell me now, Father. Does your study not have you held hard by the heart?'

'Wipe your tears, Gordan. What is it you've been thinking of doing?'

'Tell me, Father. They say He forgives everything. How can it be true?'

RISE THE MOON

'Our God is infinite, Gordan. There is nothing we can do to subtract from Him. There is nothing we can do that He does not understand. Of course it's true, Gordan. Of course it's true. Where are you going? Don't leave so soon, Gordan. We've only just begun.'

He had carried a bag of the brightest red apples one had ever seen. He took them into the confessional like they were his only possession.

David sighed. Exhaling all his air, he began to sink beneath the shallows of the lake. His feet hit the sand, and he stood up once again, heading back to the shore. A steady wind wicked away the droplets on his skin. His naked body was all gooseflesh. Lake water dripped from his hair, and he dressed again still damp beneath the clothes.

NINETY-NINE IDENTICAL CANDLES BURNED here in the chapel. David had counted them over and over again. His faith would have once chalked it up to Providence that the funeral goers in their generous number would have by cosmic coincidence left one flame for each day the girl had lived. Ninety-nine candles. They stood six inches tall in their brass holds. Wax dripped from the tops as if even inanimate things shed tragic tears.

Among those that burned for the baby girl, there was another. One tall, red candle whose mount was coated through continual, recurrent use stood at the back of the chapel memorial.

Confession was held twice a week. It was open to every parishioner and even any outsider who might decide to come for a less sacramental counsel. The latter case was rare. Indeed, the former case was scarce as well. The people who showed up tended to be the same ones. Some, inheriting an older tradition, showed up once a year as Lent rolled around. Many came with similar sins time and time again, and even if it had been a year or two David could remember what they'd said the last time. Pain tends to burrow into everyone it touches and is often a difficult thing to forget. David knew this, and saddened him when the lamb who'd returned seemed not really to be home.

Miriam Foster had come again. If ever there was another penitent in line, Miriam would stand aside. She preferred to go last and always waited in the same corner pew reading her personal Bible

JACOB KOCKEN

until the others had gone and left. Today, she did not have her Bible.

When Mrs. Foster entered the little chapel she spent a moment with her head bowed toward the memorial candles. Then she sat across from him. Miriam folded her hands, or rather, wrapped the curled right inside the palm of her left, and they began together as they always did.

"Hail Mary, full of Grace. The Lord is with Thee. Blessed art Thou among women, and blessed is the fruit of Thy womb, Jesus. Holy Mary, mother of God, pray for us sinners; now and at the hour of our death. Amen."

As Miriam recited her sins, David followed along. They flowed from the end of the prayer as if they were amendments to it, additions that would add another bead to the rosary. David too, just as the Hail Mary was rote into his head, knew everything that followed from her mouth.

But this time, David listened less to the meaning of her words and more to the sound of her voice. In regular conversation it was hard to hear; after Mass when a hundred other people were talking and shuffling around. In the silence of the confessional, he listened to its vibration. It made his lips tighten. For a long time he had thought there was something peculiar there. He'd noticed it sometime during the first year. Early on, he'd thought it was the chapel whose walls were no more than fifteen feet from end to end and made of darkened brown oak. But then other people came. They all confessed in the same room, and the wood, which in fact was porously old and softened by the usual temporal entropy, happily embraced the sound of all their supplications. Now, he regretfully recognized the difference. It was more pronounced. It was something in how the words fell from the hollow of her throat. They always fluttered back to the ear, an echo as lucid and simultaneously fleeting as a terrible dream.

She was talking of her mother again; that scene of their last day together. At the end, after she'd come to the last line of her mantral hymn and he had assigned the penance, Miriam shuffled as if she would stand but stayed fast to her chair with a look of unease about her.

"There's another thing," she said. "Not a sin. Not a sin of mine. Father, it's about my husband."

RISE THE MOON

"I was pleasantly surprised to meet him," said David.

"Meet him?"

"Yesterday."

The look she wore transformed slowly to confusion. Her eyebrows narrowed.

"We had a long talk, he and I. Didn't he tell you?" Miriam only shook her head. "He was standing by himself in the church. Just him alone beside the altar."

"He came to confess?"

"Not exactly. We talked about the sacraments briefly. He seemed quite interested."

"Interested? What do you mean?"

"He wants to join the Church. We set him on the path to confirmation."

"But he didn't confess?"

"He could talk to me, and I'd listen. But you know the sacrament is only for professed disciples." David sat back. There was a tension in the silence as Miriam seemed to mull things over in thought.

"I think Saul's been with another woman," she said. Then her face cracked like a porcelain mask.

"What's happened?"

"I can smell it on the bed, David." He blinked slowly and nodded as Miriam went on. "I found hair in the bath tub. Pink hair. And Saul's acted strange. He ripped out the carpet in our bedroom; ripped it all up. And he has this cut. I don't know what that means, but when I asked why his hand was bandaged he just stood there like a stunned rabbit."

"When?"

"A couple days ago."

"You haven't spoken to him?"

"No." She shifted in her seat, and her expression flashed everything from anger to pity within her twitching. David watched her eyes. Instead of connecting with his, they stared off into clouds of thought.

"There may be another explanation."

"There always is," she said. "But I know the one truth."

"You think it is repentance? His coming here?"

JACOB KOCKEN

"It was my reason," said Miriam. "The scene is in my heart. I can see him in regret and panic; asking forgiveness. I know it. By his calmness it's plain he's been answered." She lost some control of her breath. It came out not as a sob but as an angry rushing wind. "I'm afraid my sense for unspoken truths is heightened by His disfavor. I am not right with God. And He was so swift to save Saul. Or else how can he be at peace?"

"Perhaps he is not." David adjusted his glasses. "No one on the street can see right into our struggles. I'll say again I doubt your certainties, Miriam. As for Saul, we don't know all that's behind him. But you've both come here. It shows a willingness."

"People never change, Father."

"They do, Miriam, but only through real faith. It's a hard road to go alone; without a guiding hand."

"Is this my punishment for leaving her? All this time and I am not right with God."

"You have exhausted your confession, Miriam. That's all the help I know in this world. Remember them if you must, but leave those things behind you now. God does not permit sin just to even Earthly scales. Don't chalk it up to cosmic balance. No one has an invitation to wrong you."

They were silent for a while.

"You think he's earnest, Father? In repentance?"

"I don't know what is in Saul's heart. But he has asked for the Lord. Where else can we place our faith? Coming to me to join the Church? Unsolicited acts of commitment are usually genuine, Miriam. Perhaps it's best to give him this chance to fix things. It will sound harsh perhaps. But if the Sacrament hasn't inspired you to feel the Lord's forgiveness, maybe it will come through your own performance of the act."

Miriam's hands came up to her face. Her knuckles were white with squeezing. Then she shook her head and rubbed her eyes until the anger drained enough to speak again.

"That sounds like a task for a saint. A mere Miriam I am." she said. Then Miriam took a deep breath, and she seemed to steady. Her head nodded once curtly. "Promise me you won't say anything to him."

"Confession is a holy sacrament, Miriam. God Himself has

RISE THE MOON

cleaved my tongue."

14.
Anna Lee

APRIL 12*TH*
I was alone in the living room when Jasper came in. He was holding a shovel with dirt stuck on the end. There was no expression on his face. 'Get your mom,' he said, and the three of us walked silently out to the plateau down the mountainside. Dad's chapel is out there. He and Jasper built it when they moved to the Sierras. It's not large, but they built it with just their hands. Every bit of the chapel came from the sugar pines they took down with axes. One of those trees only fell halfway. It was the tallest pine on the whole plateau and looked like a two-hundred-foot crucifix caught crosswise with another tree. Dad was already there where the base of the crossbeam grew. His lazy eye was shut when we got there, but the other one wasn't. He was staring up at the treetops. Mom closed it with her finger. He lay across a long piece of wood with a jute rope tied on either end. The ropes were old and black as night from the upturned soil they laid in. Jasper took one and Mom took the other, and they put his body way down in the hole. Mom had dressed him in good clothes. No one said anything. He disappeared slowly as Jasper filled the dirt back in. His face was the last to go, and I watched it the whole time, but he didn't move a muscle. Jasper let the shovel fall right there when he was done, and the three of us walked back with our tears all cried out already. Up at the house, I saw Jasper look the door up and down. He did not come inside with us. Instead, he grabbed Mom by the arm and hugged her for a long time. Then he took a few steps toward his truck and dug out

RISE THE MOON

something from the bed. 'Evelyn, you got to take her in,' he said. When Jasper turned back to us he was holding a length of thick rope. This coil was new. It was a pure pale yellow without a single fraying thread. I knew he meant Nancy, but Mom stepped in front of me and pressed my body against hers and shook her head. 'For everybody's good,' he said. 'Hers too. Everybody's. I always told Claude that signs ain't always blessings.' He started marching our way and Mom pushed me inside. I heard them arguing out there. I'd never heard Mom like that. I'd never heard Jasper like that either. Then Mom came in and went straight into the kitchen. She climbed up on the countertop like a frightened animal and grabbed up above the cabinets where we'd been keeping Dad's gun. She went outside again, and then I heard Jasper's truck roar, and the next thing I knew we were on the road. Now we're on the road again; for the second time. I don't know where we're going. I don't think Mom does either. She just says somewhere less crowded. Most of me is thankful to leave the city. It's so unlike the mountains. Mom was in a hurry yesterday. She overslept and left the sink running when she walked out the door. She must have been all the way to the first floor when I noticed her wallet sitting on the table. I ran after her. The elevator was going so I took the stairs. I didn't even hear her following. The echoes in the stairwell all mix together. Mom was across the street at the bus stop. Her leg was bouncing. When I ran up she thanked me. And then her eyes drifted to the middle of the street where the cars were crossing and honking. I didn't know she was following me until Mom screamed. I could see the veins in her neck. The car that hit Nancy squealed and swiped two others parked along our building. She was lying face down on the yellow street lines. Within a few seconds everyone was around. The man got out of his car, and he was screaming too. All the other cars were honking. Nancy got up, and everyone was talking, and people were taking pictures. Mom told me to get her upstairs. People tried to follow, but we got into the elevator alone. Mom stayed down there, and it wasn't long before there were sirens. Two police came upstairs with Mom. One of them she said wasn't a police but a paramedic. They looked at Nancy and asked her questions. Mom tried to help them because Nancy wouldn't answer. She only says 'Papa, papa.' But they didn't seem to like Mom and they kept

JACOB KOCKEN

asking Nancy things. When they finally left Mom started throwing things together, and she said she wasn't going to work and that we should pack up. Despite how tall the buildings seem, the city disappeared much faster than the mountains did. No matter where we are I can always see the mountains if I look hard enough. Mom says its clouds or shadows, but she doesn't know the mountains like I do. I was born there. A hundred times I followed Dad all the way to the valley, and I know the shape of it a thousand miles away. Down in that valley it was all grass between the granite slopes. It was the only really flat place for miles. One day when we went down there was an autumn frost, and I kept sliding on icy rocks until we came to the valley. Dad said if you're going to learn how to shoot you need a flat place to understand how things move. We set ourselves right behind the chapel Dad and Jasper built in the valley. In all my life, I only went to his service once. That's all he let me. There was Jasper and his wife and a handful of strange faces who stared at me the whole time. When he was done preaching no one left. They all started talking and one of them tried to touch me. Dad told Jasper to take me home and did not come back himself until late. He didn't take me with him to service anymore. But on that day with the autumn frost we weren't there for service. We were there for shooting. Dad held the gun, and I held Nancy's hand while Jasper tipped up some busted wood from the forest. When Jasper came back I gave Nancy to him, and Dad showed me where the bullets go. He put his feet out wide because a big gun kicks you. Jasper helped Nancy cover her ears and held her with both arms. Then Dad put his open eye over the sight and fired. The sound echoed back between the mountains, and Nancy squirmed in Jasper's arms. She screamed, but he held her tight so she couldn't run like she did on the Fourth of July. One year Dad lit off fireworks that lit up the sky like the Northern Lights, but they spooked Nancy so bad that she ran into the woods. We spent an hour looking for her in the dark. She's still afraid every time it happens so Mom, Dad, or Jasper has to hold her, and the sound of the gun was the same. When her fit was over Dad loaded the gun again and handed it to me. It was a lot heavier than I thought. He said not to touch the trigger and adjusted my arms and my head. 'Do you remember where the word sin comes from?' he asked. 'Hata. Hamartia. To miss the mark. To go astray.

RISE THE MOON

Do not be afraid to miss. Just try not to miss in the same way twice. If your body is tense then remember to shoot on the exhale. If you lose control of the recoil then set the stock lower on your shoulder. You won't be good from the beginning, but you will get there. We learn from our mistakes. We are children of our sins; let us not hate our parents.' He had said something like that back when he made me pocket the rock with white crystals. Now and then he asked me if it had turned beautiful yet. I remember feeling it pressing on my thigh then when I set my feet wide to aim. While I brought the gun up he went over to Nancy and said, 'It doesn't hurt darling. Try to make it through. Make it through, and then you'll shoot another day.' And when I fired she didn't even scream. I hit the bit of wood, and it blew into a dozen pieces. I hit the target, but it was Nancy they were proud of for not screaming. Her eyes were wide in wonder, and they were patting her on the head like a dog who learned a new trick. 'Good job Nancy,' they said. 'Good job Nancy.'

15.
Saul

THE MEETING HAPPENED IN THE basement of the church. It went from 7 to 8 p.m., and Saul could hardly wait. When the hour rolled around and Miriam was up in their bedroom, Saul snuck out into the garage and left for St. Francis. He sped down the road in his eighty-four Cavalier, taking corners fast and sharp. Halfway there, while coming onto Harpen Lane, the car's alert sounded, and the lights came flashing. Saul rolled his eyes. Had the mechanical failure begun back when Saul's salary still supported such luxuries, a simple trip to the shop and a few hundred dollars might have put an end to this mysterious, iron-clad malfunction.

Saul parked his Cavalier under the long shadow of the St. Francis steeple. Entering through the large front doors, he found a staircase immediately to the right which turned downward beneath the church. The steps took him down to a dark hallway where one lone room shined with electric light. Saul stuck his head into the space to find a small group of people sitting down in a quiet circle. The meeting had yet to commence, and Saul joined them in waiting.

The walls of the room were yellowed white, and the place was tinged with the smell of dampness and ferrous pipes. The same bright fluorescent lights as in Father David's office illuminated the room. Six others, two men and four women, sat on metal folding chairs around a small circular table. The leader was an elderly woman named Pamela. She had frizzy, thin blond hair and wore both pearl earrings and a pearl necklace along with vibrant lipstick over a wrinkling mouth. It was this and the rest of her make-up that stood out to Saul. It was not entirely the right color for her skin,

RISE THE MOON

rather too whitish. And the thickness with which it lay upon the flat surfaces of her cheeks and forehead gave it all a look of crumbling cake.

Pamela spent the first eight minutes of their one-hour session telling how her shiatsu got out and ate some blades of grass. Saul could hardly listen. It wasn't her triviality so much as the look of her face that perturbed him. Beneath the cosmetic mask, a blue network of veins showed through diaphanous, sallow skin so that to Saul she seemed a woman half inside out. And her thin, faux red lips were drooping. Even when she smiled it was in that inelastic manner. Her voice was both hoarse and plucky, rising and falling in intensity as if it employed pitch and volume to distract the world from hearing what it was; dying. Then her story stopped abruptly, and Pamela made an announcement that everyone should open their Bible to Mark.

"Where is David?" said Saul. "The priest." It was the first time he'd spoken, and a couple of the others looked rattled, as if they had expected him a deaf-mute.

"Oh, Father David doesn't come to these meetings," said Pamela. She sat very straight up in her chair and smiled at him. "You're stuck with me."

"Are you a priest?" asked Saul.

"No no. Women cannot be priests in the Catholic Church. Look," she said with a hand sweeping around toward the rest of the circle, "learning already. I'm a confirmation councilor; one of a few." He couldn't stop looking at all the powder on her face bouncing up and down as she spoke, shaking looser. "Alright, the Gospel of Mark."

"Did you go to school with Mr. David?"

"Not seminary but believe it or not his grandfather was in my fifth-grade class in Davenville before his family moved away. Such a small world. Now, Mark."

"How were you appointed?"

"I asked," said Pamela. She laughed a bit. "I have been attending St. Francis for a long time. I used to keep records for the parish too, finances and things.

"I suppose I should've mentioned at the top," Pamela continued, "as you all see we have a new future parishioner with us.

JACOB KOCKEN

Perhaps a short round of introductions is in order. Everyone, who are you, and what brought you here? I suppose I just went," she laughed. "Clockwise then?"

To the left of the old woman sat a bearded man of middle age, older than Saul. "Hi, my name's Jeff. I've always been sort of religious. I guess I've been exploring for a couple decades, and now my fiancé is a Catholic woman. It's important to her; and to me; and to me, that we share a common sort of base." He clasped his hands and nodded, looking furtively at the person to his left.

That person was a woman wearing a tight sweater, red and hand-knit. It was early in the year for a sweater. She looked to be in her mid-twenties with blonde hair that she kept tied back somewhat plainly in a short ponytail. "My name is Angela," she said. "I remember being part of a church when I was little. My dad passed away though, and we stopped coming because I think it was really hard on my mom for spiritual reasons. I guess for all of us. And feeling kind of lost recently it was nice to visit again. So I'm here." She had an ordinary pale face, and her eyes wandered around the room as if looking for someone who refused to show up. Her voice had a charming lilt.

The next woman was named Melissa. She was pregnant with her first child and wanted it to grow up with a strong moral compass. Next was Saul.

"I'm Saul, and I am going to be a priest." He declined further explanation.

"Okay, good, great," said Pamela, motioning to the next man who it turned out had a deep regard for the traditions of the Church and wanted to become more involved. When all were done, Pamela put her hands together with palpable glee.

"Alright, everyone, the Gospel of Mark."

Saul paged through a copy of the Bible Pamela had provided. This section was nearly at the end of the book. When he held the pages open to Mark chapter one his left hand drowned in paper.

"Did I miss this much?" Saul asked, holding up the weighty side.

"No, no," Pamela said. "We'll just concern ourselves with the New Testament for now. Today we'll read chapter eight. About the loaves and fishes. Angela, will you start?" The woman with the

RISE THE MOON

blond ponytail nodded. Her cheeks began to glow the same rosy hue as her sweater while she read.

Saul followed the words on her lips rather than the page. She was stirring despite her plainness. Her voice quivered quietly between the words. His gaze traveled all along her. She stopped reading after one paragraph. The deep blue eyes flickered up at Pamela. Most of the group stared into their books in mock thought. Saul took the group's avoidance as license and launched himself into the narrative.

"*The Pharisees came and began to argue with Him seeking from Him a sign from Heaven, to test Him. And He sighed deeply in His spirit, and said 'Why does this generation seek a sign? Truly, I say to you, no sign shall be given to this generation.'*" His voice was strong and had risen to a commanding pitch with the dialogue of Christ. He would have gone on, but the leader of their little group stopped him.

"Thank you," Pamela said. "Saul, is it?" Saul nodded affirmation. All eyes were his way. The girl in the red knit sweater was looking at him hard. Her mouth hung slightly open, and she was even redder in the face than before. "I appreciate your enthusiasm, but just for the sake of order I'll be calling on whoever's turn it is to read. I suppose I'll go next." Pamela read the rest of the story aloud herself. Jesus gathered his disciples and sent them forth to feed a crowd. The food was sparse, but still it came continually from their hands. It was impossible, of course. It was the kind of logic that like a magnet had repelled Saul all his life, but now, flipped around, pulled on him stronger than gravity. He followed along, swelling with excitement and nearly rising from his seat.

"How many miracles are there in this story?" Pamela asked.

"Two," said the girl in the red sweater. "Christ multiplied both the fish and the bread."

"There are those two," said Pamela. "But another kind of miracle is at work. How many people did Jesus feed?"

"Four thousand," answered the bearded man.

"That's right. Four thousand people showed up to hear Jesus. It was not like it is today with radios and television programs convincing people to come listen to the Son of Man. Four thousand people who likely didn't know who He was heard about a man

JACOB KOCKEN

called Christ and decided to come follow Him that day. The miracle of the Holy Spirit delivered itself into the lives of common people. Four thousand little miracles."

Saul sat straight up in his chair.

"And isn't that what all of you are doing here today?" said Pamela. "These little ways God acts in our lives, urging us toward Him. When we accept His signs and guidance we are taking part in His miracles."

"Well, that's not really a miracle," said Saul.

"Yes it is."

"No it's not." There was a tense silence as Pamela's droopy lips fumbled over themselves. "If regular people like us can produce miracles then what is the point of God?" said Saul. "We all chose to come here tonight. That's well within the realm of free will and the capabilities of anyone human. Aren't miracles defined by the fact that humans cannot do them?"

"But wasn't it ordinary people, the disciples, who passed out the food?" said Pamela. "The miracle flowed through them as divine instruments."

This arrested Saul. She was right. The dead, powdered expression on her face belied some ignorance of her own words, but indeed the words were true.

"You mean to say *we* really do perform miracles?"

"The power comes from God, from Christ. He chose these disciples as He has chosen many throughout history to wield His power for us all to see. It is a blessing. In just the recent past there have been the Weeping Statue, the Moving Sun, the healing water of Lourdes, and of course there are stigmata accounts along with the incorruptible bodies of the saints." The stained-glass men and women surrounding the church came back to Saul's mind.

"Incorruptible?"

"They do not decay after death. They do not smell. It is a sign through the flesh that one is saintly. As is the stigmata; a mysterious, holy wound on the palm of the hand." Pamela shut her Bible and placed it inside the bag on the floor beside her. "We only have twenty minutes left," she said. "We ought to pray."

Everyone except Saul set their Bibles shut on the table, folded their hands, and closed their eyes. He followed their posture but

RISE THE MOON

kept his eyes open, observing. Pamela began to speak about Grace. The more she spoke on her own the more Saul drifted into himself. Incorruptible. Incorruptible. Saintly sign. How long had they been silent? He couldn't keep his hands folded any longer. Incorruptible. No smell. Stigmata. Energy was filling him. He needed to move. His laced fingers felt like ropes tying his hands from freedom.

Saul looked around at everyone. Their faces were calm, some brows furrowed in concentration. He studied the girl in red. Her eyes fluttered open. Perhaps it was just a twitch of the head. Her foot was bouncing. Then her chest swelled with a deep and silent yawn. He tracked the movement. He bounced. He swayed in his seat.

"Saul," Pamela's voice cut the air. She stiffened her hands and forearms in a meditative posture. The rest of the group looked at him briefly. A strong part of him felt just then like standing and leaving, running out the door. Instead, he closed his eyes and turned the fervent energy inward with silent words of inspired aspiration. He sat there in total blackness. The outside world melted away, and the ambient noise of the room became muffled behind his thoughts. He tried to put the old woman out of his mind. Steadily, his breath slowed and swung like even waves on the tide. Inside the world of quiet contemplation, he asked what was going on here, and a voice came back in answer. It was his own. As if it was an echo from some recent but guarded realm, Saul spoke and listened back in self-conversation, and without expectation, received in the sequestered form of personal experience, a small vision of mystery and splendor. In silent prayer, he saw emerge the dancing light and shadow of the world behind the eyes. A large and looming man cloaked in darkness held a naked child and spoke into its ear. *Look*, it said to the child, *Look*. But it had no hands with which to direct, only a voice. And the child had no eyes with which to look; they were always covered by its little hands, so instead, it swung a blind head all around, laughing. And Saul was filled with the playful joy pouring from the mouth of the child. He felt as light as he had a few mornings ago when he'd woken to a world washed of sin. The apparition danced on Saul's fancy, always with its vision hidden behind the hands.

They prayed until the clock struck eight, and only then at the

JACOB KOCKEN

chiming sound of Pamela's dismissal did Saul arise from his self-induced hypnosis. There was a small bustle out the door even before he gathered himself to stand. And as he did so, as he unfolded his hands from their pious posture, one of his fingers caught lightly on a loose loop of gauze. It pulled the edge of his bandage up, and before Saul fastened it back in place, he pulled the bulk of it to the side to check on his wound. It was sealed. The line was still there, but the ugliness of it had reduced. It was now nothing more than a thin, pink line. Of course it would heal. Of course it would go back to the way it had been. That was the way of things. It elated him.

Saul was the last of the students to leave. He was nearly giddy with excitement. The vision of the little child practically floated before him still.

On his way out into the basement hall, Pamela caught him lightly on the shoulder. "I like your enthusiasm, Saul, but I'm going to have to ask you to let others speak a little more next time. We've been making a lot of progress in the last few weeks, and my lessons have purposes that you might need a while to appreciate." She walked out ahead of him, smiling with just her lips. For a second he would have reacted with indignation, with a resentment fit for the stifling attitude of a woman not fit to teach Love. But in the same moment that her face turned away and disappeared behind the great St. Francis door, his anger vanished too. Transient, as all things progressively seemed to be, more than just that momentary anger evaporated. Every bit of his emotion that was not that childlike vibrance for the celebration of life and forward possibility fled from him as sunshine flees the nightfall. And so, he left the church with quite a gripping, though vague, ambition.

Saul was fiddling with his keys when he heard another voice in the parking lot.

"You were right."

It was Angela, the girl in the red knit sweater. She was standing next to a Dodge Charger a couple stalls away. Her form, half silhouetted, called to him. Her eyes shone in the streetlight. Angela shrugged her shoulders. When she drove away Saul pulled out after her and followed in the same direction. His check engine light flashed, and the car sounded its alert. "Oh, shut up," said Saul. His annoyance was piqued, but again he gave it up after an unfriendly

RISE THE MOON

tap to the wheel.

Out on the road, driving his normal route back home, Saul found he was following the girl. Her taillights were the same red color as her clothes. At each stop sign he came close enough again for his imagination to find her face flashing in the rearview mirror until at last only blocks from his own house did she pull off down a separate street only to remain a troubling linchpin inside his head.

Shortly before pulling back into his own driveway, the Cavalier once again rang with an alert. It startled Saul from his pleasant thoughts. "What in the hell," he mumbled to himself. The temperature was fine; every gauge on the dash was where it was supposed to be. The car dinged again. "What?" said Saul aloud. The alert repeated again and again. Saul looked up at the interior roof of his car and called out, "What?" And then Saul's fist smote the steering column with such force that the frame of the Cavalier shook like thunder. He felt a sharp sting as the wound on his palm split anew.

The beeping ceased. The light on the dash went dark, and Saul rolled into his garage brimming with awe. He looked at his own hands then up toward the sky and back again, laughing.

"Where did you go?" asked Miriam when he walked through the door. She was staring at him with just her eyes. They flicked up and down him from head to toe. The rest of her body stayed turned away.

"Job hunting," he said.

"What'd you find?"

"Some interesting things. We'll see what comes."

In bed that night, the lamp was out, and Saul was lying beside his wife. She was quiet except for several audible exhales. "Are you praying?" he asked.

"I'm sleeping."

"I see you do it all the time. Your lips twitch," he said. "It wouldn't bother me, you know. Every night you do it. I watch it every night. What do you say? What do you see?"

"Keep your jokes tonight, Saul."

"I'm not criticizing."

"Is the punch line here that God must be an elephant or a rabbit or something else with giant ears just to hear all my prayers?"

"What's it like when you talk to Him?"

JACOB KOCKEN

"It's not like much," she said.

"No?"

What could it mean after all that had happened that even a woman devout as this had nothing remarkable to say? The same feeling he'd had at the end of the meeting started in Saul again, the mysterious excitement; the naked child and the big person in the cloak. He almost didn't hear the words his wife spoke so softly now.

"Is there something you want to tell me?" They came out nearly dead, a whisper in the dark.

"Yes," said Saul. Again, he waited just listening and trying to see the scene inside his head. "But I'm not sure how to tell it yet. It's all still making sense."

"Then just be sure," said his wife, "when you say it, you get it right."

16.
Ira

IRA SAW THE DARK-HAIRED girl's face every time he closed his eyes. For the first couple days of class, he sat beside her in quiet admiration. She too, with the trepidation of a newcomer, kept mostly to herself. While she did not speak, her hand continued to write over page after page in her little green book. Ira tried several times to steal glances at the work, but the words were dense and rambling, and in his sidelong looks all the ink blended together. This flaunting secret made her all that much more precious to him.

Each day when the final bell rang and most of the students streamed out to big yellow buses in the front parking lot, Ira always spotted the girl moving against the general flow of bodies toward the rear exit. Outside, on the slate grey path that led out from school, she walked with her head bent down over the scrawling notes. The little book seemed her only companion. Aside from a gentle recognition during roll call, Ira had never heard the girl speak. Nor had he seen her in conversation with any of the other boys or girls during lunch or passing time. Today, as her slow steps took her down the lain-brick way, Ira found himself tailing her on his bike. He hadn't set out to approach, but the path only went on in one direction and her gait was slow and plodding.

By the time she turned onto the sidewalk at the edge of the property, Ira had caught up and rode into the grass alongside her. Just as he did, the wind moved through the wispy hairs of his chin and Ira felt a pang of nervous shame go through him. Those big eyes darted his way, and Ira wiped his palms down the front of his shirt, trying to dry an instant sweat.

JACOB KOCKEN

"What are you writing?" he asked. He coasted beside her. The buzz of his spinning gears droned on between his words and her startled, defensive glances.

"Stories," she said. Her face was kind but watchful. Then her head bent back to the paper and that curtain of dark hair closed over it.

"Are you like an author?"

"Not fake ones."

"Are you a historian?"

"Yes."

"Can I read it?" asked Ira. She paused for a moment. The pace of her walking changed, though she did not take her eyes off the paper. At length, she answered.

"No."

"Why not?"

"You wouldn't be interested," she said.

"I am interested," said Ira. "What good are all the words if no one reads them?"

The green-bound covers snapped shut and she tucked her writing into the crook of one arm. Once the book was closed, her furtive glances and hunched posture fell away as well.

"Who are you again?"

"Ira Foster."

"Have you always lived here?"

"Everything I remember is from here, but I was born in California." Anna Lee's eyes widened.

"I'm from California," she said. Her back straightened even more, and though her stride continued, she did turn more towards him when she spoke.

"Did you just move in?"

"We've been in this place a couple months."

"Do you like it?"

"I don't know. Everything is new. It's very flat here."

"We have a hill," said Ira. "It's by Lake Duval. One part of it comes over the water and you can dive off. Everyone goes there in the summer."

"I wish I'd known. Ever since we arrived I haven't done much for fun."

RISE THE MOON

"There won't be as many people swimming now with school and all, but you can still go."

"Mm. Perhaps," she said. "Did you call me Bella on the first day of school?"

"I thought," Ira began. "I was mixed up. Sorry."

"I look like her?"

"No."

"Is she pretty?"

Ira went red. He only let out a breathy laugh, and the girl mercifully dropped the thought.

They came to an intersection of roads and Anna Lee stopped. "I turn here," she said pointing off to the east. Ira nodded and said farewell as she crossed the street. "The lake sounds fun," she called out. Then she turned again, and Ira watched her shuffle along. She did look like Bella to him. But it was not in the face. Anna Lee was softer, and her eyes were too dark.

When he arrived at his front porch he let the bike fall in the grass and marched straight upstairs to the bathroom where he found his father's razor sitting beside the sink. Ira picked it up and ran his finger slowly over the metal. In the mirror, he tilted his head back, then side to side. His head was moving in one direction and the blade the other across his cheek when it broke the skin. Ira winced, and the razor went clattering into the porcelain basin. A bead of blood had formed high on Ira's cheek, not an inch off his left eye.

"What are you doing there?" His father stood at the door. Saul spoke with a piercing interest. Ira had noticed interactions with his father gaining a strange, vivacious spirit over the past several days.

"Will you teach me to shave?" said Ira.

Saul nodded. His hand came up, wiping the little stream of blood from Ira's face. Then he smiled brilliantly, and his hand moved up from the cheek and over Ira's eyes. He held it there, sending the boy into darkness. "Yes, yes, of course," said Saul. Ira heard the brittle scrape of metal as his father took up the razor from the bottom of the sink.

17.
Saul

SAUL KEPT SNEAKING DOWN TO sniff his own armpits. He hadn't taken a shower today or the day before, but so far he did not detect an odor. In passing, he may have even earlier that same day dug a curious hand into his hamper and given the old clothes a test as well. And because smell is perhaps the most imprecise of all the empirical senses owing to the molecules of air on which it relies being invisible and always fluid and mixing with all the other contents of the world so that unless the subject is particularly adept, only the most prominent aspect present will announce itself to the nostrils; because of these facts and because the most prominent smell in a house is that which is imbued into the walls and floor and fabric by the living person who breathes and sweats and exudes there, what Saul smelled was decidedly nothing at all except himself, uncorrupted, just as things had always been. And perhaps because he was restless from lately being always inside those walls, or perhaps in order to test slightly further this peculiar non-disturbance of his body by means of delicate exercise, Saul left his empty house and went out for a walk.

It was a cool day portending the end of summer. He walked west where the houses stretched further apart, and the suburbs gradually ended. The streets turned into country roads, and the sidewalk turned into prairie lands with a copse of birch scattered here and there along the road until the prairie met an iron fence behind which was the largest apple orchard in the county. Up the road, he could see the big gate with its name split on separate wings; *Summer* on the left, *Time* on the right. And out in front of those

RISE THE MOON

outstretched and welcoming iron bars was a circular driveway surrounding a patch of lawn with the oldest looking tree Saul had ever known. Its base was a twisted knot. The trunk split at ground level, warping over its own crooked, wooden fingers. Meant as a sort of folk signal inspiring interest and awe in passersby, the flagship tree outside the SummerTime gate was not even the same species as those kept, groomed, and altered inside. Indeed, it hung globular reds and oranges from its branches, but these rarely surpassed even a golf ball in size and were never considered objects for picking until a curious flutter of hunger smacked Saul's dry lips. The fruit was on its third bloom of the year, and most were still a nubile yellow green. There were, however, a handful of ripened specimens farther up in the boughs. Saul circled the trunk until he spotted one hanging near the end of a limb in reach. He pulled the branch down and walked out to pick his prize. It felt a bit firm to the touch, yet eatable. He toyed with its stem, letting it ripen just seconds more before the picking.

Just then however, rounding the corner of the block in running clothes was the woman Saul had met at the church a few nights before; the woman in the red knit sweater. He released the branch, and the fruit snapped back up out of his reach.

She moved with equestrian grace. Her body was damp with sweat. Her hair was once again done up in a tight ponytail. Saul stepped toward the woman and when she saw him her face gained a curious smile.

"If it isn't the free thinker," she said. A wry expression touched her mouth, and her eyes narrowed severely. "Are you following me? I distinctly remember your headlights on my tail the other day."

Saul shook his head.

"I'm off Lenox too. A couple streets down from where you turned."

"Are you sure I can trust you? It looks like you were about to steal one of Dad's apples."

"Dad's?"

The woman dropped her mock severity. "Stepdad. Brock married my mom when I was a pup. Honestly though," she said with a glance up at the ancient tree, "this old guy isn't nice on the tongue.

JACOB KOCKEN

You can eat as much of them as you want just don't think it represents us."

"You own SummerTime?"

"Best apples your imagination can handle. A taste envied by every candy on Earth."

"They look a whole lot different on the other side," said Saul. He was gesturing to the trees that grew on the land that was the SummerTime orchard. Sealed off by a tall steel fence were a hundred rows of blooming branches, tight and uniform. Their branches waved, but the trunks were straight and slender, a far sight from the gnarled specimen beside him.

"They are different," said Angela. "Raised different. Bred different I should say; an experiment of generations. Maybe I'll bring some to Pamela's next meeting," she said. Saul grimaced. Why must the charm of the moment become connected, even if only by tangential circumstance, with the bungling old woman? How was it that the insipid wormed so cunningly into this beautiful young lady's mind so that even here on a separate day and totally removed from her stifling presence, Pamela seemed to poke through the skin? Saul was reminded of the powdered face, crumbling almost to pieces for all to see, and the pedestrian words she sold as inspiration. His lone respite from her drudgery that whole hour had been in shutting his eyes for closing prayer. Only behind his closed eyes did the sham dissipate and make way for any experience worthy of religious terms. Saul put himself back there, in reverie of that prayer, and for just a moment, images of the child with its hands over its face and its teeth showing in brilliant smiles fluttered through Saul's imagination again.

And suddenly, by the same magic affecting him the previous night, Saul lost grip not only on the memory of the meeting but also on his frustration and resentment regarding the old woman.

"Running?" said Saul as if just now encountering this pleasant stranger.

"Marathon training," she said. "It's a month away."

"The Borlen marathon? I ran that a couple times when I first moved."

"I thought you looked like an athlete."

Saul smiled.

RISE THE MOON

"Maybe I'll get back into it."

The woman shrugged and returned his cheerful expression. She even gave him a friendly little wave as she turned to continue her jog. She ran easily, with the elegant freedom of some mythic woodland creature. Saul ambled on as well, stopping several times to look back and watch her ponytail bounce and her body rock as she trotted down the street.

18.
Anna Lee

JULY 20TH

Nancy smells like warm milk. That's what mom says. And she rarely sweats because she never does work. She doesn't have chores like me. She is lying down asleep right now. She looks just like she did when she was face down in the road after that car hit her. I can't always tell when she's sleeping. I don't even know if she can tell when she's sleeping. She never looks at anything for long. Her eyes are always far away in boredom or wonder. She was like that when I found her in the woods after Jasper came running in. I was sleeping, but he hit the door so hard it woke me up in my bedroom. I was sick that day, so Dad didn't take me out. He made me get rest instead, and now I'll never get rest again. When I came out Mom was crying, and Jasper was screaming about Nancy. Then they both went running into the woods. I followed, but they ran so fast I lost their trail and wandered off somewhere else. So I was the one to find Nancy. She was just lying there by a sugar pine with her head tilted back and smiling. I called her name, and when she looked at me her eyes were as far away as though I was on another mountain. And she smiled at me the way she does when she doesn't understand. She shouldn't have even been allowed to go practice shooting. If I knew what happened I would have left her there. I would have taken her by the hand and led her far away into the mountains so that the only ones to find her would be the wolves. But I didn't know, so I took her back home where we waited for Mom and Jasper. They didn't come for a long time, and when they did Mom had him by the hands and Jasper had him by the feet.

RISE THE MOON

Mom tried to tell her what happened and to touch him, but it was too late. And she just sat there with her big stupid eyes smiling at everything as if there's something anyone should be allowed to smile about.

19.
Saul

SAUL WAS PRAYING. HE SAT reclined on the living room couch, nearly dozing. He'd gone through this ritual the night before and again when he woke up. Without mantra or traditional words of any kind, Saul's prayer was free to morph with the whimsy of the wind. He would think up questions, things to ask or put challenge to omnipotence, then ask them inside his head and wait and listen to the reverberation of his own intention as it transformed from one thought to another.

Saul could have lived, he felt, content for quite a long time inside the experiment of his private prayer. When then, breaking the meditative dalliance, came the same scene he'd been witness to in the basement of the church. Just as one happy thought was taking form, it whirled away into the darkness of his closed eyes, chased out by the congealing blackness. Once again, the small and naked child was there, covering its eyes with both palms, craning its neck, thrashing, and searching. And all of a sudden, at the behest of a curious, imploring itch somewhere in Saul's regrettable dream, the child lifted its hands from its face and stared back at Saul with open eyes. There, in a sporadic reflection on the pupil, Saul saw something at once horrid and wonderful. What it was he could never have said, but as a person who is sleeping wakes up to find a shadow moving in the darkness beside them becomes then constrained by instinct from all thoughts or actions besides turning on the light and discovering the identity of his assailant who, had he been left asleep, could have either slain him freely or else passed him by with perfect peace, so Saul was racked by the urge to see

RISE THE MOON

again and categorize whatever it was inside the child's eyes that sent cold sweat trickling down his spine. And as some ideas find a place to hide even from their thinker, the child shut his hands down over his face again and disappeared into vapidity.

Saul went stiff in his chair. He sat up from his reverie. The image had run with the speed of a dream, and he tried desperately to fill the vacuous space with its reproduction. But of course, it was not thought in the conscious, purposeful sense that had conjured the bare child, and still less that which the child evidently saw and kept hidden behind his hands and eyelids except for that second of wanton revelation. For the same reason, it was not effortful thought, Saul discovered, that could bring it back. After many minutes of recalling only blank imagination, Saul rummaged through every drawer and cupboard and stalked out to the garage with several half-dried tubes of paint in his hand.

20.
Miriam

THE PHONE WAS RINGING. MIRIAM sat alone in the kitchen. The tone sounded five times; six times; seven times. Without even looking she knew who it was; some intuition had been working its way through her for over a week. And so, she sat there in a stiff wooden chair at the table and listened to it ring.

Then, in the middle of one of the endless chimes, the sound broke off. "Hello," said a voice. Miriam turned to see her son. The telephone was up to his ear, and he was wearing the most wonderful expression. Her gut sank.

Scratching tones issued from the little speaker. She could almost put the conversation together. Her baby's head was tilted slightly up as he spoke, showing off a freshly shaven face, newborn smooth. His eyes stared into the empty air as if he were somewhere else.

Miriam let them speak. She wasn't going to at first. She wanted to rip the cord out of the wall and lose the whole thing in the fire pit out back. But when she'd made to move toward him, she'd seen a smile. The grin was not for her, nor did it stay for the duration of their talk, but she saw it and did not want to be the one to snatch it away.

"I just started high school," said her boy. Miriam could not remember clearly if he had ever spoken another sentence to her father. "I'm fourteen. I'll be fifteen this winter. That's right, January 7th." Her son looked at her with amazement. The man on the other end knew his birthday. A man he had hardly ever seen, and who in Miriam's private heart was of an entirely different substance than

RISE THE MOON

the cherub.

What could she have expected? They lived in the same town after all. It was almost a shock to her, these worlds colliding invisibly in her kitchen. Eventually, both voices fell to a hush, and her son was there at her side.

"It's Grandpa," he said. His eyes were wide, and he stood there proffering the phone like a hopeful offering to a quiet god. For a moment, she'd seen something of Saul in her son, an expression she'd often shaken away. She regarded him a long time before accepting the only reasonable thing and stretching out her open hand. She took the phone. Instead of wandering away, her baby just stood there polite and patient, watching her talk with his hands clasped before him.

Miriam raised the phone. She held it in the clutch of her misformed hand and found the plastic still warm from her son's face. "Hello," she said.

"Hey, Mimi. It's Dad. I'm going to Mom's tomorrow to pull weeds in the garden before she tries to do it herself again," said Frank. "Will you help? She'd love to see you." Miriam's grandmother was still living in the house she and her late husband had built there sixty years earlier. Her back had gone weak and stiff long ago, but the determination that kept her alone in that house also kept her working like the thirty-year-old woman she longed to be. A year or so back, she'd strained a muscle and fallen in the garden. A neighbor boy noticed her nearly an hour later after running timidly into her yard to grab an errant football and was alerted partially by her silence that something was not normal. "You know her. She won't ask for help, but she'd appreciate you." It had been a long time since she had seen Grandma Bess and, excepting the little girl's funeral, her father as well. Since her own mother's passing, Miriam had been private. And still today, she felt the instinct to reclusion. She did not want to go. But her father's voice through the speaker was loud, and Miriam could see her son following the conversation. His little thumbs twiddled innocently in waiting. He was staring at her. Miriam rolled her spine unconsciously, tucking her chin and cheek behind a shoulder and crossing her arms over her chest. She turned further away so her son was to her back.

"Yes," she said. "Okay."

"Oh," said Frank. "Well, great. I'm going there about nine. Does that work? You don't work tomorrow do you?"

"No," she said. "I should be able."

"That's great then. I'll see you tomorrow, Mimi."

Miriam hung up the phone without saying goodbye. She could sense her son's body shifting unseen, asking for attention.

"Can me and Furke play night games?" chimed the cherub.

She nodded. "Don't stay out too late." Then, in a flash, the door was thwacking against the jamb behind him.

21.
Ira

IT WAS FRIDAY EVENING, AND the sun was falling. To the northeast, the deep red light of the setting sun found its counterpart in the sky. Three dogs were howling in triangular consort when the moon caught an ominous amber shift from its regular spectral hue. And as omens often inspire playfulness in the reckless young, Furke and Ira were out looking for fun. Their bikes rolled through the neighborhood, drifting from the house of one classmate to another.

"If the twins come out they might bring John and Andy. We could play kick the can," said Ira.

"John and Andy are up north."

"Still, the Paulsen's might come out."

As the houses swept by, the warm summer night air lulled Ira into thought. He coasted for a while and fell behind his friend. Ira's fingers kept running along the line of his jaw, feeling the smoothness of shaven skin. Everything there felt exceptionally warm or cold to the touch now. There was one nick just above his cheekbone. When blood was drawn his father had stopped it up with a thumb. It dried within the minute, but Saul would not give up the razor, and Ira was forced to stand for grooming like a doll. 'It will heal away quick enough. That's the beauty of it,' his father had said. 'Let me do the rest.'

"Hey buddy," called Furke from a block up and patting the seat of his bike. "It only goes if you move your legs." When Ira caught up Furke was eyeing him.

"What's on your mind?"

"Nothing," said Ira.

JACOB KOCKEN

They banked around a corner onto a long blacktop road. All the houses on this block looked the same; two stories, white with an awning over the four-step porch. The Paulsen brothers lived at the end.

"Did you see there's a new girl in our grade?" said Ira.

"Hard to miss."

"I saw her going home the other day. She writes while she walks. With her head down the whole time. Even crossing the street."

"Unique," said Furke.

As they rode up to the twins' house, they saw Bobby combing back and forth over the front lawn with a push mower. His head was down, and he marched forward single-minded as an ox. Their arrival was sounded by the yapping bark of a white Jack Russell terrier. "Hey, Monty," said Ira, patting the dog on the head as it jumped up against him.

"Is he bleeding?" said Furke. Staining the white fur around Monty's mouth was a ruddy color. Strands of fur stuck together in little spikes. The droning motor of the lawn mower cut off, and Bobby came walking over. He wiped the shoulder of his sleeve across his forehead where it came away dark with sweat.

"Your dog is turning red," said Furke.

"Yeah," Bobby said. "Garret wanted to train him for the CIA, so he buried the lasagna that Mom made for dinner to see if Monty could find it. He did. Garret's grounded."

"Damn," said Furke.

"We were going to play night games," said Ira. "You in?"

"Sorry," said Bobby. "I got to finish this before it's pitch dark. Mom's paying me three dollars."

"We can wait," said Ira.

"Nah. After this I'm doing dishes. Two dollars. I got thirty-two right now. Just another twenty-eight and I can get a Necromancer."

"Well, we can't hardly play anything fun with two people," said Furke. But Bobby was already back at the lawn mower, ripping the cord until it chugged to life.

"We could see about Devin and his friends," said Ira.

"I don't want to hang out with middle schoolers."

They rode around for another twenty minutes worth of unsuc-

RISE THE MOON

cessful recruiting. By then the tired sunset was bursting red.

"We could go to the graveyard," Ira suggested.

"To see the same old names again?"

"Look at the big egg," said Ira pointing off to the eastern sky where the moon was rising. "It's full. That's an omen, right? It might mean ghosts."

Furke sat up a little straighter on his bike. He eyed the sky curiously. "Since when did you call it the big egg?"

"That's what my dad calls it," said Ira. "Only when it's full."

"Doesn't that just stick with you?" said Furke. His voice was quiet as if he were speaking to himself. His gaze was still fixed to the heavens.

"What?"

"The egg," said Furke. "That he brought an egg and left it with her. They hardly talk about that on the news except to say it happened."

"It's a token."

"Some explanation there," Furke mumbled.

"He kept chickens," Ira offered. "They said that too."

"So what?"

"I don't know."

"I don't either." The gears of Furke's bike scratched together as he put himself to motion again. He stood as he pedaled, and Ira had to strain to catch up.

"Where you going?"

"To find out," said Furke simply. A moment of appraisal preceded Ira's mouth breaking into a curious grin.

"His house? What if we get caught?"

"It's all bushes and treetops out there. Who's going to see?" said Furke. "You've seen those houses from the bridge. They're all an acre apart. Besides, we'll be quiet as mice."

As the two boys rode swiftly over the Graumont bridge, the darkness fell complete, and the moon was an eerie spotlight above them. The chasm rolled by beneath. At the eastern edge of the gorge, one lone road stretched out from the bridge. On either side were undeveloped fields of tall grass in which the snakes and crickets hummed. The field eventually met a line of deciduous trees that became a forest many acres deep. Amidst the tree line there was

JACOB KOCKEN

a patch thinner than the rest which in the daytime could be penetrated by a sharp eye to the first few buildings of a small, forgotten village. At night, however, this lighter patch of forest fell under the cavernous dark of treetops.

Furke took the lead with Ira one bike's length behind. They stuck to the side of the road, covered evermore slightly by the knee-high grass. The closer they got, the slower they moved. The road seemed to crumble progressively away from the finely paved streets of Graumont, and soon their tires were flinging up dirt and sand. The boys coasted to a halt as the first building emerged from the shadowy forest backdrop.

It was a barn. The old paint was faded and flaking off in patches all across the façade. No light or movement showed in either of the two windows which straddled the doorway. The doors themselves were locked together by chain and padlock, immobile with rust. Furke lifted the lock, and the links rose all together in one corroded piece. The boys alighted, sticking close to the side of the building. The further on the forest stretched, the denser came the darkness.

Creeping around toward the backside of the building, they found that the edifice stopped short. At one point fifteen feet from the front of the barn, the sideboards disappeared, evaporated into the night. The bare oak and chipped paint transformed at this hollow end into dark, disintegrated stubs of timber. From its rear, the whole thing opened hollow like a great ashen-black doll house. There was yet a stable on either side and a loft above them, but everything else had once in the forgotten past been burned away.

"Is this—"

"The barn Daniel Pert burned?" finished Furke. "Yeah. He was an old-sider."

Little black fibers shone in the moonlight, displaying the destruction as soft as velvet. Ira touched one of the dead planks. The edge of it crumbled like sand under the weight of his fingers which came away stained black by the dust.

"Son of a bitch," he mumbled, wiping the ash on the leg of his jeans.

"Hey look, it's ol' Danny," said Furke, pointing at the ghost of black dust rising off from Ira's hand.

"Don't touch anything. This place might come down the rest of

RISE THE MOON

the way." They stood below the cover of the old, half-standing loft, peering out at the road and the trees.

"Which way?" asked Furke. As the dirt road continued, houses lingered randomly to one side or another, tucked into forest pockets.

They stashed the bikes there underneath the smoldered loft and stalked into the village on foot, keeping close to the trees. It was quieter now than on the gravel road save for popping twigs and their own suppressed curses as thin, invisible branches raked across their skin. Deeper into the village, some of the small houses produced light from the windows. There weren't more than two or three dwellings visible at any one time; such was the density of the forest and the space between properties on the old side of town. They jostled for the lead and ran from one broad backyard to another, avoiding all signs of human presence when a soft guttural sound caught their attention.

The clucks of a restless bird were calling through the brush. They approached the house from the back. Like many, it was dead black and quiet. Their target was confirmed by a circumference of yellow police tape around the yard. The boys ducked beneath this tepid barrier with cautious glances, but once on the other side, as if they had outsmarted a trap set just for them, they moved again with a curious and adrenal alacrity.

Running along the back wall of the house beside a little porch was an old wood and wire coop. Inside, one lonely hen clawed the strings of chicken wire fencing her in. She walked along the ground plucking at something. It shifted in the shadows and settled back in a lazy heap. Their adjusting eyes found the strange pattern of beak and feathers lying on the ground very much unlike the relaxing pose of sleep. Another hen about her size, whose feathers were in disarray all around and whose body was open after a series of sharp jabs, lay paralyzed in death. A wasting smell issued from the coop.

"Poor girl," said Furke. He bent down to her level and put a consoling hand against the enclosure. It startled the live, plucking hen. Her wings flapped in a torrent of droppings and feathers, lifting her inches from the ground and back into the recesses of the cage. A terrible rattling sound burst from her throat. It shook her whole body. Her eyes went wide and spherical, bulging with the

JACOB KOCKEN

force of her voice. The hair on Ira's back shot up. All his guts and nerves vibrated with the sound of her, and startled in turn by the bird's sudden dash, the boys fell over themselves, and hustled up to the dark back wall of the house.

There was a one-step porch in the center of which was a door with a single pane window. Ira peered through the glass. No sign of movement presented itself. The house was small and held only a sad abandonment now. Ira, in those few moments on the porch, found himself leaning, almost falling forward toward the house. It was Furke who'd reached the spot first, but it was Ira whose fingers found the lonely iron doorknob. The handle was loose and turned with the grinding squeak of rusted metal. The door swung on its hinges, and both boys slipped inside the empty house of the killer.

A dampened moon was all that breached these windows. Thick curtains were drawn all around, and the night's glow snuck through only at their edges. Objects pronounced themselves in vague, colorless shapes. Walls were denoted only by their tactile presence. Ira tasted the sweetness of dried and rotting fruit on the air.

A fog came into Ira the moment they were enclosed. There was something between the walls. He fancied his own breath echoed off them and never left. It was familiar, and a faint peck came on the top of his head. As soon as he listened with purpose, he couldn't hear it anymore. It was white noise. It was nothing. There was nothing to notice but his own breath on a dull and persistent echo.

"I can't see much," said Ira.

"Me either," said Furke. "Hang out. Eyes adjust."

Furke took a step ahead. Ira knew if he stretched out a hand he would probably find his friend within the length of an arm. Yet when Furke had spoken, the voice was unusual. Ira's ears did not find it coming from the other boy's mouth but rather from many directions at once, as if Furke were calling from the other end of the house and at the same time curling up over Ira's back and whispering in the crook of his ear. Then he heard the cry of the hen outside. It bubbled Ira's blood a second time. He could see her pecking at the dead one again, pecking and squawking. The image sat itself inside him, and the sound rang again.

"Go slow," said Furke. "Don't trip." The two of them waded into the darkness. Sight was still beyond them, but the touch

RISE THE MOON

of their hands began to discern the things of a small kitchen. A table with a solitary chair sat in the middle of the space. Furke found a sink. It was dry, and its old contents still cluttered the basin. Ira kept one orienting hand on his friend while the other dragged along the wall, feeling out the sink, countertop, and cabinets. This searching hand of Ira's discovered a protruding vertical handle. He grabbed instinctually, and a cool draft of air spilled over the two of them as a refrigerator door popped free. An electric light shot out, illuminating the room and casting their shadows on the back wall. Ira squinted through the brightness of the bulb. In fear that the light might travel through the forest and catch a watchful local eye, he closed the door as quickly as he could. But Ira had not succeeded in sealing the chamber before his own eye was captured by the vision of its contents. On the top shelf, directly below the harsh light, was a row of eggs laying on their sides. When the door was closed he could still see them blinking on his retina. They were round and brown and traversed by faint, structural lines. Ira halted.

"What is it?" said Furke. He spoke in a whisper and touched Ira's stiffened body. Then he took the handle from Ira and opened the door himself; just a sliver. There they were again, half-transparent eggs from the coop outside. One lone specimen peeled and bitten sat on the bare plastic of a lower shelf. It showed a body half congealed like yellow rubber. A budding, feathery texture lay in and between a series of grooves left unmistakably by human teeth. Darkness enveloped them again as the door was sealed.

"What was that?" said Ira.

"Dinner I guess," said Furke. He mocked a gagging sound in the throat. "Dare you to finish it."

"Hell no."

"Dare you."

Ira got as far as opening the refrigerator door before the sight of the baby bird and its sulfur smell now produced an earnest version of suppressed retching. He shut the door a swift, final time. Furke suppressed his own fit of cackling laughter.

"Shut up," said Ira. He choked again. "Let's get out of this kitchen. The air tastes bad."

"I want to see where he slept," said Furke. There was little else to go in the house. What could be called a living room was a small

JACOB KOCKEN

simple box of walls. There was an old lounge chair in the middle of the floor. Its cushions were flat. No photos or paintings hung on the walls. The only decoration was the grain of the wood planks as the patterns ran and crossed, culminating in staunch, black knots here and there.

Furke marched slowly over the floorboards to a hallway at the far wall. Ira followed. An open door greeted them with even more consuming darkness than the rest of the house. Without windows, this room was a void. The air felt different, warmer. Ira's leg hit the baseboard of the bed halfway through a step, and he fell forward onto sheets. Bouncing up with an acute sense of contamination, Ira wiped his face on his shirt and his hands on the wall.

"I almost forgot," said Furke. Then there was a click. A small orange light was cast over the bedchamber. Furke held the Necromancer up before his crooked smile. He moved the cigarette lighter high and low, searching the room for some curious artifact.

There were books all around. They were stacked on the floor, falling over each other in little piles. Handwritten notes stuck out from the pages. Some spilled across the floor or beneath the bed. The room smelled like sweat and parchment. Unlike the living room behind them, these walls were filled. Pages were taped and tacked all over in a scattered collage of drawings. They were made only of black and white. Some were in heavy, dark ink. Others were pencil sketches, but even these were starkly drawn. Little sign of shading accompanied the lined-out figures, and nowhere was an eraser used to clean up clumsy strokes. Mistakes lived on in plain view in the graphite. There were dozens of them. Perhaps Ira could have counted hundreds if he'd taken the time to sort through the leaves. He did not do this. Instead, he found himself quickly sucked in by a pattern. There was a familiarity here; a recursion in the drawings. There were people with spherical shapes all around them. One of them held a stick. Ira felt he had seen them before. This thought was dismissed quickly when he noticed the similarities each one had to the others. In this whole storm of papers, there seemed one prevailing wind. Ira stared for several minutes until the sound of Furke's cackling came again and jarred him from his spot.

"What's so funny?"

"What?" said Furke. He was at the other end of the room. He

RISE THE MOON

was holding something and looking intently down upon it.

"Why'd you laugh?"

"I didn't."

They looked through the dim light at each other for a moment. Ira exhaled hard and joined his friend on the other side of the room.

"Wild," said Furke, proffering the thing he held. He stood beside a small desk in the corner. In his hand, there was a thin bundle of paper.

"What's it say?"

Furke passed off the journal. Ira scanned over the words. The handwriting was quick and sharp, and it flashed in and out of legibility as the Necromancer's light waved.

"Stop shifting," said Ira. Furke reached out toward the man's abandoned desk. An iron candle holder sat flowed over the edges with ancient wax, opaquely grey and imbued with its own circulating smoke. It echoed in the room with a metallic clank as Furke fit the foot of the Necromancer into its hold and placed it back onto the desk. The flame burned straight and steady, and Ira leaned in so it stood six inches from the words. Under the iron reaper's aura, a pencil script wound light and grey in tedious longhand. As he bent in close, the heat of fire was toyed on the soft skin of his cheek.

Ira flipped the page. Words continued on its verso in vivid, declarative language. Now and then he doubled back to where his eyes had already read. There was a sound to the writing in Ira's head. It had a cadence, though rough and without the form of intention. He wrote of fire and light as one in the same in phrases laden with frightful pain. His story wandered far, far back, jumping to and from the same touchstone sentiment as a drum keeping broken time. There was a woman. She was gone. She touched him with the fire. Then Ira would hear the screaming bird. Over and over Ira lost his spot and returned to the top of the page where his eyes fixed hard on one word at a time. Furke's laugh broke into the room again.

Ira looked up. His friend was staring solemnly at the page. "We should leave now," Ira said. The tortured squawk of the starving hen cried out. The clatter of its throat was loud and terrible, and Ira could feel a shortness of breath coming. "Did you hear that?"

Furke shook his head.

JACOB KOCKEN

The ringing of the chicken's cry faded only slowly, and in its place Ira caught the ghost of a strange thought. His mind traced back the steps to the coop, to the forest, to the bridge they'd crossed. And then his memory rang in time with the rattle of the hen and a vague, black chasm that opened beneath him. His veins were pulsing, filling with pain. His wrist began to ache, and his teeth did not fit correctly against each other. The dark corners of the room became disorienting, and Ira pushed off the horrible thoughts as he stumbled toward the door. Instinctively, he swiped up the Necromancer from its place in the iron holder. It was slick with the remnants of melting wax that clung to the creases of his hand. In the half-light, Ira collided with the man's bed once again. He caught himself against the mattress with his elbows. The light from the Necromancer went out, and for a moment, with his arms in the man's sheets, everything felt hot and close. He wanted to leave, to run and escape the shadow that was on him.

The flame clicked on again, and Ira made for the door where a mark on the wall caught his eyes. It struck a low and dreadful chord in his heart. The print was distinct, black as the palm holding the Necromancer.

"Fuck," said Furke who barged his way past Ira and wiped with the end of his shirt. He spat on his hands and scrubbed at the traces of charred barn. A film of ash smeared in circles, but the prints of Ira's hand still showed stark and hieroglyphic. "Go to the sink," Furke said. "Get a rag or something."

Ira stepped out from the room into the conjoined hallway kitchen. The persistent sound of Furke's rubbing ran like mice through the walls all around. Ira never made it to the sink. On the hallway wall outside the bedroom, he saw the same ashy marks of his hand. The fridge, the kitchen table, the door, wallpaper, countertop; all were dotted here and there with the image of him. The journal as well, still glued in his grasp, had taken the lines of his flesh like ink.

His heart renewed its pounding. His breath heaved in panic as he stormed back to the bedroom where Furke still stood digging his shirt against the wall. "A bit of water should do it," he was saying as Ira passed him by. The words didn't reach Ira's ears. He was staring at the paper in his hand, dark storm clouds closing around his vision.

RISE THE MOON

The live flame caught within an instant. All at once the width of the journal was blazing. The flame stood still for a moment in that rectangular shape before Ira dropped it to the bed. A fold in the blanket caught, and little orange tongues began to crawl unimpeded in every direction.

Ira stood at the side of the bed in stillness, eyes wide and reflecting. A feeling of numbness came over his mind as well as his body. There was a comfortable heat as when the sun is just rising over the morning sky. Faintly, he could hear the sound of Furke's voice over the hum and crackle of burning things. There was a dull, wooden feeling on his back and arms, a shoving and pulling which Ira came slowly to realize as Furke's imploring hands.

Then, all of a sudden, the heat across his face turned scorching and oppressive. The room lit up with a horrible, waving brilliance that was as much shadow as light. Furke was in his face, and his distant screams turned clear.

"Run!" he was yelling. "Run!" They took off into the hallway and kitchen. The flame and its light followed shortly after, climbing suspended like a demon on the ceiling. As they barged through the back door and into the yard, the house filled with firelight, and smoke came billowing out the front where the bedroom ceiling had opened and begun to curl into nothingness.

Cool night air froze Ira's cheeks, and the two boys ran off for the woods, holding each other by the arms and clothes. They threw themselves under the police tape and barreled into the brush where the trees got dense and the world could hardly see. As they trudged under the cover of leaves, silhouettes of people from other houses could be seen gathering along the gravel road. They came like moths to the light and collected to a small crowd accounting every member of this sequestered side of town. Ira kept both eyes on the inhabitants as the rubber soles of his shoes tried not to step on dried leaves and brittle twigs. Their figures stood like irregular fenceposts, some short, some tall, perpendicular to the yard's boarder tape. Their faces flashed from orange to black with shadows always pooling into their deep-set brows and sunken cheeks. The congregating people made a distorted mass.

One of the men in a torn white shirt was hooting and howling into the night. As if in answer to his call, the woods was filled

JACOB KOCKEN

with the clatter of Yokoven's remaining hen. Its cry cut through the smoky air, and even its flustering in the form of jangling metal wire could be heard over the roaring flames.

From the center of the group, a smaller silhouette emerged. It ran with quick, light steps from the gravel road to the lawn that wrapped around the falling house. Singled out from them, her face was clear to Ira in the flickering half-light. The girl's hair was black as ever. It was the first time he'd seen her without the little green book she carried. Her eyes were wide as she rounded the back corner of the yard.

Ira halted where he was amidst the crooked, thorny arms of a growing locust tree. Anna Lee was ducking onto the killer's ground. She began to shine from head to toe as she neared the pyre. Her face twisted with discomfort. In a moment, she was nearing the back wall of the house and kneeling down before the coop.

Ira took a step further into the woods, then one back in the direction of the girl as she undid the latch on the gate. Her arms reached for the bird, but before she could even find its feathers, the thing was streaking towards the forest, a mottled white phantom through the grass.

For a second, Anna Lee made to follow it. She took a few hurried steps in its wake before it reached the denser line of trees and shot across Ira's foot. He jumped as the talons touched him. He saw her eyes find his movement, and at one and the same time was pulled at the wrist by Furke deeper into the wild-grown bushes.

Neither Furke nor Ira ever looked back. Once the light of the house fire receded behind half a mile's patchwork of forest, the boys' flight turned course back toward the bridge. In the dead of night, the emergency sirens of fire trucks and ambulances screamed their presence from all the way across town. They ran ever more frantic as the blaring of horns approached. Ira was the faster of the two, and when the open field was in sight he found the old barn and raced up to it alone. He moved in a frenzy from one corner of the barn to another, surveying the dark inner walls, covering his hands and arms once again with a thick black layer of ash. Eventually, his hand found the cool metal of both bikes. Furke, breathless, joined him in the vacant space beneath the burnt barn loft.

RISE THE MOON

By then, the red and blue lights were upon them. The gravel road was loud with the grinding of tires. Ira waved incessantly for his friend to follow, and the two hid in the soiled corners of the barn. Dust from the passing vehicles swirled through gaps in the wall. Both boys suppressed a fit of coughing as their huddled bodies couched against the remains.

Two fire trucks, an ambulance, and two police cars rolled in quick succession through the clearing and into the woods. As soon as they passed and the taillights dimmed, Ira and Furke were pedaling with all possible ferocity from the scene. They crossed the bridge and hopped curbs and sidewalks into their neighborhood. Only when they reached the street that separated their houses did either of them speak aloud.

"What the hell were you thinking?" said Furke.

"No one saw us," said Ira. "No one knows."

"What the fuck, man?"

"No one saw. It doesn't matter. No one lived there. It didn't matter. No one knows."

Furke seemed about to say something else, but Ira left. He turned down his street and pedaled through the dark silence. The garage door was closed, but the house was not dark. Ira rode into the backyard and hid his bike as best he could between a hawthorn bush and their wood plank fence. The shadow of ashes was all over him; he could see that even in the dark. He left his shoes there too, hidden away behind the hedge.

Like a peeping Tom, Ira checked the windows. His father was there. Saul was sitting in the living room, stooping over a thick book on the coffee table. Ira backed away. His head swung from one end of the house to the other. The only other door was at the front porch; both were visible from where his father sat.

He paced the yard under the cover of night. When a fallen branch from an old oak tree caught his eye he took it up and marched toward the house. His bedroom was on the second floor. The stick, seven or eight feet long, reached it barely. Ira pressed one end into the corner of the wire screen. He prodded it, and the house made a dull, hollow moan. Ira tensed at the sound, looking toward the window. His father did not come, and the neighbors seemed at peace. With a second strike, he jarred the screen from

JACOB KOCKEN

its hold. It fell several feet to the ground. Ira hid it alongside the other criminal things. Then he used the stick to leverage open the window, first from the top edge where the wood and glass met, then from the bottom until it stood wide to the wind.

Ira hiked himself up the power box from which his fingers could catch the bottom of the window frame. Again, the house sounded its deep, hollow thud as he kicked against the fascia. After a struggle, he was up, safe in his quiet bedroom. As he'd clambered through the window, there was a sharp sound of clinking glass. A pool of warm liquid covered the ground and soaked up into Ira's socks as his shoes were slipped off. The scent of fresh milk was touching him. He found the overturned glass rolling on top of his nightstand below the open window. It had been full, the final dregs now dripping off the lip. Ira set it back on the tabletop and pushed it away. He wanted nothing more than to hide himself in blankets. As Ira sat down on the bed, something hard poked into the back of his leg. The Necromancer was in his pocket. Ira opened his bedside drawer to hide the lighter. He stood up and reached into his pocket and was struck with a crippling wave of heat. Ira started pouring sweat. It stung his eyes, and in the blur, a reminiscence crept up the nape of his neck. He knew it. He felt it, as alien and familiar as déjà vu. A young boy sitting on the hard wooden floor of a shack-like house. A fire burned in the hearth along one wall, the only source of light, yet filling the room with a heat and brightness that blurred the lines of faces like a desert mirage. The boy played, a ball in his hand. Then the door pounded hard from outside. A woman ran to answer it. She was disheveled but straightened her hair right there at the door. She did so with one frantic hand, her fingers the teeth of an impromptu comb. Her mouth held a cigarette stiff and straight. The lips around it were tight, and her nervous breathing turned the tobaccos ember bright as the sun. Then the door was open, and the woman smiled up at a man whose canine teeth grinned back. 'Come in,' she said. Her hands were already on him, grasping at his forearms and barrel chest. She stood on her toes to kiss him; her head tilted up in waiting like a begging spaniel. He obliged her and took the cigarette between his fingers while their lips met. They parted, and he took a drag of his own, blowing out smoke that obscured the woman's face before handing it back to her. 'That's

RISE THE MOON

my own brand isn't it? Enchanting!' Then the man approached the boy. His voice shot from the bellows chest. 'He's learning!' The looming figure crouched down to his haunches and eyed the boy. 'Do you know your colors?' The boy nodded, silent. 'Show me yellow.' The boy lifted a little plastic yellow ball. 'Show me red.' The boy lifted the first toy's crimson counterpart. 'Show me green.' The boy lifted a blue ball. 'That one's blue!' The little boy looked around himself where he sat and, after a long moment, found the fourth ball sitting there between his legs. He lifted it halfway up. 'Ha! Mama didn't teach you that one yet?' The man stood up again and sauntered by the woman. 'Chesil! He's got to know his colors if he wants a job with me one day!' His booming voice was jocular but accusing. As he walked past the woman, his meaty hand swung around and smacked her on the backside. 'Get on his lessons once we're done.' He was touching her with one hand while the other opened a door to a vacant room. The man disappeared, and the woman hurried over to the boy, her face as red as an apple. 'You know green,' she hissed. 'Show me green.' The boy picked up the green ball. Then, swift as a falcon, the woman's cigarette was plucked from her mouth and pressed onto the boy's tender cheek. She touched him twice. 'Remember!' The child began to cry. Then she hurried away, and the dress she wore crumpled to a pile as she slipped into the adjoining room.

Ira rubbed the stinging from his eyes. The dream faded and passed. He had to catch his breath a moment. Ira made a decisive movement toward his bedside table and stored the Necromancer away in its drawer. Then he stumbled to the door. The air he breathed seemed to scald his throat. No one was heard in the hall, and Ira made it privately to the bathroom where he entered the shower with his clothes still on. He ran the water ice cold, and after some moments, the heat in his bones began to ease away. He scrubbed himself with soap. A black eddy whirled around the drain for several minutes, eventually turning grey, then clear, and Ira wrung out the things he wore one article at a time. He hid them beneath the towel he wrapped around himself and was glad he did, for he went tense at the sound of his mother's voice just as he returned to his bedroom door.

"You *are* here," she said. There was a smile of relief plain on

JACOB KOCKEN

her face. "It's late. I was about to get angry that you were still playing with Furke."

Ira shook his head. He found it hard to speak. At length, something fell from his mouth. "No," he said. "I've been here."

"Did you see your milk?" she asked. "I put it on your nightstand."

Ira nodded. His mother smiled. Her face came down and kissed the top of his head. Then she was down the hall entering her own room, and Ira shut himself away. He tossed the wet towel with his balled-up clothes beneath the bed and huddled into the sheets just as he was. Fully under cover, Ira tried to sleep, but his nerves were on edge and the terrible heat was creeping. He tossed back his blankets, now bare in the dark. The cool, soapy dampness from the shower turned to salt and grime as his perspiration soaked the mattress.

Suddenly, Ira jumped. All his muscles contracted in a simultaneous flash. He tore from the bed and swung his head in every dark direction to find the sound. Once again it came, but the room was empty. Ira came to the window and slid it open to stick his head out into the night. Every now and then, just as it seemed the world was still, it screamed again. But the backyard was bare, and no shadows moved as far as Ira could see. He turned on the fan that hung above his bed. For a moment, the moving air cooled his fiery skin though it did not seem to extinguish the source. His mouth tasted of burning things, and he could not help but smell a dank rot somehow through his sheets, feel the other house in these walls and a pulsing hand print across his cheek, and hear loud and clear the desperate loop of rattling calls from behind the chicken wire of Yokoven's coop.

RISE THE MOON

22.
Anna Lee

THE GIRL WAS COOKING. ON the stove, freshly plucked and dressed chicken was simmering in a heavy cast-iron pan; one of the items small and useful enough to earn its keep from place to place. The bread had risen hours ago and was finally cool. She cut away two slices and spread over them a thick blackberry jam with the seeds still present. Her legs had been marked in acquiring them, the thorns sharper and stronger than she'd imagined. It had been a summer for blackberries. The brambles in the thicker parts of the woods some acres behind their house had yielded half again as much as usual despite the season's lack of rain. Anna Lee wondered if perhaps the bush roots didn't stretch deeper down with such neglect from above and suck the water from every grain of sand and decomposing thing. She took a bite of the bread herself and placed it on a separate dinner plate from the other.

When the bird was cooked through she diced the breast into bite-sized squares. She kept them all on the cutting board until the steam quit rolling and the meat was only warm to the touch. Gathering it all together, she moved silently from the kitchen, down the hall, and into the bedroom across from hers. The door was usually locked from the outside with a simple brass bolt and latch, but for the moment, it was undone.

Inside the room, her sister was curled up on the bed. Anna Lee approached on the balls of her feet. She left the ceiling light off and found the woman fast asleep where she lay. The blanket was pulled up over her head like a woolen cowl. Her chest and back swelled up and fell again with the smooth regularity of the unburdened. A

JACOB KOCKEN

small, rounded nightstand stood beside the bed. Anna Lee set the plate there, and with a delicacy that would not disturb the lightest sleeper, she climbed onto the mattress. She settled herself on top of the covers, one arm draped lightly over her older sister. Nancy was still and peaceful. Though the gap had closed a bit in recent years, she was still taller than Anna Lee. Her toes peaked out of the blankets, hanging just off the end of the bed. Anna Lee nestled in a little further. Her head now lay against the flat of her sister's back. Even through the blankets she could hear the heartbeat. It was strong and steady. After lying a while, Anna Lee began to feel the rhythm of her own heart. She fancied there was a slight irregularity there, though perhaps it was simply her mind wandering through thoughts of the past or the dull pressure put against her thigh by the little crystalline rock in her pocket.

For much of the last several months, they had been on the move. Before Graumont, their nights had been spent in a dozen hotels, a studio apartment in Carson City, and on the upholstery of their family Pinto as it hummed over dreary country highways. All of these stays were cramped for space, and any time there'd been a bed for Anna Lee at all, it was shared. Now, they had separate rooms. The Graumont house was bigger than she'd expected. It came cheap as it was on the bad side of town. That was something she'd heard her mother say, and it had proved true.

There was one window on the far wall of Nancy's room. Locks were on both inside and outside just like her door. Night had fallen out there, and the glass was dark. But through the shifting forest limbs, Anna Lee could see. Their neighbor's house loomed evil. He did not live there anymore, but the mark of his dwelling persisted in form like the shed skin of an eternal serpent.

Anna Lee had encountered him on a few occasions. He was tall and his eyes were always peering out beneath the brim of a hanging hat. His mouth was always moving. Sometimes he muttered; sometimes he spoke loud enough to catch even through the walls of the house. Long before anything had happened, she'd felt a discomfort. He often walked in the woods, crossing their backyard to get to his. There was a coop of chickens back there. He tended to them every morning, and Anna Lee often watched while she tended to her sister. Sometimes he came close without an obvious purpose. And

RISE THE MOON

Nancy was always in that room. Anna Lee returned to that window often lately, judging how easily one could slip through the square. Simply enough, she thought, if it weren't for the locks.

Suddenly, Nancy made a move as if she would wake and scream. Such fits overcame her often, even during sleep. Anna Lee stroked her older sister's arm through the cotton coverlet. But Nancy needed little help in easing her troubles. Anna Lee knew as much. Still, she caressed her for the duration of the little fit. The twitching lasted no more than a dozen seconds. Then they were right back where they had been, heartbeats thumping in time.

Some minutes passed before Anna Lee got up and left the room. She closed the door most of the way, allowing a crack of light and leaving the latch outside undone once again. Back in the kitchen, she ate her own share. The rest of the food she put in the fridge. Her mother would not be home for near on an hour.

She took her little green book and sat beside a window, basking in the moonbeams that broke through the forest canopy. The trees stood sentinel all around; tall, ageless fence posts. Beyond sight were the blackberry bushes. She touched her leg where the thorns had caught her. Two long scabs lined her calf, healing over and sinking back into the youthful flesh. Her fingernails were dirty. Bits of soil crept up into the beds. She picked at the scab as if pulling blackberries from the stem. They were thin and easy to tear. Piece by piece, she began to bleed again. They ran the length of her calf, and she removed them entirely. The redness turned bright and gleamed with a soft and reticent wetness.

She opened the notebook and pressed one of the blank pages to the scratch. A thin red line soaked into the paper, and she pressed again at a new angle. She did this several times until the wound was dry. A light web of blood marked the page. It dried instantaneously, and she took the notebook in her lap, beginning to write.

ANNA LEE DID NOT STIR from her spot until the front door swung and her mother entered.

"I made food," she said.

"Thank you," said her mother. Anna Lee watched from her seat by the window. The first thing her mother did was light a candle. The scent was vanilla, and it filled the whole room from the kitchen

JACOB KOCKEN

table where it sat. The window pane caught its little orange flame and transposed the dancing light onto the darkening forest outside. The flame just sat there, deep in the thickets, a sourceless and passionless will-o-the-wisp come out to dance. The girl left off her writing and began to draw what she saw.

"Any problems?" asked her mother. She was eating the food cold.

"She's been asleep," said Anna Lee. The mother's footsteps echoed on the hardwood floor.

"Her door is open."

"I'm watching."

"That's what you said the other day. Damn it, Anna Lee." The soft sound of creaking hinges came from the hallway followed shortly by the metal click of a bolt lock. "She's asleep," said her mother, walking back from the hall.

"I know."

"But maybe I should check the woods and canyon ways on the way home anyhow."

The girl did not answer. Her head hung back down toward her book.

On the paper, she began shading her sketch of trees and bushes. The flame she left to whitespace, giving it a bold radiance against the night. Then she picked up the sentence where her pencil had left off, writing around the sketch and jaggedly framing it with words.

Her mother finished eating and blew out the candle. The smell of vanilla turned dry and smoky. Anna Lee said goodnight as her mother dragged off to bed.

When the girl looked up from her notebook some twenty minutes later she noticed the light of flame still flashing on the glass. She swung her head and saw even the stream of calm grey smoke had ceased rising from the candle wick. Pressing her brow to the window, she peered out and caught the blaze in the side of her vision.

"Mama," she yelled. Without waiting for a response, Anna Lee ran down the hall and undid the brass latch on her sister's room. She was still there; far away in sleep. "Mama," Anna Lee called out again. Her mother emerged from the bedroom bleary eyed just as the girl had snapped the bolt fast again. The two of them ran

RISE THE MOON

outdoors.

In the darkness of night, the fire was dominant. It captured their eyes with its dancing, and all down the road people from distant houses were filing into a crowd. Her mother ran ahead with longer strides. The top of the neighbor's house was bending, curling in. The wind was filled with the popping of beams and great rushes of hot air like beating phoenix wings.

Jonathan Heed was hollering a frightful delight. His tall, slender figure stood a head taller than the group that surrounded him on the roadside. His head fell back like a wolf to the moon with every ritual scream, and though he said no words he seemed to voice all that the rest of them felt, for no one else spoke in the face of the fire. Only a desperate animal squall rose up in reply.

Anna Lee had no time to watch the flames as the others did before hearing the sounds for what they were. She left the gravel road, running through unkept grass. The perimeter's warning tape was behind her in a flash, and she felt a redoubled heat thrown off the house. Gordan's coop was by the door out back.

She swam through smoke that leaked out of broken walls and windows. Even through the charred air, her tongue met a rot upon reaching the coop's front gate. When she saw what they'd done to each other her head went dizzy. The thin steel wire was too hot to hold, and it took her several frantic flicks to trip the latch. There was only one hen moving inside, white with spots of brown and black. One wing was glowing, touched by the fire. Its burning stink stung the nostrils. Its eyes were wide and unblinking. The hen choked on a final screech and darted past Anna Lee's waiting hands. In the little flurry of wings and feet the nest of hay and wood shavings she'd once sat on was upset. Three eggs were turned out and crushed against the hard dirt below. Flickering firelight gleamed off her feet as she ran away wet with yolk. Out in the yard, she flapped once and settled to the ground as if too weary or damaged to fly and ran in a straight line out from the jail to the woods.

Anna Lee hurled herself away from the house. She was coughing. There was smoke in her lungs and in her eyes. The last hen's blurry shape sped into the thick forest underbrush. And as the white spot vanished away there came a stifled sound and the quick jerking movement of a man. A ghostly silhouette lurked hardly visible

184

JACOB KOCKEN

against the deepness of the black behind. Anna Lee went stiff. The outline rung inside her as familiar, but there was nothing in the blankness to place it. Her head shot to the burning house and back again. Her eyes widened with anxious confusion. Then the branches shook and there was another person there. The dim silhouettes shifted and twitched before falling into the backdrop like surfaced fish to swirling dark water.

After a moment, she took another step in its direction. There was rustling, diminished and indistinct. She searched with cautious concern for more than a minute, her vision sweeping from left to right and back. Nothing came forth, and the woods settled to a perfect quiet.

Anna Lee wiped at her face and tried to peer out again, to penetrate the void. Just then, the first of the house's supporting walls gave way with a sonorous boom. Sparks hissed, swarming the air like insects. Anna Lee went to rejoin her mother in front of the blazing house. By the time the firemen arrived, flames had eaten into the foundation. Sirens blared and men hurried. There were no hydrants out in Old Graumont. Instead, a water truck followed the first set of lights. A second came after and two hoses pumped away, shaking like angry adders. The force of the water was enough to break some of the weakened wood from its frame. Anna Lee watched as they tried to contain the blaze, but despite their tactics and the impressive dam burst of water that washed over the house, each board that had seemed quenched reignited in moments. Like a broken light bulb, sections of the house flashed dark then bright again as they sprayed. Steam rolled up along the smoke as the rejected water was sent from the house to the heavens. The responders lost their war as the water truck ran dry. The hoses sputtered and nozzles were dropped to the mud. Firemen stood all around with shoulders slumped. Some of them took knees or sat on fire truck running boards. They stored their masks away, and, but for boots and heavy coats, they were just the same as the other civilians.

Soon only a stout limestone chimney stood, an enduring presence amongst the charred dwelling bones. For a long time that night, the people likewise stayed watching in stony captivation as the dazzling shape of the fiery house danced on their eyes even long after the flames had reached to Earth.

23.
Miriam

THE DAY WAS BRIGHT AND sunny when Miriam arrived at her grandmother's house. Her husband had still been asleep in bed when she'd left late that morning. She'd eyed his languid body with disgust, hating him. Laying there at night, she could all but feel the depression of another on the mattress; a third. It kept her up. Sinking into that shallow gorge, she cried. There was a butcher knife in the drawer of her nightstand. She'd kept it there ever since the news of Yokoven had spread. She worried in agony now that she would use it for something else, if only it was not yet another mortal sin. Saul had not come up until late. She could hear him moving about in the garage all the time. She should have struck him; demanded some answer, some reparation. But she let him sleep. Who was she to judge; she whose guilt now carried her off to pull weeds as penance of her own.

They had agreed on nine o'clock. It was a few minutes past then, and she still found herself alone in the driveway. She sat in her car waiting for Frank. Grandma Bess undoubtedly sat in the sunroom. There was a television there as well as big windows with bird feeders all around. With an otherwise empty house, these congregations of cardinals and robins were her primary company. The chair she was wont to lounge in was electrically assisted, a function she resentfully enjoyed.

After several minutes in the driveway, Miriam emerged from the car. She hardly wanted to be alone with her grandmother who was a notorious and perhaps even ill-hearted gossip, but for similar reasons she dreaded even further the judgment that would incur

JACOB KOCKEN

if her avoidance was too conspicuous. She rang the doorbell and waited. When no one came she rang again and knocked on the door. She thought of the old woman's limits and, risking some propriety to save her grandmother a spell of exertion, Miriam opened the door and slid her head inside.

"Gran?" she called out. There was no response. "It's Mimi. Dad told me to come over for garden work, okay?" Miriam ambled softly through the living room. She moved slowly so as not to startle the old woman round a corner.

She found no one in the halls and returned to the living room. The walls there were filled with picture frames. A few were landscape paintings of old life on the farm, but mostly there were photos of the family line. Each branch and generation seemed to have its own section moving organically over the wall like words across a page. Miriam found her father Frank as a baby being held by both of his parents. It was followed by Frank's senior photo. His face was hardly recognizable; before age, alcohol, and the stress of an ill wife tore the friendly smoothness from his cheeks and replaced it with sallow skin and deep wrinkles.

Next was a photo of Miriam standing there with her parents at four years old. Her sadness was piqued at seeing that the transformation in her father had already begun to set in there beside her own baby-tooth smile. And even more poignant was the glassy docility in the eyes of her mother. It was the look that suffuses a body when inevitability is grasped, that of acquiescence to sadness, the surrender, so that even in a smiling picture she could not hide her ingrown resignation.

Then something caught Miriam's attention with a strange and blank foreboding. Immediately following was the picture of Miriam's wedding, the first of the color prints and the same one that hung in her own living room. Directly below that was a void. The wooden frame was worn, light maple, and empty. It bordered only a solid black cardboard block. She stepped back, and the thing seemed to call all attention towards itself like a black hole in the room. Grandma Bess, Frank and Emily, Miriam and Saul, and then the nothingness.

It was to Miriam the kind of thing that once noticed could hardly be unseen. She left the living room in a hurry trying to put

RISE THE MOON

its opaque significance out of her mind. In the dining room at the rear of the house, Miriam heard a faint knocking sound, and there through the window finally discovered her grandmother outside wrestling with a tangled garden hose. Her old hands moved slowly through loops and coils trying to keep up with her brain. Miriam retraced her steps through the house, and on the way outside was struck again by the cavernous blackness of the empty frame.

In the backyard, Grandma Bess had made no progress on disentangling the hose. Her body was kept close under the eaves of the house to find shade from the rising sun. Her breath was not audible, but her expression was of heaving exertion. Wisps of thin gray hair fell over her face, and every now and then her frail hands took time to abandon the puzzle of the hose and tuck the locks back behind her ear. It was during such a respite from labor that Miriam rounded the corner of the house and their eyes locked.

"Your father," Grandma Bess began that instant, "is a sloppy devil. The tulips have had entirely too much sun. They're wilting all out and dying in this heat. Three days ago the rain missed us, and when I said the tulips need to be watered, and I only said it to make polite conversation because he was there and not, mind you, not for him to run outside and spray them down just so I couldn't do it right. And now the hose is a mess, and the tulips will die, and he's coming again to do more destruction." The tulips she spoke of bordered the sunroom on raised flowerbeds so that they and the bird feeders could be seen from her chair. Pink, blue and yellow petals all stood on hearty green stalks and shined vibrantly in the sunlight.

"He certainly could've wound up the hose nicely," said Miriam. "Where is Dad?"

"Suspect he's tracking down the dog that bit him. It's that time again. When he gets here we'll wind this thing around his neck the same way so he can see what a pain it causes."

"Grandma," said Miriam with a wry smile.

"I know you've wanted to do the same. God knows what he's put the women of his family through. And then he comes by my house every day now to make sure I'm not standing up too much or even thinking too hard but only sitting in the fancy chair he bought me just because I fell once; as if now all my muscles are torn and

JACOB KOCKEN

the only thing that's keeping me together is the watchful patronizing eye of savior Frank. Did I ever tell you that when he was fifteen he tried out for the football team and someone's helmet broke his leg, and he screamed about it for weeks but never let me ice him or wrap it up? He said the doctor showed him how, and I wasn't the doctor and couldn't do it, but apparently he was a doctor because the doctor showed him how to do it. Well, he could've shown me just the same way if it was that big of a deal, as if it wasn't just putting ice on swelling like I've been doing all my life and obviously done it right because here I am fiddling with this hose and that doctor that showed him how to do it was buried in the Georgenson cemetery twenty years ago and would've been the same age as me if he were here fiddling with this hose instead of being dead and buried. And clearly I ain't a doctor, but even more clear is that Frank ain't a gardener." Then her hands went back to working the maze of loops. "He took after his father that way. You never met Jerome, but he was just as bad. Wouldn't let me do a thing for him all day and then drink himself infantile all night."

Miriam looked around half hoping to see her father's red Silverado coming through a side street and half hoping he would not arrive at all.

"We're pulling weeds today right?" asked Miriam. The end of the hose dropped from Grandma Bess's hand to the ground with a rubber thud. She looked at Miriam as though a state of emergency had been sounded.

"The daffodils are maturing, and the bed is filled with oxalis and nutsedge. We better get it now before Frank rips everything apart. I don't trust him to tell the difference between an oxalis leaf and the face of his grandson." Grandma Bess began marching her slow steps toward the garden. She hunched as she walked, hips lagging behind the rest of her body.

At the edge of the flower beds, Grandma Bess halted. Her face pointed down and her knees locked, frozen. When Miriam came to recognize this posture as a preparation to kneel, she rushed up and helped lower the frail old woman. Grandma Bess batted weakly at the helping hands. She breathed a sound of annoyance, and when the bones of her knees found the earth at last she wasted no time in pulling vines and thistles.

RISE THE MOON

"Did Ira get my birthday card? I sent it with Frank, but God knows his head is anywhere at any time. I don't even know that he sees the boy much."

"Dad mailed it," said Miriam.

"As long as he has something to remember me when I'm dead."

"Grandma, don't talk that way."

"You say so? God knows I'm going to die, honey. God knows it, and I know it. The way things are going we're all in for it soon. You know what happened with that little girl?"

"Yes."

"I used to know a Yokoven. That name has been on the old side for a century, and now the last one puts the line to shame. It's a wonder God doesn't flood the world again, or at least this part with all the evil and carelessness. My contention is that's why it didn't rain last time it was supposed to and Frank had to do his watering and tangle up my hose. It's because God is saving up all the rain He can right now and just waiting for the straw that breaks the camel's back. That's why we get old in the first place. It's the accumulation of sin that takes the place of good health because that black stuff can never leave you, so every rotten person fills themselves up eventually. Then the dam breaks and floods you, and you die."

Miriam did not respond. Instead, she dropped down and began ripping weeds, tossing them onto the gravel pathway. She used only her unmangled left hand but still moved more swiftly than Grandma Bess and covered the first row of plants in a matter of minutes.

Shortly after she turned the garden corner, a sharp pain seized Miriam. She was barehanded and one of the bigger weeds was covered with small invisibly white thorns. She let out a groan of surprise and stuck the affected thumb in her mouth. The base of the invasive plant was thicker than her fingers. Several jagged leaves split out from it branch-like, and on the very top was a purple vase-shaped flower covered in as many little thorns as the rest of its body.

"Find the bull thistle?" asked Grandma Bess. Miriam shot her a look, still sucking the pricked thumb. "Those grow out in the ditch along the highway. God knows how one found its way here. Just another sign of His Reckoning. You won't pull that up with bare hands. I told Frank to get it out while it was little, but he thought it was a flower, so then I come out here a week later and it's the size of an elephant."

Just then the sound of tires rolled softly up from the driveway and silence fell as the engine rumblings of Frank's Silverado cut out. His rounded form came waddling around the house in jeans and a yellowing-white tee. His hand was raised in greeting and his head moved back and forth once over the premises before dropping down. The way his face hung it seemed a dead fish on a line. Crescent shadows underscored the pale glaze on his eyes. Miriam looked between her progenitors. Her father looked as much like the old woman in some ways as he did the person Miriam had just found in photos on the wall. Grandma Bess's eyes fell to the soil as Frank hunkered down beside Miriam at the other end of the garden.

"It's nine thirty," said Miriam.

"Sorry." Her father's voice had a tired rasp. "She hasn't bitten your head off yet."

"I haven't gotten in her way."

"You will," said Frank.

They picked at the little pigweed sprouts in the dirt for a while in near silence. A steady grating wind rose from Frank's throat. Miriam saw how the dexterity of his fingers wandered now and then over the younger, flimsier stems.

"Hey Mom," called Frank. He scanned the scattered collection of weeds, leaves, and roots strewn beside her. "You're really making a mess of this place aren't you?"

"We could use a bucket," she said without lifting her head. "You could go buy us one. There's a hardware store half an hour down the road. Goodbye."

"I think there's a few in the garage too." Frank heaved himself back to two feet and stalked toward the side of the house. His dragging feet swished through the grass. The space of a minute or two passed before he returned, holding in one hand a couple of five-gallon pails and in the other a pair of leather gloves. He walked upright now. His shoulders were set strong, and his eyes pierced through things. Miriam had seen it a thousand times before. She knew nothing special had happened there when he was alone in the garage. There was no pill or prayer. That was her father. He could be in the grip of his habits for hours and hours at a time, but

RISE THE MOON

when he wasn't, he wasn't, and it often happened just like that. He had, after all, been a teacher for many years, and a teacher has to be sharp.

Frank set one pail near Grandma Bess and scooped her work into it before returning to where Miriam knelt.

"Give me those gloves," said Miriam. Frank handed them over and she stared up and down at the stalk of the bull thistle, looking for a decent way to grab it. She started low and slid her protected hand gently up the stalk so the little needles folded neatly upward just as the bluegill's spines bend flat against the scales. She tested the pressure of her hand and found a strong grip. Miriam heaved and found the bull unyielding, nearly tipping over forward into the daffodils. She re-centered and tried again, but all that budged was her own hands stripping away the prickly leaves.

"Let me give it a go," said Frank. But the father had similar luck. "Those are deep roots." The ghost of fatigue was on his voice. "Might need the shovel for that."

"Don't dig up my beds," said Grandma Bess. She was still kneeling over in the same little patch, now sitting back on her heels as she warned them.

"This thing isn't giving, Mom. If we only cut off the top, it'll grow right back and probably spread over the whole place before winter comes."

"You came here just wanting to dig up my beds."

"I don't want to ruin your beds. I don't even want the damn daffodils I know you're going to give me."

"If you dig up one blossom, I'll put you in the hole."

"What do I get if I dig up two?" said Frank. Grandma Bess only glared as he stalked off to get the shovel.

The spade tip stopped short in the soil when Frank set to digging. The strong roots underground were wider than expected, and Frank ended up having to chop a large perimeter around the plant in order to break through and heave it from the ground. All the tendrils of root clung to the soil hard and came up with the weed. The result was a conical divot in the ground sixteen inches wide and twelve deep. Frank stuffed the thistle into their now full bucket.

"How's it look?" asked Grandma Bess, still kneeling and unable to see the crater.

JACOB KOCKEN

"Just fine," said Frank. They continued working in relative silence. Miriam worked from left to right, paying mind only to the weeds that sprouted from the soil. Frank shadowed her. Each time she scooted further on, he stretched and up followed as if tied to her by a string. Grandma Bess occupied her same quiet corner. There was only a slight breeze now and then which made itself known by the especially cool relief given to their necks and foreheads. As Frank stood to unload the weed pails into the bed of his truck, he whispered, "Keep an eye out. This sun isn't good for her."

The old woman was lagging even more than usual. Her hands were flat against her thighs, and her head was down. She ought to have a hat on, thought Miriam. She could see the top of her grandmother's scalp turning red through thin hair and resolved to finish the job quickly. When Frank returned from dumping out the first load, Miriam had amassed a pile filling half the bucket again.

"Some quick hands you've got," said Frank. Miriam gave a short nod and turned her back. She crouched down to continue plucking and sensed the great mass of her father waddling up beside her. She could hear his heavy breathing. Frank plopped down some feet away and set the bucket between them. They went on picking. Miriam came to hate the way her father worked. He was slow, and much of the time he got only the leaves when he pulled, leaving the roots behind to grow again. She stood again in a spontaneous fit of resentment and was about to stalk away from him when Grandma Bess gave an audible breath. It was a half choke on the exhale. She was bent over with both palms on the ground. Her arms shook at the elbows. Father and daughter met eyes and each set to pulling weeds with strong and fluid speed, skipping the small grasses and clover sprigs.

Soon they covered the expanse of the garden and came to either side of Grandma Bess's meticulously picked square of soil. Miriam moved toward the old woman with her arm extended and her back curved in the way one stoops over a child.

Frank shot a severe look. Miriam took notice of this, and with slightly vexed obedience, backed away from Grandma Bess.

Frank turned his attention back toward the garden and moved his hands idly around the black soil. After a while, Grandma Bess came to see there was nothing left to pick and announced the job

RISE THE MOON

was done. When Miriam tried her approach a second time she was met with the same warning expression from her father. Frank stood up with a weed stem in his hand and tossed it in the bucket which he then moved with deliberate absentmindedness near the kneeling form of Grandma Bess.

As he did this, Frank began speaking to Miriam. "Are you watching that new show on ABC? The one about the guy who's on trial for. . ." he talked on, but his words were empty, and their real meaning Miriam recognized in the way his eyes widened and his neck stiffened calling her attention to his face. She met his implicit demand, and only out of the corner of her eye saw Grandma Bess's hands reach out for the bucket beside her. The weight of her frail frame leant over the bucket. She pushed against the lid, and her trembling limbs stood her upright.

Grandma Bess's face was dry with a lack of sweat yet seemed the most plainly exhausted of all. "Lemonade," she said quite simply and began the shuffle back to the house. Frank took up the buckets and followed close behind.

Inside, they passed through the living room where Miriam's attention split between making sure Grandma Bess didn't trip in her exhaustion and the empty frame which for the third time produced an acute and uneasy feeling in her heart. In the back sunroom, Grandma Bess made it to her chair. She fell in softly and slid the electric dial back to recline. Her eyes were shut, and her breathing settled.

Miriam watched as her father closed one set of blinds but left the others which showed the flowers, bird feeders, and garden open. Then he moved to the fridge where he found a pitcher of instant lemonade his mother had made days before. He poured three glasses and gave one to Miriam. He then moved to Grandma Bess's chair carrying two full glasses in his left hand and an organized pill case in his right. She sorted through the case and swallowed two little white tablets. Frank tapped softly on another of the case's compartments. Grandma Bess nodded tiredly and reached forth again for a third medication.

"Oh no," she exclaimed when the pills were down. Her gaze was out the window and falling in a broken expression. "Look at that hole." Indeed, the spot where the bull thistle had been uprooted

JACOB KOCKEN

could be plainly seen even through the short-sighted lens of old age. It stuck out as a pock mark on a beautiful smooth face, and the old lady soured again.

"I told you not to dig up my garden. You've ruined it for good."

"It had to be taken out, Mom. I'll fill in new soil tomorrow."

"You just mean to cover up the violence you did. That's not fixing. Filling it up won't make daffodils or tulips grow there."

"You will have to go without one square foot of potential daffodils."

"I wish you'd leave and not come back to destroy the little solace I have left."

"I could run those weeds to the compost and get out of your hair for ten minutes."

"Yes, and maybe the tractors there will bury you in compost, and your body will decompose and sprout into the daffodils you cheated from me today."

"Miriam, did you want to come with?" asked Frank. Grandma Bess was going on about how her husband had been a prisoner of war before they'd met and how she envied even him when looking out at the destruction of her property.

"I don't know," said Miriam. "I ought to be going soon. I've got a boy to make lunch for."

"What's he; fifteen now?" said Frank. "Surely he can fix something himself. Just for today. He can handle that. If he's anything like his mother." His expression softened, and he looked away.

"Alright," said Miriam. They assured Grandma Bess they'd be back soon. Her scathing words rose to a new pitch as they tied their shoes and slipped out the front door.

"She'll never forget about that hole."

"If it's not that, then she'll complain about other things," said Frank. "If you ask me, I'll keep her attention on the hole."

"Next time you're going to be late, let me know please," said Miriam.

"Was she bad to you?" asked Frank.

"No, not really." They got into Frank's truck. Her father took half a minute scooting sideways into the seat. His stomach pressed against the bottom of the steering wheel until he made it all the way in. He huffed with the exertion and fixed a key into the igni-

RISE THE MOON

tion. He did not try to stretch the seatbelt around himself before the Silverado hummed down the street, leaving suburbs behind for the country. "It is awkward though," said Miriam, "standing there while she reviles everything."

"Me especially?"

Miriam shrugged. She'd not been in this shotgun seat for many years. There was a particular, boxy view it allowed of things. And the smells of her father's were trapped in the old steel and leather.

"The things she says now are like little pins," said Frank. "I notice, but it can't hurt too much. I suppose it's a trade we made. She's had opportunities to really skewer me, to dig the sword in and twist. She didn't. But her pain's still there, so when it comes out like this I'll gladly take it." Miriam pursed her lips. "You could too, you know. Every day I look back at it all and wonder where it really went wrong. But there's no starting point. It's always been in me to do the wrong thing. And even the little wrong things catch you up eventually. However it happened, Mimi; what happened to your mom; I never meant things to be like they are. And you not saying anything to me the last couple years I considered a blessing against what you could have done. But all your silence frightens me because I'm not sure there'll be any left for God to give when I finally meet Him."

Miriam touched the handle on the car door. Talking on the phone made for easy flight. A simple, invented crisis and she could excuse herself, hang up, and put miles of space between them. Here, buckled into the passenger seat of his truck, there was nowhere to leave off to.

"I keep thinking back too," said Miriam. "I miss her. But it's not any of the good things. It's only that cop waking us up at dawn with the news. And me just leaving her there."

"It's not your fault, Mimi."

Frank looked straight ahead down the road. A low radio tune and the spinning tires melted into white noise, and they bounced along for two miles eventually pulling in to the county compost. Frank backed the Silverado up to a fresh heap of comingled weeds and grass clippings. The two of them threw their work on the community pile and headed out again.

"I realize what kind of parent I've been to you," said Frank.

JACOB KOCKEN

"All this time part of me felt relief you ran away. It was less for me to have to face. I was running from you too. But I think I finally see that there isn't anything for me in that direction. And when I ran into you at that funeral and those two parents had lost their baby girl forever— Well, I guess I saw my own future in a sense." Frank raised his fingers to the front of his neck and cleared his throat for a moment. "I won't ask you to forget everything I screwed up. But I'd like to finish my years in a better way than I've been going."

"We've all done some things," said Miriam, solemn.

She put a hand to his shoulder and where at first it was stiff and waiting she could feel him ease up and steady his breath under her touch. Then she retreated. Her seatbelt had somehow snuck up to her chin, as it does for a small child, tickling and threatening to strangle. Very soon they pulled back into Grandma Bess's driveway. Miriam shook her head as she jumped the big step down from her father's Silverado.

"Is she okay here?" said Miriam. "Alone?"

"She won't go to a group home. That's for circlers she says; becoming an infant again, a dependent. She won't have it."

"She said you come by a lot."

"Well, I've never had illusions about her or Dad. Kids spend a lot of time living under their parents' wings as if they're angels. But everyone's just swollen up children I think. Dad was a drunk, you know. I hated them both for a long time until I had you and realized I didn't know what to do about it either. Then Dad died. She's been alone ever since. So I started coming around again."

Miriam was silent. She found it hard to meet her father's eyes.

"Sorry I was late this morning," said Frank. "I was setting up a crock pot at home. I don't use it much, but there's a whole beef roast cooking right now. I was going to ask if you and the boys would come for dinner." The last time Miriam had been at the home she'd grown up in, it was under police escort. When she thought of that house, every other memory was subsumed by the final one out in the gravel driveway. Even now, with her father one foot away, it was Emily who spoke.

"Alright," said Miriam.

With a nod toward the house, Frank said, "I'll take Mom from here. You'd think she resents me, but whenever I try to leave, the

RISE THE MOON

complaints get even worse. She talks outrageously just so you have to respond and stay there another five minutes. There's neighbors who drop by too now and then. But she needs her family." As Frank approached the porch, his own words seemed to trigger a thought. "Speaking of your Grandma; I was at the St. Francis rummage sale a week ago. I found an old picture frame for Mom. We hung it up in the living room. She wants a family photo of your bunch. Do you have one? It would make her quite happy."

24.
Saul

SAUL WAS IN THE GARAGE painting. He held the brush in his dominant hand which was now free from the gauze that had earlier wrapped his wound. It was, to his great satisfaction, healed. A white mark of scar tissue was forming, but he no longer noticed pain when he creased his grip over something. And so, he now sat painting with perfect concentration. His neck hung off kilter, always observing his work from a new angle, always looking for details that might rekindle his vision. He would not draw frivolously, no napkin sketches or stick men. Though he was no extraordinary talent, his serious approach yielded at least admirable pictures. The child tended to sit strong in the arms of its keeper, at times even rigid, with calm, sagacious eyes. But at all attempts, Saul could not get the pupil straight. Instead of revealing its own thoughts, the child seemed to look at something just behind its observer so that any onlooker might feel the gaze brush across his shoulder. This opacity led Saul eventually to dislike his creations, even when, at first glance or perhaps for the twentieth time, the image gave off an initial intimation of hope and joviality.

It struck Saul that his unease came from the keenness of the portraits' expression. As every child seemed to see it, it was apparent that something stood behind the observer during every contemplation. To reconcile this, Saul duplicated his work with variations on color and style and technique in hopes of conjuring up an infant with clearer vision.

After many of such portraits had been made and discarded, Saul discovered that he had to make the eyes bigger lest the de-

RISE THE MOON

sired reflection be indiscernibly cramped even if it decided to show itself. Saul took all the previous paintings he'd done and stacked them facedown so they might not influence the proportions of the new picture. Then he formed the body of the young one. He made everything the same except for the head slightly ballooned to fit the eyes which increased in the same absurd proportion. He made the irises blue with detailed, Rorschach-style variations in hue. Then he filled in the shining black pupil in the center and stood back to observe.

But the mystery that should lie in the eyes still evaded him, looking past into some inaccessible dimension. Saul let out a huff and smacked the workbench table with both palms. He pushed himself up and contracted at a sharp pain from one hand. The wound he'd suffered and bandaged some days ago had split halfway again. A trickle of blood ran across his hand, and Saul left for the bathroom where they kept the gauze and tape. Only a portion of the cut had broken nature's suture, so with the hand lightly rewrapped Saul put it out of his mind.

Back in the garage, he stood further off from his work. He paced from one corner of the room to the other, observing from all different angles and distances. But it was received just as before. So, with inspiration toddling just beyond his grasp, Saul stalked outside where the sun burned down. He took off jogging down the sidewalk; trying to clear his mind, trying to prepare a vessel for that Holy Spirit.

25.
Miriam

WHEN MIRIAM RETURNED FROM HER grandmother's house she found her own home occupied and at the same time empty. Her son was up in his room. The door was locked. He had not joined them at breakfast earlier that day, and when she knocked on his door now there was a muffled response as if he were hiding beneath the bed.

"We're going to Grandpa's for dinner," she said. Once again, the rejoining voice was weak. Miriam stalked off to her own bedroom and rummaged through the drawer of her nightstand. There she kept a key to her son's room which of late had been used more and more frequently. After marching back down the hall, Miriam maneuvered the key and sent the door swinging. Her son was on his bed. He was just lying there. Nothing illicit seemed afoot, yet, at the simple sound of the hinges, he'd started, and his face was composed, for a moment only, of anxious fear.

"What is it dear?" She rushed to his side. By the time she'd reached the bed, however, he was sitting upright and assuring her there was nothing at all to talk about.

"You just scared me," he said.

"I'm sorry, hun." She could hear past the words into the quiver of his voice and sat down beside him. He was stiff as wood and did not turn to face her but rather looked sidelong now and then at the sound of her voice. When she touched the top of his head, he flinched. There was a newspaper on the floor. She did not read the front page but saw at a glance the name continuously printed there.

"Are you reading about that man?" She brought his head to her shoulder. "That'll put an edge on anyone. Don't mix your head up

RISE THE MOON

in that." She twirled his soft brown hair between her fingers. He almost spoke, but she caught him. "Don't mix your little head up in that."

When she left him, her baby was still a stone. Miriam took the paper with her and stuffed it in the trash where the horrible words would not bother anyone.

Saul was out in the garage; she had seen him in there when she pulled her car into the driveway. He'd been sitting near the back corner where his workbench was. For many years, it had sat unused, and she'd wondered passively what on Earth it was doing there at all. Now, he was painting.

Miriam entered the garage from the house door and found him just as he had been; facing the wall with the strange looking piece of work before him. Saul did not seem to see or hear her breach the space. And so, before breaking his concentration with an approach, Miriam stood and studied her husband.

It was hard to feel anything but a threatening sadness. Sadness and anger. He sat there with his back to her, rapt in his doings. She could not help but feel as though his attention to the task was only the expression of his indifference to her, for there she was right beside him as distant as a ghost. In these intervening days, Miriam had said nothing to him of her discovery. And he had said nothing of his unfaithfulness. In the past, she had always been able to tell when he lied or held something back. Saul had simple tells in the ways he talked and held his body. In this way, she could always trust him. But with this latest lie, he did not quaver or fidget. He spoke to her freely and walked about the house with the poise of an angel. His composure seemed to intimate that the people involved in that betrayal were dead and gone beyond the grasp of reconciliation. Yet, they were not, indeed, beyond the infinite wall of death as others were, so Miriam bit her lower lip with real force and tried to contain the shame.

"Saul?" she said. "What are you doing?" She approached obliquely and ran her hand through his hair, softly caressing the crown of his head. Her fingers came away with the dank grease of perspiration. The navy shirt he wore was stained dark down the neck and back. "You're all sweaty." She wiped her hand against her pants, but the grime clung on within the waves of her skin.

JACOB KOCKEN

"I was running."

"Why didn't you shower?"

"I'm going to run again," he said. His eyes stayed on the painting before him, but the brush slowed, and he came to a contemplative halt. His eyebrows furrowed and his brush tapped mindlessly on his knee, splattering dots of dark color down his legs. "It's meditative."

"What are you meditating on?"

Saul looked up at her with a joyful grin and chuckled. Then his brush made two quick strokes on the canvas.

"What is it?" she asked.

"Can you tell me what you see in it?" His eyes trained hard on hers. He was looking up at her from his seat, almost pleading.

"I don't know what to say," she said.

Her husband's expression faltered a second. Then he took her by the hand. Blue paint rubbed off onto her palm, and she pulled away. "Please Miriam? It's spiritual for me."

He tried to hold her hand a second time, and once again she ducked him. Her gaze turned on the canvas for a moment. "I don't see anything."

"Would you like to try?" He held out the brush with blue paint dribbling off its bristles. Miriam declined.

Saul exhaled with force. He looked several times between her and the painting. She watched how with every twitch of the head his expression morphed from somber, heavy eyelids to a hopeful, piercing stare. "Do I smell?" Saul lifted his arm into the air.

"Not from here." The arm dropped down but only long enough to grab the bottom of his shirt and come back up to strip it entirely. He held the cotton tee aloft like a flag on a windless day and waved her toward his naked underarm.

"I'm not going to smell you," she said, stepping away.

His waving increased. His own face bent down and audibly sniffed. "I think it's fine."

"It's not fine," said Miriam. "I told Dad we would all come to dinner tonight." Saul stopped toying with his shirt and spun around to face her.

"You're on good terms now? All of a sudden?"

"We're going to dinner."

203

RISE THE MOON

Saul's head twisted toward the thing he'd been painting, down at his bandaged hand, then back to her. His eyebrows were raised high, and there was a smile all the way across his face. He dropped the canvas onto the concrete floor. "What time?" he asked, moving away from her.

"Six."

Saul bobbed his head from side to side, and with exaggerated movements to warm his blood, removed himself from the garage and began, once again, jogging down the sidewalk.

HER FATHER STILL LIVED IN their old house; the one where Miriam had been raised; the one where her mother had passed away. It was only a couple miles from where she lived now, out near Duval Park where a tranquil lake hid sequestered among the trees. As they drove toward the northern border of town, the houses became distanced. One side of the road flattened into farmland while trees sprang up more and more densely on the other. Frank's house was one of the last on the street. The backyard was forested with oak and pine that had long sourced their firewood.

The driveway was long and full of gravel. Beneath the weight of their tires, the shifting rocks sounded like a bridge whose mortar was failing. Miriam noticed from the moment they turned in how her father's silhouette stood waiting through the screen door.

Saul was at the wheel and seemed to take the allusion when Miriam tapped a quick, insistent rhythm on his thigh. The car slowed and did not near the house. They parked halfway up the drive.

A narrow sidewalk path connected the gravel drive to the front entryway. It hugged the outline of the house, passing below every looming board and window. Up at the top of the building, two giant windowed doors looked down at her. Miriam kept her gaze on rustling blades of grass as she led her men away from the concrete path and over the lawn instead.

Seven steps ascended to the front door. This flight of concrete stairs was, like most aspects of the place, tall and heavy, requiring a conscious effort to climb.

Frank greeted the three of them at the door and ushered them in to relax while the food finished up. A heavy scent of pot roast hovered out from the kitchen. It was a tender smell but did not entirely

JACOB KOCKEN

cover the living odor, at once pleasant and upsetting, soaked into the walls and ceilings. Miriam brought her son under the fold of one wing and clutched him as they passed the threshold to follow Frank down a dimly lit hallway.

"What's this?" said Miriam. There in the living room, instead of the couch her parents had owned when she moved out, instead of any couch or traditional furniture at all, was an old, queen-sized bed complete with base and head board up against the wall. It was worn and unmade. Two blankets lay bunched up at the foot of the bed. There was even a dresser against the far wall.

"I moved it all down here," said Frank. "With it just being me, well, there's no point in climbing all those stairs every night, is there? And the late-night programs really put me to sleep. Take a seat." He gestured to the mattress, and Miriam sat down on the edge between her son and husband. An old mahogany-framed clock sat on the mantel. Every half second, the fast hand shot back a touch as if it were broken before springing forward the rest of the way. It caused an audible and constant rocking sound in the room.

"The rest of the furniture is downstairs. The basement is really the living room." Then Frank spoke directly to the boy. "But I'm sure there's a lot in here that looks strange to you. How about this?" Frank moved to the corner of the room and ran his hand along the golden horn of a gramophone. "Ever see one of these? It plays music."

Her baby stirred beneath her arm and Miriam regretfully eased her grip. He took a few inquiring steps. Her son's reserve had carried through from how she'd found him in his room. He had hardly spoken still and the whole drive over seemed isolated by some invisible fog. Now, though, he moved. There was even a quality of happiness stirring somewhere on his face as the old man engaged him, beckoning her boy forward, inviting him toward the strange object.

Frank reached down to a small stack of vinyl. "First you hit this switch. Then lift the needle up." He set the thing into motion and the music began. Everyone's hands shot up to their ears. It was loud. Absurdly loud. Even her father looked taken aback.

"Apologies," yelled Frank over the noise. He hurriedly fingered a dial, and the volume softened.

RISE THE MOON

"You could hear that thing two houses over," said Saul. "How thick are these walls?"

"Apologies," said Frank.

Miriam pursed her lips. It wasn't the song so much as the whole of it; her father, this house, the gramophone. It got her swaying with some memory, and that was what piqued her. She could just see them dancing here like they had their habit of, her parents; dancing to old, plaintive voices, one of which was now scratching through the horn: *In the pines; In the pines; Where the sun don't ever shine.*

Frank announced he would finish setting the table and left them. For a moment, they were silent. Old memories pressed all around Miriam, and she was relieved when her husband flipped on the television.

Instead of the screen, Miriam was watching the boys. Both seemed in states near reverie. Her son sat on the edge of his grandfather's bed with his elbows tucked tight to his sides, quiet as a lamb. She rubbed his shoulder and kissed him on the top of the head once again.

Saul's attention seemed always on something off in the distance. He'd run for too long, and it was nearly six when he'd arrived tired and sweaty on their front porch. For the sake of time, he had attempted to convince Miriam that he didn't need a shower, that it wouldn't matter, and after all he was going for a run tomorrow. Eventually, he acquiesced, but the conduct of this former businessman set Miriam on the edge of exasperation at the time.

Next to the couch on a small coffee table, Miriam spotted a little photograph of their family's younger years, shortly before she had left for California. "Grandma wants a new photo of us for her wall. I'm making an appointment with Meyer Studios for next week after I get my hair done." Saul was flipping through channels on the television. She nudged him in the ribs with the little brass frame.

"A picture," he mumbled.

"We don't have anything professional of our whole family. Can you believe that?"

"None?"

"Not any professional ones."

"Not a single picture," he said again, almost to himself. He

JACOB KOCKEN

smiled at her then turned directly to her son and began tapping on his arms and shoulders. The boy stayed quiet, eyes half watching the television screen and half glazed over in thought. Her husband bent down to eye level with him and stared. Her son's gaze finally flicked over to his slowly encroaching father. Then Saul straightened up and left the boy alone.

"Just checking," he said to her. Miriam gave her husband a long inquisitive stare that he returned with playful glee. Then they were quiet and watched the screen as their son did. It showed a news team, a fire truck, and the remains of a fallen dwelling.

Just then Frank reentered the room and announced everything was set. "The garlic bread is my proud point. Don't miss out on that," he said. "Oh, and what a thing for someone to do." He was watching the news story. "I read that in the paper this morning."

"A house fire?" said Miriam.

"Arson," Saul corrected. "Some vigilante sending messages. To whom, I don't know. For Heaven's sake the man's already in prison."

"It was that awful man's house?" said Miriam. Her husband nodded. "Still, what a stupid thing for someone to do. It was probably a trove of evidence. Imagine what he's done before. And all that forever unsettled." Her face was as sharp and hard as chiseled marble, a statue to rival the armed and blinded Lady Justice. She looked to her son for agreement, but his face was on his lap.

Saul clicked the screen dark, and they marched to the dining room. The table was set with pot roast, garlic bread, green beans, and Jello squares. They all sat.

"Honestly, I sympathize," said Frank. "I'd have set that fire the next day if that was my little girl."

"It was the parents?"

Frank sat up straight and looked around the room as if searching for another suspect. Finding none, he bit into a forkful of meat and nodded. "Officially, the perpetrator is unknown."

"It's amazing, isn't it?" said Saul. "It all just burned up and disappeared into nothing. Soon that whole incident will be far gone."

"They have a good motive," said Frank. "Can you imagine driving past that house every time you take the east bridge? And what else could be done? No one should live there. It's bad energy."

RISE THE MOON

"And all that bad energy is disappearing like smoke," said Saul. "Yokoven will be underground before we switch calendars."

"They say the state hasn't given out death in a hundred years," said Frank. "But I'll be damned if they miss this chance."

Just then, a chair scooted across the floor with loud wooden vibrations. Her son left the room silently, and the bathroom door down the hall swung shut. Music from the gramophone a room over accompanied his leaving.

"He hasn't said a word all day," said Miriam.

"Perhaps some more suitable table talk," said Frank.

When her baby returned they finished the meal in relative ease. The food was well received, and despite both the long, passive estrangement from her father as well as the secret knowledge of her husband's betrayal, Miriam settled temporarily into a warm, familial humor. There was a pitcher of water at the center of the table in which slices of orange mingled with the ice; a habit of her late mother's. It gave off the faintest scent when Miriam refilled her glass; a scent that touched on recollections of summer picnics and Miriam's tender side. Her eyes closed from time to time in laughter or thought or the savoring of a particular bite. The soft sounds of silverware and conversation allowed an unwonted bliss, and in the flash of memory she felt herself a small girl at table with Grandma Bess and her parents on one of several holidays before her age of understanding. How wonderful to all be one in love and satisfaction, the generational presence eroding the very root of loneliness. Miriam breathed the old aroma. She felt so often on her own, but for a short time, with her eyes closed, she was in another world, its lucidity flirting with the possible, where her husband was her husband and her father was her father and her son was with them, and he needn't ever feel lonesome. Then she would open her eyes and the feeling was found subdued by the particulars of the table folk; the spider veins on her father's nose; the bandage on Saul's hand. All but one had already sinned it away. It was perhaps a vision reserved for the deserved.

With autumn on the way, the boys fell into predictions on the World Series, and then baseball in general. For the first time, Miriam heard her son speak up. His knowledge of the game seemed to impress both Saul and Frank. "There are one-hundred and eight stitches on a baseball; it's sixty feet from the mound to home and ninety feet between the bases."

"He used his chore money and subscribed himself to half a dozen outlets," said Miriam. "I swear every other day something with a ball or bat on it rides in with the morning paper."

"What's your position Little DiMaggio?" Frank asked. He refilled his own glass, and Miriam watched how the pitcher shook, the water inside dappled with a thousand little waves as he tried to control the tremor.

"Left field."

Frank inclined his head. His eyes blinked and there was a thoughtful grin upon his face. "We had a good glove out there when I played. Larry Lindon. He cleaned up half my mistakes himself. I was a pitcher."

Miriam saw her son perk.

"You've always wanted to pitch, right dear?"

"I can't throw a curve," her son said.

"Nonsense," said Frank, waving his fork through the air. "It's not in the grip. It's subtle things you don't learn in a magazine. Give me one week and you'll have it breaking anywhere you want."

For the first time all night, her son cracked a smile. Focus returned to him. He looked to Miriam now like he did on the baseball field; waiting for something to come his way. There was a happy wave through Miriam as she watched.

"I still have the ball that brought us to state my sophomore year," her father continued. "I struck out Jim Schuster with the meanest slider you ever saw. It was smooth. Smooth as ice. That's what I'll teach you. I've still got the ball, I'm sure of it. I'll put these dishes away and show you everything."

"You two go on," said Miriam. She gestured to the empty plates. "Saul and I can handle these." Frank gave a weak speech about the etiquette of a host and then showed her boy from the room.

Miriam filled the sink with warm water and gathered the plates and utensils, cradling them between her waist and the forearm of her bad hand. Saul wrapped up the leftover food for refrigeration.

"You ate a lot tonight," said Miriam.

"I was hungry."

"From your running?" He weighed the possibility as if never

RISE THE MOON

having considered the cause of appetite. "What's got you into running? And painting now too?"

"Something gave me a thought the other day. I feel different."

"What happened?"

Saul's soapy hands stopped scrubbing the plate beneath the faucet. His mouth hung slightly open, and his gaze was focused on the shifting shadows out amidst the trees through the backyard window. "Oh, it's not suited to conversation really."

As Saul avoided her eyes, Miriam felt the contentment she'd had during dinner drain away. Then her husband perked up.

"Want to go for a run together?"

Miriam went silent for a moment. A dirty plate sunk into the water; it oscillated right and left like a leaf in the wind.

"No thanks," she answered.

"It really clears one's mind," said Saul. "It's relaxing. Perhaps you could use it."

"I could use it?"

"It's good stress relief. We could go down to the park and run where the wildlife is. You can see deer there. It's beautiful."

"Is there anything you want to tell me?" she blurted. Immediately, Miriam felt almost ashamed. But the laxity in his lies angered her. Saul's body came to a halt, and his face contorted as if trying to take in something he could not comprehend.

His lips bounced and grasped at words, and Miriam's stomach sank at the thought of opening this mess here in her parents' house. This was not the place to hear it. Her head swam. Then he laid one hand around her shoulder and pulled her face toward his to kiss. Her lips deflated against his like an old rubber tire. "Miriam," he said. "Temper yourself. You're speaking with a man of God."

26.
Ira

IRA FOLLOWED HIS GRANDFATHER THROUGH the hall. For the space of fifteen or twenty minutes, Ira had gotten to think of fast balls and home runs; he'd gotten to impress his folks and the one grandparent he had left. He liked the way his grandfather spoke of the sport. The old man spared details. He knew things, and three years of work had passed for Ira without a successfully thrown curveball. So, Ira had been glad for all the dinner talk of baseball. But now, up from the table and treading through a strange house, the cruel thoughts were creeping in again. When Ira peered into the living room there was a flashing fire. It was gone in a blink, but his heart still jumped like a fawn at a gunshot. Little tendrils of smoke rose from ordinary objects as they walked through the hall. A phantom sting was on his cheek. In moments of stillness, Ira could often hear the plaintive sounds. When he had nothing to think about, these reflections encased him. So, he took as much refuge as possible in the little sights of the house that could occupy attention. Mostly, he tried to study the figure of the man who led the way.

The face he'd been imagining these past two years was almost right. Juvenile memories of the old man floated up sharper features than the bulbous ones he saw now. Still, there was a familial draw to the look of this stranger.

There were no family pictures at home, though now, as they moved through this front hall, Ira saw the reverse was not true. Ira saw many photos of himself decorating the entryway in little gold and silver frames. They hung on walls and stood on shelves above the shoe rack. They were old, from when he was young; a new-

RISE THE MOON

born in some, no more than five in others. His mother was in some of them. Frank was in none. Ira had always known somehow that his grandfather lived here in the same city. He did not remember ever asking. You could tell something was important when adults wouldn't talk about it. Then his grandmother died, and a lot of things became silent. That was the only time they'd met before, at his grandmother's funeral. That was the only other time he recalled the presence of his mother's parents. His father, Saul, had pointed him out. 'That's your grandpa. We'll talk to him later.' The old man's face was gloom then, a rugged shadow of Ira's own mother. She had the same color eyes and sharpness of the lips. Her hair was different. Ira discovered where that had come from through pictures and mourners' remarks. The casket remained closed. They had met with Frank briefly after the wake, but Ira remembered no talking. All he seemed to recall besides the image was that this man had once been a teacher.

The back door of the house opened into a yard surrounded almost entirely by trees. A rectangular lawn extended for twenty yards before meeting a line of oak and pine. The wilderness was dense. A wending, stomped-out path was grown over with grass and wild brush. It ran in what Ira knew to be the direction of Lake Duval. He had heard his mother speak now and then of times long past at the lake, and for a moment now, standing beside her old home, he saw her in his mind's eye as a child running barefoot onto the path and disappearing amongst the pine trees.

Near the back of the property, the iron gleam of an axe caught Ira's eye. It leant beside a wide oak stump that was cut flat a foot from the ground and whose face was littered with a thousand slits. Split-up trunks and limbs were stacked along the eastern property line in a long, chest high row.

"Are you building something?" asked Ira.

"Just chopping down," his grandfather said. "This way." Frank gave a twitch of the head. He led them around to the side of the house where the space between the trees widened out. Frank stopped halfway down the length of the house where a pair of rusted bulkhead doors lie covering a stairwell to the cellar. The old man stooped, grasping one of the iron handles with both hands. A grinding, high pitched squeal came from the hinges as the old door

JACOB KOCKEN

swung up and fell to the ground again with a heavy thud. The way was dark. Plank steps descended below the house. Ira followed his grandfather into the hole where faint, hollow echoes bounced in the stairwell. There was a strange smell to the dank basement air; something sweet and harsh mixed together with the dust and dirt.

His grandfather's balding head had to duck to clear the threshold and again at the landing. Ira felt a wooden brace above brush his hair as he stepped beneath it with the slightest of bows. He looked up to see this heavy, horizontal beam. The wood was old and lined with dark splotches. Mildew was growing on the bottom and creeping around the sides. It was ugly, cracking, and in the way as one trod upon the final step. Down at the bottom, Frank pulled a string of metal beads, and a lone hanging bulb started humming with electric light.

Storage cabinets lined one wall. The living room furniture Ira's grandfather had mentioned before sat in the center of the room; a solitary sofa, one weathered, leather reclining chair, and a coffee table. The concrete floor was covered by boxes of former upstairs things. Each box was unlabeled, sealed crosswise with yellow tape, and stacked in hoarding towers along the back wall.

"Emily's things," Frank said. "Clothes, pictures, knickknacks. Stuff I couldn't toss away or live beside. Come on over this way." Ira's grandfather showed him to a decorated hutch along the wall. On one shelf there were pictures of a faded athletic past. The young man at the center of every photo was accompanied by bat and mitt. Up at the top, a soiled old baseball scribbled upon by some forgotten Hercules sat upon a three-pronged aluminum stand.

"This," said Frank, choking up on a long wooden relic that had stood leaning beside the hutch, "is the very one Babe Ruth used to call his shot. That's what some conman in Philadelphia told me anyhow. Turns out it wasn't even game used. Now I call myself a Louisville Sucker." Frank chuckled. "In here," he pulled open a drawer, retrieving a dark blue binder, "are the cards. I stopped playing years ago, but collecting is an old man's sport. The good ones are all there. Ken Griffey. Paul Molitor." He flipped through pages, pointing out particular prizes and reminiscing. He stretched the book out for the boy.

Ira almost took it. The outer cover brushed the grooves of his

RISE THE MOON

fingers when all of a sudden he tucked his hands behind his back, cuffing one in the other. His heart began to beat in his neck. Heat licked his skin. He fancied a finger of smoke was rising off the page as if the cigar Babe Ruth held in his mouth were really alight. Ira could smell it for a moment. Then it vanished like a candle's fragile flame in the wind. Instead of holding the book, Ira leaned over it and peered down at the cards as if he stood near the edge of a canyon. Frank leafed through a few more of the pages before setting the collection on the flat of the hutch.

"This was my first real glove." Frank took up a folded clump of leather. It was cracked with wear and stiffened by disuse. It was the same dark shade of brown all around and finally resembled a mitt only when Frank burrowed the bulk of his adult fingers into its pocket. "My last glove too actually."

"Why'd you stop?" Ira managed to say.

"There were other things I thought were important and that turned out to be something else. I started smoking, drinking, and partying too young. Things that gave me the air of danger I enjoyed. Gals loved it, so I leaned on the persona. It was probably a mistake. But hell, that's life. And if I hadn't, I never would have met Emily. I'll bet it was on her the last time this was used." A pleasant chortle bubbled out of Frank as he handled the mitt. "I remember she wanted to learn to throw like a pitcher. This was the only glove we had between us though, so as we tossed the ball back and forth we'd have to fling this thing over first. It was silly looking. Ridiculous. I think Emily just liked throwing the glove. She was full of that beautiful nonsense." He proffered the mitt, but Ira only looked away slightly until he heard the dull sound of the leather falling back in place on the hutch beside an empty twelve-ounce bottle.

"What's that got to do with baseball?" said Ira. The glass was brown and smoky with age. Any label that might have once been attached had long fallen to the wayside.

Frank hunkered down and opened the cabinet at the bottom of the hutch. From there, he pulled up a tub glass and another, larger bottle full of sparkling copper liquor.

He sat down on the sofa and poured a third of the glass. The spirit swirled, and Ira's nostrils flared. There was an excited na-

JACOB KOCKEN

scence, a profanity. The boy approached like a small animal who knows not yet to fear human kind. He sat on the sofa beside his grandfather and picked up the drink. The glass was dirty, almost opaque with old prints from fingers, lips, and evaporating liquor. Frank watched him lift it level with his eyes and examine the shifting amber hue.

"It smells hot," Ira said in a low voice. The liquid flashed bright orange like a torch in the night. Ira shut his eyes tight. The spirit filled his nose, and sweat pooled up beneath his cotton shirt.

"It stings a little on the nose," said Frank. "Stings more on the tongue."

"Can I try?"

"I don't think you should," said Frank. "My father used to call it his medicine and take one every day at breakfast. It didn't seem to cure him though. All the same, if you don't have anything to cure I can't see how it should help you." Then he took the glass away and stopped it abruptly just before his own lips. His eyes narrowed as a change came over his face. Ira watched his grandfather in silence while the world seemed to shrink and danse macabre on the surface of harsh brown water. The joviality from those articles of athletic history evaporated, and Ira saw there an expression of resignation that he had only seen on one face before, that he had seen repeatedly along with every man and woman of Graumont for nearly two weeks. Frank firmed his grip on the glass and brought it to his mouth, swallowing half. He licked his teeth and pointed back at the old empty brown bottle.

"I swiped that stuff from my dad one night. I'd won us a ballgame and was riding kind of high. Me and a girl named Marsha went back to that same diamond and sat in the outfield looking at the stars. And it worked." Frank chuckled.

"Worked?"

"For a while. I kept seeing her, and then one night at a party we both had too much to drink and got into a fight."

"What about?" asked Ira.

"Not an argument," said Frank. He sipped his drink and made a grimacing face as he swallowed. "I hit her. It doesn't matter why. Everyone heard pretty quickly, and I was kicked off the baseball team. A lot of my friends stopped talking to me too. I was bad to be

RISE THE MOON

seen around." The old man was staring into his glass. He rotated it, making the liquid swirl all around. Ira looked down at his own lap. "But then I met Emily. You remember her, right?"

Ira's face fell and his shoulders rose up to his chin.

"Sort of."

His grandfather's expression of resignation lingered. In the dim basement light, the lonesome aspect of the house he'd burned flickered through the walls. His lips and mouth went dry, and he ached for something to quench the heat in his veins. His grandfather made a funny noise, and Ira saw his lower lip push the rest of the weathered face up into a tremble. As he listened to the old man's words, Ira's breath turned to panting.

"I can tell you're kind like her. You've got her hair," said Frank. "One day she caught me after school and asked why I did it. I gave her some bullshit about who started everything. A few days later, Emily asked me to get ice cream. She asked me again why that fight happened. I gave her some bullshit about fairness. Then another day I walked by the diamond and saw my old team playing. They were up thirteen to nothing; biggest lead I'd ever seen. When I walked away Emily came out of the stands and followed and walked all the way home with me and talked. When we got there she asked how I felt about Marsha now. That was the first time I ever cried in front of somebody who wasn't my own mama. I could tell she disapproved like everyone else, but also that judgment wasn't the end of all things for Emily." Frank took another sip and kept shaking his head back and forth. The whiskey went down, and another liquid streak shined from his face. "She had a way around that fixation we have for bad things." Frank pointed at the cramped staircase they'd climbed down. "That ugly beam at the bottom is low. I've always had to duck not to knock my head. Its edge is square sharp too. I know that from one time twenty-five years ago when I was in a hurry and split my crown. Just one time. The doctor had to stitch me up and all. Now it's all I can think of every time I take that step. I can remember good things too, but I have to try. Once, Emily crowded all our friends down here for a surprise party. That was a really wonderful thing to walk into. But the reflex every time is still to remember how I knocked my head once. I'm starting to think God meant our two eyes to be split in front and in back, but

JACOB KOCKEN

somehow we put them real close together, so we only see one thing at a time. That's what people are best at. Fixating. It's involuntary; almost physical, how being right there makes me relive it. I'd have that beam removed entirely if it wasn't weight bearing. But Emily didn't get all stuck up on things like that. She could just dance the bad away. I never liked to dance before I met her. To be honest, I only liked it afterwards when she was there with me. And I don't dance anymore. Only with her. Only with Emily. She got me to move all kinds of ways I would have been embarrassed of otherwise; graceful at times or wild and free like a colt on the prairie. You met a girl like that yet?"

Ira shrugged.

"I remember early on when I first fell for her; we were on a little date. I took her to this nice Italian restaurant downtown, and she wore a dress that the angels sewed around her; sleek and black with sleeves like some French aristocrat. It was a fine thing, and you could tell by the slow, conscious way she walked into rooms how proud she was to wear it. Well, this little restaurant had a pair of musicians in the corner. They played low, romantic songs on cello and grand piano. I remember how they watched Emily instead of their own notes as she bobbed her body back and forth on that seat. She was always swinging to the music if there was any. Then just before the entrées came she stood to fix herself up in the restroom. Her dress caught on something in the chair, some tiny, jagged edge of metal. It caught and ripped like paper across the front from hip to knee. What she wore underneath was black too, but you could see it like daylight anyway. She must have been embarrassed. She was at first. Her cheeks glowed red as the wine we drank as soon as it happened. But you wouldn't have known if you'd looked a second late. Instead of crying or running off, she just swung her hips to the plucky sound of the cello. She grabbed my hand and pulled me up so we were standing on this wooden floor and dancing as if it were a ballroom. I saw how everyone gaped, and I'm sure she did too, but just like that she was natural as ever. We just jigged together until they asked her to leave. That was Emily. I wish you'd been able to know her too. I wish you'd been able to see what she was like.

"But most people don't have what she had. They can't just dance away from their troubles all on their own. I suppose that's why they

RISE THE MOON

burned that house; those parents," said Frank. "How could you ever think of anything else with reminders like that standing up in your town?" The whiskey smell was strong as Frank raised his drink. The diminishing glass went from lips to lap several times.

Ira sat still as a tomb. There was a terrible hot and dry knot pinching his throat. "Do you think they'll go to jail?" he said.

Frank shook his head slowly. "No, I imagine even the law is about ready to be rid of that whole thing." With a long sigh, Frank downed his cup and tipped the big brown bottle over it again. Ira's nostrils flared. "He dropped out of my class," Frank said. Ira looked up at him. "Did you know I was a teacher once? Well, I remember the name. I had him, and he dropped out. Not only from mine; all of them at once. You don't really remember all the students. But he was bright. I gave him good marks."

"He quit?"

"It was a medical problem. I remember the notice but not the particulars. Something chronic. Mental or physical I can't recall. He had it when he came and left with it worse. He was a bit peculiar. He always seemed occupied with something up in his head; never took notes. But his exams were quick and clean. I swore his answers were word for word as I'd taught them. I might as well have graded my own prep sheets. So, I let the daydreaming slide. And one day he dropped out. We never saw him again; at the university, we didn't. I did. There was a meeting for people like me; if you know what I mean. I'm sure your mother has told you all about that. Well, he spoke, but his problems were different. I don't know why he was there except to talk to people. I never went back. I didn't want a student seeing me that way. Even a former one."

His grandfather was staring at the glass. It had been drained to empty again. He set it aside and brought the big brown bottle to his lips. He held it up with both hands. There was a deep hollow sound from the neck of the container as Frank relinquished.

Then, as his grandfather twisted back the top, Ira saw the old man's eyes darken. It got quiet enough that the wind catching leaves outside made whispers in their ears. Frank's chin was on his chest so that a hard stare pointed down upon his battered hands, shoulders rolled forward like a frozen, cresting wave. He was a man trapped in ice blocks.

JACOB KOCKEN

Ira, on the other hand, was heating up again. His hands snapped back from out before him to his lap as he felt the whip sting of flame from nowhere. It licked and licked at him, and each time, Ira flinched. He rubbed his arms where he felt the pain. He rubbed all over his neck and face, pushing the sensation from place to place across his skin.

"I burned that house," breathed Ira. His grandfather's stiffness melted slightly.

Frank turned slowly at the neck. "Is that so?"

Ira nodded. His grandfather's eyes were turning to foggy glass like the cup in his grasp.

"Why?"

"I don't know," said Ira. "I was just there. And it was awful."

An audible breath passed through the old man's nose. "I can believe that," said Frank. "Your parents don't know? Your mother?"

Ira shook his head, and his grandfather regarded him for a long time. Finally, the old man broke his slumping posture and draped the back of Ira's neck and shoulders with a gentle hand. He looked about to say something, but his mouth fell dumb and left his head to toddle.

"Are you going to tell her?"

"Shouldn't I?" said his grandfather. Ira hung his head and heard Frank clearing his throat. "My boy, you must be going on fifteen years old, and today is the third time I've shared your presence. Do you know why we've seen so little of each other?"

"Not really."

"There's some things I've done, but more so than that, there's some things I haven't," he said. "I wouldn't want you to join me in failing to do right by your mother. I hoped tonight would resurrect something old; something we used to have back when she was in the bliss of youth. Before your grandmother got sick. Before I really started drinking. The thing you've still got with her. You've got it, but you can't give it to me. The best you can do is keep it for yourself and for Miriam. Promise you will, Ira."

"I promise."

"That means telling her yourself what you told me," said Frank. Ira looked out just below his heavy eyelids as he gave a jagged,

RISE THE MOON

hesitant nod. "Good."

"Tonight?"

"Whenever you're ready," said Frank. "People have to balance their reasons and actions alone. I won't presume to do your accounting." Ira nodded slowly. An ambient tension in his muscles eased. "Why'd you tell me?"

Ira rubbed a palm across his face. "I don't know."

"Well, your secret's safe. I won't tell. Even if I happen to remember it tomorrow." He swirled the jug in his hand.

"Is there any more baseball stuff?" said Ira.

Frank clicked his tongue. "Not for tonight." His grandfather patted him on the back and stood. He stocked the glass and bottle back in their cabinet. The wooden door clattered and bounced open again off the jamb.

They ascended the stairs to find night falling in the yard. Back inside, his mother and father were standing in the kitchen. The two were looking quite seriously at one another.

"Need some help?" asked Frank. He took up a hand towel from beside the oven and gave a full body gesture toward the dishes, most of which were still on the table or sitting submerged in one side of the sink. These words from the grandfather seemed to pry Miriam out of some strange spell.

"Thank you," she said, turning away from Saul to face the chore. Ira watched in the corner of the room as his father peeled away. A tension in his shoulders had fallen when the woman's back turned and now he moved off, an autumn leaf blown away to the living room.

"I'll put the things away," his grandfather was saying. "I keep where things go pretty usual. There's no real system, only a habit." The old man rambled on about the dishes and about the house as he turned each cleaned article over in his towel and found its place in one cabinet or another. Miriam was mostly quiet, and Ira noted quite surely how her nose rankled now and then. Frank grabbed the plates to dry; her face twitched. He came back to grab the pitcher, and her every feature flashed in and out of a scowl. There was intensity in her eyes. When everything was put away she asked Ira if he was ready to go.

At the door, Frank came to wish them farewell. There was

JACOB KOCKEN

a strong handshake and stiff embrace with the parents before he turned to the boy. Before Ira knew it, the two of them were chest to chest. His grandfather spoke. With their faces so close together, the volume gave Ira a start. And even with the words already out and past him, something of their essence stuck on the air as Ira breathed in the fermentation.

"Bring your glove sometime. I'll teach you everything I know."

27.
Saul

SORENESS HAD TRULY BEGUN TO settle into the muscle of Saul's knees, thighs, and groin. He'd gone running six times in the past four days. On the exterior, he appeared the same, but under the skin his atrophied body was now tearing down deadwood to be rebuilt under the scourge of a blind and searching captain.

When he started to cramp, his wife suggested potassium. She bought him bananas and he ate them grudgingly. He'd been contemplating a fast and hoped he would not become too reliant on earthly medicine such as food. A cup of water accompanied Saul at all times as he attempted also to rehydrate. This he overdid and found the pressure on his bladder perpetuating the cycle of movement. He ran to the bathroom as often as he ran for his own higher purpose. And then his dry mouth would convince him to drink again. So, it was with a body feeling both drained and bloated that he started up his Cavalier.

It was Wednesday again and nearly seven o'clock. The sun was still high and yellow but had lost the heat of the day. He drove the few blocks down to St. Francis church for this second meeting with the group of confirments.

The lightheaded rush of his physical exertion still lingered in Saul's brain. He parked the car along the great stone wall of the church and his engine cut off. He sat there in the stillness, enjoying the humming sensation throughout his body. Other cars had arrived. A small trickling procession of bodies pushed through the heavy oaken wood doors. Saul watched them. The faces were the same but seemed only distantly familiar. The clock on his dash

JACOB KOCKEN

ticked. One minute to commencement. Yet, he sat. He was waiting, vacillating between watching the faces which were now all closed inside and looking out to the street where headlights drove. He watched every car, expecting them to brake and turn down the long St. Francis driveway.

But invariably, they passed. As the minutes stretched on, his legs and hips stiffened in the seat. He had not seen her walk in; the woman in the red knit sweater. Angela. And perhaps she was simply late, like him.

The sun ducked behind the steeple and cast a premature setting over Saul. His eyelids fell. In the hypnagogic warmth of the car, Saul's exhausted body began to drift. An image of himself rose up. He was descending a staircase into the nave of the church. The lights were dim, and she was sitting there all alone facing away from him and toward the lectern. At the entrance beside him, a large stone piscina was set into the wall. The limestone basin was wide as a small bath and bone dry. Saul ran his fingers through the bowl, and they came out white with dust.

As he approached the beautiful woman, the other initiates materialized as well. Their round and hazy features pointed up in unison at the podium where the old woman stood talking, hanging over them and looking down, a warding gargoyle of some abandoned gothic cathedral so grievously misplaced. Her voice echoed indistinctly in the cavernous church hall.

Saul came up to the woman he'd been looking for. Angela. He touched her shoulder, but she did not move. When he came around to face her, she seemed made of wood. Her features were smooth and beautiful but cold. Even her hair was stiff as marble. Those around her were similar statues.

He cupped her face but found her wholly gone. Even the eyes would not notice his presence. Saul followed their wooden gaze up to the lectern and marched swiftly up the set of steps, passed the altar, and stopped beside the old woman. When he came close she faltered in her speech. Her lips quivered at the sight of Saul and small pieces of her face began to crack and fall to the ground beside her. She spat at him. Her frail old finger waved from the group of statues to him and back. Her other hand covered the Bible which was splayed open before her. Saul stepped closer without

RISE THE MOON

answer, and the old woman's hand came straight out, pressing its weathered pads into his nose and mouth. He shoved the hand away with his own. She stood level with his eyes, boosted by the lectern platform. He stepped up and the weight of his body rolled her back to the edge. For good measure, his hands found the rounded scapular bones of her shoulders and shoved the old woman off the stand with all his might. Her body sailed backward as if caught in the wind, tumbling and thrashing. Just as the body came crashing onto the hard laminate floor, it vanished entirely into powdered particles of dust, lending even its existence to the lectern's new officiate. 'Where are you? I am here. Where are you? I am here.' Along the back wall, the piscina bubbled and holy water overflowed from its edges, slickening the ground and turning it into a great mirror. Trickling water came to touch the feet of those paralyzed novitiates. Like flower petals unfurling for the sun they unwound from their tightness, life and love returning to their vacant eyes. And when she stood, she flushed to the hue of her clothing. Their eyes connected and he left off his pontification. The cool water livened his soul as he ran. He was barefoot, splashing in the flowing shallows. He took her by the waist. They coursed with grace from pew to piscina, and Saul cradled her neck as her head was lowered into the surging well. He kept her there under the surface, and she eased back, her spine curling over the concrete lip and slipping with the rest of her body into the narrow pool. Saul followed, losing his clothes on the ground and crawling headfirst into the watery nook. Very soon he was enclosed in darkness and the drainage walls at his shoulders caused a claustrophobic panic. He felt around for her, but he knew only a pulling sensation in his chest, and he awoke there in his car. The windows were closed, and the air was stuffy. His clock read seven thirty and his stiff legs felt the stagnant wetness of urine trickling down his calves and soaking in the fabric of his seat.

Saul cursed and drove toward home. As he pulled out of the church parking lot, he saw the Charger he'd followed the previous week. It was dark and empty now, and the doors to St. Francis were sealed.

On a garage shelf back home, Saul found a purple bottle of foaming carpet cleaner. But upon further inspection, whether due to the gallons of water he'd been drinking or to his spiritual advancement, Saul detected no terrible smell or discoloration of the Cavalier and decided there was no need to waste the product. Despite the painful threat of muscle cramps, he resolved not to drink so much water.

The house was quiet, and Saul snuck into the laundry room, exchanging his wet clothes for some sitting in the dryer. He went straight up to his room where he found his wife awake in bed.

"Out job hunting again?" she said.

"Yes."

"Well?"

"It's not for me."

"What?"

"I told you at your dad's place. I am walking with God."

"Saul," said his wife with an inflected silence. "You have to get a job. Do you plan to sit around here doing nothing?"

"It's not nothing. My contemplation is purposeful. I am on a spiritual journey."

"We all are, Saul."

"Not like me. I need time to explore things; to think."

"People don't get paid to think."

"Your father did. Frank was a damn philosopher. All they do is think."

"He was a professor. He got paid to teach."

"Yes," said Saul. The sense in it arrested him for a moment. He sat on the edge of the mattress to ponder. "Yes, perhaps I do need a student. I've been learning lots of things about Him; about God. Want to hear?"

His wife sighed and turned away from him. "It's late, Saul." She pulled the blanket up to her shoulder, and for the rest of the night as far as Saul could tell, she was out.

As he laid his own tired body into bed, he took up the Bible from his nightstand. His bookmark was in II Samuel. He read one sentence and shut the cover again. With the book resting on his chest, and his searching hand fingering the indented letter on its leather cover, Saul fell asleep.

SAUL WOKE UP THAT MORNING with Miriam gone to work. There was a pulsing discomfort in the bed beneath him, and he rolled over

RISE THE MOON

to find the Bible putting a crook in his spine. He opened it up again to his marked page. The words were blurry in his morning eyes. He stared for a moment at the scripture but was pulled immediately away by the sound of rustling in the hallway. Saul jumped up from bed and found his son getting ready for school in the bathroom.

"Boy," he said. "You need another shave."

The toothbrush in Ira's mouth stopped working back and forth. "I do?" he said through the foam. Saul retrieved the razor while his son rinsed. Ira reached for the blade, and Saul pulled it away. He raised his finger. "Let me guide you through it again."

"I have to get to school soon."

"No matter," said Saul. He tilted the boy's head back to assess the situation. Only the upper lip and the cusp of the chin showed any growth from the first shave he'd given some days ago, and even there it was sparse. The stubble, thin and light as it was, could hardly be seen by the eye and was only detected by the pad of Saul's probing thumb. Then, in the mirror, Saul noticed his own budding beard much further along than his son's. He let go of Ira's face.

"You're becoming a man now, Ira. It's a strange concept. It requires wisdom. I am sure this seems like quite a time of change for you. A frightening time. Well, let me tell you something I have discovered." Saul ushered the boy toward the little bathtub wall and had him sit. Ira complied. The boy placed hands on his impatient, bouncing knees and looked up at the teacher.

Saul brought the razor to his own face and began slowly shearing from right to left. "There is a powerful illusion to the world. It is one of decay. Things seem all the time to be breaking down. Leaves fall from the trees; the carcasses of deer decompose on the roadside; we get older, running involuntarily toward the edge of a cliff. This is a confusion brought upon us by the limitation of our minds. Take for instance, those trees who lose their leaves. They appear dead. Wooden skeletons. If they were to fall from the base, their bare branches on the ground would resemble the rotting corpse of some fossilized giant. But of course, they stand all through the winter, appearing as dead as dinosaurs when all of a sudden the spin of the Earth shows them a little more sun and spring rolls in. In no time at all, they burst back into life. And then consider the deer on

JACOB KOCKEN

the side of the road. It is dead. Yes, finished. Its body disintegrates. It falls atom by atom into the ground and leaves nothing but its bones for the world to remember. It has become the ground. But do not despair. Even if you are the dead deer itself, do not despair! Its material, decomposed but organic and living still, becomes the soil; becomes the grass. And the next season, when another loping animal comes around to graze, that decomposition makes a journey down the throat to integrate once again with a body so similar to the original it can hardly be a different process from a man who goes to sleep at night and, due to his digestion and the constant cyclical forces of entropy, wakes up the next morning with a slightly different physical composition. Death would not trouble these creatures; pain and sin would not trouble these creatures if only they had the foresight to know they will soon enough come back around to their true, essential state. And so it is with the soul of Man."

As he spoke, the razor moved in neat columns over his features. The stubble lifted away, baring smooth, clean skin until his face was as hairless as Ira's.

"If we too held a proper perspective," he went on, "we would see then that the long term and the short term converge. The human soul, created by God, is incorruptible. Our bodies are designed for death, but our human essence is an eternal thing. And all things pale in comparison to eternity. You, for instance, were a crier, Ira. When you were a baby you screamed and cried all day and night. One would think you were tortured or that the fear of terrible and imminent death was always upon you. Do you remember? Do you remember that?"

"No."

"Precisely. Pain; fear; these are temporary things that with faith can be wiped away like dirt from a window." Saul set the razor at the edge of the sink and admired his shave. "Do you understand?"

"I'm really going to be late to school."

"Do you understand what I've been saying to you?"

"I think so."

"Good. It's imperative you understand the things I teach you. I'm passing them down for a reason. I've spent a lot of time listening to myself, and I've come to undenied answers. If you learn the ways of the world like I have, you can pass by that which does not

RISE THE MOON

matter and find anything open to you. Any goal, any sum; whatever you most earnestly desire."

His son looked him in the eyes. He was paying real attention. Saul smiled down and grabbed him softly by the head with one hand.

"Your first lesson," he said, "is to know that whatever you desire will be yours if you place yourself within God's abundant mercy. It is yours to claim, but you've really got to mean these things, Ira. You can't just wish gummy bears and ice cream. If you want God's concern, your request better steam out from your soul. Understand?"

Ira nodded.

"Say it with me then," said Saul. "I will ask for God's abundant Grace."

"I will ask for God's abundant Grace."

"A little more gusto at the end. You should say important words with feeling."

"God's abundant Grace."

"Good," Saul smiled. "Now shave up and run along to school."

There was a livened, ambitious feeling in Saul having had such a talk with his son, and when Ira exited the house he became restless. Saul settled in the garage where he directed himself once again toward painting, toward his drive to capture through art the mystery lurking behind his excitement.

This time he experimented without the brush. The pads of his hands mixed yellow, red, and blue paint into unique secondary hues. Each finger and knuckle he dedicated to a different color of the rainbow. Lines made by fingertip were thicker, less precise than brushstroke. But they did possess a particularly human texture, and the ridges of his hand transposed onto canvas as part of the coloration itself.

However, the elusive vision Saul chased was no more successfully captured by this intimate technique. In fact, with the imprints of his own carnal pattern dwelling inside the child's features, Saul found the impression of his subject grotesque.

When noon came around, he opened the garage door and began immediately to run. The first several minutes were stiff and painful. There was a knot of latissimus muscle where the Good Book had

JACOB KOCKEN

sometime during the night before migrated and spent several hours shifting his spinal alignment. His blood felt cold and resistant, but Saul kept on running. Very soon sharp aches appeared in his feet and abdomen. He ignored it all in accordance with the newly acquired conviction that strong belief does more shaping to the physical world than the world could ever do to belief.

He did not think much about the route he was taking even if he accidentally kept recalling it; down Cherry Street, toward the prairie, past the big apple tree. And once again by some willful chance he encountered the woman. Angela.

She was running down the long county road in the opposite direction, and he crossed the street to meet her. He stopped there, his hands akimbo and his legs spread in an attempt to stretch the fiery muscles.

"Well, hello again," she said. To Saul's delight, her posture loosened, and her feet stopped in the dirt. "Are you full of paint?" There was amusement in the words. Her smile was warm and quizzical.

Saul looked down at his blue and green and orange hands. He was reminded momentarily of the disappointment those colors had brought him only a short time earlier. But standing here in the magnetic presence of this woman with her swelling lungs and sweat-beaded skin, the vision he sought seemed nearly within reach again. Saul displayed his mottled palms. "I am." Angela laughed a full and hearty laugh.

"Why?"

"I was painting."

"And now you're running."

"I've been out every day."

"I love that," she said.

"Were you just starting?"

"I've done a small loop," she said. "I was thinking to head down to the east side of town. To check the wreckage."

"I haven't seen it either," said Saul. "Do you mind if I tag along? A little partner training?"

"Fine by me," she said. The two started off on a trot back in the direction of Old Graumont.

"You missed the meeting last night," she said. Angela seemed

RISE THE MOON

to glide across the pavement with quick steps, her white running shoes still pristine as if she trod only over clouds instead of dirt and blacktop.

"Yes," said Saul holding up a purple finger. "When training for a marathon it's best to run at a conversational speed. It keeps the breath in check." He slowed their pace to something he could manage. Already there was the tightness of a threatening cramp in his hamstring. "I decided not to go in. I was there in the parking lot. It felt wrong."

"Avoiding me?"

"Why do you run?" he asked abruptly. "What are you scared of?"

"I'm not running away from anything," she laughed.

"Right." Even at the slower pace his breath was somewhat labored. "You're chasing something. A goal."

"I suppose."

"Running to, not from," said Saul.

"Yes."

"That's why I didn't come inside to that meeting last night."

"What goal are you chasing?"

"Some other kind of calling," he said.

"Mysterious."

"You couldn't understand it."

"Try me," she said.

"You can't understand it because I can't say it. The very fact of it is synonymous with ineffability. It's like seeing a ghost. You can't convince anyone else because there is nowhere to point."

"Don't mess around about ghosts," said Angela. Her expression, unbothered by the strain of this comparatively light jog, was quite serious.

"Certainly," said Saul. "It's a bad gamble to underestimate the power of what one himself defines as supernatural; much better to align yourself with the world of the impossible so that when God finally decides to put His finger to Earth it is to help rather than smite you."

"You're kind of funny talking philosophical with paint on your face."

"Is it on my face too?"

JACOB KOCKEN

"Yeah," she said this laughing, but her tone did sober. There was a pause where the only sounds were the rhythmic thumps of their feet and lungs heaving in unison. Then she spoke up again, venturing some and only meeting his eyes with sidelong glances.

"When I was six," said Angela, "my father died. A car accident. I don't know. I can hardly remember him now. But I was so scared. I remember that part. I remember crying. I remember going up into a tree house in my backyard to hide. And one day when I climbed up that ladder, by God, he was there. He really was. For just a few minutes. He told me everything was okay. That he was in a safer place. That I was. . ." she stopped, catching her breath.

"Yes," said Saul. He turned his head toward her as he ran and kept it there until she looked. Her eyes were touched with a lost wonder, and he simply stared back.

"Sorry," she said. A laugh was forced. "It doesn't matter."

"My parents died when I was young too," said Saul. Then Angela was behind him. She'd slowed the pace and when Saul turned to see her she had stopped entirely. Her eyes were shining with water atop an expression of great tenderness. "Keep running," said Saul. He did not slow or return to where she stood. Instead, he plowed ahead toward Old Graumont and kept pushing with all his might until he heard the quickened steps and breath of the woman catching up.

They had crossed the bridge and jogged now in relative silence until the tree tops looked down above them. They first encountered an old barn half consumed by some past flame. They stopped to examine the scene and determined quickly enough by the tufts of tall wild grass growing within the abandoned place that this was not their destination. The pair of runners continued on down that singular dirt road. When they did finally come to the former Yokoven property, Saul recognized it immediately as such. Yellow police tape marked it from a hundred yards away and the dry smell of cinders lingered in all the surrounding area. They came to a rest beside the rubble. Black and grey ash covered everything. The whole property was a foot deep mound of dark dust. Even the tree trunks close by were painted black by the wind. A stout brick chimney was all that stood erect, a dark obelisk standing stolid in the ruin.

"Wow. Not a whole lot to see," said Angela. "What are you

RISE THE MOON

doing?"

Saul had bent down and ducked beneath the tape onto the property. Once again, he raised his purple finger to her and kept moving. His feet sunk into the ashes, and he tripped over half disintegrated beams as he approached the chimney. It stood taller than him, and he got so close that his still labored breath disturbed its powdered black coat. Then he laid his hands against the brick and pushed with all his might. Saul closed his lids in concentration. His mind's eye brought forth in a vivid inward manifestation all the empirical sensations of his wish. It began with a slow and shifting tidal wave of sound; the gritty, milling hum of tectonic movement. The temperature of his hands began to rise as Saul rocked back and forth into the pillar; so hot they may have glowed as a lighthouse beacon does for every wandering Rachel, every ship lost in the fog. As he pushed, he could hear her voice. It pursued him. Then the mortar slipped from its decades of fixed grip on every chimney stone. Cement and boulder tumbled alike in an avalanche before him, colliding with and pulverizing each concomitant piece of the old tower in the midst of its descent. The Earth shuddered. When finally the dust settled pure as a winter snowfall, Saul opened his eyes.

The great brick mass still stood as if anchored to the center of the world. Saul tried a second time with all the weight of his raffish body to shake the thing from its foundation. But his feet only slid across the ruinous ground and, eventually, he stood back and returned to where Angela was waiting outside the line of tape.

"What on Earth was that?" she said. But Saul just shook his hangdog head and started jogging back to town.

Saul was lost in thought until they passed the old barn and the bridge back to Graumont was in sight. In the corner of his vision, he could see the woman looking at him as she ran. They were in even step, and as they came up over the bridge he saw her head turned toward him again. It was captivating; Angela's plain face.

"I know what you mean about seeing your dad," he said.

"You do?"

"I believe you."

"I don't know," said Angela. "I don't even believe myself all the time. It was so long ago. And it's crazy. Grief can do strange things."

JACOB KOCKEN

"If you don't believe yourself, believe me," said Saul.

"You have strong faith, huh?"

"It's the only option for people like us. How can you doubt your own most meaningful experience? Because it's impossible? Perhaps impossibility is the realest thing of all. It constitutes the boundaries of the real. How does something come to exist? Coming into existence necessitates creation from something that was not it. The cause has to differ from the effect or else everything would be just a mirror image of itself. So how could we be comfortable with the position that what we know to be possible is all there is? Do you follow me?"

"I don't know," she said.

"If I told someone I live outside the constraints of possibility they would scoff. Do you know why?" he asked. Angela shook her head. "Solipsism."

Angela's eyes were alight. "Keep going," she said. And so they ran and talked of other things, and along the loop they came eventually back to the gates of the SummerTime orchard. Angela's house was just on the other side of the street, and they completed the circuit with a sprint, collapsing side by side on the step of her front porch.

"Nearly five miles," she said. "Just twenty-one more."

"And I've still got to run home," said Saul.

"You'll just out do me on race day then." They sat; two chests heaving in and out until the shock of their final sprint had worn off. "Do you believe all that stuff you said? The crazy stuff?"

"I speak as one with authority," said Saul.

Angela nodded. "Can I ask you one more thing? Even if it's personal?"

"Certainly."

Her breath was still rising and falling, quavering some, and making her words undulate like breaking waves. "You said your parents died when you were young? How?"

"Oh," said Saul. He straightened his back. He put his hands on his knees. "It was a car accident. Like your dad." His lungs chopped, and he brought a hand up to rub over his chest. "Man, that was a swell run, huh?" Angela nodded again, but this time she did not fill the silence with talking. Her eyes were soft and unmoving.

RISE THE MOON

"I'm sorry," said Saul. "I haven't talked about it in a while."

Her hand touched his. It did not grab, only rested. "What were they like?"

Saul looked up at the sky. The clouds floated by on slow streams of wind. "Well, I was young," he said.

"How young?"

"Five."

Angela had a quick intake of breath, a gasp that even through its tenderness startled Saul like a deer. "Do you remember them?" she asked cautiously.

"Yes." Saul tapped the concrete step like an amateur pianist plucking out a bastard tune. "I remember things. Once there was a bee that stung me. I was out on the swings, and a bee stung my foot. My mother pulled the stinger out. I remember I was scared because I didn't know what happened. All of a sudden I was just in pain; on fire. And then she scooped me up, and she pulled out the stinger. There was an ice cube. She put an ice cube on the spot. She smelled good. Warm and good. And she told me about bees. She said what they were and why they sting; to protect the other bees. She said she would sting too if she thought someone would hurt me. I remember that she smelled good. She might've only held me then for a minute, but in my memory it seems like my whole childhood. A year. That's how long she held me."

"Oh Saul," said Angela. "That's sweet. Very sweet. And your father?"

"I remember he had black hair." Saul began rubbing his knees again. Then one hand came up. It grasped around the other arm up at the shoulder and squeezed. His heart was beating as if the run had never ended. Angela was looking at him kindly. Her small frame leaned in to support his as it tipped to and fro.

"You really don't talk about it much do you?" said Angela.

"No one's ever asked."

Saul stood abruptly. He let out a long exhalation and embraced Angela honestly when she stood. "I ought to be going home," he said. She nodded, understanding.

"Will you come to the next meeting? On Wednesday."

"No," he said.

"Off chasing something?"

JACOB KOCKEN

Saul nodded. She nodded back.

"We could do this again," he said.

"Yes, okay." Her eyes brightened. She offered her hand for a final goodbye. Saul shook it. His sweat had loosened some of the paint which rubbed off green, blue, and yellow on the back of hers in the loose shape of his thumb. He took off jogging and halfway down the road was seized by a faint muscle cramp. He stopped for a moment in surprise, but the tension receded, and he went on running.

28.
Ira

IN THE FEW DAYS SINCE the fire, neither Ira nor Furke had spoken a word of it to each other. When the subject was breached around them they listened. Nearly everyone was in agreement. The nameless vandals were celebrated. The frightened and mourning town had been avenged. The monster was in prison awaiting the probable sentence of death, and now even the traces of his mark and memory were snuffed away. Though the children squealed mystified delights, the often-eavesdropping Ira found the sounds set him to startling. Whispers swung round him, tickling the hair that stood out on the back of his neck. He knew the feeling for not the first time. When they laughed, or gasped, or cheered it was always with a foul abruptness that rattled the immediate air. And to join the thoughts of fire burning, a troubling vision continued to rise from the depths of a guttural pit. He thought abysmal things, or, that is, felt them falling seamlessly in and out of awareness. It was strange and impossible as a bad dream, lacking the comfort of transience.

Ira came to school with the Necromancer in his pocket to return to Furke as soon as they met. But his friend was not at the lockers before the bell, and Ira walked to class with a weight on him. He could not stop replaying that night in his head; the house, the fire, the girl seeing him frozen in the forest. For the first time since she'd come to Graumont, Ira dreaded his hour sitting next to Anna Lee Lac.

On this Monday back to class, two things happened that put all of Ira's nerves on edge. First, when the class filed in and Ira took his seat, he found the head of the room occupied not only by his

JACOB KOCKEN

geometry teacher, Mr. Callan, but also by a police officer dressed in his full blue suit and cap. The officer stood facing the desks, his hands tucked patiently behind his back. He had beady black pupils that touched each one of their faces as they strode past. The students settled themselves with more order than usual.

"You will all have heard by now," said the officer, "that a fire was set on the east side of town. I say set because the fire department has confidently concluded the thing was a purposeful act. I know where emotions lie, and rightfully so. Arson, however, is a crime. The fire was sparked in the middle of a forest; a recipe for disaster. It happened that the wind blew in the direction of luck that night. But danger is not the only problem here. As an investigator, I will refrain from making assumptions, but the most obvious circumstance here is a motive of frivolous revenge; a man is arrested for heinous murder and some member of the community takes it upon themselves to illustrate their displeasure, to enact their own moral code. Yet, there is a trial to be had. Should the culprit by some act of Satan, procedural misconduct, or legal argument be let off the hook for what he's done and evidence that could have secured his deserved fate was lost to that conflagration, our vigilante would be the one responsible. I hope whoever it is never has to answer to God for letting a monster loose." As he spoke, the policeman scanned them. He examined the children's faces one at a time, looking directly into their eyes and holding the contact just long enough to haunt his words with private intention. Ira's spine turned still as a board.

"The reason I'm telling you all this in person is that though the structure of the house was lost in totality, there was discovered at the rear end of the property a set of footprints in the soil. They lead from the house to the forest behind it. Based on the size of the shoes and the space between prints, it can easily be determined that they were made by someone running. This someone was either an underdeveloped adult or a person roughly your age. I would invite the offender to make a confession to your principal by the end of the day. Now, I know how word travels in a school, so I am also more than willing to hear out anyone who has information on the topic. Anything that leads us to the perpetrator will be met with a worthy reward."

RISE THE MOON

Ira's skin had gone blighted, and the officer was bearing down now. The man's heavy boots clapped the hard flat floor with a deliberate pace. He approached the rows of desks and a second, deeper silence fell on the room.

The dull taste of ash was on Ira's tongue. His dry lips stuck together. He felt at his neck as if he might choke. The authority's forefinger found the corner of his desk. The hands were spindly for the man's stature, and the needle finger tapped loud enough to keep time with the second hand of the entryway clock. He was looking down at Ira, or so, at least, Ira felt, for he could not raise his gaze to see the man's face. Every muscle in his neck felt fused to bone. The uniform before him loomed to the ceiling. He wanted to run. His stomach began to churn, and Ira felt he would be sick. There was a noise to his left, a cough. It was delicate, and Ira heard its voice from instinct. Her shape shifted in its seat beside him. He began involuntarily to hold his breath.

A vague thought intruded. It made Ira deeply sad and hung over his neck like a yoke. It was like the thoughts he'd been having for several days. There was nothing directive in the feeling; except for that it was about his father, Saul. And in the way that thoughts connect invisibly to one another and arise from the depths of the soul, Ira was struck with a remembrance, a vignette in a flash, of a once smaller boy holding up a little green plastic ball. 'Chesil!' boomed a voice at the back of Ira's head. 'I have something for you.' A shack door creaked open, revealing a man's silhouette. He had enormous shoulders that grew even larger under the light of the room. 'Hey there, little guy.' The child sat on the floor again. His hair was longer now and a natural blonde only the sun could have bleached. The man set a box down in front of the child. It was filled with fruit. 'SummerTime!' said the voice of a woman. She was standing beside them now. She appeared clad in rags. Her dress was all of a piece and white once upon a time but filled now with the grime and wear of a life on the brink. Smoke crawled out of her mouth. There was a lit cigarette held between two of her fingers. It waved and caught attention like a magician's wand. Her eyes were trained up on the man while the toddler crawled about below. 'The newest product,' said the man. 'You'll be the first to try.' 'Oh you're so good to us,' said the woman. The child already had an apple in

JACOB KOCKEN

his hands. He'd taken it out of his own curiosity before the mother snatched it away. 'Gordan!' she scolded. 'What do you say?' The boy was stunned for a second. 'Please?' he uttered. 'That's right. Now ask him nicely.' 'Please, sir.' 'Ha! Eat up lad. Quickly, tell me what you think.' As soon as the child bit his head recoiled. The bite of fruit fell from between his teeth and down to the wooden floor where it clattered like a rock. 'Pick that up,' said the mother. 'Eat, and don't be rude.' The mother took her own share from the box and bit. She ground it slowly like a cow and swallowed. 'No, no,' said the man. 'It's all fine dear, not rude at all. Are they sour?' 'Only a bit.' 'Well that's fine. They're an experiment! One must experiment. Please, don't finish.' The big man took the bitten apple from her hand. 'Leave the rest for him.' He picked up the box and set it on top of the counter. 'Give him one every day, Chesil. Hear me? Good. I'll have to be off now.' 'So soon? But you've just arrived.' 'I'll be back,' said the big man. 'I'll be back in a few days. You still have those lesson books I gave you?' 'Oh yes, Gordan does them every day.' 'Grand! How's he doing?' "Well,' said the woman, 'he's doing fine. Fine. We're on the second book.' 'Only the second?' 'He's really getting it though. I promise.' 'Hm.' There was disapproval all over the big man. 'He'll get it. He will. I know it. I'll make sure of it.' Then he pulled the cigarette away from her and puffed on it himself. His nostrils filled with the recycled smoke leaking from between his teeth as he turned the burning tip on the back of the woman's hand and pressed. 'See that you do.'

    Ira took his hand out from his pocket. Furke's lighter was there, bulging slightly through his denim as he looked up to see the police officer bearing down on him. The officer's badge reflected a spotlight onto Ira whose eyesight danced with a dozen forms; white, purple, and orange even after he'd shut them.

    And since Ira was too confused and nervous to think any kind of straightforward thoughts, he latched onto his most recent advice and prayed. That's what his father had said; prayer was salvation. He prayed like he'd never done before even when his mother brought him to Sunday Mass. He prayed without thought, without direction. He prayed for the eyes of the world to leave. He prayed to be forgotten. Beads of sweat dripped down Ira's forehead as if he'd been dipped in the Jordan. From an open corner window, the

RISE THE MOON

breeze rushed past and swept the heat from his face.

The officer's finger stopped its tapping. He turned on his heel and had a short word with the teacher before striding out of the room.

Ira's held breath hissed away, and should the room not have regained a portion of its usual levity, the class would have all been drawn to the sound of his panting. A rush coursed through his head. Mr. Callan's voice was muffled. It was well into their geometry lesson that movement returned to Ira's body. When relief came to stop the pounding in his ears, he found his relaxing posture twist askew. She was already looking in his direction. Ira snapped back to the front of the room. Her face had been expressionless, but the big, solemn eyes caught him all up in a glance.

The second of the notable classroom events came soon after the policeman had left whereupon there erupted a game; initially between the students who smoked cigarettes and later on even among those who didn't.

Ira was sitting; Mr. Callan was lecturing. When the teacher turned around to demonstrate his concept on the blackboard, a small click went up from the right side of the room as a boy struck his lighter and held the flame aloft. The boy was in the second row and nearly everyone saw it. Several smirks broke out, and the lighter was down in his lap, safe and cooling by the time the instructor spun back to them.

Andrew Steele, the boy with the lighter, a poor student with a rich sense of humor, raised his hand and asked the instructor a pointed question about the graph on the chalk board. When the teacher turned to reiterate the lesson, Andrew once again struck his lighter. Ira's shoulders tightened at the quickness of the spark, the grating scrape of the metal.

The motion of the rebel was mimicked immediately by another student and then by another shortly after. A murmur of laughter rippled through the room. The game developed among eight of them. Those who had no cause to carry a lighter watched with general glee. Ira was one of these, though no mirth rose from him. Instead, his stomach plunged. They were only little flames, smaller than the tip of a finger, gone with the same twitch of the thumb that struck them. But these little flames lingered, climbing up the periphery,

JACOB KOCKEN

imprinted on Ira in dancing purple and white light.

THE GAME SPREAD QUICKLY AND flames were sent up in other classrooms behind the backs of other teachers. A boy named Terry Demrath was caught in final period after setting the edge of his homework alight. It was smothered quickly, but the smoke was dark, and a burning smell loitered on the air. He was ordered swiftly to Principal Monroe's office. "And take that singed up paper with you to show him," scolded the teacher. Terry Demrath pushed his chair back and obediently stood. Halfway to the door, however, he stopped, and the lighter flashed out from his hand a second time. The students roared, and Mr. Callan scrambled to strike the paper to the ground where he stomped a strong six-inch flame against the hard tile floor. His fury was lost among the hooting of the children, and the game continued on with the most brazen students winning a mindless, rebellious glory.

Terry's infamy was carried on wild whispers the whole rest of the day. When the final bell rang, Ira headed to the school's back entrance where he was accosted by his best friend. Furke grabbed him round the arm with a powerful, enthusiastic grip, ushering Ira and his bike down the brick path toward the football field.

"What's going on?"

"You'll see," said Furke.

As they passed the gate that led toward the bleachers, Ira saw several kids hanging a large banner. It was white with blue lettering and zip tied across twenty feet of the chain link fence. *Homecoming 1994*, it read. *Football Friday, Dance Saturday.*

"The homecoming dance," said Ira. "Are you taking anyone?"

"You know I don't go to those things."

"Then what about it?"

"Nothing," said Furke. "That's not what I wanted to show you."

"Well, what was?"

"I said you'll see."

As they walked, Ira recounted the incident of the lighters. "They did that in my class with Mrs. Landon too," said Furke. "Even in gym, Deandra did it during volleyball games before serves. Now look."

As they rounded a bend of the path, Furke pointed a finger into

RISE THE MOON

the distance. The football team's practice field came into clear view where a ring of people stood down at the far end zone. A couple dozen heads were leaning in at the center of the circle, their bodies jittering on impatient feet. None of them, however, were clad in helmets or pads, only the t-shirts and backpacks of an everyday student. The boys came closer, and the familiar voice of Bobby Paulsen was answered by a chorus of excitement. Then from the center of the circle, a bright orange fire rose up and the bouncing crowd erupted.

"I am the king of ashes!"

"King of ashes! King of ashes!"

"I lay waste! I am fickle as the flame! Bring sacrifice and gain the favor of the fire!"

Bobby stood in the midst of the group. Both his hands were raised overhead; one holding a long and familiarly ornate metal lighter, the other holding a red notebook being slowly consumed by licking orange tongues. Then he opened the burning pages, and as the fire turned brighter, he tore the smoldering leaves from their binding at random.

Garret Paulsen was facing the little crowd and circling his brother with long energetic strides and one outstretched hand soliciting the onlookers. He stopped abruptly as one of the children thrust a loose white paper into the ring. Garret took it, and with a swift inspection hollered, "Math!" The surrounding students gave an instinctive chorus of snickers and censorious hoots. Then Garret passed the paper to his twin who clicked the Necromancer's ignition and held the devouring flame aloft.

The students grew louder and many of those surrounding boys and girls threw their book bags to the ground and filled the air with the sound of shuffling paper. Garret took one, then another of the offerings. He passed them on to his brother as fast as the fire could eat. Ash and spark rained from Bobby's hands.

Ira once again began to sweat. His tongue turned dry and clung to the roof of his mouth. The most delicate breeze was in the air, playing with the shape of the flames in Bobby Paulsen's grip. They danced orange and bright on Ira's eyes and their heat was in him. Ira shuffled uncomfortably beside the multitude. They yelled and cheered, and somewhere amidst the screams a throat rattled with

JACOB KOCKEN

pain and pitiful longing. Ira swung his head from end to end. Every face was aglow with a pleasant passion. They bellowed and shouted in joy. Yet clearer and clearer sounded the call of the hen. As Ira mixed himself into the throng, their noise surrounded him. It wheeled and repeated like the bones of a melancholy song.

New flames were preceded by exhortations from the crowd; "Necrotize mine! Oh, king of ashes, necrotize my test!" Every cry seemed to catch distant ears so that soon more and more students came inquiring around the corners of the school. With each passing minute, the throng of students along this normally vacant back path grew in number proportionate to its revelry. The frenzy stirred and the excitement of the children sucked them body and soul into the devilish ritual. So eager were their hands for the freedom of destruction that it was no wonder when without malice or even without intention an open notebook was snatched directly from the hands of an unsuspecting girl whose mind was down in its pages and whose hands never ceased their marking even as she passed the yowling crowd on her way home from school. Her scream when the flames began to climb over the cover spasmed Ira's body. It was Furke who first reacted and jumped into the center of the ring. His fist caught Bobby Paulsen's face, and the two boys scuffled over that burning sacrificial paper. Then both went tumbling in struggle and the crowd shouted louder than ever.

The girl raced to the ground where the book's burning face had fallen. Her hands slapped down on the flames and her mouth contorted in agony. Then, in a moment, she was up, pushing through the cheering bodies and running far away.

Ira took pursuit. She had disappeared at the end of the sidewalk, but he knew the route she took and pedaled hard in search. His head swung side to side, peering through yards and bushes.

When he rounded the next corner of Anna Lee's route, he saw her. She ran with her arms clenched horizontally across her chest. He called out to her. She looked back and, after a moment, halted where she was. She bent down to the ground, and as he approached, a stone came hurtling into his chest. The pain was sharp and hard. Ira nearly fell from his bike. The girl was poised to throw a second chunk of gravel when Ira shed his wheels and caught her by the arm. She did not fight him. The rock fell from her hand onto the

RISE THE MOON

concrete.

Her tears dropped into the burnt front pages of the little green book. It was now an irregular shape, scorched from the bottom up. As she opened it, flecks of charred paper fluttered into the wind. She let it all fall to the ground beside her. Then her tears became loud. All the weight of her body fell into Ira and clung to him. Her hands pinched through his shirt, and she pressed so close to his chest that Ira could not see her face. Dark hair caught in his grip as he tried to console her shaking body.

"Don't cry," he said. "You can write the things again if you remember them. Do you remember them?" The girl's fingers dug into the skin where she held him. Ira winced. "Do you remember what you wrote?" When he tried to step back and look her in the face she came his way, still gripping with all her might as if she too might flutter away in the wind.

"I remember what I saw," she said. Every part of Ira went still. His mouth moved but formed no words. The girl stared. Her unblinking eyes arrested him. The sun was shining bright on her dark walnut rings. He could see himself in there; his own face peered back distorted, grotesque, and transparent as window glass. Her fingers dug into him; needles burrowing. "I saw the people in the forest."

Ira shook his head. "What?"

"There were two of them," she said. "When the house was burning. I saw them. I know who it was, Ira."

His body felt a mile away. His stomach churned and tied a knot. He stood paralyzed, sewed in by her embrace. His hope had been false. His account had been made. With nothing else to do, Ira turned his face away from the gazing sun and hid beneath her veil of hair. He prayed the same dizzying plea as before.

"That's who it was, wasn't it?" she urged. "The twins. They set the fire. They burned his house and ran like rogues. There were two of them. I saw two. They burn things."

Ira hugged the girl as hard as he could. Her body, despite its feminine adolescence, was hard as stone. The world was blinding dark beneath her hair.

"You're right," he said.

"It was them?"

JACOB KOCKEN

"I don't know." His eyes were closed. Ira craned his neck back, and her head tucked beneath his chin. He pressed it there so she couldn't look up. "It makes sense."

"Of course it was. It was the Paulsens. I've hardly known them a month, but I can tell who's a vagrant."

"It makes sense," said Ira. "It makes sense." That was all he could find to say on unsteady breath. Anna Lee relinquished the hold she had around his chest, and Ira felt his weary legs wobble. He clasped his arms over himself and furtively searched her face for any deceptive sign.

After some time, Ira noticed the hand that hung at her left side. It too was burned. The palm where she'd held the book was red and very sore looking. Blood was rising up around several small white blisters.

"You're hurt," he said.

Anna Lee tucked her arm away.

"Come with me," said Ira. He urged her on, and she leaned against him as they hustled over the sidewalk. Ira nearly ran, guiding her down the streets until they came to his doorstep.

The house was empty except for the two of them. Ira wrapped a wet washcloth over ice from the freezer. She flinched when he touched it to her wrist.

"How bad is it?"

"It hurts."

"Maybe you should see a doctor," said Ira. "Bad burns scar."

"That's okay," said Anna Lee. Her eyes kept flicking to the opposite wall. "Can I use your phone?" Ira nodded, and she paced quietly over to the counter where the white and yellow pages sat. The book leaves turned beneath her methodical hand, and she took up the phone from the wall. Ira heard the dial tone twice before Anna Lee's clenched fist shot the receiver back to its hanging dock. She stood facing the wall. Ira approached to see the book open to the police department's page.

"We can just forget about it," said Ira. "If you want." The girl was shaking her head almost imperceptibly. Her mouth was a hard line of frustration and her burned fist was clenched. Her grip was so tight it threatened to stay that way forever. "Or I could do it."

Her eyes went gratefully round. "Really?"

RISE THE MOON

"If you want."

She verged on tears again. "I just don't want them to come asking me." Water welled in the corner of her eyes, and Ira swiped the phone in hopes that would dry them. He dialed and pressed the plastic to his ear. It rang twice before a woman answered.

"Hello," said Ira. "I have a tip on the fire. From this weekend."

"Can I ask who's speaking, what the information is, and how you came to acquire it?" said the woman on the line.

"It was Bobby and Garret Paulsen," said Ira. "I saw them."

"And what is your name, sir?"

Ira hung up the phone. It missed the dock at first under his shaking hand but eventually steadied as Ira exhaled a long breath.

"Thanks," said Anna Lee. They sat there for a moment without a word before the girl spoke again. "His house was next to mine." She pushed a strand of night black hair behind an ear. "I knew there was something wrong."

"You did?"

"He talked to himself. The day we moved in he was outside mumbling and holding eggs to the sky. I said 'Hello, what are you doing?' and he turned away and went inside. The door slammed so hard I could feel the noise. He hated those hens. He kicked them."

Ira turned to move, not to be away from her, only to shake his nerves. The girl began to speak ferociously, as if they were drifting apart on separate rafts, a deep, abysmal ocean spreading between them.

"And one day," said Anna Lee, "I went for a walk out in the woods, and when I came back through his yard he was there and yelled out asking why I was so sad. I wasn't even crying or anything, but he kept standing there with his arms dangling and saying that, 'Why are you so sad?' I didn't understand, so I went over, and he asked did I want to help gather victuals. He led us to the coop and asked why I smile in pictures."

"Why you smile?"

"Yes, and I said, 'What pictures?' and he said, 'Are you in school, and don't you take your picture?' So I said, 'Yes,' and he said, 'Do you smile?' Well, I do so I told him, 'Yes I smile,' and he asked why. I didn't know what to say, but he just kept looking at me like I should answer, so I said, 'So people can see I'm happy.'

246

JACOB KOCKEN

He said that was right and asked had I ever seen a picture from the eighteen hundreds? Did those people smile for their pictures? 'Yes,' I told him; I had seen those pictures. 'No, they didn't smile at all.' Then he crouched down almost to the ground beside the coop. The hens started to flap their wings, and they all moved real quick over by their eggs and sat down on top of them. He said, 'Back then pictures took a long time to take, so you had to be only yourself the way you were all the time or else you'd move and ruin it. And that's why everyone looks mean, and sad, and blank. There was no way to tell untruths on a camera.' I didn't know what to say, so I stayed quiet and tried not to look at him because his voice was getting lower. He had a strange voice. I can hardly describe it. 'Were you especially happy when you smiled for your school picture?' he said. I shook my head. 'But all the pictures in the world are of people smiling, and in a thousand years, when God pulls the next catastrophe and all the good things are gone, the sad people of the future will find your pictures and cry at all the happiness someone else had because look at all these pictures of this little girl who's always happy, and we are always sad. And even if it's not true and you can't really be happy, at least you can trick the world into thinking you didn't get duped the way they did.' I wouldn't say anything, and I wanted to leave, but he put his hand around my arm. He squeezed and shook until I looked up. But he wasn't watching me; he was staring into the coop. Then he undid the lock and crouched inside. Those hens squawked louder than ever, and he tried to push one off its nest. It pecked him back, so he kicked it with his boot. That's when I ran back into the woods and went for a mile all the way around to the road on the other side of my house. Two days later he killed that girl."

 Ira was silent, and after a moment, she stood up and once again fell forward wrapping her arms tight around him. She did not weep this time. Instead of rushing labored breaths, what Ira felt both against his chest and in the palm against her back was the soft and steady pounding of her heart. This time there was no reason to struggle, nothing to hide, so he stood there feeling the warmth of her body and resting his chin ever so slightly on the top of her head. He closed his eyes and thought of nothing but the smell of her hair, the curve of her spine, the sound of her voice swimming through

RISE THE MOON

his imagination.
    Then came the squawk. Ira jumped. The little hairs all over his body stood out. He let go of Anna Lee, and when the air seeped between their broken embrace its fluid loneliness slipped all the way through him. Then the rapping of a fist began, and Ira knew the sound he had heard for the doorbell. Someone had simply rang the doorbell. Anna Lee's big eyes were opened in full alarm as the pounding at the door persisted. Ira rushed up and saw a familiar freckled face through a little column of the entryway window.
    "Don't tell Furke about the Paulsen's," he said. "Fewer people is better. Promise?"
    She nodded, and Ira opened the door for his friend to lope inside. There was a piece of lined paper in his hand, written over, front and back, and charred at the bottom corner.
    "Where'd you go man? That girl who writes," Furke was saying but trailed off when his eyes found Anna Lee standing back in the kitchen. He walked past Ira with the paper held out. "This was on the ground." Anna Lee took it with her good hand and thanked him.
    "I didn't mean to read it or anything," said Furke. "But I picked up that your dad has guns, and you should just know he doesn't have to do anything drastic because I already kicked the living shit out of Bobby. He'll be nursing a broken rib in detention after somebody rats on him for burning all that school stuff."
    "Is he really hurt?" said Anna Lee.
    "Hard to say," said Furke. "The weasel cries every time I have to hit him. All I'm saying is it's taken care of so please no dads and no guns." Anna Lee's eyebrows rose up, and Furke met her with an unbroken stare. She reassured him.
    "Okay," she said. "No guns."
    Furke pointed to the wash cloth over her palm. The ice had begun to melt and was dripping onto the hardwood floor. His eyes widened.
    "Are you hurt?"
    She turned out her palm.
    "Damn it, Bobby," said Furke. "Two broken ribs will be all he can handle."
    "It's okay," said Anna Lee. "I'll be fine."

JACOB KOCKEN

"Honor demands I bash him."

"I will be okay," said Anna Lee. The corners of her lips were lifting. "It's already feeling better. Thank you for bashing him once."

"It was just the thing to do," said Furke. "Stick with us and your stuff won't ever get necrotized again." Then Anna Lee leaned into Furke and hugged him with her good arm. In the seconds of their embrace, Furke looked straight to Ira; his eyes brightened, and his big mouth stretched, flashing a row of crooked bottom teeth.

"I should be home," said Anna Lee quite suddenly. She tucked the loose paper back inside the notebook and swung her backpack to a shoulder. "Thank you," she said, dropping the ice and washcloth into the sink. For the first time, as she reached the door and said farewell, Ira saw her truly smile.

"You crushing?" said Furke. Ira realized he had been staring at the empty doorway. His friend's head was cocked, one eyebrow raised.

"What?"

"I just mean," said Furke, his hands making vague little circles, "you brought her here. A girl. All alone. What's it been, half an hour? That's a long time."

"No, no," said Ira reflexively. He looked down, hiding his flushed cheeks. "It's not like that. She was hurt."

"Saint Ira," sighed Furke. "Well, I got some shit to do. Guess I'll see you at school."

"Wait," said Ira. His friend stopped halfway to the front door and turned back. Ira withdrew the shining chrome lighter from his pocket. "I still have your Necromancer." His open hand proffered it up, but Furke simply shook his head.

"Throw it into Lake Duval," he said.

"What? You paid all that money."

"I don't want it. It burned down that house. It's evidence now. No one knows it was there, but still. Plus, now that the Paulsen's have one it's got a whole different flavor. That's bad juju all around; as good as cursed. Get rid of it for me, will you?" Furke tucked his hands behind his back and gave a final glance to the metallic magic man. "Thanks, brother."

29.
Miriam

HER HUSBAND HAD GONE OUT running again and was now so sore that he couldn't leave the couch. He lied like a man made of straw, his muscles stiff with strain but impotent.

"Have you been stretching?" asked Miriam. She was filling four large plastic bags with ice from the freezer. She wrapped each in a dry washcloth and placed them beneath his calves and hamstrings. He was reclining on the far end of the couch and groaning.

"I never used to stretch," he said.

"You're not a kid anymore."

"Ira," Saul was calling. The boy emerged from the other room where he'd been doing homework. The pencil was still in his hand. "Help your mother set the table. I'm out of commission tonight."

Miriam had her son set the table for two. It was hardly a job at all. From the kitchen, she could see Saul reaching for the remote on the other side of the couch. He did not strain or dislodge the ice bags to grab it. Instead, he simply sat there with his arm outstretched like a magician about to bend the physical world to his whim. He held this way a long time until Miriam left the kitchen and got it for him.

"Bless you, dear," he said. "I'm in good hands."

She thought of the butcher knife she kept in her nightstand drawer. She thought of sticking his leg; then he would move with no problem at all. Instead of the knife, she brought him silverware, and when the food was ready, fixed up a plate.

Miriam and her son sat at the dining room table. The garlic potatoes had a nice browning crisp on the top of the dish. She doled out servings of everything to the two dinner plates at the table. With the fork on its way to her mouth, Miriam was arrested by the conspicuous force of her husband's throat clearing in the other room.

"Let me lead us in prayer," he said.

"What?"

"That's right. Does Ira have his hands folded and his eyes closed?" The dining room wall blocked his view of the boy's side of the table, and so Saul was looking expectantly at her. She turned toward her son who, to her surprise, was sitting straight-backed in the chair. His eyes were closed, and his palms were together before him. His head bowed slightly until the upper lip grazed the tips of his fingers. His chestnut curls hung still and serene. Miriam gave a look of affirmation to Saul who nodded back and assumed the same position, leaving the hot plate on his lap.

"Dear Lord," he spoke. "Thank You for Your Grace in our lives." Miriam, who had also closed her eyes, waited in the ensuing silence. For a decade and a half she had worked, slept, and eaten beside this man and never heard a word of religious veneration. Now, over the last few days, it populated his every thought. Only two nights prior, she had woken in the middle of her sleep to hear his lips atremble with murmuring. She had begun to inquire, but the muttered words, whether in answer to her or some hypnagogic ritual, were ceaseless, and in the dark bedroom, his state of consciousness lay under a blanket of Schroderian ambiguity until that vocal pitter-patter turned eventually to white noise and lulled Miriam herself back into dreams. Here at the dinner table, she opened one lid slightly and saw that Saul was sitting there with his eyes on the television. She put her own tangled hands down and watched as her son too came out of the spell.

"Were you finished?" she said. Saul seemed hardly to hear for a moment. Eventually, his head bobbed in her direction.

"Yes," he said from the other room. "Ira, prayer is salvation, understand?" Miriam looked at her son whose eyes were lit and whose head was nodding deep and slow. "Does he understand?" said Saul again. The sound was more direct, and Miriam saw she was again tasked as intermediary.

"Yeah," she said. Saul nodded approval, and the meal went on in relative silence. They finished up, and her son went off to his

RISE THE MOON

bedroom. Miriam fixed her immobile husband with another glass of water.

"You didn't touch your food," said Miriam.

"I'm fasting," said Saul. "Fasting has long been a tool of enlightenment." His languid body sunk like a load of bricks into the cushions of the couch. But his eyes were always on fire.

"Are you doing alright, Saul?"

He shrugged.

"It's the groin that's the sorest right now," he said. "Lateral movement."

"I got a look at some of your paintings in the garage."

"What do you see?" His eyes widened with renewed focus.

"I see a man who's trying to express himself. Desperately trying," she said. "Whatever it is you're working through out there. Well, I don't know, Saul. All the pictures are the same thing really, but I can't tell what it is. You've been different."

"I feel different. In fact, the day-to-day congruence of any identity at all is progressively baffling to me."

"I don't know what that is supposed to mean."

Saul blinked slow and deliberate. Then he raised a finger as if to quell some impending objection. "What's the difference between a second and a thousand years?" he asked.

"One's a lot longer."

"Play along. Play along. What is longer; ten minutes or eight hours?"

"I'm very sure eight hours is longer," she said. But her husband shook his head.

"Every night I fall asleep, and eight hours goes by in a second. Less than a second really. It goes by entirely unnoticed. Entirely. If I slept for a thousand years, I wouldn't know the difference. Nobody would. The passing time isn't real for me. And if eternal life is truly our future, then I find it very hard to say there is anything that is Saul Foster; only a cloud of experience that sees through these eyes and hears through these ears; the same cloud that dissipates when I fall asleep and congeals again a thousand years later to discover that nothing is ever really different as it ever has been." Miriam sat down on the armrest of the couch beside him. She ran her hand from the front of his crown to the back. His neck was stiff,

JACOB KOCKEN

his tendons corded steel. The skin of his face was pale as if exhaustion had drained the blood away.

"You've run too much," she said. "I want you to stop."

"I can't stop."

"I know what it's like to run away, Saul." He met her eyes, and for the first time in days, his burning gaze was dampened. His straw-man composure announced itself again as he sat back in wait. "And I know what it is you're running from." Saul shook his head against the straining muscles, though his eyes betrayed something.

"God understands," he said.

"Next time I go to see Father David," she said. "Come with me." He seemed to weigh the thought. Then his countenance fell. "Will you come to bed?" asked Miriam.

"No. The physical consequence has set in," said Saul. "I am confined to the chair tonight."

"Pillow?"

"No, the headrest is too high as it is. Only a blanket." Miriam cleared her husband's full plate and came back a minute later with a long fleece. She flipped it out over his body and tucked the edges in around his feet and shoulders.

"Swaddled like a babe," she said. "Goodnight." Miriam left him wrapped there in the fleece. The lights went off, and he was in the dark.

30.
Saul

THERE WAS A SMALL GLARE on the television screen that reflected the light of the moon trickling in from the kitchen window behind him. In the image, he could see his dark shape on the couch, wrapped up and quiet. His muscles and stomach shook with aching. Miriam's voice rang in his head of its own accord as it sometimes did. He had been lying there a while, unable to sleep.

There was something she'd said that caught him like a hangnail. *Swaddled like a babe.* The words were uncomfortable. They stirred him. Something was trying to emerge in his mind. He rocked back and forth. The motion felt ever so slightly like the rhythmic bounce of jogging. *Swaddled like a babe. Swaddled like a babe. Swaddled. Swaddled.*

Saul leapt to his feet. The blanket he left trailing in a twisted pile on the couch as he stumbled blind in the dark. His footsteps were heavy and plodding and kicked the corner of the wall as he fumbled around for the light switch. The time spent lying had made him stiff.

Out in the garage, the night air was humid, as if rain were coming. Saul stilted through the mass of boxes in the back and found the old, now incomplete, nativity set. He picked up the Messiah wrapped in swaddling clothes and held Him to the light. The fluorescent beams swirled in gleaming webs over the curves of His face and garment. The little boy was covered in a blue robe. Only His face and one tiny hand reaching up to the sky were exposed. His ceramic features were hard and smooth as riverbed boulders. The eyes were brilliant blue. Saul stared into them.

JACOB KOCKEN

The Christ was doing it too; His gaze was fixed so very nearly on Saul's eyes, but no matter how he twisted the figurine into and out of the light, it looked just past him. "Oh, Redeemer." Saul studied the pupils. The tiny black beads were reflective, and there was something in them, some diminutive shape reflected but always obscured by the sliding beams of light.

And so, to combat the glossy enamel, Saul took up a brush and stroked black acrylic over the entirety of each of the Savior's eyeballs. The wet paint too had a sheen of light inside it that would drain away with drying. All of Saul's paintings had finished with a matte surface that bothered him at first for its lack of brilliance, but perhaps now the darkness would bring clarity. He set the babe aside to dry and fell asleep back inside on the couch with his neck bent uncomfortably on the arm rest.

31.
Ira

SHE WAS GOING TO COME to Lake Duval. Furke would be there too; his bike had pegs, so those two would come together. Ira stirred privately that evening while his mother made dinner. He didn't want to ask if he could go out. She might say no and have reason to keep a watchful eye. So Ira tried to wait. He had to keep moving, however, both in body and mind. First, he tried his homework. He even tried chores. While he was moving, things were mostly fine; as long as his mind was occupied. But when he stopped, when his mind wandered off by itself, Ira felt the heat. Blistering points of pain that erupted here and there on his arms; his neck; his face. They always came alongside the ugly thoughts. He kept returning to the mirror expecting to find his skin rough and red from the summer sun. But he found no burns on his person, no scars.

Then Ira had tried taking showers with the water set to cold. At first, the frigid shock seemed it might provide a quenching. Cool rivulets washed down his dreadful body, relief running through to his toes. But soon enough his mind would adjust. The water was not so cold anymore. He could stand under the stream without gasping. Before long he began to shiver at the bones, and his skin turned white with chill. It would take a quarter hour under blankets in bed to lose his shaking. And still he smoldered, waiting for the evening to fall.

Anna Lee said she would be out at eight. The hour had come by the time his mother's evening meal was served. Ira ate as fast as possible and told his parents he was off to bed. His mother, as she was wont to do, kissed his head of chestnut hair. "Good, sweet

JACOB KOCKEN

baby," she'd said. Before allowing him off to bed, his mother heated a glass of milk and pressed it into his hand. "Drink up, baby." Then Ira scrambled upstairs, slung a pack to his shoulders, and climbed out the window.

In as big of a hurry as he was, Ira had a stop to make. He had looked all over his parents' house but didn't find a drop. Every cabinet, cupboard, and pantry shelf was searched and found devoid, so instead of going straight to the waterfront, he took a detour through the neighborhood where the houses spread out and the old growth showed between them.

His grandfather's house was on the corner of the block. Out back, several acres of wooded land separated it from everything else. As Ira coasted soundlessly into the driveway, the tops of these trees peaked up and then slowly receded behind the height of the house. It had a tall second story at the center of which were two quite large and long-sealed master bedroom windows, each on hinges left and right like a swinging gate. Their height seemed as though the architect had meant for a balcony but left only a wall of glass. Ira, passing beneath their purview, dismounted and stashed his bike in the dark front corner of the open garage.

A loud thwacking sounded from the backyard. Ira peeked out through the grime of a garage window and saw his grandfather out behind the house chopping wood. The iron axe, bespeckled with rust, rose up above the old man's head and swung back down with the weight of his body. There was a small explosion and the log fell in two clean halves off the splitting stump. The old man tossed the pieces in an empty wheel barrow, the sound like a deep metal drum pounding the subtle percussion of a patient song's prelude. A new log was placed upon the stump, and he went on chopping.

Ira ducked from the window and snuck around to the side of the house. He went immediately to the basement stairs. The room grew darker with his descent, the sinking sunlight funneling dimly inside like the mouth of some winding cavern. Everything was shadowed. The wall of his late grandmother's belongings loomed over him with irregular towers. He found the cabinet easily enough despite neglecting the light cord at the landing and took three of the bottles at random. Their glass clinked sharply in the empty room as he zipped them up inside his backpack and made for the stairs.

RISE THE MOON

Ira moved silently back to the garage, peeking around corners and always finding he was alone. The cracking sound of splitting wood still came intermittently from behind the house. Ira hopped back onto his bike and followed the tree line until the street forked into an old county road toward the cornfields and a smaller dirt path into Duval Park.

The ambient suburban sounds disappeared under the forest's umbrella. The closer he got, the faster he raced. But they were there already when he arrived, and there was a frog in Anna Lee's hand.

"Furke jumped in the muck to catch it," she said. The frog was green and white with black flecks all over. It had golden rings for eyes and a small vestigial nub of tail still shrinking into the body. Furke lay stomach down at the water's edge, his face and hands hovering out over the face of the deep. He had his shoes off and pants rolled up to his knees. Thick black mud covered his feet.

Anna Lee held the thing up for Ira to see. Her other palm, at her side, was wrapped in gauze. The faint color of blood showed through its layers.

Ira ran a finger over the head of the amphibian, conscious not to touch the girl who gripped it. "Hello, frog," he said. "Did you confuse Furke for your mama?" Anna Lee laughed; a sweet, golden giggle that made the blood rise up in Ira's cheeks. Then Ira saw his friend's narrowed eyes. They were directed momentarily right at him.

"I knew it," said Furke.

"What?" asked Anna Lee.

"That one's evil," said Furke.

"Evil?" exclaimed Anna Lee.

"Only a real demon could make Ira insult someone. I should've known when I saw it swimming. You find good frogs on land. Guilty things hide in the water."

"Then what'd you catch it for?" she asked.

"That's just what you got to do." Just then his hand shot down into the lake. It came back up clenching a dripping ball of muck. "Damn."

"Another frog?"

"A fish."

"No one can catch a fish with their hands."

JACOB KOCKEN

"I do," said Furke. "I do it all the time."

"You need a pole for that," Anna Lee insisted.

"Pole fishing is lazy. It's for the blind." He chuckled to himself and peered down into the dark water. "People who fish with hooks can't see what they're grabbing down there. It's just clumsy hope."

"I like pole fishing," said the girl. "We used to do it a lot." Furke's head was nearly stuck halfway into the muck, and Anna Lee looked at Ira when she said this.

The lake was long and wide. At intervals all around its ring, little campfire flames announced themselves. Frogs were croaking in regular rounds like the ticking of a clock. The sun was breaking the horizon over the lake and casting glows of orange and purple on the undersides of small white clouds.

"It looks like it's sinking. Right down into the water," said Anna Lee. "Swim fast, frog. Come back with the sun tomorrow morning and Furke will stop calling you evil." Her lips puckered and kissed the frog on the top of its head. She brought their catch to the edge of the water where its legs started to whirl. Just before she let it down, the frog's throat bubbled up and a quick guttural groan peeled out. Ira jumped. Then Anna Lee loosed her hand and the frog slipped away smooth as wind. A croaking continued in the distant dark. There was another thunderous splash.

"Oh, I had it!" yelled Furke. He threw a dismissive gesture at the lake and pushed himself up to standing. It was only then that Ira noticed his friend's dress. The pants were black rather than the usual tattered jeans and his shirt was a collared grey button up with silver pinstripes.

"Why are you wearing that?" asked Ira.

"I had an interview."

"At Betty Blossom's?"

"Yeah."

"What's that?" asked Anna Lee.

"A flower shop," Ira answered. "Did you get it?"

"No. Do you remember the grand prix?" asked Furke. Ira nodded and Anna Lee looked quizzical. "A few years ago Ira thought he could beat me in a bike race."

"Which I won," added Ira.

"By default."

RISE THE MOON

"Default?"

"You have a better bike."

"That's not what default means. And you're the one with a better bike. Yours has pegs."

"But mine only has one gear."

"So does mine. It's stuck on gear six."

"It wasn't during the grand prix."

Ira turned to Anna Lee. "You should know that I got that bike at a garage sale for one dollar because it was broken. I had to get a new chain for it, and—"

"You should also know," said Furke, "that my handlebars are loose, and a screwdriver won't tighten them. So I'm at a real handicap in—"

"Or know that an Allen wrench would tighten them, but he just keeps trying to use a flathead."

"Or know the fact that Ira grows his hair out so long to hide the fact that he has a flat head."

Anna Lee was smiling. A sputtering laugh escaped her, and she held both hands up like stop signs. Her head mimed a dizzy bounce back and forth. Then she centered between the two of them and crossed her eyes so the left looked right and the right looked left. "I can only know one thing at a time," she said.

"Okay," continued Furke. "Ira did win the grand prix, but the point is that the course turned from Linden Street to Belmont right where Betty Blossom's is. They have a big front property, but it's all just grass that makes for an easy short cut.

"Well, it's not all grass," said Ira.

"It's flowers."

"You rode through the flower beds?" said Anna Lee.

"It looked like a tractor harvesting corn," said Ira.

"It did not!" said Furke.

"I'm kidding. It really wasn't that bad."

"Well, however bad it was, Mrs. Betty remembered who I was."

"I'm surprised she even saw you then," said Ira. "With all that winning speed your face should've been a blur."

"Shut up." Furke gave him a friendly smirk. "So, she wouldn't hire me."

"Why do you want to work at a flower shop?" asked Anna Lee.

JACOB KOCKEN

"It's just the only place that's hiring minors."

"Maybe you can convince her. Or someone else will start hiring."

"Maybe," said Furke. "But you only get one reputation, and mine's lousy."

Mimicking Furke, Anna Lee took off her shoes and rolled the legs of her jeans up to the knee. "I don't know. I think you get as many reputations as people who know you." She sat on the grass, dangling her feet into the water. Ira followed suit. As he sat, he swung his pack with the pilfered bottles to his lap.

"Oh, it's cold," said Anna Lee. Her foot shot in and out of the shallows. "Not going in tonight then."

The boys sat on either side of her. The attention of the whole night swung from one side to the other with the glance of her eyes as if she was the fulcrum of the Earth. The soft, tidal splash of Anna Lee's rhythmic sole against the surface of the water joined the ambient chorus of croaking frogs. Then, without warning, Anna Lee kicked the water hard with the flat of her foot splashing, water tall and wide, striking both boys in the face and speckling half their bodies like one caught in the rain.

"Are you asking to swim?" said Furke. He stood up and ripped off his shirt; then, wading into the shallow water, grasped at her kicking feet as she laughed and thrashed on shore. Her utter joy arrested Ira, and he watched her, consciously guarding his adoration. She had thin legs that curled and struck with a playful verve. Her face, so often shadowed by the curve of her shoulder or a pileous black curtain as she buried it in the pages of her book, was now thrown back against a bed of green grass ringing laughter and condensing into dimpled cheeks and other indescribable revelations of delight.

Furke let go of her feet. His rascal smile only broadened as he splashed his way back on shore and thumped down into the grass beside them. In short order, a small orange flame lit the twilight, and the pungent white cylinder of a cigarette was wagging up and down out from Furke's froggish lips. He held an old lighter, one of cheap blue plastic, a quarter at any convenience store. Tobacco smoke made a mild haze over the water as Furke sat back on the heel of one hand, his shoulders lax and his eyes glossy with content.

RISE THE MOON

Ira jumped. A sharp, burning pain touched his cheek. He shot a palm into the cold lake and brought it up to splash his face.

Anna Lee, without a word of permission, or even inquiry, reached forth with two fingers, straight and delicate as chopsticks, and removed the cigarette from the tall boy's possession. Furke's mouth remained open as it had been, once to draw the smoke, now in surprise. Ira saw his friend's face go rosy. He himself thought it was rude for Furke to have lit up so close to a girl and waited now for Anna Lee to rub its burning ember out in the grass or flick the whole thing into the lake where the water would kiss it dead. Instead, she lifted it to her own lips. The orange dot glowed intensely with her inhale. She suppressed a small cough and let the smoke trail out of her mouth slowly, tasting each ghostly tendril.

Furke was giving her a long look, appraising. She took a few more drags before Furke slid a second cigarette from its box and another ember began blinking, two fireflies lost and signaling. The three of them sat for several minutes among the sounds of the lake. Frogs croaked; turtles surfaced; the wind ran hushing through the trees. The smoke from the two of them hovered over Ira. It got into his nose and mouth. The taste was poison. Furke did not offer a third cigarette.

Now and then amid their silence, Anna Lee's eyes would touch on his and Ira would be struck with gusts of private elation. Then, swift as a sparrow, she would move off him, alighting here and there on treetops, lily pads, and the celestial specters unfolding slowly in the nascent night sky.

To catch her, and bring that coveted gaze back to roost, Ira undid the zipper of his book bag and chose one of the stolen bottles. He cradled this spirit, sealed like a genie, in his delicate hands. His fingernails clinked a luring rhythm against the glass. The sound sliced high and pure over the lake, and both the tall boy and the beautiful girl stopped what they were doing to look at him. Ira thought he saw the burning end of Anna Lee's cigarette go dim as if she'd thrown it down into the soil.

A botanical scent suffused the air as Ira unscrewed the gin. He took a sip from his bottle, holding it high up into the confluence of dying sun and rising moonlight. The liquid was clear and reflected inside the glass with a silver sheen. Cool fire tickled the back of his

JACOB KOCKEN

throat. He winced. Ira pressed his tongue into the bottle neck to stop the flow, but even then after a second it set his tongue to burning. When he finally lowered it they were both looking curiously with round eyes and flared up nostrils. He proffered the bottle to Anna Lee, and she took it. Her hand searched around a bit on the smooth curves of the glass before tipping to her mouth. Then a cloud of silver mist sputtered from her lips. She coughed into her chest.

"Are you alright?" said Ira. Before he could reach for the bottle, she'd already brought it up again to drink. Then she set it down between them.

"My tongue is being poked by a thousand little needles," she said. And then she said it again, twice more under her breath. "Thousand tiny pine needles." Ira leaned past her face and tossed the bottle up to Furke who stood now in the water sending little ripples in every direction. They passed it around the circle a few times, each taking sustained draughts under quiet, adolescent pressure.

"Like it?" asked Ira. The spirit was not long in acting, lightening the sense of his body and circulating a comfortable, phantom warmth through every vein.

"It tastes kind of horrible," said Furke, sucking his teeth. Despite his words, Furke drank the most and held the bottle neck in his laddish, possessive grip the longest. Already Ira sensed something swimming in his head. It was pleasant, and he felt like laughing.

"The smell reminds me of sugar pines," said Anna Lee. "They stood all around our old house."

"In California?" said Ira.

"You're from Hollywood?" said Furke. He belched and one loose fist shot up to cover his mouth. Anna Lee smirked at the crudeness and went on.

"We've lived a lot of places. The last one was a city with too many people and not enough room. But I was born in the mountains out west." Her feet curled beneath her, and she looked past them over the parochial expanse of the lake and forest. "The sugar pines are so tall there. One day I watched Dad and his friend take down a dead one, and we had to stand on a plateau hundreds of feet away to be clear of the fall."

Furke belched again, this time his hands moved to his stomach.

RISE THE MOON

"It's getting to you, huh?" said Ira. He gestured to the spirit in his friend's hand.

"What's getting to me?" Furke raised the bottle again. Moonlight poured with liquor down its neck and into his for several seconds. Then he tossed the remainder to Ira who fumbled the catch, spilling gin over the dark green grass. Ira swept it up as quickly as he could for a healthy swig. His eyes watered under the juniper punch. A fuzzy feeling overtook his tongue. But amid these trivial discomforts, there was a phantom warmth, imbibing him with soothing, rocking arms.

"Why do you move so much?" asked Ira.

"Because," said Anna Lee.

"My dad moved here for work. Did yours?"

"No."

Lake water sloshed back and forth on the bank as Furke climbed up on shore. He refused the bottle from Ira's hand. "I think I need the restroom," he said and stalked off toward the trees, stumbling as he went. Ira shared such an unsettled, churning belly and stored the bottle back inside his bag.

"Well, sorry you had to move in next to a murderer." He zipped the gin away and set it between them. Out in the night sky, looming just above the southern tree line stood the silhouette of a dark and lonely tower. Ira pointed to it. "That's jail," he said. "They watch the yard from up there. And they got guns. If he ever tried to leave, they'd get him. They'd shoot him."

The girl was quiet. She stretched out again with her feet dangling. There was a sharp inhalation as her eyes found something on the ground beside her; a small rock cracked in half where the hollow inside revealed dozens of tiny gleaming crystals. She collected it quickly and pushed the fist deep into the pocket of her shorts. When Ira next returned his gaze to her face the lunar glow gleamed off her wet eyes just as it did the surface of the lake. She sniffed as if holding back tears and rummaged into the pack Ira had just fastened, taking up the gin again. Then like a fountain, her lips circled up and she spat out in one long and far-reaching stream. "Thousand tiny pine needles."

"It's okay. He's locked up now," said Ira.

But she only went on the way she was, staring into the wilderness beneath the penitentiary tower. "Do they know what they do?" she said at last. Her foot slapped the water. Circles swam far out along the shore.

"I don't know."

"I always know," she said. "A few months ago I was so mad at my sister I wished aloud that we hadn't been born. My mother said not to say those things; she said it was bad for the soul. But I stormed out furious and heartbroken. I planned to run away. When I came back later to take my things I heard a sound and followed it to Mom's room. She was on the bed looking up. Her pillows were torn in half, and she cried so hard. I stood right in the doorway, and she couldn't even see me because she cried so hard." Anna Lee stopped holding back and bent over on her knees. Her teardrops rippled on the lake.

Ira's heart raced. His swimming head went dizzy when he came close to put an arm across her shaking shoulder. When she didn't move away he held her more firmly.

"I didn't even mean it. I was just mad."

"It's not your fault."

"Then whose is it?"

Ira found his lips were numb. "It can't be your fault. If you didn't know."

"I hardly know anything. That means I'll do it again. Something else. Not that because I know it broke her heart. But something else. And once you do know it's because it's too late."

Ira was looking at the rings of her eyes. Their brown was so dark and thin it melted into the pupil. The chemical warmth inside him set to massaging his muscles, and it was a long moment before his eyes blinked away a bleary mist. "Everything's okay," he said.

She leaned into his arm and they both fell back against the ground. "Ira, the stars are turning. I don't feel good." For Ira too, the alcohol had begun to swarm. His face felt numbed, and when he closed his eyes it was easy to imagine they were floating in midair. But for Ira, it was pleasant. He lay on his side with one cheek against the grass, not even noticing the blades that stuck into his ear.

The girl was only inches away. Her head rested on his arm. Her eyes were closed, and her mouth was open. Her chest moved slow-

RISE THE MOON

ly up and down like the tide. Ira, watching in wonder, began to stir. He bent one knee up to hide himself and it met the smooth skin of Anna Lee's leg. Ira went dizzy. The girl's head tilted his way and her eyelids opened. He went stiff beneath her neutral gaze.

Then there was an ugly noise from behind them. Anna Lee jumped like a startled rabbit. She removed herself from Ira's arm and looked back into the woods. With her leaving went a large piece of Ira, and he filled it back up immediately with what he could suck down from the silver bottle. Only after his chin was dripping with gin did Ira stand to see Furke bent over his knees in a shallow ditch some thirty yards down the path. His head heaved back and forth, and there was the hoarse, guttural noise again. When he made his way back to them Furke was wiping his hands over mouth and shirt. He smelled like guts and bile.

"You okay Annie?" said Furke. She was holding her stomach and rocking side to side. "It's a lot better when you let it up." He pulled her forward by the elbow. When her head came all the way in front of her she covered her mouth. "Let it up."

Furke helped the girl stay upright over the bank. "Give it up," Furke said. "Give it up and you feel a lot better." Then there was the same hoarseness as in the ditch, swallowed by the lake. Ira could feel his stomach churning too. It crawled upwards. He clenched his jaw and fought it until the height of the feeling passed. There was acid in the pit of his throat that he could hardly swallow down.

"Feel better now?" said Furke.

"Yes," said Anna Lee. "But tired."

The three of them sat and looked at the sky. Ira lay with his back flat to the ground. Blades of grass tickled at his neck and ears, but again he did not feel them at all. There was no pain now; no fiery sensations on his skin. There were no intrusive thoughts either. After a while, the voices of his companions became a droning hum, an enchanter's lullaby, and Ira found himself several times drifting off through reverie toward sleep. Ira's calm could not be perturbed by the shine of celestial lights above. The moon was half dim, and the turning stars burned very, very far away. Soon, darkness gathered him up.

IRA WOKE TO THE GENTLE hand of Anna Lee shifting him at the

JACOB KOCKEN

shoulder. Her face hung over him. Furke was stretching tall and cracking joints. "Time to go," said Anna Lee in a distant, muffled voice.

The three of them walked together down the veiled forest path. It was darker now than when he'd fallen asleep. Ira's first few steps were wobbled as a fawn's though his gait straightened out by the time they were reaching the main road. A cloudy mist was gradually leaving Ira's head as well, replaced by a dull, portentous headache. They walked on that way for nearly an hour. When at last they came to the trailhead, Ira's mind was clearer. He was hearing things with crispness again. Down the old country highway, the bunch split up. Ira, feeling only just sharp enough, saddled his steed and set off in one direction. Furke would take Anna Lee home. He was allotted this task because Ira's bike did not have pegs.

He traveled alone for only the space of a few minutes before reaching his pit stop again. A warm light flicked on the window glass of his grandfather's house. It came from the fireplace in the living room where the old man slept. The garage was closed this time, and the sounds of the outside world were all lying down to sleep. Inside, however, the gramophone was on. It was loud, and the air hummed with a muffled, melancholy song.

His bike stayed at the side of the house. With the three stolen bottles in his pack, Ira approached the basement's bulkhead doors. A black, abysmal hole stood out even against the darkness of the night.

Ira snuck into the dark stairwell. His feet fell slow and soft on plank steps. The spirit of gin was still in him, and Ira gripped the railing hard for support as his feet bumped against the ground. Waves of musical sound vibrated through the walls and ceiling of the basement. A drum was pounding time. Several brass horns wailed in melodic loops.

Down at the landing, he could see the gleam of a small metal bead dangling on the light bulb's pull chain. When Ira got there he passed it by, walking cautious and feeling his way toward the cabinets on the right-hand wall. With his eyes adjusting in slow degrees, he could just make out the frame of the hutch and liquor cabinet. His careful feet slid with quiet grating sounds across the concrete floor. When he reached the spot he stopped and patted the

RISE THE MOON

wooden fascia until his palm met the coldness of an iron handle. Ira undid his pack and drew out the first of the three liquor bottles he'd taken. As the cabinet door opened and his unsteady hand clinked glass against glass, another sound, quiet and shifting like his own footsteps, brushed Ira's ear. He turned and peered back into the depths of the room where the sound continued to circle. A shift in darkness, a veiled but moving shape announced itself in silhouette. It was flat and wide; then narrow and waving like a flag in the breeze. The fabric hung suspended with no body inside. Its ghostly bounce continued, swinging and jumping in time with the muffled music through the walls. Then it turned and began to separate from the darkness. There were two of them. One had the frame of a body. Two glistening stones shone as the eyes caught moonlight. The head rose from its shoulders as the body turned toward Ira, and a voice rolled like shifting gravel.

"Darling."

The bottle came loose in Ira's fingers and tumbled off the edge of the shelf to the concrete below, shattering with a sharp, reverberating ring and spilling the pungent spirit. The piney scent was as strong here as for one lost in Pacific wilderness. The word came again, "Darling. Emily," and where the moonlight trailed through the stairwell Ira could see a vague and labored figure swaying in the middle of the room. His own head swam. Ira's blood went hot, and again he could not see true. The basement shadows whirled, and Ira fell to one knee, feeling sick. The wet smell of pine needles climbed up the fabric of his pants where he knelt. A razor of glass poked through into the skin below his knee.

Then the light shot on, and there was his grandfather standing halfway between the stairwell and the old couch and coffee table. He stood with a strange, paunchy posture. His head and face seemed they would fall to the floor. His lips hung open and from between them there hummed a low and rhythmic song. As the sound faded, the subtle swing of his body came to a halt. Hanging from one hand now was a woman's dress. It was black and sleek. There was a rip across the bottom half. In the light, this open spot stretched wide, and the dress hung off-kilter. Frank's other hand still clung to the light bulb's dangling cord. "You've been missing," said the old man.

JACOB KOCKEN

The spell of dizziness waned in Ira, and gradually he gained his feet, standing level with Frank. Both of them squinted in the harsh new light. On the little table, Ira saw a large, transparent bottle. There was no glass with ice this time, only the bottle at the end of its life. A trembling, squinted expression sat on his grandfather's face. The old man dropped the dangling cord. His arms at first hung dead from the shoulders as his circular body came nearer. Then they began to swing. Frank's body dipped in consort with the movement. And he hummed. For a moment, Frank passed between Ira and that only source of light, shielding his face with a dark veneer. Then he was close to Ira and turned so as to be revealed again. His once blue eyes were all glazed over. The pupils, despite the light bulb above, were vacuous black spots. A rosy color shone over his skin like bad make-up and gave something of a mask to his bloated cheeks. His nose was round and circus red.

Frank dropped the dress that trailed in his grip. It bunched into a pile of streaming folds on the concrete, sticking momentarily to the rubber of Frank's passing shoe. It was an Oxford on his foot. Indeed, all of his dress was formal. He wore black slacks and a suit jacket. A necktie was looped through his collar. The knot was still tight.

Frank took another step toward Ira and the cabinet. His foot came down in the puddle of gin. The old man looked at the floor where a dozen points of coruscating glass shattered his tranquil expression. "Oh no," he said. "Broke." With one arm out against the hutch, Frank lowered himself to a crouch. A swift rush of air went through Frank's nostrils. It wrinkled his whole face. Then he came down on his knees, and his face turned level to the floor. His hands were half submerged as was his necktie.

"Grandpa?" Ira breathed. But the old man was far away.

Frank's lips puckered slightly and came down into the spill. He kissed where the dust and liquor mingled, and when he came up for a second Ira heard the juddering of his throat. Then the old man was back with his face to the ground.

"Grandpa?" Ira said again.

His knees straightened out, and Ira tried to stop him. He lurched forward to grab the old man around the waist as Frank's body stretched and came down pelvis first on the wet floor. Up in

RISE THE MOON

the house, the gramophone began to skip.

"Stop," said Ira, but his throat failed him.

The darkened hue of water climbed up Frank's clothes. His chest was flat on the ground. His mouth was moving back and forth with hungry sounds.

Then the harsh botanical scent of gin was dulled and mixed with an odor familiar and rank. Beneath them, the puddle grew, and Frank's passionate tongue went on licking. His torso worked against the concrete. He was too heavy to lift or slide from the spot. The weight of him was like a sandbag, and Ira succeeded only in rocking his grandfather side to side. For a moment, that balding head turned back. As the horse brushes off gadflies, Frank swatted and returned to the trough. There was a darkened red streak down his chin, which, upon seeing, sprung Ira away from the old man's midsection.

Kneeling down in the wet gin, Ira began to sweep through the puddle with the palms of his hands, displacing fluid and sending jagged shards of glass over into safer, darker recesses of the basement. When Ira flexed his palms they stung with burrowing, microscopic glass. A plaintive moan came from behind the bleeding lips. A weak and wrinkled hand protested against Ira's sweeping arms until it brushed the flowing chestnut wave.

Frank went still. His mouth stopped its greed, and his body reared back. The darkened hue of his soaking clothes was a void in the dim light. The old man pushed himself slowly up to his knees; then his feet. His eyes were glass and looking all about with slow, wandering oscillations.

He reached a calloused hand out and touched the top of Ira's head. It was a heavy palm, and Ira could feel the thumb moving in tiny, caressing circles through his hair.

"Dear."

Ira pulled away, but the old man was large, and his strength was equaled by his weight. The thick hand atop his head dropped down the nape of Ira's neck and found a powerful, flat grip against the bump of his spine. The other hand found Ira's hip.

"Grandpa," said the boy. Ira could hear his own hurried breaths on either side of the word. Then the old man's weight leaned in. They tipped and steadied, tipped and steadied. The scent of dank

JACOB KOCKEN

perspiration was on his clothes beneath the gin. It transferred to Ira, wicking away the heat that radiated off the fat man's body. Ira kept his own arms to the side voluntarily at first. Then Frank bore down with his force. Ira tried to squirm but could hardly move. The hand on Ira's hip began to rub and travel. "Grandpa," he said again, louder. The old man's breath came down over his face, and Ira felt saliva. The soft flesh of lips pressed onto the top of his forehead; his nose.

Ira kicked. He jerked back hard, breaking one arm hold from the leader of the dance. A few strands of long brown hair that had tangled in the old man's palpitating hand tugged at Ira's scalp. The old man breathed heavily, trying to keep hold. A swell of air sucked through the spider-webbed nose. Frank sniffed Ira's angel hair, and it lifted like a candle's trailing smoke. With that breath, he stopped again.

It seemed to bring Frank to life. He stood up a little straighter in his suit. His eyes focused quite intensely on the wisping brown locks between his fingers. Ira watched his expression harden and soften with new thoughts. The old man looked from Ira's face to the hair in his hand and back.

"Boy?" said Frank.

Ira nodded. His body was locked with tension, his arms together at the waist.

"I was alone."

"I'm sorry," Ira started to say.

"What are you doing here?" mumbled Frank. "Leave us alone, boy."

He slunk from the cabinet back to the couch in the center of the room. His body dripped, leaving a slug's trail in the wake. Human dexterity neglected him, and he used his elbows to lie flat on the cushions. Once there, he turned an expression on Ira. The boy could hardly tell if he was even seen. But the eyes were on him; angry, momentarily sharp eyes.

Frank sunk like a stone on the sofa then, and his mouth reared open, expressing the slow, even breath of a sleeper. The swinging melody still skipped through the basement walls and ceiling. And there flashed from out the shadowy stem of Ira's mind the image of a woman lying indecent on a broken old sofa. In her hand was a

RISE THE MOON

cigarette that burned bright and orange; the sun that lit the thought. She looked up under a glaze of the eye and grinned. His heart sunk as her once suckled bosom arched off the cushions and swung hypnotic shame.

Ira ran up the stairs without a thought. Outside, Ira mounted his bike and pointed home. The gramophone blared one broken and incoherent syllable over and over again as he fled. He looked back to find the cellar door open. He did not go back to seal it. There was an orange but waning glow in the window above. Fire felt licking at Ira's bones yet had seemed to leave his grandfather's den and now only smoldered in the hearthplace.

For a second night in so short a span, Ira came home through his bedroom window. He fastened the door locked and did not turn on the lights. The curtains he drew closed. Harsh, swampy vapor filled his nostrils when he slung off his backpack and wrenched open one of the two remaining bottles. Ira tossed the thing back violently. Swirling contents climbed up and down like hourglass sand. It was all he could do not to cough it back up beneath the bed's thick down coverall. Ira drank and drank until the numbness of the lake found him again. The buzz crawled over him from head to toe. He drank past the pleasant feelings until he could no longer find his mouth and the power to think washed clear.

32.
Saul

IT WAS ELEVEN O'CLOCK ON Friday morning and Angela was meeting him here. He had suggested it on their last run as they'd passed by on his street. Only later did he feel a strange sense of unease about the situation. But he let that pass as all trivial things do.

Saul was in the garage reworking blue pigment into the eyes of his ceramic Savior. This little statue drew the attention. Its pastel blue wrapped around the Babe's whole body, tucking Him tight like a chrysalis. Saul had painted only one part of it. The eyes were solid black now. They carried an atavistic vacancy; holes that one could not help but peer into. But the black-eyed Babe had yielded nothing to Saul, so he reasoned to pursue the colors.

The sun was hot again today. Such heat usually loosened muscles automatically, but this morning Saul had awoken on the couch feeling mangled. His left leg had fallen off the cushions, pulling half his groin down and twisting his spine to a tight spiral. Now his legs felt as if each belonged to a separate mind, unable to harmonize with the rhythm of the body. And his neck, bent sharply against the armrest of the couch all night, resembled a broken pipe, an iron pole bludgeoned into a right angle with a heavy bat or hammer. The left side of his neck pulled down on his head while the right froze at full extension. His whole body felt strained, but the stiff neck was worst of all. He looked out of his eyes sideways because of it.

The new orientation somewhat changed his visual experience. When he wanted to see something, he felt compelled now to turn not only his head and eyes; he moved this morning as a soldier in drill with small, pointed steps that aimed his entire frame. As a

RISE THE MOON

normal person is blind to his back, Saul was now blind also at the flanks, the feet, and to all that flew above the reach of his periphery. His eyes yet had free range, but they did not go far before bringing on the pounding threat of a headache.

"Hey you."

Saul spun his whole hunching body to face the driveway where Angela now stood. Her hair was up. She was ready to run.

"Hello," said Saul. He gave her a little wave, but she did not see it. Angela was looking at the house. Her head tipped right and left and all around. A soft smile was on her face as she approached the garage. She had the focused expression of one who is present, taking things in. She looked at the windows and the door and the porch.

"Hey!" He proffered up the Babe. Angela was drawn like a magnet.

"Jesus."

"I've had a vision, Angela."

"A vision?"

"You said your father appeared to you after he died." The woman nodded in silent affirmation. "I've got something trying to reach me too."

"A spirit? Who?"

"I don't know who, but I was given a glimpse some days back. It appeared to me, and then it was gone again. But I can still feel it stalking me."

"Why this?" she ran her hand along the Baby's robe.

"It appeared inside me where everything is dark and hidden. I want to put it out here in the real world. To see it and know it."

"The eyes," she said. "It's all you painted?"

"Eyes are like telescopes and mirrors. I want to know what they see when they look at me." Then the two of them met each other's gaze. Her eyes were a light ocean blue. They looked intently at his. Again, Saul tried to straighten his neck and looked upon her more naturally. But the spasming muscles hardened like a statue. Saul had come quite close before he'd frozen. The air moved, and he could not tell if it was the breeze or the breath from her open lips.

JACOB KOCKEN

Then Angela's hand left the statue of the Boy and caressed the grotesque bend at Saul's neck. "Are you hurt?" she asked.

"There is no pain," he said, "for a saved man." Then her fingers pressed into the tension near his spine. A great gasp of excruciating relief escaped him. He lurched forward some, nearly dropping the Messiah, then leaned back into the pressure of her hands.

"So tense," she said. "You're in no shape to run today. You need to put a hot pad on this and work yourself out. Do you stretch?"

"I'm not a yogi," he said.

"Can you move your neck?"

"Hardly."

"We'll start with the arms then." Angela crossed one elbow over her chest, and, pulling it into her body with the other, instructed him to do the same. "Loosen your shoulders up first. Everything in your body is connected, and the problem isn't always just were the pain is." Saul mimicked the motion. There was immediate tension, but the pose loosened some carnal rust.

"I have been thinking about your decision," said Angela. "About not continuing that Church program. I might not either. I don't know. I guess it's just not entirely what I expected."

"Why'd you join?"

"I've always been the spiritual type. Ever since Dad died. But it's always been a thing I kept to myself. Part of me always thought it was supposed to be that way because he came back to me and no one else, and why would he do it that way unless it was supposed to be a secret? Also, I knew no one would believe me. We didn't go to church after he died. I don't think it ever crossed anyone's mind. I think Mom's an atheist now. I don't even know. It wasn't a thing to talk about." They switched arms, and began to stretch the other side. This side gave Saul a tremendous feeling that the knot was being undone.

"You joined to tell your story?"

"I wanted to experience that revelation again. It was the clearest, most powerful moment of my life, seeing him. I'm done living disinterested. I want that gravity again. The meetings; well, they've lacked a bit of luster."

"That woman doesn't know what she's talking about."

"The way you speak about things, Saul, it gives me that same

RISE THE MOON

mysterious hope; like there's some passionate miracle to tap into." Her hands dropped down to her sides. "Put your hands together now behind your back," she said. "Try to thrust your chest out. It'll stretch the front part of your shoulders."

"The Bible," said Saul, following a concentrated pause from Angela, "speaks of a chosen people. There are some who are God's elect and commune with Him. My impulse to join the Church was, I think, the same as yours. But I have been met with tedium and condescension. We have received the unequivocal blessing of the Divine and yet are treated there like children learning the ABC's. It's a backward world. The Holy Spirit ought to be our guide, not these self-appointed politicians. They constrain the mind. How is it that we, who have communed directly with the Lord's Grace, go unheard under His own roof?"

Angela nodded.

"The chosen people have always been denied and persecuted, and yet always emerge victorious over idolaters," said Saul.

Angela had stopped her instructions. One of her arms still held the other but had fallen to her waist. Her eyes were wide and full of wonder. She looked at him for a long time, and there was a rosiness in her cheeks when suddenly she cast her eyes away. They came back with a guarded smile.

"Do you want to sit?" she asked, moving herself toward the door that led through the garage into the living room.

"Oh," said Saul. She kept walking. She was at the door with her hand on the knob when he took off in the other direction. He looked back at her as he ran into the driveway and pulled her with his gaze. She caught up to him halfway down the block. Excited breaths escaped her as she poured over with gaiety. Saul fought against his locking muscles until, to his delight, they found warmth and pliability. They ran for an hour down every suburban block with the sun kissing their skin to a late summer tan. Saul kept the pace faster than they had run before. Small conversations of passing sights and thoughts were had such as their lungs could allow. But for the most part, they ran, syncing one's body to the rhythm of the other.

When they circled toward the edge of town Saul steered their course toward her house beside the SummerTime orchard. They finished the jog with a strong sprint to the driveway and ended

JACOB KOCKEN

bent over hands to knees at the porch. Angela hung there stretching while Saul walked about. There was a pounding ache beneath his ribs, and he paced the driveway trying to breathe through it. Eventually, the throbbing subsided, and he took a seat on the porch step. Angela was some feet away, leaning one hand against the house and pulling up a foot to stretch her quads with the other. Saul bent forward and reached out for his toes where he sat. A sharp tension seized him through the legs and back, and Saul eased out of the stretch into a forward slump. Soon, Angela came to join him, taking a seat on the concrete step. Their bodies were close. Angela first broke the silence.

"You believe what you said before?" she asked. "Are we chosen?"

"Our own experience is the only truth we can know. I know mine to be the divine truth of revelation. I cannot speak so surely for anyone else." She was listening. It filled Saul with happiness, and he straightened out of his slouch for a moment to lay hands on his chest. "But my feelings of your role here come from this same vessel which was touched by the Lord. So, I have no fear of doubt."

"I am chosen?"

"The One tells that the joy in Heaven will be greater over one sinner who repents than over ninety-nine righteous people who need no repentance. If this gospel is true then surely its inverse is true as well. Those who squander the gift of God are more an affront to Him than the black sheep who go without Him all their lives. Your experience of the Lord was a gift, and you've left it behind in the past.

"No," she said with worried haste. "I haven't abandoned."

"You spoke already of the fog that lies between you and the Lord's gift."

"It was so long ago," she cried. "I don't know how. Help me."

"We will experience Him together. You will look upon a great force and be filled with the ecstasy of His power."

"When? How?"

"That is not up to me. It is the Lord who gifts Grace once you turn back to Him. Let us pursue Him, Angela. Instead of the meeting on Wednesday, come to me."

33.
Ira

IRA HAD WOKEN THAT DAY in a blur. His bare foot found the purloined bottle on the floor beside his bed. It went spilling, and Ira had to use a shirt from the laundry basket to wipe it up. The cap was still up on his nightstand, and the liquid line was at the glass's halfway mark. Seeing it there was a shock at first. It scrambled his pounding head, and for some minutes he lay blank in stupor. He held the bottle up and peered through the glass. The room before him curved and distorted. What was such a thing doing here? He tried to think of the night before and his head began to pound. In little bits, he relived the day. He'd gone to school. He'd come home and finished his chores. There was dinner. They'd eaten chicken. Then he remembered his grandfather's house, sneaking into the basement while the old man chopped wood. And lastly there was Anna Lee. He got a flash of the two of them at the lake. They lay down on the grass. Their faces were close together. She had the scent of pine trees on her breath. Her head lay on his arm, and their faces were so close together. There were her lips. A nervous excitement came over him.

Then Ira noticed the dryness in his mouth. He tried to swallow, but his throat rejected. He coughed and his insides began to burn. There was a terrible taste in the depths of his gullet, and Ira moved to find water. As soon as he stood, his vision reeled and sent him to a knee. The bedpost he clung to waved back and forth like a pendulum. It was several minutes before he made it to the bathroom where he lapped hungrily at the lukewarm tap. But when the water hit his stomach it began to churn. There was an awful ache travel-

JACOB KOCKEN

ing up through him, and Ira spun quickly to the toilet. He lurched forward and what came out of his mouth was black as tar. It dripped from his lips onto the porcelain, an oil spill over clear water. His throat burned and his eyes were filled with water. It came up again, the same viscous blackness.

Back in his room, Ira opened the window as wide as it could go. The smell of whiskey hung there, swirling slowly off as the breeze rolled in. Ira twisted the cap back onto the bottle and slid it to the far corner underneath his bed. As he was coming up, there was a loud and horrible sound. Ira jumped and struck the top of his head hard on the underside of his bed's wooden frame. He yelped in pain and things went blurry again. When Ira regained himself he looked around in near panic for that shrieking, rattling sound. It was only his alarm clock.

The day came and went in a malaise. Ira was pulling out of it quite slowly. Furke and Anna Lee were quiet at school. Their eyes were red, and the lot of them dragged along under a weary pall. It was around the second hour that Ira felt the heat creeping in again. It was on his skin, low and crackling. He could ignore it for a while; for whole minutes while his attention was on something. But his mind always wandered off and found it.

The heat came especially bad at the end of fourth hour. The bell had rung, and students were dispersing into the hallway when a large body came opposite the current. Ira blushed at the sight of the police officer he'd seen just two days before. The man was in his uniform again. He stood at the doorway. Gun, baton, and handcuffs were hanging at his sides where his hands rested akimbo. The flow of children slowed as the officer walked up to Mrs. Vue, the science teacher. His words were quiet and curt. The teacher straightened her back and nodded. Then, before they could disappear into the crowded hallway, Mrs. Vue grabbed the shoulder of each Paulsen twin. They were never surprised to be held back by a teacher, yet Ira saw confusion on their faces at the sight of the officer bearing down. The door shut as Ira and the rest of the students were ushered out by Mrs. Vue. One thin rectangular window showed Bobby Paulsen proffering up the shining silver of an expensive lighter toward the officer's waiting hand. Then Mrs. Vue blocked the way, and Ira ducked into the stream of students with his head down

RISE THE MOON

burning hot from the inside out.

It was decided not to do anything after school. Anna Lee said she still felt sick. Furke was going back to the flower shop. So, Ira turned homeward on his bike alone. The sun was out again today though the summer temperature seemed to be departing. He wore a t-shirt and shorts, and over all the exposed skin, Ira thought he saw the color rising. He touched a finger to his arm and pressed. It may have left a comparatively pale imprint. It may have been his imagination. Ira was never sure. He was sure, however, that there was a special relief in the breeze when the wind decided to gust and then a consequent, dreadful return to normal when the air turned still.

Somewhere down Phoenix Street, the gears on his bike began to scratch. It was not a thing he'd ever noticed before, but as his legs pedaled around and around, there came a rhythmic squeaking. The first few squeals caught him by surprise, and though he now recognized the innocent source, they would not fade from attention. Ira did not like the sounds. They made him nervous. He spent long stretches of the ride home pedaling in a quick fury and then coasting down the long blacktop streets. As long as he did not pedal, the bike did not squeak.

About half the way through his trip, Ira turned onto Lennox Avenue. It was the longest road in town; the one that followed the dried up river, straddling the old and the new sides of Graumont. The cavern where the river once was sank away some thirty feet off from the road. Ira could not see far down into it from where he sat on his rolling bike. Only the lip of the gorge was visible, yet his eyes followed that line. It was all grey rock and black dirt. Here and there some spray-painted word or symbol flashed by where the children over the years expressed a small recklessness. As Ira coasted beside this tract of land, he was set upon by a strange state. Things looked far too familiar. He'd had **déjà vu before**, but it was seldom so unsettling. He slowed and eventually came to a stop in the grass along the sidewalk. For a while, he listened. The only sounds revealing themselves were the wandering wind and the slow tick as his rear tire spun lazily on its side. Ira walked further up toward the gorge. Spray-painted walls fell out before him into the earth, and Ira jumped when he heard something sharp. It was the violent sound of flesh. He came closer still to the ledge and

JACOB KOCKEN

began to scan left and right, for he heard faintly the squeal of distress. But no one was there for as far as he could see. The chasm floor was bare but for a trickling of ancient stream. His eyes followed the water toward the bridge until something arrested his eye. Something he'd seen a thousand times without note but now bled out from the chasm wall as if Ira had put it there himself. A ball of crimson red was painted on the rock face. Dirt clouded its vibrance from years of wear. The sphere was cradled in the hand of a silhouetted person. The head was bowed toward that ruddy ball. Below, at the figure's feet were others; one of blue, of green, of yellow. The mural continued further down with a woman who held a stick of fire. Then Ira knew a voice in his head. Again there came a violent sound and Ira jumped back in pain as his own cheek began to sting. And then the sun was hot, burning a hole through his tender cheek. Ira shut his eyes hard. In quick succession, a dozen images came to him along the chasm wall with the familiarity of a dream. And the sun seared hot. It burned so bright Ira felt he could see straight through his lids.

He ran back to his bike and pedaled hard. Ira passed by the old stone bridge in a flash and did not stop. The squeaking gears of his bike rose to screeches that spurred him on even faster. He did not even check for cars as he sped through corners of his neighborhood. The wind was always on him now, yet somehow it had lost its pleasant touch.

Ira left his bike lying on the lawn. His father's Cavalier was in the driveway, but he saw no one as he came bounding up the stairs to his room. The lock shot into its hold in the door jamb behind him. Without a thought, Ira hit the floor. He fell flat on his stomach and inched into the narrow space beneath the bed. As soon as he had the bottle in grasp he was trying to stand back up. Again, the top of his head collided with the heavy wooden frame board. He doubled over and fell back sitting up against the side of the bed. He shut his eyes tight as the crowning bruise pulsed with pain, holding the bottle to his lips with both hands.

Liquor wet his lips, his tongue, and his throat. The liquid he drank did no quick quenching. Still, Ira sucked at the tip until he could take no more. It was coursing through him, washing things. Ira went to the window, hoping the air would pour in swift and

RISE THE MOON

cool. He was sweating from the forehead. Little beads ran down to his neck. Ira still held the bottle in his grip, and he tipped his head all the way back to take another draught. A minute passed and his mind began to swim. Ira paced the room slowly from the window to the door. Each time he reached the far wall the bottle was raised to sip. Again and again. Soon Ira's footstep faltered and the line he paced went crooked. Whiskey sloshed around in the glass cylinder as his arms flung out to balance.

Ira capped the bottle again and let it down longways on the floor. He kicked the rounded glass as gently as failing dexterity could manage and watched it rumble across the carpet where it disappeared back in its hiding place. Clinking sounded from under the bed where the rolling progression was stopped at the wall. It was a quick sound, high pitched and sharp. But this time Ira did not jump. This time Ira hardly noticed a thing.

A numb and pleasing buzz was rising to his head. Ira moved from the bed to the window and looked out at nothing for a long time while the numbness traveled his veins. The window was wide open. Outside, clouds were rolling in. There was no wind. Ira closed his eyes languidly and simply stood. In his dark, private world, the burning drained away. No longer did he taste the whiskey on his tongue, nor ash, nor anything unpleasant. And for many minutes there was nothing at all to make him realize the comfort of where he floated, for only the disturbance of equanimity draws the conscious eye. Ira had not known this warmth for almost as long as he had lived. The heat was gone, and a calmness remained. It was numb. Comfortable. Unnoticed.

Then Ira began to sway, unconsciously at first. His drunk head tipped him from side to side. There was a heartbeat rhythm to his leaning. He closed his eyes, and soon his feet began to pitter patter softly beneath. Ira could hear something absently in his head; a gramophone. He didn't know the song, but its melody was trapped in him. It was slow and longing. He swung too with the thought of it there beside the open, breezeless window. His thoughts began to rain from somewhere unknown, and he let them. Then the song welled up, and Ira could not stop thinking of the girl he'd lain with. He moved about with that same longing swing soaking into his bones. He swayed and tipped.

JACOB KOCKEN

There was a knock at the door. Ira started and composed himself. The world was bleary when vision returned. Ira checked the floor again to make sure the bottle was hidden safely away. Then he paced to the door, the brass handle looking fuzzy and having none of the expected cool, metallic feel to the hand as he let his father into the room.

"Come with me," said Saul. "We have a project."

His father was gone as quickly as he'd spoken. Ira followed down the hall to the master bedroom. He did his best to walk straight and upright, but his shoulders still dipped clumsily left and right as though he were a poor dancer.

There at the end of the hall, he encountered a thick, expansive carpet, rolled into a thick cylinder and leaning on its long end against the wall. Ira had little occasion to enter his parents' room, and so for the first time, noticed the floor was stripped of its old look. The furniture inside stood on bare plywood.

"I need you to help me move everything," said Saul. His voice was loud, and there was a childish smile across his face. He did not even notice Ira's fumbling around.

They first went for the dressers. His father had not emptied the shelves inside and the weight of them was almost more than they could handle. Ira's fingers fumbled over the edges of things. It took him long seconds to find a grip. But he was strong enough still despite the spinning in his head.

"When did this happen?" asked Ira, gesturing to the floor with his foggy gaze as they came to the doorway with the second dresser. His father stood in thought for a moment, trading his glance from Ira to the barren room.

"Twenty years ago I put red carpets down every hall in my hotel. Today, I'm putting red carpet in my bedroom. Jesus Himself was a carpenter; did you know? I've heard that somewhere." Then he directed Ira toward a heavy, cherry wood nightstand.

"Is that why He washes people's feet?" asked Ira.

"What's that?"

"To keep the carpets clean? At church there's a painting. Jesus washing people's feet. There's a window of it too. Stained-glass."

"Ah," said his father with a long breath out. "Perhaps it is, dear boy. Perhaps it is."

RISE THE MOON

With everything out but the bed, the two of them brought the carpet inside. It was already cut for the dimensions to fit perfectly into each corner. But when Saul snapped off the plastic wrap and began to undo the roll, he stopped in his tracks. Puzzlement overcame his face.

"It was supposed to be red," said Saul. The carpet they had before them, instead of the ruby color, was as black as night. The shag was thick and comfortable to step on, but consternation still filled his father's expression. Ira stood in silence while the two of them contemplated the calamity. "It was supposed to be red," said Saul again.

"Black looks nice," Ira offered. "At least it won't stain."

His father ran a foot over the carpet. He wore shoes as black as the new fabric, and when Saul pressed his foot down it disappeared amongst the shag. Ira had to shake his head and blink to rid it of the image that his father dangled over the invisible firmament of a great abyss.

Saul's expression changed as he looked down at his blended foot. "Okay," he said. "Yes, it could be good, Ira. And we've already moved everything after all."

As his father unwound the onyx color, Ira lifted one side of the bed and then the other until the roll was pushed through. Sunlight beaming through the bedroom window seemed to lose intensity soaking into such darkness. The whole room dampened.

Saul stood in the doorway where the glow of the hallway entered and died. "Black is a beautiful color, Ira. Don't you agree?" Ira nodded in compliance with the rapture of his father's voice.

"Yes," the boy replied.

"You've got good taste then. Like me."

"Must be in my blood."

Saul looked like he'd been struck. "Blood?"

Ira shrugged lazily, wondering if he had said the wrong thing. His father's face had gained a new expression. He was staring off into the distance, reading some invisible sign. Then in a sudden movement, Ira was grasped by the hand and led to the bathroom. There his father rummaged swiftly through a cabinet on the wall, and taking something in his palm, turned again and led Ira through the hall and down the stairway. They came immediately to the ga-

JACOB KOCKEN

rage where Saul stopped before the workbench. A dozen tubes of paint and an unblemished canvas sat waiting.

"Red," Saul began, squeezing the boy's hand with real force, "is the true color of a man. Did you know that, Ira? No? Well listen. I've something to teach you. I'm sure you've heard it said that God created man in His own image and likeness. Yes, of course you have. And that man He first endowed with breath He named Adam, didn't He? And what does that mean to you? You don't know? Has our generation so lost sight of the Word that you don't know? It means redness, Ira. This!" Here he left off squeezing Ira's hand and touched him on the cheek. "It means to show blood just like you're doing now." Indeed, Ira felt flushed. He hadn't noticed before, as it was a part of the pleasant and lulling warmth. He saw in turn that his father's face was tinted rose. "Excitement, Ira. Passion. This is when we show blood, our true color. Blood is the image of God. That is the likeness He gave us. That's it. That's it."

His father produced something from the hand that had searched the bathroom cabinet; a razor. Ira started in momentary alarm, but his father moved so quickly there was no time to object. There was a scar on the older man's hand that Ira had never noticed before. It ran the length of his palm which now lay open and displayed to him. The corner of the razor then followed that thin white line and opened it. His father did not wince, but his teeth did grit in a grimace of terrible zeal. He dropped the blade onto the workbench table and clenched his fist around the wound. Drops of hot red blood began to fall like rain onto the empty canvas.

Saul was muttering something. His eyes were not watching the blood as Ira's were. Instead, they were closed, and he went on with some private incantation.

"What do you see?" The words were spoken aloud in the midst of his invocation. Ira shuffled, unsure how to respond. "What do you see on the canvas? What picture is it making? Don't force a thought. Just say what you see."

The blood fell from an unsteady hand, and the drops spread in broken circles. Little veins ran out from each splash, connecting through the blank space all mottled and webbed. There was no fixed item to see. Now and then another bead would fall and change everything of the picture's presentation as wind does to the form of

RISE THE MOON

clouds. And with no real form of its own, the thing conjured up its beholder's concern. It emerged all at once like a Signac. Up close, it was dots. From the wide view, its gestalt struck like lightning. Ira's blood stirred as it always did when he saw her. Though the hair was red and not black, and though many of the features were only blank canvas, he saw Anna Lee clear as crystal.

"It's a woman. A beautiful woman," he said. Ira kept the specifics to himself and looked on with wonder. His father did not press him further. A confident smile broke onto his face and Saul quit his murmuring to turn up his palm. Blood ceased to fall. Then the two of them were eye to eye.

"If you need something," said Saul, "if you want something, your Father will oblige. No, don't look at me that way. I am not your Father. It's a title of vanity for a man. Your Father is the same as mine, and He obliges true disciples. Follow your passions; for He passed them on to you." Saul gestured toward the canvas. "In His own image and likeness."

34.
Evelyn

EVELYN CARRIED A SMALL ALUMINUM ladder. Its hinges were tight enough only so that it stayed open for the first few seconds after being lifted off the ground. Once its four feet were flying, the little bounces from Evelyn's plodding over the grass jarred the pieces from their lock and the front half came swinging in. Each time it did so it struck with force enough to whack one or other of her ankles. Every repeated strike reminded her of the pattern with such a sting that she cursed her forgetfulness aloud through grimaced lips. If it went on any further she thought for sure she'd have the bruises of the chain gang, and the painful step as well.

She set the ladder now underneath the full and twisted branches of an untouched tree. One of the other women set a ladder on the opposite side of the trunk. "Estan listas," said the woman. She spoke not directly to Evelyn but rather into the air, upward at the tree and its hanging fruit. Her eyes flicked like a shadow toward Evelyn who gave a soft, panlingual smile in return. Then they climbed their respective ladders, first reaching all they could from the first and second rung and placing them delicately in their burlap bags before hiking up to the third step, the fourth, and so on.

The day had been long. Evelyn could smell her own odor every time she reached forth for an apple. The shirt draping her shoulders had once been white. She wore it here most days, and now after a summer's worth of dirt and sweat, the color had dulled into patches of grey like the clouds of an incoming storm.

Weight was piling up in the sack dangling from Evelyn's left hand. With a grunt, she hoisted it up to where the ladder legs con-

RISE THE MOON

verged into a wide, flat top step; in this case, a table top. It sagged over the edges there, the little round contents sinking toward the earth. But with the help of her leaning body and one hugging arm, Evelyn managed to keep the sack upright long enough to fill it near the brim. They were paid by the pound, and more time spent picking instead of hauling sacks from tree to scale meant more money at the end of the week. Perhaps soon it would mean enough extra money to get herself a new shirt.

Evelyn had money, of course. Not a lot. All her recent time on the road precluded any type of steady income. There had been jobs here and there. But always they'd been short stints. Twice she was forced to leave before the pay period came. One of those checks hit her bank account. The other didn't, and eight full days of work went down the drain. She could have called and tried to straighten it out. She'd thought about it several times. But Evelyn had disappeared for a reason, and a chipmunk rarely calls out to the hunting hawk no matter what she feels she's owed. Rather, she'd taken to frugality. For herself and her children. Two daughters; and one even as small as Anna Lee was required a lot. While Evelyn neglected even a moderate work wardrobe for herself, it was out of the question that Anna Lee be ragged at school. Penny-pinching was often a necessity, but little would make her a stronger magnet for the scrutiny of her peers than wearing the same old sweat-stained tee day after day. Nancy was fine. Nancy didn't get dirty. She didn't stay dirty.

At the top of the ladder, Evelyn held the mouth of her apple sack with both hands. The contents nearly glowed with color. It was a red that reflected the sun so strangely, almost iridescent in the way a direct beam would break across the skin. Evelyn's fingers had to curl with all their might to hold the heavy bag steady while she lifted. The pressure of fingernails pressed into her palms even through the burlap. It took great care for her to turn around on the ladder steps without falling or dumping the loot, and a good deal more was needed to make it back down to the ground. Then began the walk. The weighing station was some hundred and fifty yards away, nearer to the center of the orchard. Every muscle in her arms began to burn quite quickly. Now and then, Evelyn set the sack down to stretch out her hands and regrip. She saw some of the others carrying toward the station as well. There were about twenty

JACOB KOCKEN

of them in all.

"Necesitas ayuda?" said a voice behind her. Evelyn had let one of her hands slip and half a dozen apples bounced to the ground. She recognized the man who'd spoken. He was tall with a kind looking dark face. His eyebrows were raised expectantly. Some of them had been there all summer, but this one was new. He'd started a couple weeks ago, and on only his second day, he'd handed her the loveliest pink blossom from one of the trees. Several of the women had taken to decorating their hair with the petals. Their stems were just long enough to lodge behind one's ear. She had kept to herself, and it was the first time one of them had approached her. She'd taken the gift cautiously and remembered how the women had watched. Some smiled when she'd set it into her curls. Some had narrowed their eyes.

Now, the same man had set his sack aside and was scooping up her lost apples. All six of them balanced easily in his one cradled arm and he let them roll softly back where they'd come.

"Muy llena," he said, gesturing at her sack. Evelyn guessed at the meaning of his words. His own bag was less than half full, the bottom part swinging lazily in his grip.

"Yes," she replied with a nervous laugh. Then she began to grip the edges of the sack again. Her aching fingers dug into the small fold of burlap and her arms flexed with all she could muster. But before she could lift, a gentle warmness lit her wrist. The man had stopped her with his free hand. There was an easy look on his face, the kind, steady eyes telling something. Then he proffered up the bag he held and gave it a little wave in her direction. Evelyn's gaze traded between their separate loads. Her lips tightened at the suggestion.

"There," said the man in a broken accent. One of his fingers was raised and pointing to the weigh station near the center of the orchard. "To there." He set his apples at her heel and took up her full pack with a swift pull. "Ooo." He grunted the expression with a mock severity on his face as he rocked the sack to and fro, weighing it. Evelyn slung the other bag over her shoulder, and they began to walk.

He was a handsome man. Evelyn enjoyed the look of his taut arms gleaming with summer sweat. They walked side by side and

RISE THE MOON

looked now and then at each other. It was a quiet trek over the grass but pleasant. He had the natural aroma of something softly sweet, and Evelyn was mindful of how the breeze brought him to her. She was reminded of her husband. Her late husband. She closed her eyes a while and listened to this man's feet swishing through the grass, his scent bleeding through the air. Suddenly, her face began to quiver, and she opened her eyes again. They were struck by the sun's pin needle beams and her pupils contracted in pain.

They had arrived at the weigh station. A line of workers led to a small brick structure. It was a cube of ten-by-ten feet or so jutting out from one of the largest buildings in Graumont. The station was open halfway up by means of a retracted door that spanned the façade's full length. Two men sat behind the little wall at a desk taking bags and jotting notes. They were uniformed in all white except for the black SummerTime script across the breast pocket. They worked quickly, rolling the bag's contents onto a wide steel scale and picking through the pile for damaged goods before repackaging them in cardboard boxes and sending them off on a conveyer that disappeared into the belly of the building. Evelyn's eyes, however, were on the man beside her. He had not given her bag back yet. As the line in front of them diminished, she began tapping him on the arm.

Trade back," she said after swinging the lighter bag off her shoulder and holding it out to him. For a moment he simply stared ahead, the kindness on his face half shrouded by profile. Evelyn's tapping fingers turned to knuckles as if his arm were a thick walnut door. Just as the woman ahead of them had her weight recorded and sack returned, the tall man broke. He turned toward Evelyn with a charming smirk as if he had pulled off a riotous joke. He set her full bag down, leaning safely against her leg and took back his paltry pickings. Evelyn let out a breath of relief and looked at him with an intensely furrowed brow. His smile grew even larger, pressing his young skin into the folds of an eighty-year-old prankster.

"Next," said one of the men behind the partition. The handsome man took a step back, and with a little bow of the head, made way for Evelyn to go first. Before she hoisted her bag to the desk top however, Evelyn grabbed four apples from the brim of her stack and stuck them into the loose, gaping mouth of her new comrade's sack where it hung open under one of his brawny hands. She gave a quick nod to his surprised expression and turned back to the men in white.

They took her load of apples and spread them into the scale's bowl. The needle read just over thirty-two pounds. "Name?" said one of the men in white as he took up a pen and bent over a clipboard on the desk.

"Scarlet Lac," said Evelyn. The man found her line and recorded the numbers.

"Off you go," he said, handing her the now empty burlap. Evelyn turned away, and the man who'd helped her took the place.

The grass was a solace for Evelyn's exhausted body as she walked back toward her work. The softness of it was exceptional, almost preternatural in its fullness and how it eased the step even through the rubber soles of her shoes. Her arms were aching to the fingertip and her back felt near to spasms. She wanted little more at that moment than to wipe the sweat away from her eyes and lay down on the earth.

But on she walked until the boughs of the apple trees darkened the sky above her. Before she could come to the place where the ladder awaited her climb, there was a soft but hurried sound behind her. It was the handsome man again. He was holding two burlap sacks. One was his own, and with the other draping his hand he gestured between Evelyn and the expanse of green lawn behind them. She had dropped it somewhere along the walk.

"Oh," she said. "Why, thank you." When he offered up the bag to be taken, their hands touched. Seeming to catch the longing in her eye, he reached forth again, and this time grabbed her other, free hand. It fit easily in his gentle grip. He turned his palm upward then and raised the back of her hand to his bowing head. He kissed the middle knuckle quickly and when his face rose again it had flushed inside with color.

"Mañana?"

"Sorry?" said Evelyn with a tilt of the head. She too had gone rosy around the cheeks and might have known the word somewhere in the back of her brain but wanted secretly to protract the moment.

"Mañana," he said again. This time he looked once over each shoulder and found the sun beginning its descent. He let go of her

RISE THE MOON

hand to point at the Phoebean king and indicated a slow orbit with his finger until he had passed the horizon and the ground beneath them and ended up back at the summit of the circle. Then he pointed in quick succession at her and at the ground where they stood.

"Yes," said Evelyn. She twisted the burlap sack into a tight cylinder between her fists. Suddenly, she had been flooded with energy. She felt young again for a moment, though she was not particularly old. "Yes. Mañana. I'll be here." She mimicked his pointing at herself and the ground. The handsome man smiled. Then someone called out and his head snapped in the direction of the voice. An older man some thirty yards away was halfway up a ladder with both arms raised in the air, one of them picking an apple from the branch and the other waving impatiently at he who stood beside Evelyn. The handsome man touched her shoulder once more. It was a light touch, but so strong and warm. Then he nodded at her a final time and trod off to join his people.

Evelyn watched the definition through the moist back of his shirt as he left. When at last the breeze had ushered off the scent of him, Evelyn returned her thoughts to the task. She lifted the aluminum ladder to bring it to another fruitful spot on the tree. Again, the far legs swung shut as she walked and slammed the weight of it into her shins with the dull clang of metal on bone.

"God damn it," she muttered through her teeth. The blood that had risen in her cheeks some moments ago rushed out and filled in at the front of her leg as the site began to swell. Another spot added to the litany of aches as she set the ladder in place and began to mount it again. At last, she came near the top and turned her sights up to the canopy. She looked around to find the fullest of fruits. She leaned into the steep angle of the remaining rungs to steady herself as she plucked the heaviest looking apple around and let it drop into her empty burlap sack.

By THE TIME EVELYN WAS in her Pinto rolling back down the road toward Old Graumont, the sky had gone indigo with the diaphanous haze of twilight. The sun sunk away in her rear-view mirror, and the trees welcomed her as she passed the burnt barnyard that led down the only forest road. The neighborhood was as desolate as usual. The few houses she passed were still and quiet, their slipping

JACOB KOCKEN

foundations the only sign of movement past or present. The breeze was quelled by thick wilderness. Birdsong had ceased for the day. Engine thrusts and the crunch of broken pavement under tires was the extent of the forest hum.

Soon the scent of ash overpowered her, announcing an arrival home. There was a light on in their house, the only one as far as the eye could penetrate. Evelyn parked along the side of the house so close to the frame that Nancy's window could only be seen through those of the Pinto. The aches in her feet renewed when she stood up from the car. The grass here was no solace.

Inside, her daughter was sitting at the dining table. There was a pen in the girl's hand, and her notebook was open to a half-scrawled page.

"Hello."

"Hello," said Anna Lee. All the while she did not look up from her work.

"Did you eat?"

"I heated up the soup you made on Tuesday."

"Nancy?"

"That. And bread. She didn't spill. I helped her."

"Thank you."

"It might still be warm."

Evelyn opened the refrigerator and removed a wide black pot. Beneath the lid there sloshed a drying puddle of broth. A few waterlogged carrots and onions floated in the soup while others clung to the sides of the pot. She dipped a finger in to find it a liquid patchwork of warm and cold spots. Evelyn's stomach was tight with hunger and neglecting the stove she poured the last of the portions into a dime store plastic bowl. It tasted mostly of water and salt. But Evelyn ate. All this while, the scratching of pen on charred paper underscored the silence with its jagged rhythm.

"What are you writing about?" asked Evelyn.

"Dad."

"About anything in particular?"

"Yes," said Anna Lee. "The thunderstorm."

"When you two didn't come home all night? And you stayed in a cave watching the lightning?"

"We saw it hit one of the trees. It burst into flames and burned

RISE THE MOON

in the rain. Dad said he'd never seen it happen before. I was his lucky charm. Only good things happened to him when I was there. That's what he said."

"Yes," said Evelyn. "I know, hun. I know." Anna Lee's head lowered even further. Her face was nearly flat with the table, and the scratching of her writing had made an abrupt halt. Evelyn let her spoon fall, splashing in what was left of the shallow soup. She stood and bent over the backrest of her daughter's chair, hugging Anna Lee from behind and rubbing the girl's knobby shoulders. "I know, baby," she cooed. "Baby, I know."

Evelyn buried her own face into the crook of her daughter's neck. She kissed the skin and squeezed tight several times. Anna Lee's long dark hair fell over both of their faces, and they sniffled under their private veil. Her daughter smelled vaguely like milk and fresh baked bread. She always had to Evelyn though it was subtle now beneath the scents of perspiration and notes of perfume.

"Are you still hungry, baby?" Evelyn asked at last.

"Yes."

Evelyn stood back again, letting her hands trace the nape of Anna Lee's neck before she stalked back into the kitchen. There was a jar of peanut butter left in the pantry. When Evelyn picked it up it felt light and hollow. She dug a rubber spatula out from one of the drawers and placed both on the table beside Anna Lee. "Finish that off for now." Evelyn left for her bedroom to change into cleaner clothes. On the way there and back, she observed the fastened bolt lock on the outside of Nancy's door. Before returning to the main rooms, she undid the lock and poked her head into her other daughter's dwelling. Light trickled in from the hallway, throwing a golden shadow over the bed where Nancy lay sleeping. She was at as perfect peace as ever, her body sprawled mindlessly across the mattress so that one leg and one arm hung off opposite sides. The girl defined that same calming scent of warm milk that suffused the air all about the room. Evelyn blew a kiss from where she stood and closed the door with care.

"I'm going to run to town," she said to Anna Lee back in the kitchen. Evelyn wore a sweatshirt now, one with a hood that stuck out past her face even though the night was sultry. "I didn't realize how low things were."

JACOB KOCKEN

"Okay."

"Is there anything you want?"

"No."

"Nothing special? Ice cream again? It's not expensive."

"Not this time."

Evelyn squeezed her daughter's shoulder and was on the way out into the evening air with car keys in hand when Anna Lee's voice sounded again.

"Mom?" she said. Her voice wavered, venturing. "What about a bathing suit?"

"A bathing suit?"

"I was going to go swimming tomorrow. Someone invited me."

"Who did?"

"Just some school kids."

"Swimming where? Their house?"

"No," said Anna Lee. "There's a lake. On the other side of town."

"You mean Duval Park?" Anna Lee nodded. Evelyn slipped her ring of keys from her hand back to her pocket and rejoined her daughter at the table. Anna Lee looked up with soft eyes. Evelyn smiled fondly. She took a seat across from her daughter. "I used to go there too, you know."

"You did?"

"Everyone here did at some point. When I was young, your grandfather used to take me out on the water in a canoe and paddle around to catch the turtles. It's a big lake. There are so many little pockets where it bends around the trees. The best place to find turtles is by shore though. That's where there's lily pads or fallen logs for them to bask in the sun. I remember once we were sneaking up on a family of them. There must have been five or six all balanced on a floating old oak branch. Your grandfather could paddle soft as a swan so they wouldn't notice. He always let me hold the net and sit in the front of the boat. Well, we were gliding in, just about in reach when all of a sudden there flashed in front of us the pink torso of a sunburned boy. He'd run from up on the shore and jumped straight out at the turtles."

"He jumped on them?"

"Ha ha!" cried Evelyn. "Almost! He almost jumped on us too.

RISE THE MOON

But no, he crashed into the lake stomach first and sent up a splash that scared every turtle around for miles and left both me and my dad half soaked. I was furious. After the confusion wore off that is. I was furious, but your grandfather threw his head back in laughter because when that boy broke the surface again there was the mama turtle squirming in his grasp. A chorus of excitement came from further up the shore where a dozen bare-chested boys were cheering."

"They sound obnoxious," Anna Lee said. She'd cracked a grin though.

"Obnoxious doesn't begin to describe what that boy would be to me," said Evelyn. "Do you know what his name was?"

"What?"

"Claude." Anna Lee's eyes shot wide. She dropped her pen, and the grin that had begun to crack on her face turned into a fully fledged smile.

"Dad?"

"That's how we met alright," said Evelyn. "Then I hit him with the net for stealing my catch. He looked so alarmed. He was so focused on his jump he didn't even see us in the canoe. At least, that's what he told me some years later. I never believed that though. I think he wanted to splash me."

"Years later? Why'd it take so long?"

"He ran away after I hit him!" Evelyn cried. "That was the first time we met. We went to different schools though, and I didn't meet him again until a long time later. Shortly before your sister was born actually. He stole my heart quickly. Just jumped out and grabbed it from someone else like it was a basking turtle."

Anna Lee's eyes had the varnish of thought. There was tenderness on her expression as she looked out into nowhere. Then, when she came away from reverie she picked up her pen and straightened the notebook in front of her.

"Can I put that in here?" said Anna Lee. "That story?"

"Of course, dear." Evelyn stood. "You can add that he was in his underwear. That's what a lot of people did back then at the lake. But I'm sure it's not the way nowadays. I'll get you a bathing suit, Annie. I'll get you one. I'd better be going. It's getting late."

Evelyn left the house in warm spirits. The joy was tempered

JACOB KOCKEN

some by the sight of the former neighbor's yard. It was less than a skeleton, a graveyard of destruction. Evelyn could feel heat still running off those ashes.

The drive into town was quiet. Evelyn was lost in her thoughts, and she did not turn on the radio. When the bridge was behind her and the length of Lennox Ave along the old river began also to recede, there emerged from out of the ground a labyrinth of lights, passing cars, and buildings large enough to rival that at Summer-Time. She stopped first at the mall.

Evelyn flipped up the hood of her sweatshirt and entered through the big glass doors. The entryway was capacious and cold, marble tiles all around swimming in a draft from industrial air conditioners up above. There was only a smattering of people walking about the main drag of the mall. Most of who she saw were dressed in uniformed polos for this or that boutique and restaurant. The ceiling lights directly overhead were still on, but to the right and left there sunk into the walls several rectangular chasms. These dark tunnels were fortified by bars. The cage doors had come down in front of more than half the shops, and Evelyn began to step more swiftly through the hall. Her head swung side to side looking at neon signs above the thresholds. The whole stretch was blinking into darkness.

"Closing up ma'am," said a security guard as Evelyn came to the end of the passage and stopped, looking back at what she may have missed.

"Already?"

"Afraid so."

"Isn't there anything open?"

"Mall closes at eight," he said. "It's eight."

"I'm only looking for a bathing suit. I'd be very quick."

"Apologies. I don't run the stores, just clear people out when it's time."

The corridor turned even darker and emptier on the way back out. Soon Evelyn could hear the clapping of her own feet echo against the flat, barren walls. The happy mood she'd left the house with had been quelled entirely. When the big glass doors shut behind her they connected with the magnetic click of a lock, and the big ceiling lights that lit the way powered down to a dim glow.

RISE THE MOON

Evelyn found much of the rest of the city was closing up shop as well. There were lights in every direction, but they belonged to traffic, gas stations, hotels, and restaurants. She looked around for anywhere that might sell clothing late in the evening. Finding nothing yet, she pulled into the grocery store.

Evelyn filled her cart with care. She bought necessities and staples. Bread, milk, eggs. She bought cereal because it was cheap and shelf stable. Nancy loved Lucky Charms, so she got those along with others that claimed less sugar. The chicken breasts cost less if they were still on the bone. There was a sale on ground beef. Cans of beans. Iceberg lettuce. When she had scoured every isle and came again toward the front of the store, she found a man in a red vest counting endcap inventory.

"Excuse me," said Evelyn. "I know it's probably the wrong place, but you don't happen to sell summer things at all, do you? Bathing suits?"

The man pointed to a small shelf between the door and register. "There's some miscellaneous things there. Sunscreen for sure. No clothing though, unless you're looking for sun glasses. Styles for all ages. Would you like me to take you to eyewear? There's a rack just that way."

"No," said Evelyn. "Thank you." She brought her cart to the register and unzipped her purse while the cashier scanned her things. She fingered through a scanty bill collection while the beeping of the scanner went on, keeping a daunting pace.

"Sixty-three dollars and forty-eight cents," said the girl behind the drawer. Evelyn counted out her money. She counted again.

"Can I put that back? Yes both boxes."

"Fifty-four eighty-nine now." Evelyn handed over what she had. "Eleven cents, your change." The girl handed Evelyn a dime and a penny which she stowed away in her purse's protected inside pocket.

Evelyn stashed each of her bags in the trunk of the Pinto and went to return her cart. As she did so, another woman exited the store. A harsh clangor vibrated the air as their carts collided. Evelyn doubled over her handle bar and saw the twinkling lights of silver and bronze as it rained down to the ground below.

"Oh no," exclaimed the other woman. She was fumbling with

JACOB KOCKEN

a coin purse and a large box between her arms, balanced on top of an overloaded haul.

"I'm so sorry," said Evelyn. She crouched to the ground, reaching in every direction as she picked up loose coins. The other woman bent down to join, and the box she had been steadying fell to the ground as well.

"Damn it," the woman said. Evelyn retrieved the rest of the change while the stranger checked on her other fallen goods. It was a box Evelyn recognized. She had seen hundreds of them today alone. *SummerTime,* it said on the side. Beneath the bright lights of the grocery entry, that red and yellow script she so often saw seemed to shine and taunt her. Little globes of idyllic red were rolling away across the concrete.

When everything had been collected Evelyn had two fists full of mixed metals. She stood up as the woman reset her things and pulled out the coin purse again. "Thank you," she said curtly as Evelyn slid a pile of coins into the open pouch. The woman stalked off as soon as the clinking had ceased.

The lady's back was already to Evelyn when she muttered, "Ma'am," and the clatter of a cart across the parking lot cobblestones rang between them. Evening embraced the other shopper, and she was a faceless silhouette when she turned back.

"Did you say something?" Evelyn stood there with a fist clenched tightly around the other dimes and nickels.

"Just sorry," she said.

"It's nothing," the woman assured her. Then she continued her walk through the lot, and Evelyn moved in the other direction toward her car. Back in the driver's seat of the Pinto, she secured thirty-five cents somberly in the pocket of her purse.

All light from the sun had left the sky, and stars were beginning to blink on distantly. Evelyn fancied she could hear a jingling from the passenger side where her purse sat as the Pinto rolled out of the city and back onto the long stretch of Lennox Avenue back toward the suburbs. She contemplated driving to Holcomb, the next city over. Perhaps there she might find a department store with later hours. But no. The drive would cost gas, and even if the needle were not already a quarter from empty, she had only a pittance left in her purse that couldn't hope to buy a bathing suit off anyone's

RISE THE MOON

shelves. This time she turned on the radio, trying to distract from the thoughts in her head. Aside from her daughter's wishes, Evelyn's mind was piqued by her run in with the woman and the cart. It was not the thirty-five cents, though she did feel a lowly shame. Nor was it that the face of the woman was one she'd seen before; one from the years she'd spent growing up in this town, whose sense of recognition had the mercy not to reciprocate. It was that she kept picturing the scene, the two of them bent to the ground, one picking up loose coins; the other, loose fruit. *SummerTime*. The words and the logo had faced her there on the ground, glowing in the grocery store light like a neon sign amidst the rest of the darkened cityscape.

And as Lennox Avenue ticked by and the bridge back into Old Graumont coalesced from the black backdrop, Evelyn kept her foot on the accelerator and breezed by down the road that she traveled nearly every day into the prairies and the endless farmland beyond.

Silver moonlight colored the landscape as it flattened out. From somewhere in the hidden distance, a wolf or coyote or perhaps a canine of other nature let loose a howl to the sky. It stretched on like an animate medieval bugle announcing arrival of some king or emissary. It ceased as Evelyn's Pinto slowed to the side of the road. She parked along the great iron-wrought fence, stopping just before the gate that split the SummerTime words. Through the iron fence posts, the orchard was serene. No movement disturbed the trees. Even the wind seemed blocked from the property. The building at its center loomed in the night as a behemoth shadow. Its blocky form during the day was molded now so that its edges softened and appeared in its rising and falling sections like a beast in crouch, held back only by the iron bars of its cage.

But Evelyn did not approach the SummerTime gate. She turned instead to the opposite side of the street. Directly across the way, there were two buildings. Houses; one with a modern appearance in its squared-up shape and plastic siding, the other a more Victorian build with its height, spires, and a steep rooftop cap with an intricate latticework of black gables. Evelyn walked up to this older, larger house. Its front porch was wide and swung around the length of the building. There was an aged creak as she trod up the steps and onto these first wooden floorboards. A wide overhanging

JACOB KOCKEN

roof stretched above her that would have cast everything into shadow if not for the single light beside the doorway. The bulb gave off a yellow, incandescent glow and revealed a heavy iron knocker fixed to the center of the door. Evelyn took the cold metal backward and swung it three times into the wood. Dull thuds carried into the house, and after several seconds, they returned in the form of profound footfalls that could be heard even through the walls. Evelyn stepped back as the door opened in front of her and a mastiff of a man leaned into the jamb.

"Ms. Lac!" barked the man with a private grin. "Ms. Scarlet Lac." His voice was loud as always and made her twitch like a startled rabbit. His muscular frame towered nearly all the way to the top of the threshold. The dress upon him was informal but rich. A robe of dark purple satin draped the boulder shoulders. It came together partway down his body, revealing a mat of straight black fur over a powerful chest.

"Hello," said Evelyn. She found herself looking at the ground and dragged her eyes up to meet his.

"What brings you here?" He began to say. Then he waved a hand and cut himself off. "No. No. First thing's hospitality. Come in, my sweet." He held the door with one of his mammoth arms and she entered the home.

It was larger inside even than it appeared without. The ceilings were tall, fifteen feet at least. As soon as the door was shut behind her, the feeling of evening disappeared. All around were lights. A chandelier of a thousand crystalline pieces hung above them in the foyer. The walls of the room were white with gold trim. The carpet was a pristine ivory color even at the entrance where worn shoes lined the wall. But what drew Evelyn's attention foremost was that which did not seem to fit within the immaculate atmosphere. From the eastern wall of the house, a smell of damp earth floated subtly among the other scents of living. That entire wall was transparent. Tall windows traversed its length that in the daytime would have filled the room with all the natural light one could bear. And standing along this glass façade were a dozen planter pots. Each one was two feet tall and at least as wide. Sapling trees of various ages and conditions stretched up from the black earth inside the pots.

"Experiments," said the booming voice of the giant man.

RISE THE MOON

"Here, look at this one." Evelyn took three strides to his one across the capacious room. When they came to the third plant from the left the big man crouched down to his haunches. "Feel this," he said. His two great forefingers stretched out and stroked demonstrably across one of the little tree limbs. She followed his instruction and felt the bough. Its bark was smooth and well bodied already. The tiny buds and leaves sprouting out from it were a deep, lively green and stood out strong and straight as if they were reaching for the moon.

"Know what that is?" said the man. His eyes glistened with admiration. "Water retention." Then the two large fingers that had stroked the tree bough turned downward toward the earth packed into the ceramic pot. He dug with a delicate motion, revealing a tangle of spindly brown veins, roots searching their limited space and gripping the ground around them. "It all happens out of sight," he said. "It's a complicated chain, this directed evolution. I can't tell you how many generations these went through; shrinking the pot size, restricting water, breeding still for high root density and bifurcation. But they get better and better every year, and now here we are looking at it. Exciting! Ha! They're mighty heavy. You can't tell by looking but these thirsty demons drink three times as much as their originals. I have to water them twice a day at least! If one snapped at the trunk it would spray like a hydrant. Imagine that! Enough water to wash away the world."

"Fascinating," said Evelyn.

"Yes, you were never one for science talk, were you? Forget it, my sweet. Put it out of your mind."

They stood, and a hand that spanned her entire width pressed the small of Evelyn's back. He guided her this way into the belly of the house past the first walls and into a dining room whose ambiance, due to ancient wood paneling and the soft golden glow of candles, was less imposing than the front of the house. The table in the middle of the room, however, was enormous. There were twenty seats in all. The man pulled out a chair for her just adjacent to the head. Each one of the backrests was carved into flowing arabesques of wood. All were ornamented in their own fashion, some with gold, others with glittering colors of emerald or sapphire. Still others were not inlaid with precious things, but rather displayed

JACOB KOCKEN

with portraits of ravens or wolves carved in detailed relief. Evelyn sat down and felt a ring of pearls circle her spine. The man gestured for her to wait and left the room a minute before returning with two glasses filled halfway up with an aromatic red wine. He swirled both glasses in opposite directions and held them out to his guest. Evelyn picked the one in his left hand and sipped it. He smiled and took the seat at the head of the table.

"Now," he said. "What is it that brings you here so late an evening?" Evelyn could feel his voice in her hand as it vibrated the wine glass.

"I need a favor," she said.

"Oh, you're full of that need lately, Ms. Lac!" He said the name with a special inflection. "You're not finding the work to your liking? Is it the pay? Does someone know you?"

"It's not the work."

"No need to pussyfoot Evie. I know what it's about."

"Do you?"

"It's your handsome fellow!" He slapped the table with a heavy, jovialar laugh. "Ha! Yes, I can see from my window. I'm hard at work upstairs but it doesn't take long to see. He adores you, doesn't he? What spell did you learn, my dear? How did you enchant him so? Carrying your load all the way from the trees. Ha! What did you talk about as you walked? Does he know enough words to speak of Chopin? That's your favorite, I know. Say, do your fingers still know the dance? Want to give it a go? *Fantaisie-Impromptu?*"

"I'm afraid they don't," said Evelyn. "They're more used to picking apples now."

"Nonsense," the man barked. "Leave off the excuses. Leave off the pedestrian. Come. If you can play it, I'll give you what you came for. The favor. To the best of my ability. No questions. Come. I haven't had someone sophisticated in so long. Come." As quickly as he had sat her down in the chair, the enormous man pulled her up and ushered her to the end of the long room where a grand piano sat reflecting candle light off its smooth ivory teeth.

Evelyn sat on the little bench. She could feel rather than see his weighty presence standing directly behind her. There was a book of Chopin already on the music stand. She flipped a few pages further in and found the title. The man was breathing hoarsely through his

RISE THE MOON

mouth, she could hear it. To cover the sound of his panting, Evelyn began to play. Her fingers were still nimble but out of practice. Reading the music came back easily as embodied recollections do. The first measures began easily enough. Her time was irregular but close enough for the notes to match the memory of their perfect form from some years back. For a moment, Evelyn loved the song again. Then however, the pace increased, and the complexity of the composer overtook her rusted abilities. Her fingers lost their place first, then her eyes. She tried to reset and start from the beginning of the troubling measures several times. But it wasn't to be done and soon enough the sheet music went flying upward, swiped off the stand from overhead by the giant. He closed the book and set it neatly on the lid of the piano.

"Close enough," he said. There was still a sense of satisfaction in his voice as he once again stood her up and placed his hand around her waist to lead the way back across the room. His touch felt warm and damp even through her sweatshirt. They came back to the head of the table and took the same chairs again. Evelyn began to speak but he sprang ahead, cutting off her words, "Not yet! Not yet! Talk first. Just pleasantly. I haven't heard anything of your life yet. Not the job. Of course, I know what happens there. But you! Your daughters, how are they my dear Evie? How are the pups? Are they healthy? Are you keeping up? Are they staying out of trouble?"

"They're well," said Evelyn. "Healthy I mean. You know Nancy. Anna Lee has been better since school started. Less gloomy I mean. It's been hard on her, on both of us, since Claude…"

"Ha!" the man exclaimed. This time it was more a shout than a laugh. "I knew it! It comes around so quickly. Back to your handsome man. You're lonely! What a pair you'd make. I'm sure he speaks a sort of sign language though, something anyone can understand." The man's eyebrows raised at the suggestion. "Ha! Apologies. I'm indecorous. Of course, you're lonely and want a replacement. He may even be younger than you. Have you asked? Veinteocho, that's my guess."

"That's not it," said Evelyn.

"Older you think? Younger?"

"I'm not looking for a man."

JACOB KOCKEN

"No?" said the giant. "No. No, of course you're not. You can handle that, an attractive lady such as you. Well then, fine, out with it. No more dallying. We'll work something out. What have you come for?"

"Two things," said Evelyn.

"Two things? Half a song for two favors? Two asks? You're always so ambitious. Well, do the easy one first. The one about the money."

"Yes," said Evelyn. "I need money."

"You said you could pick apples!" The man was having riotous fun. "Labor was your pick!"

"I need more for the kids."

"How much money could they suck? Two children. Two even? There's the first one. Nancy you decided to name her? Well, come now. Is there any expense but food? And the other one. She's so small."

"I need more."

"Yes, well, of course you do. I know. I know. I'm only toying. It's mean of me. It's indecorous. We can find another job. A promotion! That's what it is, you know. A promotion!" Just then, amidst the giant's hollering, there was a sound of descending footsteps above them. The staircase was tall and wrapped around the outside of the dining room, surrounding them with the sound of quick little pats like a distant snare drum.

Then the tapping ceased, and a woman emerged from behind the partition. She was older than Evelyn though her skin still glistened with a youthful animation. Her hair was a washed out yellow and was tied up behind her head in a long, sleek pony tail. She was dressed exactly as the tall man in a robe of dark purple satin. Dangling from around her neck was a fine necklace with one shining pearl. She pulled the opening tighter below the neck when she saw Evelyn, and her eyes narrowed.

"Company, Brock?" said the woman.

"A surprise my dear," said the giant man. "It's Evelyn Pollard. You remember the name?"

"Yes." She did not approach them.

"Evie," he said with two graciously gestured hands and a slight bow of the head. "This is my Chesil." Evelyn greeted the woman

RISE THE MOON

but was not returned the kindness.

"Evelyn came to discuss business. She wants a promotion."

"Isn't that something to do at work? During business hours, so to speak."

"Ha!" the big man howled. "She plays with words. Evie, you get to hear my Chesil. She's really very clever with words. Very clever. She's a talent. Look at her blush! Is that a smile creeping out? Yes, you can't stay sour so long you little devil. Come here!" The woman's hard face tempered some and she came waltzing over almost at a skip. The man put a heavy hand upon the curve of her backside and said, "Where did you come up with that one? Business hours! Ha!" Chesil was overcome with giddiness. Her arms scrunched together before her chest to contain a bursting verve.

"It just came to me," she squealed.

"It certainly did you little devil," the big man said. "You little hellhound. Now, of course you are right. It's unusual to have such a talk as this at night. And in our house, at that. It was indecorous. Indecorous! But we've had talks about your jealousy, haven't we? Yes. And after all, it was a surprise for both Evelyn and I. She was just driving by, and the feeling overcame her. You understand that, yes? A spur of the moment. You must forgive us. Yes? You forgive us then?"

"Oh alright," said the woman. "I do. I forgive you." There was a wry smile across her happy cheeks, and glistening eyes lit alternately on Evelyn and the giant.

"That was easy wasn't it?"

"Easy," said the woman. "Did I hear Chopin? Were you playing?"

"Yes!" roared the big man. "Evelyn was. *Fantaisie*."

"I can play Chopin!"

"Yes you can! Better than anyone! Darling, please exhibit. Evie, listen. You must hear her play. Chesil is a demon on the keys, an angel." The giant's woman blushed and fluttered over to the waiting instrument. But the moment she sat down another set of steps sounded from the hall.

A second woman, blond with similar dress to the first entered from around the corner. "Brock, dear," she said. "What's this?"

"Rachel!" The giant waved her in. "We have unexpected com-

JACOB KOCKEN

pany." But the woman turned slightly to reveal a phone held up to the other side of her head.

"I've got Angela on the line."

"Oh! How's my baby girl?"

"She's got a man in her life," the woman's eyes widened with excitement.

"Does she now?" The mastiff of a man faltered. Then a smile was forced out across his canines. "How wonderful. We ought to meet the young pup. Give her my best." Rachel nodded with exuberance before ducking away again behind the partition.

An exaggerated clearing of the throat came from the direction of the piano. Chesil looked hard in their direction, calling the audience's attention back to her. Then her fingers found the page in the music book, and she began to play.

Evelyn sat still, listening to the melody slowly build. The notes were pure, and Chesil's thin, naked fingers kept perfect time. When the music took its sudden rise in tempo the room was filled with the beauty of her playing. And beneath the sound of *Fantaisie*, the giant leaned to Evelyn and spoke for the first time tonight in low, whispered tones.

"I'm glad you've come tonight, Evie. I'm glad you've come around." Then the enormous hand left its resting place on the table and found Evelyn's leg. He caressed her up from the knee. "Finish your wine." The glass still sat on the table beside her over half full. Evelyn took it by the stem and opened her throat. She swallowed it all in one bitter cascade. The sting in her mouth was strong and covered most of the pain as the big man took up one of the knives from the table and opened a small slit across the palm of her hand. The hand she held the empty glass in lowered down to catch the stream as the man squeezed. Evelyn's fingers turned a purplish red and drops of blood ran down to join the dregs of cabernet.

"The music slows here," he said. His breath was wet on her ear, and his hand explored to the rhythm of the piece. Then his chair rumbled across the floor, and he was behind her. The second hand found her waist. "Come again tomorrow, my sweet Evie," he said. "Chesil is one of my favorites. She plays this every night."

35.
Ira

IRA WAS IN THE BACK seat of his father's Cavalier longing for the ride to be over. The air conditioning had never worked, and the windows were up. His parents didn't seem to mind, but as the young day progressed, Ira had begun feeling stuffy and hot again. They were driving back home from Meyer Studios, a small professional photographer. The man who had taken their family photo was the same one Ira recognized from his head shots for the school year book. Mr. Meyer was a stocky fellow with a clean-shaven face except for the great, tar-black moustache on his upper lip. This facial hair was comically thick and drew attention away from his eyes when he spoke. When he prepared to photograph the children at the beginning of each year, this bouncing bush aided the coaxing of genuine smiles from his subjects. It was silly. Today, however, Ira found none of the usual amusement at the man's appearance. His mind was elsewhere, and indeed, his parents seemed hardly enthusiastic either.

They'd tried a few different poses on the studio dais, Ira always acting as the focal point whether sitting in the middle or having his parents' bodies turned open to face him. Mr. Meyer had some trouble finding a way for the three of them to fit naturally together, a shape that would look nice in the frame. Blinding camera flashes went off a dozen times before Mr. Meyer dismissed them from the little stage.

Miriam took a look at the samples and pointed her finger to a few before deciding. She placed her orders for wallet-sized and wall piece photos and was told they'd be ready in just a few days.

JACOB KOCKEN

When they arrived home at last, Ira hustled to his bike. He went first to Furke's house and found his friend lathering himself with sun block.

"You want any?" Furke offered the plastic squeeze tube.

"No thanks."

"Yeah, you don't burn so easy, do you? Not so easy as me. I got one brown spot for every day the sun saw me." Furke's long, freckle-mottled limbs were able to bend around and spread the sun screen over his spine and shoulder blades unassisted.

The water would likely be cold. Despite the daytime heat, as the days marched toward autumn, the night chill snuck in more and more. The boys told her people stopped swimming halfway through September, especially in the lake whose depths once shed of summer heat refused all efforts of the sun. But Anna Lee had said she wanted to swim.

Anna Lee did not own a bike, so they had arranged to pick her up from the east side of town. The two boys could not bring her one to ride, of course, but Furke's bike had pegs. Furke and Ira only got as far as the bridge that centered Graumont before finding her. She was sitting on one of the wide stone ledges above the gorge. She was dressed in usual clothes. Her dark hair and loose blue t-shirt tossed back and forth in the hesitant, late-summer wind. She was bent over something held in her hand. When the boys came within easy earshot Anna Lee looked up from her muse. She stuffed something in her pocket, and when the empty hand came back out it shot into the air, waving at them with girlish exuberance.

The boys crossed the bridge, and in haste their tires skid over the eastern side's gravel road. She was still sitting when they came to her, and Ira was struck by a visual echo. The way she dangled her feet as she sat at the edge, wagging them lazily into the depths, rebirthed a blurry vision of some nights ago how she sat at the edge of Lake Duval. He got the sudden urge to sit beside her. They had lain together that night with their faces close together.

"Hey," she said.

"You ready?" said Furke. Anna Lee nodded and stood up. As soon as she did this, Ira let his bike drop. It clamored on the ground as the gears rattled together, and in the space it took to fall, Ira was beside the girl, hugging her. His arms were wrapped tightly, one

RISE THE MOON

up at the shoulders, the other down around her waist. He could feel Anna Lee was caught by surprise. She simply hung there for a second. Then her arms came around him and squeezed back, and the dreamy memory he had of lying together sparked again. Ira inched even closer and felt his shoe cross over hers, their legs ever so slightly entwined.

"Careful," said Furke's voice. A second pair of hands took hold of Ira and pulled. "Don't fall now." Ira looked down at his feet and noticed their proximity to the ledge. One of Anna Lee's heels was suspended. She gave a little gasp of fright and wobbled as Furke pulled the two of them into prairie grass safety.

"Thanks," said Anna Lee. She was looking up at Furke. Ira stepped deliberately in front of his friend. Now she was looking at him. Anna Lee smiled.

"Well, let's get going while the sun's up," said Furke. He remounted his bike and pointed it in the direction of the bridge. "Annie?" Furke twisted his body, gesturing at the pegs on his back wheel. She took a step in that direction when Ira broke in.

"You should sit on my handlebars."

"Sit on handlebars?" said Furke. "You really are trying to kill her today."

"People do it all the time," said Ira. "It's easier to sit than stand. And then she doesn't have to look at the back of your head the whole time."

Anna Lee gave a giggle, and to Ira's surprise, she lifted his bike from the ground and steadied it, finally looking back at him and waiting for him to mount. Ira jumped to the bike seat. He kept both feet firm against the grass as Anna Lee turned her back and hopped over the front tire onto the handlebars. She tipped back and forth some trying to collect her balance until she made contact with Ira's chest. He thrust it forward trying to support her like the backrest of a chair.

"To the lake," the girl cried out. Furke shook his head and pedaled in the lead. He went slow and trepidatious, looking back every few seconds at the condition of the tandem riders.

Ira pedaled forward as best as he could. As long as they went straight, he could manage. But such extra weight on the front made the tire dig into rifts of uneven earth. They went bumbling along over the prairie field. Ira had to stretch his neck to see over the girl's shoulder and support her with his own body all at once. They began to gain speed. A sound or two of discomfort issued from Anna Lee as they went over bumps in the ground, and when they came upon the bridge the right-angled turn proved too tall a task. The tire came to a halt as it caught between gravel chunks. Anna Lee reeled forward a second before swinging back and falling straight over the handlebars into Ira's lap. He stuck a foot down to keep them from falling, but the girl's feet were already on the ground. Her torso lay across him, bouncing with nervous giggles.

"I don't think it's going to work," she said through her laughter. As she stood up, the weight that Ira had been supporting lifted. Without trying, he pushed himself in her direction, and when their bodies collided he felt the cool wetness of her lips press into the rise of his cheek. Ira went stiff.

Anna Lee stood back still stifling her laughs from the fall. Her fingers came up and touched her mouth lightly. Her face had gone rosy red, and her furtive eyes met his. "Sorry," she said.

36.
Anna Lee

SHE STOOD ON THE PEGS of Furke's back wheel. The wind tickled her face, and her hair floated in trail like a jet-black flag. Her hands held his bony shoulders, and when they tilted into a turn, she clutched and leaned against his back. Ira rode beside them. His hair also swung in the wind, now and then covering his constant gaze. She saw how he looked at her. Furke too. Both boys sent her such secret signs as she had begun some years ago to understand as different. The first time she'd discovered the romantic advance was back in California. A boy named Timothy had been paying particular attention to her. She was fond of him in a child's way and would spend many of her afternoons fishing at a creek alongside him. She was squeamish of hooking the worms, so he always performed the piercing. Then one day, with the slime still on his hands, he leaned over to where she sat staring at the rush of the current and kissed her cheek. She was taken aback by the kiss though not offended or alarmed. Then his fingers entwined with hers and they sat there like that until a tug on her line brought them to their feet. Later that evening when Anna Lee was back at home and contemplating her friend, she sought out her father. The only talks of romance she'd ever had had come as portentous quips from her mother, light hearted and teasing, and indeed part of her felt she ought to reach out to a woman first; yet, though she loved and trusted them both, it was her father whose degree of compassion and eloquence soothed her uncertainty. They talked for a long time about love in all the ways the word was used. He told her how he'd started seeing their mother; how he came to know he was in love with her, and that

JACOB KOCKEN

even though there was no one time or reason for it, it was, once acknowledged, undeniable. He asked her about Timothy, and as she spoke, he gave her the freedom to explore the possibility of her love along with the courageous, respectful duty to either seize it or admit it was not there. She wished now as she let herself flutter in the wind that her father was here to talk.

"You have to do a back flip by the end of the day," Furke was saying.

"I can't!" Anna Lee cried. "Ira, tell him I can't do a flip."

"Ira used to be scared too," said Furke. He turned his head to the side and yelled the words over his shoulder at her and the other boy. "But last year I gave him a shove off the cliff, and he did at least three before reaching water." Anna Lee laughed. It was a brief, yet free and joyous laugh.

Ira sped ahead of them and led the way down an old county highway. He pulled off onto a walking trail that was swallowed by a forest of oaks and conifers. Anna Lee, standing tall on the bike pegs, had to duck now and then to avoid the rogue, spindly branches of the backwoods trail. One of them caught her across the forehead, and she buried her face against the nape of her driver's neck. He smelled of shampoo and a subtle summer sweat.

When the path opened up ahead, the surface of Lake Duval was shimmering with light. Only one scattering cloud was in the sky, and such direct sunlight contended with a soft and cool breeze over the temperature of the day. The three friends passed the little stretch of ground where they had only some nights before sipped on stolen gin. There was a collection of vibrant purple flowers scattered around the forest that Anna Lee had not noticed under the nighttime shroud of her first visit. She indicated them with a squeal of delight. Furke pointed out how strongly they grew near the ditch where he'd been sick.

"I must have a green thumb," said Furke. "I can make geraniums!"

"I thought those were violets," said Anna Lee.

"Just the color. But they're geraniums."

"They looked like violets to me."

"I'll bet anything."

"Why are you so sure?"

RISE THE MOON

"It's my job to know," said Furke. "Didn't I tell you two? I got that gig at Betty Blossom's."

"What about the grand prix?" asked Ira.

"Yeah, the trampling!" said Anna Lee.

"I studied flowers and cactuses and all that shit from a book in the library at school," said Furke. I memorized every one I could to impress Mrs. Betty enough, and I finally stopped in again yesterday."

"Did you knock her socks off?"

"We didn't even talk about plants."

"What'd you talk about then?"

"My mom," said Furke. "She asked why I wanted to work bad enough to come back there, and I told her. I only got one parent left, and what if she gets fired? We've got an ungrateful sister to put through college, and I know Mom doesn't want to be on an assembly line for the rest of her life."

THE LAKE WAS OF IRREGULAR shape, and when they came around one jutting peninsula Furke indicated their spot with a long, pointed finger. Up ahead, a rock face undulated across one section of the water, sometimes fifteen to twenty feet up before grading back down to the shoreline. The outmost crest of these reached out slightly from the bank to where the water was dark and deep. Soon they came to where the rocks began to rise.

Ira clutched his brakes as the incline of the trail began to plateau. Furke came to a coasting stop behind him, and the two leaned their bikes against either side of a thick oak tree that seemed to Anna Lee to lord its magnificence over all the surrounding forest. Beside them, some thirty feet away, was the overhang of the cliff. Furke was the first one undressed. His socks were tucked into his shoes and placed beneath the bike while he racked his shirt on one end of his handlebars. Ira mirrored the procedure, looking away from her while removing his clothes. This bashful action struck Anna Lee and reflected its cautious, reverent spirit in her when she began to lift her own garments. She owned a bathing suit back before they moved, but it was not among the precious items taken when they left. As she disrobed, Anna Lee stepped behind the cover of the great oak. She dressed the other end of Furke's han-

JACOB KOCKEN

dlebars with her shed garments and leaned for a moment against the weighty trunk of the tree. Out of nowhere her cheeks were hot. She could feel the blood rising in her face as well as the faintness of a lost breath. Nothing unexpected had occurred, yet she now regarded her own body with more gravity than usual. She wore a swimsuit new to her; white with floral prints. The style was old, a generation past, and the once red color of the flowers had faded to a milky pink. The yellows were almost gone entirely. It was something of her mother's presumably. The woman had been gone still when Anna Lee fell asleep the night before. But when the morning sun had woken her, the gift was found draped over the top of her dresser. It fit, but loosely. She had to tie the back strap tight.

When Anna Lee emerged from behind the tree the boys were standing some distance away, occupied with a pale and staccatoed conversation. They each looked her way in an instant like squirrels to a foreign sound. Her eyes focused on the ground as she came toward them. Her feet found acorns dropped by the oak over summer whose dry husks gave a conspicuous sound even beneath her bare heel. She walked slowly towards them. With each step, an acorn pressed into her sole, stretched with living tension, and popped.

"Shall we jump?" she said, treading past the dirt trail and onto the outcropping of limestone. She came to the edge of the cliff to look out over the scene. This was a flat country where she'd lived these last few months, and she was glad for the elevation however slight it may be compared with the mountains in her head. Some ten or fifteen feet down, the water lay still and tranquil. It was nothing much of a drop off to her. A cool wind stirred and raised the little hair on her arms. Before she could brush them back down there was a loud whoop streaking past her, and Furke's freckled body was twisting through the air. His splash nearly reached the edge of the cliff, and before his head reemerged, Ira had gone diving past her too and was being swallowed by the same depths. They both surfaced with a gasp.

"How is it?"

"See for yourself," called Furke. A handful of lake water came at her, streaming from the palm of his hand and breaking into little dappled bullets. She let out a shriek of surprise and mirth and jumped in as they hurled more rain her way.

RISE THE MOON

She plunged several feet into the lake to where her toes touched the tall, waving weeds. Fields of grey blue flooded her opened eyes. Odd, lonesome fish darted somewhere in the distance, and two pairs of legs churned above her. The water was cold indeed. Her body tensed and hurried to the surface where she took as deep a breath as her lungs would allow.

"You didn't flip," said Ira.

"I don't know how."

"There's not much how involved," said Furke. "Fall any way except straight." They swam toward where the high rocks sloped back down into the shore. There was a little path where the boulders could be climbed, and the three of them went as fast as they could, dripping all the way until they were off the edge of the cliff again. Ira jumped first, waiting until gravity took real hold of him before his body tucked and spun all the way around. It was graceful as a swan she thought. Then Furke stood himself at the edge and turned around. His knees bent low, and he sprang backwards with a yelp. They cheered her from below, but as Anna Lee jumped, all coordination left her. Her legs flailed and she came around halfway when her spine smacked the flat of the lake. There was little pain; the worst of it was the water collapsing into her nose as she sunk. Anna Lee came up sputtering, shaking her head to clear it.

"We'll work on that," said Furke.

The three of them talked of passing things while they tread water, drifting thoughtlessly into the deep parts and back again. Anna Lee found her body acclimating to the cold, and soon she could have believed it was a bright day in the height of summer. They developed a sort of game by alternately losing each other underwater and surprising one of the other two with a tug on the ankle, a monster dragging them down to the doom. She felt a thrill in the waiting, every wave and shadow in the water around her was suspect. A giddy peel of glee erupted from her whenever one of the boys got hold of a foot. It was a surprise every time even though she knew it must be coming.

The boys quarreled over who played the better monster. Furke was the stronger swimmer, but Ira could really hold his breath. Both were essential qualities for a creature of the lake, and she gave only this equivocation when she was asked to settle the debate. With

JACOB KOCKEN

continued talk of their abilities in the world of water, they circled eventually back to skill of cliff jumping.

"All you got to do is tuck your knees," said Ira. "That's what makes you spin."

"As soon as I jump I'm in the water," she told them. "There's not enough time to tuck my knees. There's not enough time to spin."

"If time is your problem, then I know a spot you can fall for a lot longer," said Furke.

"There's a bigger one?"

"The Mountain. Just around that bend." He pointed to another of the lake's peninsulas. More from curiosity than any wish to accomplish the stunt, Anna Lee agreed they move on.

Back at shore, they left the bikes where they were and trod up the crags on foot. The boys walked on either side of her, speaking back and forth on the subtleties of their acrobatics. She noticed a beautiful rhythm in their exchange, a union of thought and spirit that heartened her and drew her admiration simultaneously in two directions.

Indeed, this second cliff was higher. As the incline kept grading upward, she wondered how it had remained hidden to her in a terrain so flat. Though not reminiscent of her Californian mountains, she found herself eye to eye with some of the smaller treetops in the distance. The height of their drop had doubled at least, she thought, looking down at the lake. This new spot did not hang over the shore as the first one did. Instead, the rock face angled steeply toward the water as it went down.

"If you dive here you've got to really jump and clear the rocks," said Furke. "But the water is deep right where it starts."

"That's kind of far," she said. Furke nodded.

"I've done it before though," he said. "Even with a flip." Anna Lee looked out over the edge again where the little waves crashed into the cliff face and back to him. She felt her eyes widen reflexively.

"You could die."

"I'm not afraid."

She sensed by his voice that he indeed may not have been afraid, or at least that he was willing to make the assertion come true. Before she could respond, Ira popped up.

RISE THE MOON

"I'm not afraid either," he said. His tone was as if in contest to Furke, yet he looked the whole time at her.

"You always were," said Furke.

"That's a lie. I'm not afraid. I've never been afraid. I could do it backwards."

Furke's eyes narrowed, and his mouth parted. Anna Lee tried to step between them, but Furke was faster. She bumped into the tall boy's shoulder as he squared up to Ira.

"Go ahead then," Furke was saying. He pivoted, clearing a path for his rival who strode to the edge of the limestone.

"Wait," she called. Ira turned to her; his mouth was a hard line of determination as he awaited her words. She searched for something to take the place of their daring, and from the corner of her eye she spied a dart across the water. "I want to do that."

Down at ground level and some fifty feet away, there was a man standing knee deep in the water. His pant legs were rolled up and just barely keeping dry while his upper body was entirely bare and twisting lazily. A shirt and a black and white collar were tucked into his belt, flapping with his movement like a barman's rag. All he wore above the waist was a thin pair of glasses. Now and then a stone shot out with a flick of his wrist and skipped across the glassy lake.

She sighed inwardly as Ira left his post at the edge of the cliff and leaned forward with a squint at the man.

"That's Father David," he said.

"A pastor?"

"Isn't there a rule against seeing a priest's nipples?" said Furke. This time Anna Lee did not laugh. Neither did Ira.

"My Dad always chopped wood with his shirt off." Anna Lee turned back inland to the dirt path. "You two stay," she said when the boys began to follow. Her voice was soft but serious, and the command froze them both at the top of the little mountain.

Now and then her view of the man was blocked by trees or boulders as she wound her way back to ground level. The place she emerged on shore was covered in little zebra shells that broke under her feet just as the acorns had. Anna Lee tread slowly over them, fearing the crunching sound might startle the man who stood alone and bare in the shallows.

JACOB KOCKEN

He slung another stone and watched it bound across the water. Long after each toss, he stared absently at the place it had sunk before bending low to the sand where his fingers came up with another rock. As this ritual proceeded, Anna Lee waded into the lake behind him. Her steps quickened the closer she got. She was nearly running, her little legs churning water into whirling eddies when the priest stooped again and saw her upon him.

"Hello there," said the man.

She stopped and looked up at him with wide eyes. A certain rush drained from her face, and her arms hung limp. "Can I throw?"

The man smiled. It was a youthful, boyish grin. At the same time, a sort of shadow passed over him, and he pulled the shirt from his waist. He shifted the stone in his grip and handed it to her while he shook out the shirt and slipped it over his head. The thin, religious collar came next, fixing all his clothes in a proper place.

Anna Lee tried to mimic the lazy twist he had when he threw. Her rock sailed out on a small arcing path and slid underwater on first touch. A pang of disappointment ran through her but evaporated quickly under the calm smile of the priest.

"Ever skip before?"

Anna Lee shook her head. The man bent to the ground again and came up with a whole handful of little stones.

"That one wasn't flat," he said, sifting through the collection with his forefinger. He plucked three specimens and turned his open palm down, letting loose a little rain of sand and stone. "I like the ones with corners and notches. They give you something to handle." He gave her one of the stones and showed how he held his with just three delicate fingers, the tip of his pointer fixed on an edge. "Throw flat," he said. "Even downward if you have to. And really let your wrist flick." Another example came slinging from his hand. Anna Lee counted seven jumps. She tried again, relaxing the muscles in her hand as he'd instructed. Two skips.

There was a hearty grin on the man's face. She motioned toward him for the other stone he held which was given up gladly.

"Are those your friends?" said the man. His neck was bent back a bit and pointing up the hill to where Furke and Ira stood watching.

"We were swimming," she said.

"I know the Foster boy. Ira. Who's the other one?"

RISE THE MOON

"His name is Furke."

"Furke? Is that a nickname?"

"I don't know," she said. "I just met them really."

"And what's your name?"

"Anna Lee Lac." She paused, looking down at the ripples she made in the water before meeting the priest's eyes again to say, "Anna Lee." She adjusted the stone in her hand, finding a comfortable fit. "Yours is Father David. That's what Ira said." Anna Lee flung her third stone. She felt it leave her hand with a ferocious spin. It hopped four times on the water. "Let the wrist flick."

"That's right," the priest laughed. "Are you new to Graumont then? I know Ira's been here a while. I baptized him a couple years ago." Anna Lee furrowed her brow. Her head tilted.

"Not as a baby?"

"That's when his family joined the Church. It's never too late to come to Christ."

"Was it here?" Anna Lee stopped stirring in the water upon the thought that this might be holy ground. But the priest only peered curiously and shook his head.

"We only do Baptisms inside the church."

"Oh," said Anna Lee. "Mine was in a river. My father pointed out the spot every time we went there."

"Oh really? What kind of Church do you claim?"

"My father's."

"Do you know the denomination? Baptist? Pentecostal?" His eyes narrowed in mock severity. "Did they handle snakes there?"

"It was my father's Church."

"I see. That was somewhere else? Does he preach here now? I ought to know my competition."

"No," said Anna Lee. "He's still back there."

"Mm. You miss him?"

She nodded.

"I'm glad you've got friends then," he said. "Ira's a good young man from what I hear."

"I like him a lot."

They continued to skip stones for a while in silence. She enjoyed a certain comfort in his presence, the good man standing tall beside her, giving advice and encouragement in their petty pursuit.

JACOB KOCKEN

With only a small amount of practice, Anna Lee had conjured a modest ability. The priest's throw still far outdid hers in both distance and number.

"Why did you baptize Ira?" Anna Lee asked at last.

"His mother requested it be done."

"But what does it do?"

"It washes away the sin that we're born with."

"Now Ira can't sin?"

"He can sin. That's a necessary part of humanity."

"To sin?"

"To have the capacity."

"Will you baptize him again later?"

"No. There are two kinds of sin. There's the general inherited kind and then the specific kind we make with our own hands. The rite for those is reconciliation. Confession. When we confess our failings and contemplate the goodness lost by them, the roads to Heaven and Hell fall under a bright light."

"But for people who don't understand?"

"I'm afraid I don't know what you mean."

"Is it wrong to get baptized again? To just wash it all away from you? If you can't confess, I mean. If you don't know what you did wrong; that you hurt somebody."

"If it stops you from solving the root of your issue. If the washing allows you to act without the pang of conscience. Then perhaps it is. That's supposed to be our compass through life after all."

"My dad said it's the mother's job to bring you into the world and the father's job to get you through it."

"I like that formulation," said the priest. "In a symbolic way. It's nice to have a guide to show you the way. Of course, you won't always have someone wiser around. People come to me for help a whole lot; especially when they're desperate. God's always the last hope. But sometimes they have difficult problems, and I don't know what God would say to them; what He wants me to say to them. There's this one woman in particular I just can't seem to help no matter how much time I spend out here trying to pray and listen for answers."

"What's her name?" asked Anna Lee.

"Gillian," said the priest. His face got a bit fallen. "At some

RISE THE MOON

point, you're all on your own. In that case, think of your body as the mother of your soul, giving it life in this world, and your mind as its father, guiding it through. Recognizing how things played out is all we've got. That's all a person does to get wise is remember."

"You talk like my dad," said Anna Lee.

"I hope that's good."

"Once I threw a rock at my sister. She wasn't hurt, but I wanted to hurt her. It was a very pretty rock with crystals on the inside, so Dad put it in my pocket and said to carry it with me wherever I went to remind me of what I did. He said I would feel bad and guilty, but that after a while I would be happy because it would also be there to remind me that I hadn't thrown it again for so long. And then it would be more beautiful than just a gemstone. I'd show you now, but it's in my pocket back there." She pointed down the shoreline to the place where the boys had stashed their bikes.

"I think your dad talks better than me, Miss Lac."

Anna Lee smiled softly. Her eyes were sparkling like the top of the water, and she broke that surface to reach down and pluck two stones from their bed. She handed one to him and kept the other, tossing it with all her might and watching the tap dance it made across the lake. It was her best throw by far and filled her heart. She turned to see if the priest would out do her again, but he was not poised to throw. The stone she'd given him was still in his hand. She saw now that it was too round and not good for skipping. Still, the man contemplated it, and instead of bending down to find another rock, he pocketed the round one he held. It bulged out at the side of his leg beneath the rolled up pants. His hand rested lightly over top. Anna Lee found a better, flatter stone and handed it up to him. This one he took and skipped with calm perfection.

They continued tossing stones at leisure when the reflection of the bank caught Anna Lee's eye. Up at the top of the little hill were Ira and Furke. They were sitting now, right next to each other with their shirts off and one of Furke's arms draped across Ira's shoulder in a comfortable fraternal posture. They were looking out over the expanse of the lake and talking. All the tension that might have been there before seemed gone away. They looked timeless.

Then one of them saw she was looking. They both stiffened almost imperceptibly. Ira was the first to stand up, as if the pose

JACOB KOCKEN

might help him see or hear her better, followed quickly by Furke. She smiled softly up at both of them.

"Are you married, Father?" she asked the man.

"In Catholicism, priests are married to the Church." He lifted his left hand to bare an empty ring finger. Then he gave a slight tug to the collar fastened at his neck. There was a final stone in his hand which he gave a mighty heave into the sky. It carried farther than any they had skipped and crashed down with a gulp into the belly of the lake. Then he dipped his hands into the water and brushed them together, washing off the sand and sediment. "I had a girl long ago when I was young. But that seems like a different lifetime now."

"What happened?"

"She left," he said.

"Was it bad?"

"Yes."

"What do you—"

Just then there was a splash loud and deep as a timpani drum. The water around Anna Lee's ankles seemed to vibrate, and she looked back just in time to see one boy jumping off the cliff in pursuit of the other. The second body fell thirty feet and entered the water with the same thunder as the first. Then the two heads bobbed up a short distance out and began crawling with eager arms in her direction.

"I see what you were going to ask," said the priest. "And I'm sorry to leave you without any clarity, but I think perhaps you're better off with anyone else's advice but mine here. Good-bye for now, Miss Lac."

37.
Saul

AS ALWAYS, DURING THE DAY, Saul was alone in the house. He had spent a good deal of time admiring the dried blood on the canvas board in his garage. The previous works of art were nothing now. His attempt to coax something valuable from the Savior Boy was shattered when he saw how the paint had dried with cracking waves instead of the deep, contemplative stare he'd hoped to produce. The humid air had formed paint bubbles which chipped away under the pressure of Saul's thumbs as he rubbed the ceramic face. The final effect displayed a more opaque and confused expression than anything.

He rolled the figure over in his hands and let it drop into the garbage can where the Messiah cracked from hip to shoulder. He took his other painted works and piled them out back over the fire pit. They went up in mere minutes on smoke tainted with the artificial scent of acrylic.

When it was done, he returned with a mind to study the blood. But all the moving had taken a good deal longer than expected. Saul was still constrained in most every muscle with a soreness nearing spasms. So instead, he went to lie down on the couch and fell asleep for an hour or two.

When Saul woke, it was to the sound of thumping at his door. The knocks came again, and his stiff body rolled off the couch to answer.

It was Angela. She was holding a cardboard crate.

"I brought apples," she said. "Say hello to SummerTime." Saul stretched an arm against the door jamb, barring her way as she took

JACOB KOCKEN

a step toward the threshold.

"I'm fasting."

"Oh, you did say that before. Aren't you done? You shouldn't fast too long, especially when you're running so much."

"I'm on the brink of something," said Saul.

"But it can hardly hurt. It's not a meal after all. Only a treat. You've never had a SummerTime snack; anyone could tell by the dullness of your eyes."

"By what?"

"The glaze of ignorance is over them. You don't know what you're missing out on. Everyone perks up with a bite of summer." Saul regarded her and the box of fruit. She wore lipstick today. It was the apples' hue; a deep sunset red. He nodded slowly and ushered her inside. She set the box down on the kitchen table. It was full to the brim with dozens of hearty, softball sized apples.

Angela took one and rubbed it clean against her bosom. It gleamed with a smoothness seldom found in nature. Saul didn't even take it in his hand; she simply lifted the thing up to his mouth to bite. His teeth sunk in easily. Its grain was soft as a ripened plum. And so sweet.

"Cotton candy," said Saul. His eyes got wide, and he took another bite from her hand. "How?"

"Well," said Angela, "for some strange reason, when rainclouds pass over the orchard they turn from black to white, and instead of rain, it's sugar that falls to water the trees." She giggled and took a bite from the other side of the same apple. "My stepdad explained the techniques to me once. Apparently Brock's family has been breeding plants for generations. You know, like the way they breed dogs. With a little intention you can turn things into whatever you want."

Saul took another bite and smiled as he chewed. It was wonderful. The flesh inside was white as sugar. So sweet. So unbelievably sweet. Red color from its skin began to run off like wet paint when the juice released. It stained Saul's lips like gloss. Angela held up a new shining red globe from the box. Once again she fed him, and several drops went running down his chin as his mouth hung open in astonishment.

Saul's head was swimming. He leaned forward, bypassing the

RISE THE MOON

fruit in her hand and kissed her on the lips. Angela dropped what she held and wrapped both arms around him, bringing him close and kissing back.

"Let's go," said Saul, nearly bouncing where he stood.

"Go?"

"Run."

"Now?"

"Yes," said Saul, and he led her by the hand out the front door and sprinted as fast as his body would let him, ignoring every ache, twinge, and threat of cramp to run and run through the streets of the town.

38.
Miriam

THE SUNDAY AIR WAS THICK with moisture that had not fallen all summer. Miriam had spritzed herself with perfume before church that morning. The bottle was old and purple. She could not remember the last time it had been used; certainly more than a year. The scent was of jasmine; rich and sweet. People in the pews around her seemed to notice. When she shook their hands after the Lord's Prayer they smiled warmly. For a time, she was just as contented. Then the Communion gifts were presented. While the servants of the altar marched, Father David took up the censer. Redolent smoke crawled over the crowd, and Miriam bowed her head.

When church let out she took her son to see a matinee. They'd spent so little time together lately just the two of them. She bought popcorn and a large soda, and situating them on the arm rest between their seats, shared both with her boy. After the movie, they went down to Meyer Studios. The family photos were ready. She'd ordered one for Grandma Bess and another for their own house. They were big; twenty-four by eighteen inches. One of them she had paid to be framed; the second one, wrapped only in cellophane, lay on top of the first in the trunk of her car. She and her boy decided to drop the gift off right away. He carried the photo while Miriam held open the door to Grandma Bess's living room.

"Grandma," Miriam called out. "I have something for you."

"Frank?" The hoarse voice came from the sunroom. They entered the house, and Miriam pointed to the empty spot on the wall, instructing her son to prop up the photo.

"Take that blank frame down and see how it fits," she said.

RISE THE MOON

While her son prepared the casing, Miriam moved to the sunroom and found her grandmother there sitting in her chair surrounded with bundles of tulips, daffodils, and geraniums. Many of them were standing all together in vases and jars of water while others lay strewn across the small table beside her.

"It's so colorful in here."

"Oh, Miriam dear," said Grandma Bess. "Well, since the garden was ruined I figured to take them all up to give out to people. Is Frank with you?"

"Not today. But there's a surprise in the other room."

"I figured it would be him because he usually comes by around noon, and when he didn't come yesterday I thought to give him a call, but I'd just be pestering, so I waited until today and still haven't seen him at all." She stood up slowly and followed Miriam. Her boy was fixing the photo plate back into place when they walked in. He tipped it up and smiled as if posing for another picture.

"Oh, you're all so beautiful," said Grandma Bess. They hung it up and stepped back to admire the whole scene. "With them all up by each other, you can still see my granddad's ears all the way through to Ira."

Miriam had to chuckle. Her grandmother was right. The old patriarch's features transferred so faithfully from one photograph to the next it seemed beyond a doubt they belonged to, rather than genetics, some platonic form of the family that would have stretched on backward through each generation as far as time could see.

"You sure are one of ours," said Grandma Bess, reaching a tiny hand up to the boy's shoulder. Miriam was warmed upon seeing a smile spread across her son's face.

"So true, sweetie. So true," Miriam said, kissing the top of his head.

"Wait here now," said the old woman. She held up a finger and shuffled away leaving them alone in the living room. When she came back a minute later it was with three bouquets from the flowerbed garden; twenty blossoms in each bundle of tricolor vibrance. She approached the boy with the loveliest of the three. "You give these to some special girl, and we'll be hanging up another photograph in no time."

Miriam laughed aloud.

JACOB KOCKEN

Then Grandma Bess handed the other two sets to Miriam. "One, of course, is for you Mimi for all the help you gave taking out those evil weeds. And you run these others to Frank since he's decided not to visit anymore. Even though he ripped up half the beds, God knows I'll still be generous with him."

"Is something wrong with Grandpa?" said the boy. His smile had fallen away, and he stood there stiffly, clutching the flowers with both hands on his chest.

"Where to begin with what's wrong with Frank."

"I'll make sure Dad gets them," said Miriam. She gave her grandmother a hug and watched her son do the same before leaving.

"Is something wrong with grandpa?" Her son asked a second time when they got out to the car.

"She's always hard on him. He needs space now and then," said Miriam. Her boy was not looking. Rather, he stared up and to the right with his eyes, tracking down a dust mite thought. "But I'll run the flowers to him tonight," she said.

When they arrived home Miriam put her son in charge of finding a vase for the flowers. "Put a few pennies in the water with them." He nodded. He had been quiet on the ride back, his eyes constantly out the window or looking intently down at the petals, breathing their delicate fragrance.

As her son went off with the flowers, Miriam retrieved the new family photo from the trunk. She hung it in their living room on the wall opposite the front door.

In the conjoined kitchen, Miriam found a box of SummerTime apples open on the table. One of them, half eaten, was lying on the floor. It bled thick red juice everywhere. "What in Hell?" she said to herself and threw the leaking thing into the trash. Paper towel soaked up the rest of the mess, but its deep color had penetrated the linoleum, and no soap or liquid cleaner was taking it out. Miriam popped in a strip of spearmint gum and clenched her jaw tight as she scrubbed.

There was the sound of footsteps down the stairs and her baby came in holding a large glass vase in both hands. He filled it at the kitchen sink and set it, brimming with floral beauty, on the countertop before disappearing once again upstairs.

RISE THE MOON

Miriam gave up on the stain. She put the lid back on the SummerTime box and was stuffing it on a pantry shelf when the front door opened. Saul walked in limping and sweaty. He collapsed on the couch.

"Did you go running again?" she said. "You're going to hurt yourself."

"I was inspired."

"Did you leave a half-eaten apple on the floor?"

"What?" said Saul.

"One of those sugar traps, Saul. There's a whole box, and I sure as Hell didn't buy them."

"Fruit is important, dear."

"They're candy, and everyone knows it," said Miriam. Her husband shrugged.

"We can just throw them away if you like," said Saul. "Did you get yourself flowers?"

"They're from Grandma. One is for us; I'm bringing the other to Dad." Then, grabbing one bouquet from the water and sweeping her purse to her shoulder, she headed for the door.

"You're going now?"

"I'll go afterward. It's Tuesday. Dad lives close to the church."

"Oh," said Saul. "Yes, of course. The priest." She nodded and headed again toward the door when his voice called out. "Miriam. Come here a moment."

She stalked over and his languid body sat up on the couch some. He looked her up and down, smiling for several moments.

"Can we be quick," she said. "It's nearly six."

"I don't think you need to go see him anymore."

"Thank you for your opinion." She turned to leave again, but Saul caught her by the hand and pulled until she sat beside him.

"I know you've been in pain for a long time now," said Saul. "And I know I've got a role there. I'd like to fix it."

Miriam's expression softened. Her husband's face was earnest though she fancied there was something held behind his serious eyes; shame perhaps. That's what she would feel. She could almost feel that string of hair she'd found in the shower wrapping around her fingers again. Miriam set her things down on the coffee table. With her hands and attention free, she took a patient seat atop the sofa's armrest. Her heartbeat changed; quickened. Saul's mouth quivered as if he were about to speak, and Miriam found her spine already leaning in with anxious anticipation.

"You can tell me, Saul," she said, unconsciously hushed. "I want you to. Did you want to come with me? Do you want to see Father David with me?"

"It doesn't all make much sense, Miriam. I'll have to ask for your faith."

Miriam nodded very slowly, almost to herself. It fell in line with something, what he'd said. Father David had said something like that; something about faith and change and forgiveness.

"Fair enough," she said.

Saul shifted in his place on the couch. "Sometimes when bad things happen to you, or when you do them, bad things I mean, they stick in your head, you know?"

"I know."

"But it doesn't have to," said Saul. "It doesn't have to stick there. I don't mean to say I know precisely where it goes. But you can let it out. You can let it pour right out." He gave her his hand, and she took it. There was a long cut on that hand. He had it wrapped up in gauze again. Saul had said he'd swiped it across the broken edge of the one nightstand in their bedroom. It had been healed up a few days ago, but today it was wrapped in gauze again. "It requires real faith though," Saul continued. "The things you can do to let it out. They require faith. A lot of faith. I'm sorry, I'm talking in circles, aren't I?" His finger too was making circles, following the pale mark on his left ring finger around and around. Hers was still bound in gold. The ring was too tight these days. It pinched.

"Saul," said Miriam. She squeezed the fingers of his offered hand with both of hers, careful to clear the dull red line showing on his wrapped-up palm. "I understand. My confessions with Father David always dance around." Miriam sucked in a breath and closed her mouth. She looked away from him, hoping her directness did not startle the moment away. But when she found her husband's face again, he was at ease. He smiled. There was something innocent about it; something young that she had not seen on him in a long time.

"I'm happy to hear that from you, Miriam. That's a wonderful

RISE THE MOON

start. But we need not think so much about that anymore. This is about something bigger."

"What?"

"You don't need to do that meeting with him anymore. You don't need to talk to that priest."

"Saul, I don't know what you're getting at, but it'll be better if you just say it. I know, Saul. I understand. You can tell me. You can confess."

"I have no fault to tell, Miriam," said Saul. "That's what I wanted to share." Miriam did not move. She felt the blow strike her heart, and she steeled herself with a blank expression.

"That's what you wanted to share?"

"I can help. I can help you."

Miriam dropped her husband's wounded hand. Her pounding heartbeat skipped once and returned to the steady, usual rhythm of her life. She lifted her head away and looked at the blank white wall for a while. Then she stood.

"Saul, I'm going to meet with Father David now."

"I can help you, dear. You said you'd give me your faith. Don't be so unfaithful." Her whole body straightened up, tense and angry. Miriam opened her mouth to yell, but it barely reached a whisper.

"I'll prefer to keep that between me and God."

He stood to meet her, and something seemed to close tight on itself in one of his legs. He winced and buckled to the floor, catching himself on the fallen knee. Miriam took a sharp breath and came close. In that propositional posture, Saul shook off the pain with gritted teeth and took her hand in both of his. They were soft fingers, and warm and sweet as melted honey. With his head bowed close, Saul must have caught a ripple of jasmine on the air. He touched the tip of his nose to one of her rounded knuckles, then another. His crown tucked into her waist. She began to ask if he was alright. But her husband pushed back those words with his own.

"Why should things crystallize and sit there weighing your head down? Close your eyes. Follow me in a prayer. Please, Miriam." Saul's eyelids fell, and he tipped back his head, speaking softly to himself. His mouth moved on faint incantations. And as he spoke, he bounced to the rhythm of his lips, rocking her side to side.

Miriam wriggled from his grasp. "I'd like you to sleep on the

JACOB KOCKEN

couch again tonight," she said. He looked up at her from just below his half-closed lids.

"I can help you," said Saul. "Let me help you." Miriam could see little cramps threatening her husband's limbs by the way he held statue stiff.

"In that case," she said, "I'll be the one to stay elsewhere."

"What do you mean?" Her husband's expression lost its tension. She'd seen the resigned look before; all over newspapers and television screens.

"I don't know. I'll sleep on a damn church pew or something." She spun away, leaving him there where he knelt. The front door thwacked behind her, and she drove to St. Francis in a flash.

Before turning in to the church parking lot, Miriam lowered the window and spit her ball of gum into the grass. Her jaw worked unconsciously back and forth now, loosening to the summer air. The stale spirit of the spearmint faded in the warmth of her mouth, and Miriam tried to calm herself with a hum.

When she came through the hallway, Father David was in his office. There was a pen in his hand and a book of Webster's intermediate crosswords open on the desk. He blinked out of reverie. "Hello Miriam. Sorry, I'm putting a homily together." He closed the puzzle book. "I'll come to the chapel in a minute." She left him to his business and walked the rest of the hallway alone. Her throat began absentmindedly to hum again, then to speak and even sing a low and mournful tone to herself as she entered the chapel.

The room was small, a fractal of the larger sanctuary save for the stained-glass windows. Here, the light tunneled through a single round skylight in the roof. When the sun went down, it was the quiet, immortal candles burning at the head of the room that gave the prayerful illumination. Weeks ago, after the infant girl's funeral, there were ninety-nine new candles burning in her honor. It had looked like a million fireflies in the dark. Several days later Miriam watched them blink out of life as she prayed with Father David.

Miriam approached the empty chapel's dais. Those little gold candle holders lined the entire platform. Streams of dried wax coated their grooves, and the wicks had all burned to the ends. Only one flame still waved, though it too was approaching bottom. This one live flame stood at the center of the platform in a holder larger and

RISE THE MOON

more ornate than the rest.

The chapel door opened, and Father David entered. Another candle was in his hand. The cylinder was two inches thick and nearly two feet in length. "It's a changing day I believe," he said. Miriam nodded her head and took the candlestick from his hand. They knelt down together on the wood floor, and Miriam lowered the fresh wick over the dwindling one. Its flame redoubled in size, traveling off to the new host. Father David took what was left of the old candle from its bracket, and Miriam fit the new one in its place. He held the dying one up to Miriam, and after a moment's regard she emptied her lungs through the flame, snuffing it into a wild trail of grey smoke.

They rose from their knees and sat down on two small chairs facing one another. Then they closed their eyes, folded their hands, and spoke in unison.

"Hail Mary, full of Grace. The Lord is with Thee. Blessed art Thou among women, and blessed is the fruit of Thy womb, Jesus. Holy Mary, mother of God, pray for us sinners; now and at the hour of our death. Amen."

Miriam brought her hands back to her lap. "Dad called again," she said. "After we had dinner at the house."

"Did you answer?"

"Yes," she said. "He asked about my son. That's the only thing we talk about."

"Ira's a good kid."

"Now and then I still hear her voice through the speaker instead of Dad's. It always startles me at first, and when I hear him again I pretend it's her on the line. When I can't see Dad's face and I'm telling him about me or the boys, I pretend I'm talking to her."

"You mustn't continue, Miriam." There was pity in his eyes, and Miriam looked to her lap. Her hanging head weighed down like a boulder on her neck. "Your mother was a beautiful woman with the soul of an angel. She loves you," said Father David. "You should be happy to think of her now. The anguish on your face must mean it isn't her you are remembering."

"She called so many times, Father. I could have helped. And what about when my boy learns the truth? We told him Mom was sick and that's how she died."

JACOB KOCKEN

"She was sick, Miriam. That's a basic fact."

"It's not the basic kind of facts that constitute truth."

"No," he said unequivocally. "No, it's not the basic kind. Would you like to take the sacrament again?"

The fight that was always in Miriam's expression dropped away momentarily. "No forgiveness has touched my heart since the first time. Perhaps it really is her voice from Heaven on the phone so I might always know what she thinks of me."

"Your mother sees clearly now, like the Father. She does not dwell as you do. She sees your remorse and triumphs as strongly as any failing. She knows what's in your heart. I know what's in your heart. You know what's in your heart. There is no reason to keep dwelling other than your loving, desperate, remorseful heart. You are forgiven, Miriam. Consider your own son. Do you think only of Ira's failings?"

"He's a good boy."

"He is young," said Father David. "Should he go all his life without sin? Will you expect that of him? One day he will hurt you, betray you; if not you then someone else. He will cause the world injury. And for a short time or a long time, people will have cause to hate him."

"He's a good boy," she said again.

"Life is too long and complicated not to be a sinner. But Heaven forgives, Miriam. Heaven forgives."

"Not the mortal things. Father, I killed her. If there's a Heaven and a Hell then mustn't God have a line?"

Father David removed his glasses and sighed. He rubbed each lens on the clean white fabric of his robe. It moved in little circles, removing every scratch and smudge. Then he returned them to his face and searched hers for several moments. "I don't know, Miriam."

"Gordan Yokoven? Guilty of the same consequence; is he forgiven? I'd burn forever before attaching his freedom to mine."

"I want to punish him too. But you had no intent. Your cause was not direct. That's enough. It must be. Please, Miriam. Please find that it's enough."

"Yet we produced the same effect. I took life; I will not be given life. I will burn like him." When she said the words her eyes

RISE THE MOON

flicked over to the memory of her mother dancing orange and hot above the wax.

"Suppose Ira was that monster," said the priest.

Miriam's nostrils flared. "What if I did forgive him? What would it matter? The mother of the victim would want him damned with equal fervor. Imagine you had asked me to suppose he was the child murdered in his sleep. The same love I would have once forgiven with now fills me with hatred. There is no fair place to stand. Forgive me Father, but I cannot forgive myself. I know what I have done. When someone hurts me and my heart tells me they are sorry it is an easy step to make. It's a feeling not a choice. Two years have passed, and not a touch of Grace has entered my heart. I look for it and do not feel it. We may do the sacrament every day, but I believe I have received His answer in silence."

She was breathing heavily. Her cheeks were as red as the candlelight beside them. Her eyes were bent on him. David saw how they waited. Rehearsed words bubbled in her throat.

"Perhaps you are right," he said.

"What?"

"It was indirect, but you could've done otherwise. You didn't."

"How on Earth is that supposed to help me, David?"

"I'm trying to face facts."

Miriam stood and pushed back her chair. Father David did not argue. Instead, he mirrored her motions and nodded with those same soft and pitiful eyes.

She caught another long look at the bright orange flame atop the new candle. In two weeks it would fall to the bottom, and she would have to come again to save it from death. Then again a month from now. Then again. And again.

The chapel doors swung open and closed. When she reached the exit at the end of the hall Miriam turned to see Father David emerging behind her. He did not follow. His head was down with one hand up around his face as he strode silently away toward his office.

Out in the car, Miriam was almost surprised to see the flowers lying on her passenger seat. The daffodils were bright and yellow, smiling at her and the falling sun through the window. Miriam picked up the bouquet and smacked it hard against the dashboard.

JACOB KOCKEN

Three flower heads popped off and littered the air with pollen. Thin, golden petals fell to the floor, lingering on Miriam's lap as they twirled down. She whipped the bundle again. There was another soundless explosion of yellow. The hearty stalks cracked. Their life water leaked down her clenching knuckles. Then Miriam put the car in gear and began to drive with one hand while the other squeezed flower stems to stone.

THE FIRST LEAVES OF A premature autumn had started falling on the front lawn and driveway. Miriam drove in. Loose gravel groaned under every tire. She kept her gaze fixed on the ground level, and when she knocked at the front door there was no answer. She did not see Frank in the backyard, but his Silverado was in the garage, so she knocked again. The door was unlocked, and after another period of waiting, she entered on her own.

"Dad?"

The television was off. The gramophone was off. There was no sound of habitation. The flowers she left on the kitchen counter as she moved about the house. When Miriam went to the living room she found her parents' old bed frame. It was still tucked against the wall beside an old, wooden dresser. But the mattress was missing. "Dad?" she called out again.

Miriam came back around toward the front door, and for the first time in two years, she leaned past the dividing wall to peer up the staircase. It was dark and lost light the more it went upward like an inverted hole in the ground. Something twinkled halfway up the flight. It was the silver frame of a picture that had fallen from the wall and lay face down on the carpeted step. Miriam mounted the stairs. Frank had kept photos of them hung along the way; the three of them. Miriam could not help but stop momentarily at seeing her face on the wall. "Mom?" she called aloud. "Dad? Dad are you home?" Her feet went faster. The steps creaked from disuse and plumes of dust rolled out from her feet.

She knocked on the closed door of their bedroom. "Dad?" Unlocked again, she entered. He was there in their old room. The mattress from the bed downstairs was on the floor with two blankets and a pillow. The rest of the room was bare. There was no dresser; no clothes in the closet. There were no belongings, and nothing

RISE THE MOON

hung on the walls but old eggshell paper.

He was lying down on the bare mattress very close to the windows. Their spectral glass stretched from floor to ceiling. Frank's head turned toward her, and a groan issued from his throat. She approached him quickly and fell to her knees, tripping on a length of carpet lying frayed and folded over.

"Dad. What's going on?" His face was very pale, and when she took it in her hands to see she nearly fell back. His eyes were not weary like his voice but rather wide and filled with crimson fury. His shaking hands came out from under the blanket and reached for her face. All his skin seemed sunken, and the veins raised up round and blue to the surface. He was visibly thinner than he had been, as if most of the liquid had been drained from his body. The wisps of hair that had recently rounded his head were scattered in a broken ring around the floor.

"It's me, Dad. Miriam." She felt the fever with the back of her hand. "What's going on? How long have you been up here?"

"Don't sit there," he said.

"What?"

"Don't sit on that lip." He grabbed her hindered hand and squeezed. Tufts of carpet were caught under his fingernails. The rest of his body started shaking. His grip on her hand was tight. He looked hard at her and squeezed, but the rest of him started shaking like paper in the wind.

"I'm calling an ambulance." She tried to run for the stairs, but he held fast to her wrist.

"Don't leave," he breathed.

"Dad!" She broke free of his grip and raced downstairs to the phone. Paramedics were sent. When she came back up Frank was still there, sitting up now. The great windows were open, and a gentle breeze rolled in. Frank was still shaking at the shoulders and talking aloud in mumbles as he inched closer to the open air.

"Stop!" Miriam tried to grab him, but her bad hand could find no purchase. She stumbled into him and saw the darkening sky outside enlarge as her head lunged into the open window. By grace she caught herself against the frame and shoved her father away from the edge. She clutched his arm with both of hers and dragged him to the mattress. She laid her weight across him so he could not

JACOB KOCKEN

move. Frank was wet with stale sweat. His whole body vibrated. He cried and she cried with him, and with her foot Miriam reached the window doors and swung them shut. Only a few minutes later, the ambulance arrived.

    At the hospital, Miriam waited alone for two hours. She called the house three times without an answer from her son or husband. She left a message every time. When the doctors let her in to see him, Frank was sleeping. They said not to worry; he was getting intravenous fluid, and the waking dreams had ceased. She talked to Grandma Bess on the phone and said she'd pick her up in the morning to come visit. Miriam hunkered into a chair beside Frank's bed. Almost all of his hair had fallen out now. His scalp showed significantly more even than when she'd seen him last. Now he lay there in peace, and Miriam sat the whole night through waiting for him to wake or for her husband to return the call. Not a moment of sleep came to her.

39.
Saul

THE SUNDAY AIR WAS THICK with moisture that had not fallen all summer. His wife had stepped out once again to see the priest. She'd slammed the door behind her. Only minutes after she left did Saul follow suit.

He now met Angela at the SummerTime gates. Saul had called and asked her to walk with him. It felt right when she suggested the orchard, and Saul arrived holding a long plastic tube.

"What is that?" she'd asked immediately.

"You'll see soon," he answered. Her coy smile accepted the waiting game.

Angela punched a series of numbers on the press pad, and with an audible metallic click they were let inside. "New security system," she said. "A few months ago I saw someone come through in the middle of the night. He came through and started picking straight from the trees, holding them in his shirt. It was hard to see, but I think it was that man. There was something awfully familiar about his face when it kept coming up on the news."

"He stole from you?"

"He was evil after all. Him breaking in here and running away, it could've happened a thousand times. The scavenger. Can you believe we're feeding him? It almost makes me feel responsible."

Inside the gate, the orchard spread for several acres. The grass, which Saul had known from his outside viewings, was pristinely kept. The depth of its green color was unmatched, not a blade had been bleached by the sun all summer. What he did not anticipate was its softness. Rarely had he ever complained of a lawn as hard

JACOB KOCKEN

or brittle, but felt now, after a moment's walk in SummerTime, that every other field would henceforth be criticized or pitied for its lack of fullness. It was an earthly cloud, a king's carpet. Angela seemed to see, or even expect this revelation from him. She smiled easily and kicked her feet to remove the pair of thong strip sandals she wore. Saul followed her lead, undoing his shoes. He left both socks rolled up beneath the tongue of his sneakers and walked barefooted through the garden. Even the breeze felt divine, refreshingly cool after such a brutally warm season. Saul also undid the top two buttons of his shirt, letting the wind breath down his naked skin.

A driveway ran through the orchard's middle up to a large, brick building where Angela said her stepfather worked. It was tall and pure black as if the bricks were stripped from the throat of an obsidian mine. Angela led Saul away from the drive and the building toward the trees.

"There are nineteen sections in all," said Angela. "Different flavors." The rows were symmetrical; each tree fifteen feet tall and in a late summer bloom. The branches of these famous trees, Saul noticed, did not grow straight forward. Each of them wended side to side like fractal forms of the great sibilant letter. The bark was smooth and equally patterned, even amongst such turning spines, with a grey-brown diamond hide. The fruit hung like yuletide ornaments, round, red, and voluptuously full, so heavy in their ripeness that the boughs bowed down to the weight of water. Living limbs on the cusp of cracking were corrected by twine twice tied to the trunks. Among the more rubeus orbs there hung in scattered scene some smaller, undoubtedly sourer, more hoarfrost ones, as if the immature flesh inside showed white as snow through a transparent skin.

"Why are they so different?" asked Saul, gazing up at the fruits of the tree.

"They haven't been sprayed," said Angela. "They're naturally white like that. Brock doesn't like it. I think he tried to sell them that way before, but people are averse. White on fruit; I don't know. It reminds people of mold or something. But they're not rotten at all; quite the opposite. They've just been born."

"What does he spray them with?"

Angela shrugged. "He does it himself."

RISE THE MOON

"All the chemistry?"

"And the labor," she said. "He comes out here once a week and showers all the trees with a little arboreal make-up. We've asked before, but Brock always says it'd be useless to tell now. He's still working on the formula after all, and it's subject to change. But you should see when it happens. They color turn right away like light bulbs. You'd think it was magic."

Then the woman stepped in front of him and reached forth to one of the lowly serpentine boughs. Each one of her hands plucked a glorious globe, and she handed one to him as she bit. Saul followed suit. Saliva sprang from his glands as he sucked the sugar sweet streams of apple blood that dripped from the tip of his upper lip. The tension he'd carried so long in every muscle fiber below eased out of his mind like a running river. The fruit held the impression of Saul's teeth, collecting pools of juice between the ridges of his bite. Saul licked these deliberately clean until nothing more soaked through, and he chewed out a new spot of red. Angela took him by the other hand, and the two waltzed further into the orchard.

"It's so strange how everything works out," said Angela.

"How?"

"I was feeling so alone that I ran to the Church for some kind of better purpose; and I got it, sort of. Every service and group meeting and charity event I went to I learned more and more about myself. It was kind of wonderful. But then you joined. And now today I'm happiest of all precisely because I'm not there. I was still alone. Finally someone is around to share things with."

"Sharing," said Saul aloud. He thought for a moment. "Yes, the entanglement of our identity with each and every experience is muddy and tedious. Something that I experience with or through another person is not mine. It exists only in a sort of communal space between us. If someone asks me who I am, it would be ridiculous to respond by naming those shared experiences. They're only as much a part of me as is an idea that pops randomly into my head which I choose whether or not to adopt before tossing it back into the unconscious abyss. And if I change my mind, I'll rein it back, but it is not a component of Saul; for if it were, I would be diminished when I threw it away, yet here I am not believing or being many things I once was and still am as solid a man as ever

JACOB KOCKEN

has been."

"How did you get so wise?"

"The great scientists of the past achieved their deeds by working within a shrouded frame of truth. Edison did not harness electricity into the light bulb by a stroke of luck. He knew the relevant principles of the physical world and commanded great intention to harmonize them. He followed the framework of science as discovered by other men; I follow the framework of the Lord as disclosed to me by inspiration."

"Can you teach me?"

He stopped and kissed her there surrounded in the cover of a thousand arboreal guards. Saul swelled. His chest rose, and something giddy escaped on his breath. Then he sat her down cross legged on the ground. He was across from her and brought out the long, plastic tube he carried. The end cap popped off, and out slid a cylinder of canvas. The new edges still held their curl when fully unrolled on the grass between them. It was perfectly blank. Angela stared.

"It's empty," she said.

"It's ready," he corrected.

"Ready?"

"Yes."

"Did you bring paint?"

"Yes."

"Well, what are we going to draw?"

"That part," said Saul, "is not up to us."

"No?"

"Not entirely. But I trust it will be to our liking." Saul then began to unwind the mess of gauze wrapping his hand. It had yellowed over the last few days of wear, and when the base layers were reached it wrinkled Angela's nose.

"That's a nasty cut," she said. "What happened?"

Saul smiled. "Should I so simply reveal His mysteries? No. I think He ought to." Saul's other hand reached into his pocket and returned pinching a silver razor blade. Angela stiffened when Saul put it to his cut.

"Saul, don't—"

But he hushed her. His stolid expression calmed her wor-

RISE THE MOON

ry while his fist tightened into a ball. It opened again, and blood rained down from his fingers like a plague. "Look at the canvas," he said. He had to scold her with his eyes when she refused to look off of his face. "Tell me what you see." His fist balled again and squeezed. Another spurt of blood fell onto the canvas, speckling it red. The little pools touched each other and began to run in organic patterns away from their original splash marks. The uneven grass below made miniscule peaks and valleys that sent the blood drops rolling. Then Saul tipped up the corners here and there to direct the flow. He made two legs; two arms. "See how it moves to Nature's accord? That's Him. Read it."

"Like the Rorschach thing?"

"Tell me what you see." Angela looked. Her head was turned slightly askew, and her eyelids trembled halfway down. "Does the sight make you squeamish?"

"When it drops," she said. "When it comes out."

"It's okay. Don't look for a moment then." One of his red fingers came up and tipped her head back so she was looking up at the sky. "Take a few deep breaths." Angela followed his instruction and gasped on the third inhale as he poked the blade into the palm of her hand.

"Oh, Jesus," she exclaimed. "Saul don't—"

Her expression had turned toward the pain which lay an inch above the canvas. Her palm dropped just a few red dots before she snatched it back. But her eyes stayed stuck on the ground. Saul saw her focus in. The depth of her pupils showed. Then she looked back and forth between the canvas and the sky. The shifting clouds had rolled in above.

"Let your mind perceive what comes," said Saul, "and don't run away. Believe it. There. Did you see?"

"See? No."

"There he was."

"Who?"

"It looked like a man," said Saul.

"Oh. Maybe." Angela was squinting, and her eyes flicked back and forth between the man on the canvas and the man in the sky. "Oh, was that his arm?"

"Indeed, I think it was. Look there."

JACOB KOCKEN

"Yes," said Angela. "Is that his head moving to the right?"

"Oh, yes."

"Who is it, do you suppose?"

"Don't ask me," said Saul. "You're the one seeing him after all. You tell me, Angela. Who is it you see in the sky?"

She didn't say anything for a long time; she just looked up there at the turning white vapor. Her mouth opened slightly, and her head rocked softly back and forth as Saul entwined his fingers in her long blonde hair. It was in a ponytail as it always was when she ran. Saul snuck a finger through the elastic tie and slipped it off so her hair spilled over the grass. Then Angela stopped moving. Her face was hooked on the heavens. She squinted as one from the crow's nest lost at sea when the shimmering waves mirage. "Oh my God," she said at last. Saul smiled ear to ear and kissed her again.

"You did it, Saul," she said.

"I did?"

"I see him. I saw him. He was in the clouds." Her eyes became as misty as the swirling sky.

Then he got up and climbed on top to kiss her. They stayed there amidst the SummerTime apples as the sky drifted from light to dark.

When they took to their feet and returned to the front gates, evening was fully upon them. Her house was there straight across the street, and because she asked him, Saul did not return home that entire night through.

40.
Ira

THE SUNDAY AIR WAS THICK with moisture that had not fallen all summer. The flowers from Great-Grandma Bess were standing strong in a vase on the kitchen table. He planned to go after dinner, but his mother had not come home from her visit to the church and his father had gone without explanation. Ira thought perhaps that was best. He no longer wished to eat for his stomach was cramped with nerves.

He'd found a mason jar to use as a vase and dressed himself in his good amber shirt; the one people said made his eyes glow. He'd worn it not long ago, but now it felt tight in the shoulders and high on his wrists. When he tucked its ends into his pants the extra material pushed his belt just a bit off its regular notch so that it was too tight for comfort. He owned a neck tie too. It was white with little black dots. Ira slung each end over a shoulder and went to the bathroom mirror. It had been fastened around him on only a handful of occasions, most recently a wedding for a friend of his mother's. He pictured her before him now, how her hands looped the thing over and around itself. It was hard to concentrate on the task. His image in the mirror was fuzzy and he kept blinking hard at himself. Circles of sweat darkened the underarm fabric. His skin had been smoldering under the long pants and polo for a few hours prior. There was a hint of color all over him. He must have gotten burned at the lake.

Ira reached down and grabbed the bottle he'd taken from its hiding place. Only a few draughts were left. The minty flavor of the toothpaste he'd just used was washed away in the whiskey sting.

JACOB KOCKEN

He took another sip and blinked.

Ira's unpracticed knots with the necktie were guesswork, and he undid them all just as soon as they were made. He left the thing folded over itself on the bathroom counter. Finally, he took up his father's straight razor. He cut slow and careful, coming away as clean as the day he was born. There was more of an Adam's apple than he had ever noticed before. He moved as delicately around the uneven surfaces as possible, but when he came to the far side of his neck the sharp edge caught skin and dug. Ira flinched and dropped the razor. A little stream of blood came down to his collar. It wiped away easily enough with a square of toilet paper, and Ira pressed on the wound until it clotted. He shaved off the rest of his budding hairs and checked his nick in the glass. It glared bright and garish with simple imperfection.

He palmed the now empty whiskey and marched to his room. He'd had the intention to stash it back underneath his bed, but when he saw the flowers falling in several directions over the wide mouth of their mason jar, he slipped them instead into the narrow-necked liquor bottle.

Then Ira set off for the town across the bridge. The sun was going down, nearly at horizon. Above him, the nascent moon, surrounded by dying orange light, ushered him on. The walk to Anna Lee's house was being made longer by his slow, nervous steps. The flowers bounced haphazardly around the narrow neck of their glass container. He tried not to sweat.

"Homecoming is soon," he spoke beneath his breath, beneath the sound of his striding feet. "There'll be a dance."

He didn't know how to say it. All he was truly sure of was the fear that the flowers were cut and would most certainly die and decay right here and now. The thought crossed his mind even not to knock on the door but simply to leave them out front and run, and to go on living contented with the imagined scene of her joy upon finding them. His heart, however, dismissed such thoughts. The butterflies did not calm. Every step only brought him closer to her. And that growing proximity dizzied him in the same way that panic strikes one standing near a precipice. He began to hum to calm himself. It was unconscious, a beautiful and melancholy melody.

There was the bridge up ahead; the last piece of town. Ira felt

RISE THE MOON

for a moment he might be sick. He stopped and held his stomach. The feeling did not pass, so he strode on, trying to picture her happy. Her smile, even artificially conjured, soothed him. He went on.

Ira's feet fell numb against the gravel road as he crossed into the shade of the Old Graumont forest. His hand ran repeatedly through his hair, smoothing it out whenever the breeze untidied him. He saw the earth pass by below as his eyes bent down upon the daffodils. Then as if time had skipped a beat, the smell of ash touched him, and Ira knew he was there. The girl's house stood some forty yards away from the razed one, and before he knew it, Ira was on a one step concrete porch knocking on her front door.

He stepped back and waited. There was movement in one of the windows, and Ira heard the tones of urgent steps and voices. Still no one came, and he knocked again. The longer he waited the more he began to sweat. He was wiping his forehead dry when at last the door creaked open. A woman Ira had never seen before poked her head out. She was tall and thin with grey blue eyes and hair as long and dark as Anna Lee's. The woman gripped the door with both hands at first. There was dirt beneath her fingernails. The trepidation on her face softened when she took in the scene.

"Hello?" said the woman. Her voice was questioning but kind. Ira noticed only now that she was breathing quickly as if she'd been on a run.

"Is Anna Lee here?"

The woman didn't answer at first. She let go of the door and stood up straighter in the space between it and the threshold. Then she brushed at herself as if the dirt embedded into her shirt would fall away under the simple touch of a hand. She looked back at him, and Ira could see her eyes trained on the daffodils. A deep breath came through her nose, and she said to him, "Wait here."

She left him there at the door step, and another minute passed in the silence of the forest before the door opened up again. Anna Lee slipped out. She seemed nearly a miniature of the woman before, except for the darkness of her eyes and the pretty sun dress she wore in place of a soiled shirt and denim. Her curiosity was plain as her eyes traveled all over him.

"Ira," she said.

"Hey."

JACOB KOCKEN

"What's going on?"

She too was looking at the daffodils. Birds and crickets waxed in the silence. Ira clicked his feet together as he took little, motionless steps. "Do you want to go for a walk?"

Anna Lee smiled, and the two of them stepped off the little porch. She led him toward the backyard where a path ran through the woods. It was only just wide enough for the two of them to walk side by side. Ira found his hand and shoulder grazing against hers now and then as they passed beneath the oak and aspen branches.

"It's been quite hot this summer hasn't it?" said Anna Lee as the trees thickened to a curtain that blocked all sight of houses in the scattered town behind them.

"Yes," said Ira. "Yes, quite hot."

"Is it always like that?"

"No. Usually it's better. Not so hot I mean. You're probably used to it, being from California. Just wait a couple months. It'll get cold fast. Winter is longer than summer here. It usually snows by November. Have you ever seen snow?"

"Of course," Anna Lee giggled.

"Does it snow in California?"

"Well, I wasn't from the beach. I don't know if it snows much there. My family lived in the mountains. The Sierra Nevada. It snows a whole lot in the winter."

"I can't wait for winter."

"Why's that?"

"No reason," said Ira. "It's just been too hot this year." The path they walked took a turn to the west, and they went on back in the direction of Graumont. As they passed tree after tree, the two of them searched for signs of cooler weather in the leaves. They were still a deep summer green all around until Anna Lee gave a little gasp and pointed to the sky. Up ahead of them was an oak. Hidden in the midst of its emerald flora was a single gold harbinger rimmed with red.

"Look," she said, pointing.

"I see it," said Ira. "It's beautiful."

"Soon they'll all be like that. Then I'll come out here in the middle of the day and see the sunset all around me." Anna Lee appeared rapt by the thought of the changing colors. She stared up at

RISE THE MOON

the single yellow leaf for a long time. And as she did so, Ira stared too. He stared at the whiteness of her dress; the blackness of her hair; the redness of her lips.

"You know what else it looks like?" said Anna Lee. She started walking again and looked quickly back at him over her shoulder. Ira saw her eyes dart down to the daffodils he still held in the whisky bottle.

"I got these for you," he said quickly as if he'd only just remembered. He jumped to catch up with Anna Lee along the path and held the flowers out in front of her.

"Did you?" she said. Her eyes went playful and wide. "I thought you might have. Were they from Furke's place?"

"What?"

"The flower shop Furke works at. Is that where you got them? Did he give you a discount?"

"They're not from Furke," said Ira. "They're from me. I picked them. I picked them myself. I did."

"Oh. Well, yes they're nice. They're nice, Ira. Thank you." She took them from his hand and admired the radiant color. Her nose bent down to sample the fragrance. Then Anna Lee turned quiet. They went on in the direction dictated by the path, the girl's eyes constantly down on the golden petals. After a few minutes of walking, the sky ahead began to open up. The forest path widened slightly, and the thickness of the trees diminished. Then the woods were behind them, and Ira found himself wading into tall prairie grass. The great fissure lay a hundred yards ahead of them and the town of Graumont to the west was glowing red on the sunset horizon.

Anna Lee's dress trailed on the tips of bluestem. "These could use some water," she said holding up the empty bottle that cradled her daffodils. Then she turned and walked toward the west so that she seemed to tread right into the sun.

"Where are you going?" asked Ira.

"There's a stream down there." Anna Lee pointed to the gorge. They followed the line of broken earth until they came near the old stone bridge. A group of jutting rocks in descending fashion made for a natural staircase there. Ira and Anna Lee peered over the edge into the chasm. With the sun so low, the hole appeared bottomless.

JACOB KOCKEN

The tranquil trickle of water could still be faintly heard.
"Anna Lee?" said Ira.
"Yes?"
"Do you know what Homecoming is?"
"Sort of."
"You've seen the signs at school?"
"I know there's a football game. And a dance."
"Right," said Ira. Her eyes had finally come up off the daffodils. She was piercing him. He hesitated. Her eyebrows began to knit. Her lips tightened. Ira waited for the words to come up from his chest, but instead of his own voice the thing that found his ears was the cyclical squeaking of steel.

Both Ira and Anna Lee seemed to have heard it. Their faces left each other's and found a figure on the other side of the gorge. For a moment, he was a silhouette as he pedaled across the setting sun. Then the light bent around him and revealed the freckled face of Furke. His long limbs moved in rhythm as he coursed over the sidewalk toward the bridge. Ira saw he was still dressed as he did for work; black pants and a long button-down shirt. Today, he wore a bowtie. Ira had never seen any such adornment about his friend before. But what was particularly new and perturbing was what balanced across the handlebars. In the steady grip of Furke's left hand was a bundle, a bouquet of flowers, roses red as wine wrapped in protective plastic from Betty Blossom's with a thin white ribbon around the dozen stems. Ira stepped closer to Anna Lee. As Furke came nearer the bridge, his face raised and pointed in their direction. Then his arms went somewhat lax and his legs stopped pedaling. A whine from the gears of the bike wound out on the air.

Anna Lee gasped slightly as Ira took her by the arm. He bent his face to hers and kissed her hard on the mouth. His other hand clutched her waist, and he brought the girl toward his body.

"Ira," she said. He could feel the breath that spoke his name. It touched his own lips as soon as it left hers. "Ira stop." He kissed her again; harder, so that she could not form the final plosive sound. Then Ira felt her pull back, and he went with her. They stumbled a bit on the uneven prairie ground. The weight of gravity shook her loose and Ira grabbed. She was slipping away. There was a sudden sound of tearing and Ira saw the skin of Anna Lee's leg travel up to

RISE THE MOON

her hip beneath the torn sundress. He held one end of it and yanked. The girl fell toward him again, pulled like a dog on a leash, and he wrapped his arms around her body.

"Ira," she said. This time it was louder with displeasure ringing through her voice. Ira reached down and grabbed her. He felt her legs clench together. The muscles in her limbs went tight, and when he tried to kiss her again there came a pounding blow to his ribs. The wind blew hard and sudden at his back, distorting all sound into a blind and confused stupor. The clapping of hurried feet had come and stopped. There was a shattering of glass as the girl lost grip on the bottled flowers. Ira let go of Anna Lee and pushed back like a bull at the other boy. A sharp pain came across the nape of Ira's neck as Furke fought back. Perhaps he reached out to plead or simply to grab hold of someone or something as he fell toppling to the ground. But no ground was there to hold him. Rather, a gap in the earth stretched hungrily, and a long way down, the tall, froggish boy went spinning with all the force of Ira's desperate fury.

In the dying light, Ira rose to his feet, only slowly regaining a sense of clarity and shaking violent tears from his eyes. They were both gone; one fallen down below and the other slipping away in Ira's confusion. When he stood all the way up he had instantly to fall back again to his knees and shake and heave at the glimpse of the red spotted rocks. They declined with their coloration down to where the darkness ate them, and the Earth's trap door hung limp. The wind had settled. There was no sound in the night other than a hoarse, choking breath and the steady trickling of a stream that had been dying for years, set to evaporate entirely with the heat of the coming day.

Ira cried. Then he ran.

He ran across the bridge and a quarter mile down the road before a guilty fear reeled him all the way back. He looked down into the gorge and saw it again. A groan came rattling out from the pit, and Ira hurried away a second time. Back and forth his head swung, searching for rescuers to call and witnesses to purge. Headlights appeared, turning onto an adjacent street. Ira called out, and when the car passed by he chased it. His hands arced frantically overhead as he stumbled along, the vehicle diminishing in the distance. Then it was gone, and he was alone again with the body in the gorge.

JACOB KOCKEN

Down at the edge, right where the world dropped away, something shimmered gold. A group of daffodils harkened, their petals caught beneath a pane of glass. Ira came to them. The bottle had split and shattered like the Virgin statue he'd once seen his father pouring penance over. One large broken piece lay alone, its long edge razor sharp. Ira remembered the words of his father and fell down on his knees, directing anguish upward. He held the edge to his open palm, but before the skin could break, his guts went rumbling. Ira quivered reflexively and bent over at the stomach. A sticky, rank black discharge splattered the wild meadow grass. He wretched a second and third time in painful purging. The sharp, cracked-off piece of glass tumbled out of his grip over the edge of the gorge, chiming off the steep rock slope. And in his head, Ira prayed. The sky turned black with evening, and the stars stayed back behind the darkness.

Then on the other side of the gorge, emerging from the trees of Old Graumont and running like some injured and disjointed mule, came a strange shadow. Ira stood beside the bridge waving again, calling out toward the thing as it approached. They were holding hands; one in front and hurried, pulling her bewildered companion like a half-moored anchor through the prairie grass. Ira started running up to them but halted when the twilit crossbeams revealed two unforgettable faces. That one was the same as in all his recent reveries. The other was of ineffable quality; porcelain skin so smooth it shown off her cheeks and forehead like a clean china plate; and as pale and round as the harvest moon. She stood tall and grown as a woman save the hanging mouth and anxious, inquiring expression.

The closer they came the more the sound of their feet swishing through the prairie grass transformed to Anna Lee's hushing whispers. Ira moved toward them again, but in the closing space he met her tortured eyes and was so struck with pain that he did not follow as she led the tall, bumbling woman down the slag stairs; down into the gorge. The only sound amidst the crickets was Anna Lee below the earth, crying and pleading without words.

Peeking over the edge of the bridge, Ira saw only their shapes. Shadows hid the blood. The big one moved the most. Anna Lee whispered to her. Her voice kept going, asking, pleading. The other mounted his body. She lay down on top of him, and a moment later

RISE THE MOON

she was up again, and Anna Lee was speaking louder and crying and standing. Then the shuffling sounds of feet and rocks crawled up the slag and the two of them were up again out of the gorge holding hands, leading and being led, running back down the gravel road into the woods.

Ira watched them run. She didn't look back at him, and he didn't chase. When he looked down into the gorge the shadows were different. He ran to where they had climbed and tread down into the pit. He whipped north and south, and though it was dark, found a conspicuous nothing on the ground. He went one way, then the other, pacing and searching. He passed the walls of graffiti whereupon his face began to sting in a thousand places. The pores all across him flushed with sweat.

Then Ira saw him. He was sitting on a rock against the gorge wall. He was on the other side of the bridge now, looking up at the stars blinking on in the night sky and rubbing his knees and arms and face with long skinny fingers.

"I'm cold, Ira. Aren't you cold?" said Furke. His skin seemed paler than usual. It was smooth. His freckles hid behind the rock face shadows.

Ira froze before the voice. Then he melted and fell into his friend's chest, embracing him. Ira hung there, unable to squeeze. Potency abandoned him. They sat there at the bottom of the gorge for a long time looking up at the lights and not talking. The night air was dank between the rocks, and they leaned against each other's warmth. Finally, Furke stirred. He tried to stand, but Ira clung to him, and he was unable to move. Ira's head slid against the cool limestone wall. Three times Ira cocked his head back and struck the stone before Furke pulled him away. A bead of blood rolled down his nose from the crown where the skin had broken.

"Hey," said Furke. He held Ira tight between his arms. "Stop that. Are you hurt?"

Ira could hardly breathe.

"Can I let you go? Will you stop hitting your head?"

"Yes."

Furke's grip softened, and Ira found his legs. "Come on. We should clean you up," said Furke. Ira simply nodded. They climbed up out of the hole and began walking in the direction of home.

JACOB KOCKEN

Their sojourn was long. Furke pushed his bike by hand. The streets seemed to stretch out forever. Furke dallied, always looking around; looking hard at the lights, and the trees, and the grass, and the houses, and even his own shoes as they trod. An expression of wonder was always budding.

"What happened?" asked Ira. His friend seemed not to hear. Furke stared off into space, his head tilted. Only many moments later did he turn and acknowledge Ira.

"What?"

"That girl. What did Anna Lee say?"

"Anna Lee isn't here," said Furke. His eyes flashed sidelong in each direction. Then his face went blank and contented. They walked for a while in silence.

"Take a picture," said Furke.

"What?"

"You keep staring at me." Furke's eyes were full of reflected starlight. It covered up the green iris color almost entirely.

"Am I crazy?"

"Yeah, I think so," said Furke. "Because of Anna Lee?"

"What?"

"Were you going to ask her out or something like that? Is that why we came all the way out here? My stomach says that." Ira found nothing to say. "You like her, huh?"

"No," said Ira. "That's not it." Furke's froggish grin was visible in the pale moonlight. His hands were together, and he kept popping knuckles as they walked.

"Oh." Furke blew an audible breath. "Because. Well, I know she probably thinks I'm a dope. But I kind of think…"

"Yeah," said Ira.

"Yeah."

They came eventually to the corner of Lennox Street where Ira hugged Furke so tightly that his friend had to push him off in the end. They parted ways, but Ira stood there a long while watching Furke saunter tall and happy into the night.

When Ira reached home himself he found it dark and quiet even for a late evening. There was no one bustling in the kitchen or relaxing in the living room. Upstairs, he turned on the hallway light and saw even his parents' bedroom empty.

RISE THE MOON

Ira locked his door and collapsed to his stomach beside the bed. He had to crawl on his elbows under the beams where there was just enough room to tip the final bottle to his lips. It dripped and pooled onto the carpet, fading quick as if borne down on by the desert sky. Ira didn't stop until the libation sucked dry. But the bottle was close to its end. Air filled the whole container quickly, and Ira could not get a proper dose. The scenes refilled his mind, and all night long he was plagued with the sensation of falling.

41.
Ira

WHEN IRA WOKE THAT MORNING the house was still empty. He got out of bed in the same clothes he'd worn the night before. The good amber polo had stains of black streaking the front checkers. It carried the smell of a stagnant pond. Instead of the laundry bin, he discarded the shirt in the bathroom garbage. Ira did not raise his face to look himself in the mirror and left for school without eating. Buses had not yet filed in when Ira got there.

He encountered Furke at the back doors. The Paulsen twins were there. The three of them were yelling over each other in argument. The debate was explained to Ira in their brash, boyish way. He heard none of it until the twins mentioned how they'd been summoned to the police station for questioning. The cops thought they'd burned the Yokoven house. They'd be damned if the pigs pinned the thing on them just because of Bobby's innocent after school stunt as King of Ashes.

Even so, Ira only stared at Furke, waiting for one of the boys' shouts or shoves to wake him from a dream. When the morning bell rang it sent a spark down Ira's spine.

In the classroom, Ira sat at his desk and watched the clock. Kids started to appear slowly and then all at once, but the seat beside him remained vacant. Halfway through class he excused himself. The halls were a square, white tunnel through time and space. Ira roamed from door to door in silence. Each time he passed one of those wooden frames, he peered through the window into the other classrooms. But the portals were void, and she was nowhere to be found.

42.
Saul

A FAR AWAY SOUND. CRYING, muffled beneath his hands. He caressed her. The woman smiled and her eyes swung from his hands to his eyes then out to the blackness. He kissed her. He worshipped her. He pressed her torso between his hands, compressing as she shrieked with glee. She did not watch as he watched. She seemed not to notice the wonder of it. Her eyes flicked between somethings and nothings out off the world's edge. Then it was flat, and he kissed her from head to toe and pulled at her clothes until they fell like scales from her new body. Her teeth were pearls, and they could do nothing but smile.

Saul woke and was met by the reposed figure of another woman. Angela blinked slowly. The sleep left their eyes, and she leaned over to kiss him.

"I like that," she said. "Waking up beside you."

"Yes," said Saul. The girl's room was strange. He hardly recalled the details of the house from the night before, and now he found it disconcerting. There was a lot of pink. "I ought to get out of your hair. It's nearly nine."

"Are you in a rush?" she asked.

"It's Monday. I shouldn't keep you from work."

"You're not."

"You don't work Mondays?"

"I don't have a job at all right now."

"No job?"

"Brock pays for this place. He owns SummerTime after all; supporting me is hardly a burden. I help out around the orchard

JACOB KOCKEN

when there's something fun to do," she said. "And speaking of him, I have a surprise for you." Saul had been circling his thumb in a light massage over Angela's arm as she spoke, and when the hand traveled up to pinch her cheek his knuckles found dampness straightening her long blond hair.

"You're wet," he said. "Did you shower already?"

"Yes."

"And then came back to bed?"

"Saul, I have a surprise for you," she said. "We're having brunch with my mom and Brock."

"What?"

"I called them to come over. You were so precious sleeping I didn't want to wake you. It's not until eleven, though. We've got a couple hours."

"No," said Saul. "That's not necessary Angela. Not necessary at all."

"Oh, but they'll love you," she whined. "Come on, up then."

Saul had only the clothes he'd worn the previous night. They carried the smell of soil, and grass stains were on the legs and elbows.

"It's really not a good day for me," said Saul. "I've got things to do."

"Really?" said Angela. "What are you doing?"

"Well," said Saul, "lots of things. I've got lots of things to do. They'll probably take all day."

Angela laid a hand on his shoulder. It was soft, and even through his agitation Saul melted into its caress. "Are you nervous?"

"What?"

"Lots of people get nervous about meeting my stepdad. SummerTime made him the richest man for miles, and everyone's scared of making a bad impression. I get that. But you've got nothing to worry about."

"No?"

"After Dad died and Mom married Brock, I got pretty aloof. I didn't like him. He wasn't really my dad, you know? And he's not exclusive with Mom. I don't know how she accepted that. Anyway, Brock put me up in this place as a nice gesture. To try to win me over, I guess. But I was always cold. It was hard to get close to any-

RISE THE MOON

one. I didn't even talk to Mom about anything important for a long time. Actually, it was only very recently that I called her up and broke that ice. I told her I loved her, Saul. I do love her a lot, and I just hadn't said it in years because... I don't know why. She said it too though. That she loves me. I've hardly ever felt so warm and happy. We got to talking about things; about Dad. I told her I was sorry for not being able to move on. She said she was sorry too for marrying so quickly. She and Brock just had a connection she said. Something spiritual. And do you know what Saul? That day that I called her was the day we went on our first run, and I understood everything she said." Then she kissed him tenderly on the lips. "A week or so later, I told her about you. I've never heard Mom cry from happiness, but she did right then. You've got nothing to worry about, Saul."

Angela fit so easily when she leaned into him. Saul closed his eyes and rubbed up and down her back with his good palm. She was not heavy though Saul could tell he was supporting all her weight. He let out a big breath and squeezed her. Then he kissed the top of her head.

"Thank you, Angela."

Her soft pupils were large and dark. They found his, and Saul felt a knot rising in his throat. His neck was getting hot. So were the corners of his eyes. But before any tear could form and drop, Saul was arrested by a sudden, uncanny silence. Some heretofore unnoticed sound had left them, conspicuous now by the chasm it left in its wake. Saul sat up in the bed and looked at the door. It stood open a crack. Across the hallway was the bathroom.

"Was that the shower?"

"Sorry," said Angela. "Brock's had an issue with his plumbing the last couple days." Saul pulled the top sheet off the bed and up over his naked chest. He looked to Angela in confusion and then back at the door.

"Your stepdad?" She nodded.

"Sorry again. I know it's a weird way to meet. We ought to get dressed."

Saul stood in anxious brooding for a moment while Angela eased herself around to the other side of the room. She was mostly dressed already he saw. Her pants were on and there was a shirt at the ready on the bedside table. Saul, on the other hand, was struck all along his body with the sensitive touch of morning air when he finally threw back the blankets. He turned to climb off the mattress and shut his eyes before the rising sun as its rays poured through the window. Angela's bedroom was on the second floor and Saul kept peering out through squinted eyes at the distance of the drop. It wasn't terribly far. One might be able to jump without breaking a foot.

Just as Saul had done his fly and pulled on his shirt from the night before, there was a hollow tap from the opposite side of the room. It rapped three times. Angela checked quickly on Saul's state of dress and took herself to the bedroom door. She swung it smoothly open to reveal a sea of purple.

The man who stood in the hallway had the chest of a behemoth. Water dripped down from a head of black and grey dappling the folds of a royal purple robe. His shoulders took all the space between the jambs and upon his face he wore a set of thin-rimmed golden glasses. At first, the giant man looked only on Angela. He asked her how she was and thanked her for the use of the shower. His voice, Saul knew. It was uncommonly loud even though he did not yell with excitement. And when at last the man looked off of his stepdaughter Saul recognized the face as well.

"Hello," said the SummerTime owner. "You must be the man I've heard so much about. Angela has spun quite a thread on you. I could hardly wait to make your acquaintance." He smiled. He looked Saul up and down one quick time before holding him by the eyes. "I hope you're all she says you are, Saul. Our Angel deserves it." He offered an enormous hand, waiting for Saul to shake. When he did, the big man enveloped him, surrounding Saul from thumb to pinky.

"Are you hurt?" said Brock. His powerful grip still held Saul by the hand. It was the bandaged palm he'd shaken with, and Mr. Nabers pulled it up closer to examine.

"Just a cut," said Saul. "Nothing special." He made to pull back the hand, but it did not come. The giant held him by the wrist, an amiable concern on his face.

"Do let me see," he said. "Angela tells me you've had this wound for a while. Perhaps it's nothing. But you can never be too

RISE THE MOON

careful."

"Brock might be able to help," said Angela. "He's a scientist after all."

"It's fine," said Saul. But the big man did not let go, and his fingers found the end of the gauze.

"I insist."

Saul felt a prickling pain as the wrap around his hand loosened and the adhesive of the bandage below was peeled up. The skin beneath appeared bleached. Only in the center of the palm was his wound red. Most of it had healed again, but the space of a centimeter or two was red and puffing.

"How long has it been?" asked the giant.

"A few weeks."

"More than a month?"

"I'm not sure."

The orchard owner grumbled over thoughts and kept changing the distance and angle at which he inspected Saul's open wound. "Angela has told us you were a man of God."

"Yes?"

"Don't you know what this is?"

"It's a cut. Just a cut."

"Ha!" The giant relinquished the hold he had on Saul. "I won't let you escape so easily, sir. You've got something special here and you know it. Don't you? Don't you? You must. A man of God such as yourself. A learned man. Don't tell me you don't know. Can that be true, Saul?"

Saul caught a look from Angela by the door. Her loving gaze was on him, hope twinkling on her eyes. He stood up straighter than he had been and took the wounded hand into the other. "No," he said as he began to redo the wrappings. "No, I know. I know." Once he'd said this he looked down at his hand, down at the floor, away from the piercing stare of the giant man in his purple robe.

Then the sterile scent of soap interrupted Saul's breath as the big man came close to him. Inches away, the orchard owner spoke for the first time with a voice unprojected by the bellows chest. The whisper tickled every little hair inside Saul's ear. "You are the soul mate for our Angel?" He did not step back after speaking, and Saul was left to stare at the purple ocean of satin in front of him. There

JACOB KOCKEN

was gold stitching that followed the edges and wrote just below the left shoulder the letters *B. Nabers*. When Saul tried to peer up to the man's face he felt himself shrunken as if the body before him were a mountain whose shadow looked down on the clouds.

"Are you saying that of your own accord?" Saul answered in equal whisper. He looked again at Angela where she stood patiently. Her hair was down. It fell gracefully over her shoulders, shining yellow in the reflection of the sun all around her head. "Or did she say it of me?"

"Am I her heart?" the giant answered. "She herself has brought you here. Brought you to me. Have you given her good reason to believe it?"

"I am a man of the soul," said Saul.

Mr. Nabers smirked and continued in his undertone. "That job offer is rescinded. I've got other plans for a man like you." A moment of silence passed between them. Then the big man stepped back, and his voice returned to the powerful barking pitch he'd spoken with before. "Ha! Come, the both of you." He paced into the hallway and waved toward Saul with a wheeling hand. "I've got something for that wound of yours, my boy."

Saul hesitated but followed and met with Angela at the bedroom door. She welcomed him with an embrace and did not fully let go as they walked side by side in the wake of her stepfather. Angela's arm rested into the length of his, and her hand intertwined with Saul's unmarred one. It was warm and pleasant, and Saul found himself smiling in private wonder all the way down the stairs and out into the daylight. When they crossed the lawn to the nearest house, one large and towering compared to everything Saul had seen in Graumont, the burly man instructed them to wait on the porch. He entered the house alone and came back out several minutes later. In his arms, he held a pot filled with black earth. From out of the dirt there grew a sapling tree. It's thin trunk stood four feet tall with spindling branches winding out around the upper half. It had dark green leaves and was already budding fruit. Saul recognized it as a fractal of one of the many SummerTime trees he'd seen the night before.

"Take this home with you," Mr. Nabers said to Saul. "Eat from it as it blooms. I believe you'll find your ailments fixed. Whatever

RISE THE MOON

they may be." He handed the sapling over to Saul who buckled momentarily under the weight of it. "Can you carry it?"

"Yes," Saul assured the man. Mr. Nabers chuckled, and Saul took it for approval. Then the big man pressed Angela by the hand.

"I'll see you two for brunch?"

"Thank you Brock," said Angela. "We'll see you at eleven."

"Very good," said the giant. He brushed the front of his body where dirt had fallen from the potted plant. It fell away easily from the satin, leaving the purple robe immaculate once again. "See you soon, Saul." Then he turned and reentered the mansion.

Before Saul knew it, Angela was at his side. She ran her hand up the nape of his neck, and he melted into the caress of her fingers through his hair. They embraced, and she stood back with a giddy smile. "I think he likes you," she said.

"Yeah?"

"I've never seen him give anyone a sapling before." The miniature tree stood with them under the shade of the porch awning. "Shall we bring it home?" asked Angela. Saul's eyes darted to the house across the lawn where he'd slept the night. "I mean your home, silly. It's yours after all."

"I don't know," said Saul. "Maybe it should stay here." The tree's little fruit hung pale from the branches and Saul toyed with one between his fingers. He did not mean to pick it, but the stem was thin, and his twisting was all it could bear. As he rolled it between his fingers, Angela bowed her head toward the apple. He felt the supple edge of her lips across the folds of his hand as she bit down. She'd taken a quarter of the little fruit with her teeth and looked up at Saul with satisfaction.

"Still sweet," she said. Saul followed her example and tried the thing for himself. It was candy on his tongue. There was none of the acid sour most premature fruit takes on. They bit back and forth in bliss and before Saul realized what was happening the apple was down to its core and his mouth was on Angela. They kissed there in the bliss of the shade several times.

"Let's go," said Saul. "I'll need a change of clothes anyhow."

The two of them walked side by side down the long road that led past the SummerTime orchard. They had thought at first to drive but could not fit the young tree inside Angela's car. It would've had

JACOB KOCKEN

to lay down and spill its dirt. The branches would have bent and snapped. The budding orbs of fruit might have gotten crushed. So they walked; this time side by side but without hand in hand for Saul needed both arms to lift the weight of the tree. His good hand hooked the bottom of the pot while his wrapped one steadied the trunk. It leaned against his body for support, and Saul felt an instant sweat break out across his crown, washing down into his eyes. The ubiquitous soreness he'd lived with since taking on the habit of running flared in every muscle. Saul leaned back and forth trying to find comfort.

"Are you sure you can carry that?" asked Angela.

"Yes."

"The whole way there?"

"I've got it," said Saul.

The day was overcast, but a light breeze from the north was pushing clear skies in fast. For much of their route, Saul and Angela walked with the wind and had no cause to notice anything at all except the rhythm of their bodies and the frequent infatuations of the other. But as they came to the end of the fields where the suburbs began to rise, there was a terrible constricting in Saul's right calf, and he went down hard on the concrete. He kept the sapling upright most of the way down, but it tipped as it struck the ground. Jet black soil went spilling from the pot.

"What is it?" said Angela breathing hard in his face. Saul's leg folded involuntarily at the knee. He grimaced in pain and tried with little avail to stretch it out. Angela ran her palm down his leg and found a knot the size of a golf ball. He yelped when she touched it. "I'm trying to work it out," she said. "Hold still." She turned him over onto his stomach and pressed her thumbs back and forth over the cramp as Saul's face tossed across the sidewalk in anguish.

When finally the tension eased and the pain subsided enough, Angela helped Saul back to his feet. He took a few tentative steps under her support and then began to walk by his own strength. Again, he carried the sapling, hugging it tightly around the pot and leaning back as he walked to hold it steady. He looked up periodically as he went, watching the top of the tree sway before the sky. For a moment, he forgot the ardor of his task, and looking up at the swirling clouds through the branches of a tree, he felt himself back

RISE THE MOON

in the SummerTime orchard the previous night. The taste of sugar was still in the recesses of Saul's mouth, and the heavens above appeared as pale cotton candy. He stared into the edges of their twisting shapes, forming here and there an image in his mind before the wind rearranged its canvas. Suddenly, Saul was struck by something he saw. It was fleeting and when he looked again it was gone. He had not seen the face since he was child, and for many of those early years he'd wondered in vain if she were looking down on him from there. But Saul dismissed it, and dropped his head to watch his feet plod over the concrete. His body felt heavy now; as heavy as the tree he bore.

Saul was losing feeling in his good hand. Beneath the weight of the potted sapling it had turned white. He tried to prop it against his stomach and simply balance things with his forearm while he shook out the exhausted hand and wrist.

"Let me help," said Angela.

"I've got it."

"I can help," she insisted. "We'll do it together. Tip it this way." The woman grabbed one of the thicker lower branches and bent the tree sideways. Shoulder to shoulder they went, Angela with one hand on the trunk and one on the lip of the pot, Saul hugging the base and hoping not to lose much soil as they bounced. Splitting the weight between two sets of arms allowed Saul to stand more comfortably. But though his spine and muscles felt eased, his face still dripped with sweat from the exertion. He had to give up wiping his brow with the back of his hand for it too had become coated with water. Here and there Saul found the time to hold the heavy pot in the crook of one arm while he lifted the torso of his shirt to his face. Saul toweled off this way and noticed on the fabric, just as he had in the clouds some moments before, how a face stared back at him. It was lined by sweat that darkened in the shape of his face. Within the image, patches of dirt had fallen from the pot and stuck to the dampness of this canvas giving a value and texture that stood out from the cotton as all too human.

Saul dropped the shirt and hid it again behind the tree he carried, longing most strongly now to be through with the voyage when they had only come to the halfway point and were equally barred from returning as they were from forging on.

JACOB KOCKEN

Twenty minutes of labored walking passed. The pain that Angela's assistance had leavened returned now under their long and continued march. Saul kicked the ground hard and tempered his will against the shooting aches until his left hamstring seized up and he went falling to the ground once more. "You see?" said Angela. The sapling had fallen again with him, and one of the branches had cracked with a sharp sound against the sidewalk. "You're past the limit, Saul."

She turned him over again and massaged the cramp. This one was larger and more difficult to knead. Saul cried out several times and saw through the bleariness of pain as several faces appeared in the windows of his neighbors' homes.

Finally, he stood again and promised Angela no more strenuous activity. He saw there on her face a tear. It traveled down one cheek and trembled at the base of her chin. This arrested Saul and he sat up to wipe it away with his thumb. "I just hate seeing you in pain like that," she said. Saul found he could not swallow. But he did not want to cry in front of Angela, so instead, he kissed her and held on until the feeling eased. Then he stood and announced they ought to be on their way.

The sidewalk they'd been on was surrounded by hardened dirt from the sun on one side and the blacktop road on the other. However, it was only another hundred or so feet to a lawn of plush green where Saul could lie and recuperate. They walked slowly side by side until the goal was nearly in reach. On impulse, Saul tried once again to hurry. His shoulders shot back quickly, pulled on by several horrible muscular tensions. And Saul fell a third time.

"Saul!" Angela nearly screamed.

Mrs. Vargas, a nearby neighbor, came out onto her porch. "He okay?" The old woman waddled out to the lawn where Angela knelt beside a crumpled Saul. The knots were in his back this time, and Angela had to remove his shirt to work them. Once his groaning had ceased, they tried to stand him up. But now even the weight of his own body was setting off spasms of cramping all around. He grimaced at every movement and asked to sit. Angela, along with Mrs. Vargas, sat him against the heavy sapling. The lip of the pot stuck into the small of his back, but Saul found he could rest comfortably enough against the young trunk.

RISE THE MOON

"Will you get water?" said Angela to the kindly neighbor. The old woman left and returned with a glass from the tap and dabbed a wet rag over Saul's forehead. The cool water was welcome on his skin, and he drank the rest of it greedily. As soon as the liquid hit Saul's stomach he felt himself groan with hunger. It momentarily replaced all his muscular pain, and he remembered what the giant man had said to him. Saul reached forth over his head and plucked one of the premature bulbs from its branch. He bit into the still pale flesh and let the sweetness wash him. His tongue jumped and vibrated with exaltation. His mouth watered for more, and Saul bit half a dozen times until the little apple had disappeared.

Without noticing he'd drifted near on to sleep, Saul opened his eyes and sat up straight. He could not move quickly for his muscles still strained, yet he found it could be ignored for the time being while the taste of sugar still coated his mouth. Saul centered on elation and told the two women to take him up. Each grabbed him by an arm and pulled. On his feet again, Angela propped Saul up upon her shoulder and walked down the Fosters' block while old Mrs. Vargas struggled behind with the sapling tree.

At last, they came to the house where Saul had spent a decade. Angela told the kindly neighbor to leave the plant on the porch. She thanked her profusely and took Saul's body inside. She helped him into an upright position on the living room couch. Then Angela reclined the seat slowly until he could stretch out and bear the weight of his torso without another cramp. "Does this help?" she asked, rubbing at his neck and shoulders.

"It's lower on my back. Just let it rest," said the immobile Saul. "I could use another drink." Angela showed herself to the kitchen, opening cabinets and eventually finding glassware. She came back with water.

"Thank you," said Saul.

"You're in no shape even to drive," said Angela. "Mom and Brock can pick us up here for brunch. I'll give them a quick ring." She stalked briskly off toward the kitchen.

"Not necessary, Angela," Saul called out. But the shouting caused such a threatening tension in his neck that Saul had to give up all his breath to gasping. He could hear the little buttons beep on the phone as Angela dialed and spoke eagerly to her mother from the next room.

Saul drank half the glass of water while he waited. Even the tension of swallowing produced a flash of seizure at the back of his neck. Angela returned.

"They'll come here," she said. "They'll pick us up in half an hour."

"Angela, really. It isn't necessary. They ought not to come. Call them back. I only need a moment to rest." There was no surface beside him other than the cushions of the couch, so he tried to hand the glass back off to Angela. But she did not take it. She was looking up somewhat, almost at his face but off to the side a bit and over Saul's shoulder. There was a familiar twinkle in her eye, and Saul nearly spilt the cup.

"Who are they?" she asked. Saul tried to turn his head to see what she saw, but the tension came again, strong this time with a lasting and warning pain. So, he simply stared forward at her. "Who are they?" she asked again.

"Who?"

"Are you married?"

"What?"

"Are you divorced?"

"What? No," said Saul. "What?"

"Is she...dead?" Saul forgot himself a final time and tried to stand up, to grab her, to bring her face back toward him instead of off in the guarded distance. And the tension took hold all over his body; in both legs, the spine, and the neck. He cried out and crumpled back into the seat. Water went spilling down his stomach and pants. Angela took the glass away and tried to settle him. It took several minutes for the pain to go, and Saul was left still as a statue.

"Oh God, I need rest," breathed Saul trying not to agitate himself. But Angela was moving. She went behind him where he could not see, rustling and scraping at something.

"Angela? Come back."

And she did. Against her waist, taking up a large portion of her wingspan was the framed photo removed from the wall; Saul, Miriam, and Ira.

"Who are they?"

"Angela," said Saul, "what is this?"

RISE THE MOON

"What is it?"

"What is it?"

"Did you have a family, Saul? Honey?"

"Close your eyes," said Saul, "and pray with me."

"Pray with you?"

Saul closed his eyes and thought. He began to speak soft words of contemplation and devotion to a God of great power, but her words were louder.

"Do you have a son?"

"Pray with me. Concentrate."

"No," said Angela. "Answer me."

"Trust me Angela," he said. "I love you. We're one spirit, aren't we? I love you. Our answers are in prayer."

"Saul, are you married?"

"It's best to close your eyes when you pray."

Angela let the picture drop forward. "Oh my God," she said. The photo came to rest there spread half over Saul and the couch while Angela backed away. "Oh my God." She turned and covered her face with both hands. "Oh my God."

"Come here," said Saul as Angela drifted across the floor. "You don't understand." But then she was out the front door and gone. "Angela!" he called. She did not return, and so Saul closed his eyes and prayed, resigning himself to private devotion.

43.
Miriam

MIRIAM SAT BESIDE HER FATHER'S hospital bed. They had him on an IV with a mild sedative. The doctor said it was probably the first good sleep Frank had gotten in days. He looked at peace, flat on his back and slightly upright on the inclined bed. His skin was still sallow and sunken around the eyes, but the tremors had stopped.

She'd been up the whole night. Dreams were working their way into her waking thought. Alone, her mind wandered. Despite his bald and aged head, now and then when she looked up toward the bed Miriam thought she saw her instead.

"Blood work doesn't show anything else," said Dr. Betts, "but even by itself the symptoms of withdrawal can last a week; sometimes more depending on the patient's history of habit."

"So he'll stay here?" she said.

"Yes, until the major symptoms disappear entirely. I'll give you some information on places that help with the psychological side. That's the longer road."

"Right. Thank you. Am I able to come and go?"

"Yes."

"And you think he'll sleep for a while?"

"Everything looks stable."

Miriam called the house. It was the fourth time she'd called since arriving the previous day and still had not gotten hold of her son or husband. So when she got the answering machine once again, Miriam grabbed her things and drove home.

Saul's Cavalier, she saw, was in the garage as usual; Her boy should be at school. That's where she'd go next, to pick him up.

RISE THE MOON

She had keys already in hand, but found the front door unlocked. Inside, Saul was sitting on the couch. Their new family photo lay across his lap. She stalked up to him swiftly and saw the marks of stress and sallowed skin almost as strongly here as on the old, hospitalized man.

"What is going on?" demanded Miriam. Her arm swept around at the scene. "Didn't you get my calls?"

"What is this?" said Saul. His tone was low and dismissive.

"I called four times. Did you not even wonder where I was all night? Dad is in the hospital. Come on. We're all going to be there for when he wakes up. Let's go." She turned to gather some things but noticed her husband did not move with that same urgency. "Saul!"

"How is there a picture of me? This is not okay." The accusatory tone arrested her. Miriam turned back to face him.

"Excuse me?"

"That's a piece of me," he said. "Me."

"What are you saying? Get up. We have got to go."

Saul started tapping demonstrably at his chest. "I'm here, not there." He tipped the frame back and extracted the photo from the glass. Then with a clean stroke he ripped it down the middle, severing their son's face ear from ear. Then he squared the pieces up and tore again.

"What on Earth are you doing?" But Saul went on tearing until the pieces fell around the couch like dying autumn leaves. "Saul! Stop it! What are you doing?"

He stopped ripping and both stared at each other breathing hard when there was a knock at the door. It was light and only hit twice. It was so quiet the sound of Saul's ripping would have covered it. Then it came again; two more knocks. Miriam glared at him and said, "Let's go," between her teeth as she turned to answer the door.

Standing on the porch was a woman with a face that Miriam vaguely recognized though she could not in the moment place it. She was average height, probably in her mid-twenties, and had a head of vibrant pink hair.

The girl looked down at the ground. "Is Saul here?" she asked as timidly as she'd knocked.

"What do you want? Who are you?"

JACOB KOCKEN

"I have to talk to him."

"Who are you?" Miriam asked again. But the name mattered little. Miriam's hindered hand began to ache as it clenched tight, the flesh itself remembering a ball of pink hair it once solemnly held.

"Darla. I used to work at the Bedalaus hotel. I have to talk to Saul."

"Well, there he is," said Miriam, opening the door fully so the girl could see in across the room. Darla took a step forward, and her head snapped up as Miriam barred her way. "I don't want you in my house."

"I have to talk to him."

"Then talk. Quick."

The girl's lips closed up tight, and she seemed as though she might cry. Her youthful voice rattled when she spoke. "Saul, come here." But he did not stand. Miriam waited there with her arm blocking the threshold. At the other end of the room, he just sat there on the couch looking at the two of them with a strangely contorted expression. He closed his eyes and began speaking to himself. Miriam could see his lips moving, but no sound came out.

"Saul, please," said Darla. But he just kept on sitting and speaking to himself there on the couch. His eyes were shut. "Saul, please," she said again. "Saul, I'm pregnant."

Miriam let her arm fall and walked out the door to her car. She got behind the wheel and watched the crying girl with pink hair enter the house as she peeled out of the driveway.

44.
Saul

"I'M PREGNANT, SAUL," DARLA WAS saying. She was standing before him with her arms crossed on her stomach repeating that over as if it were his ears rather than his body that were incapacitated. He only stared back at her for a long time. She was ghostly pale. Saul waited for the breeze to roll through the window and disperse her like a vaporous cloud.

"What are you doing here?" he said at last.

"I'm so sorry to come like that." There were tears on her cheeks. "But I didn't have your phone number or anything, and I'm pregnant."

"I can't move."

"I need help, Saul. I'm going to keep it, but I don't even have a job. I quit the hotel a few weeks ago; did I tell you? And they already got someone new. They won't take me back, Saul."

"I can't move."

"What am I going to do, Saul?" He tried to sit up and made only a very little progress before slouching back into the reclined position. "You do think I should keep it, right? Right, Saul?" He could not bring himself to answer her directly.

"It's a lot to dump on you right now, I know. I didn't believe it at first either, but I went to the doctor and everything. My parents want to meet you," she said. "It doesn't have to be today if you need a bit to take it in." But Saul just sat there silently. Darla curled onto the couch with her head on Saul's lap. He could barely feel her rhythmic shaking. They stayed like that for quite a while, huddled and disconnected.

JACOB KOCKEN

"Darla," said Saul after his head had cleared some. She snapped up from where she lay across him. Her eyes were eager and pitiful. He moved to stand again and felt his muscles lock. "In the garage. There's a razor. It's on the workbench beside the door. Bring it here."

"A razor?" A look of horror passed over her face and she looked down at herself.

"For me, Darla," he said. "Trust me."

She went out the front door. Saul could hear platform shoes slapping the concrete walkway to the garage and back. Light flooded the room as the door opened again and Darla stood there beside him holding the blade in two manicured fingers. Saul stretched out an arm, and she placed it in his palm. Her gasp was near screaming when he carved open the recent scar.

"Quiet," he said.

"Saul, stop that. You're going to kill yourself. Stop it!"

He wiped off the edge of the blade on his wrist and stuck the thing in his pocket. Then he displayed his empty hand, and she saw there was nothing to worry for.

"I want you to go home and go to sleep," said Saul.

"But this is important. Saul, it's yours. It's yours!"

"Do you trust me, Darla?" She gave an equivocal nod. "Then return home. Go to sleep immediately. When you wake up I'm sure you'll find a more tranquil state of mind."

She protested, but Saul waved her off. As he did so, a stream of blood fell from the pool of his hand. She cried out in disgust and anxious fear. He gave her his phone number so she would not have to arrive again in person, and with a voice as soft as velvet, he reassured her all would be better soon.

45.
Ira

THE BELL RANG FOR LUNCH, and as all the kids were leaving class, Ira saw Furke amongst the crowd. His friend walked with the same nonchalance as always, his lanky, froggish arms swinging lazily at his sides. But instead of his usual glower, he glowed.

"Have you seen Anna Lee?" asked Furke. Ira shook his sullen head.

"She wasn't in math."

"Must be sick," said Furke. "That's probably why she wasn't with us last night." Ira said nothing; he only looked at Furke in wonder and then away in shame. They joined the flow of students toward the cafeteria. As they passed by the school office, the blur of a waving hand caught Ira's attention. Behind the glass door was his mother. Ira's heart sunk. His chin hit his chest. The stink of dust and sweat was still on him. He felt as guilty now as he did down in the gorge. Her expression was low as she quit the office.

"Come with me, baby," she said. He could see on her face the suppression of many things. His face went hot and flushed. He shot a look back at Furke, expecting his friend's body to crumble with broken bones. Ira clicked his dry mouth as his mother came towering over him.

"I'm sorry, Mama." The skin of his face felt it was being pulled down in gravity's clenched hand.

"Grandpa is in the hospital. We're going to visit him." Ira looked back and forth between his mother and Furke.

"What's wrong?"

"Just come with me."

JACOB KOCKEN

She turned and stalked out of the busy hallway, and Ira followed.

Grandma Bess was in the car, sitting up in the passenger seat. She was saying something intensely when she caught a glance from his mother and stopped talking.

"What's wrong with Grandpa?" said Ira.

"Dancing with the devil," said Grandma Bess.

When they got to the hospital Ira's mother led them to the room where Frank lay sleeping. There was a tube feeding into his arm and he looked far away. A doctor came by and talked with them for a while, addressing most of his words to Ira's mother. He gave her some papers, and she thanked him. So did Grandma Bess.

He saw his mother put the stack of papers down on a little table in the corner of the room before she took Grandma Bess by the arm and the two of them walked out into the hall. He could see them talking and his mother's eyes getting red. They stayed out in the hall for a long time.

His grandfather was immobile on the bed. Ira did not look. He sat on a metal chair along the wall, head in hands, listening beneath the hum of hospital machinery for the sound of breathing. He closed his eyes to pray. In that private darkness, something ignited. He was unconvinced of its truth but could not shake it. He saw Frank lying on that basement couch in a stupor still as death. The spark was painful, and Ira grabbed his head with both hands.

Then the door clicked open. His mother and grandmother, solemn, reentered the room. The two of them went to the side of the bed. They were talking about Frank and then about flowers. Eventually, their low tones trailed away, and for a long time the three of them sat waiting for God's intervention. It was Ira who broke the silence.

"Where's Dad?" Neither of the women answered for a minute.

"I'm sure you'll see him before long," said Grandma Bess. "Focus on Frank."

And as the old woman spoke his name, her son began to stir.

"Ever think I'd finish the race before you, Mom?" A choppy breath escaped Miriam and she clasped her father's hand in hers.

"Dad," she said. "How do you feel?"

"Old," said Frank.

RISE THE MOON

They talked for as long as Frank felt up to speaking. Within minutes, he turned visibly tired and once again drifted off to sleep. None of them left the room for many hours. The three visitors sat down around a small end table. They talked of other things in scattered, dispassionate exchanges. A game of rummy cycled through many rounds of shuffling and dealing, attention always split on the son, the father, the grandfather beside them. He stirred several times, mumbling through thoughts unconscious. His eyes remained at rest. They waited. In time, the sun, hidden behind a field of approaching rainclouds, fell over the edge of the Earth. Purple twilight shone through as a tap came at the window. Little raindrops streaked the glass pane, and Grandma Bess began to cry. She put down her cards and stood at the side of her son's bed, holding his hand. The rain would not let up all night.

The doctor assured everyone of Frank's condition. They took the IV out, and he slept unencumbered. With no beds for the visitors and the hour turning late, Grandma Bess had to be driven home. Ira stayed. It was not a long drive. His mother would return soon enough.

Ira was twisting chestnut hair between his fingers when the old man stirred again. He stood, watching over his grandfather.

"I'm sorry, Ira." Frank's voice was gravel. He stared with clarity; no bleariness of sleep lingered in his eyes.

"Sorry?"

"I was in a bad way. My mind isn't always with me when I'm with the spirits. I'm so sorry." His deflated lips labored to shape the words. They quivered then even when he'd finished speaking. Ira stood still. He thought back to the night they'd had dinner. It had been a fine time. There was garlic bread. They'd talked of baseball. Down in the basement, he'd seen his grandfather drink. He'd told of the fire.

"You okay, son?" said his grandfather. Ira shrugged. They looked into each other's eyes a moment. "You don't remember?"

"Remember what?" asked Ira.

His grandfather sighed, and all the air in the room was displaced. "Well, I know a thing or two about that. I won't have you down this old road, Ira." The old man's ears pricked up at the sound of the rain outside. "Open it." His head tilted toward the window,

JACOB KOCKEN

opaque with running water.

"Grandpa?"

"Open the window."

Ira slid the pane gently up. The breeze rushed in, and water ran down the wall from sill to floor. His grandfather groaned as he pushed himself up some on the bed. Frank was halfway between sitting and lying when he gave up and his trembling hands left the bedrails. He was blinking hard. His head kept moving from Ira to other corners of the room. His eyes were bright blue now; the same color as the hospital gown across his shoulders. Again they flicked from Ira to the wall; from Ira to the door; from Ira to the window; and back.

"It was raining," said Frank. He spoke almost out of breath, but the words kept coming and you couldn't tell if his gasping for air was to go on living with or to go on talking with before there wasn't any time left to live or talk.

"It was raining that night, Ira. The thing I remember is that it was raining. Most of the time she was fine. Same old Emily. Then in the middle of her words she'd be gone, and all scrambled up. It's not for a young person. Old people fall apart. There's homes, of course. Pills and bed pans. But I kept thinking of those early days and how much I loved her and couldn't let her go. Everybody said it wasn't good, but I kept thinking on the early days, hoping and pretending. At some point I couldn't pretend anymore. I couldn't pretend, and she couldn't help herself. She didn't care if the lawn was mown or if the dishes were done. I was doing all those things for a while; keeping our house in order, trying to talk sense. But she couldn't be about that kind of conversation anymore. She was somewhere else like a kid caught up in imagination. So I got like that too the best way I knew of. Because in our conditions it was just like we were stupid little kids again. And at night when I was gone and she was gone we'd be gone together and happy. Why not spend the promised time happy? Yes, I imagined better ways to be, but each one was out in the future where we might not live to see it. There's a guarantee and a gamble. What kind of fool gambles away his happiness? So those days came more and more with both of us gone and happy together. In that way, we could dance like the day we were married and trip over ourselves or each other and laugh

RISE THE MOON

even if we went tumbling into the china cabinet. We could talk for hours even if our words weren't straight. I could wake up the next day and feel terror for what was happening, but when the sun fell down and the time came again, when I could stand there and see my wife falling apart and pity her or we could dance again like children, there wasn't any choice to my mind. And that last day I woke up with authorities in my house and the window wide open. It was so cold because it was open all night long, and I was so gone it didn't even wake me. Then she was really gone in entirety, and try as I did I couldn't remember how it happened. God Almighty, every day I think and dream back and every time the vision is different. That's the thing about it, Ira. I can't remember. I can't even do honest penance. It would have been an accident, but God help me I cannot remember the night. Or maybe she fell. Or maybe she jumped. I just can't remember anything except that it was raining. By some cruelty I can remember that. I drank real hard afterwards, trying to get back to the place where we were just kids and maybe she'd be there. But there's no place to arrive at really. I kept trying it even though I knew. I always knew why I couldn't remember. It was for the same reason that I can't remember the last decade of Mimi's life either. I knew it fifty years ago already. But a person gets good at persuading themselves; at fixing little reasons together so they cover up the big ones." He began to choke.

There were paper cups beside the sink. Ira filled one and brought it to the bed. Frank sipped it empty. "More," he said, and Ira filled it again. But when he came back with the cup of water his grandfather was tossing off the papery hospital blanket. He was thinner. The skin of his jowls hung loosely. He stood and went over to the window where the rain was splashing. His elbows leaned on the sill and his head hung in the open air. He kept rubbing hands over his bald head as the rain poured down on him. With no hair to cling to, the water washed over his scalp and dropped away. When he finally left the window his eyes were even brighter and the gown they gave him was soaked to the waist. The water ran off his chin, marking the floor like ephemeral paint in quick, irregular drops. Frank's bare feet dragged through the spill.

"Do you remember your first Mass?" said the old man. Ira nodded.

JACOB KOCKEN

"Grandma's funeral."

"Some years before that, when we first met you and your dad, Emily insisted you get the sacrament even though you could already walk and talk and had hair down to your shoulders. Your mother wouldn't hear it. Then all of a sudden Emily was in the ground and Miriam had you back in the church leaning your own head over the basin. I don't know what she said to the priest to have him do it right then. Did you see their faces, Ira, those people in their mourning clothes as they filed away?"

"No."

"Their faces were all screwed up and you could just read people thinking, 'What on Earth is that priest doing washing up a full-grown child?'"

46.
Saul

IT WAS RAINING HARD FOR the first time in months. Saul was forty miles down the east road out of Graumont when the engine light on the dash of his Cavalier flicked on. The alarm bell dinged every couple seconds until Saul gave a few good punches to the steering column. Things went silent again just as he pulled into the parking lot of a roadside motel. The rain was so hard on his windshield he could hardly see. There was something about a hotel wrapped up in all of this, he thought. It may be a fitting place to try again.

The soreness still plagued him. He walked slowly and was soaked through by the time he reached the entrance of the building. He would have to make use already of the one change of clothes packed in his duffle.

Saul had made his prayer some hours ago stuck there on the couch for a long while after Darla had left. He'd spoken the words of his first plea so far as he could remember them. When the blood stopped running under the pressure of his folded hands he quit his supplication as well. In the time afterward, he eventually made his way to an upright position. The muscles had calmed, and he was free to clean himself. When the blood was washed and the gauze was set, Saul was brought back downstairs by the ringing telephone. It was Darla. She had slept she said, and nothing was different. She wanted to talk with him. Saul let her speak into the receiver, but he had little to say himself. 'It will be better,' was all he said. 'You have to believe in me.' When Saul hung up the phone he found himself uncomfortable in the room. He dusted away the

JACOB KOCKEN

shredded bits of photograph that covered the couch and marched upstairs to the hallway closet where beneath a pile of towels he found the overnight bag he'd packed some weeks ago.

Now, several dozen miles down the first road he'd seen, Saul couldn't raise his eyes to the woman at the check-in desk. When he walked in he half expected to see Darla standing there at her post.

There was only one floor to the motel. He got room 102. The hallway lights were dim, and his key card took a few tries. The room went dark as the door closed behind him. There was an old, dank stench, exacerbated by the heavy rain outside. The white walls were grey with age, and a bare iron water pipe ran the length of the ceiling, oxidizing to a tired turquoise color. The carpets and mattresses were flat. Water trickled from the sink in a broken stream even through the closed brass valves. There were many things Saul found undesirable; many things he would have had fixed or changed.

From the window, Saul could see nothing but trees and meadows. There was little hint of civilization in the direction he'd been driving. He closed the curtains before removing all his clothes to kneel down beside the bed. From inside the pocket of his discarded pants, Saul retrieved a razorblade. He pressed it between his lips to hold while his free hand peeled up the layers of tape and gauze.

HUNGER PRESSED HIM THAT MORNING. The motel had a small continental which he abused, leaving only one muffin on the counter. The rest he ate or stuffed into his bag. He'd called home and gotten no answer. Then he'd called Darla who picked up right away. He hung up at the sound of her hysteria.

Saul's eyes were bloodshot; he'd hardly slept during the night and his raving thoughts were practically manifest on the dingy motel mirror's reflection. Perhaps he would drive south toward Missouri. It was warmer there at least.

The lobby and hallways smelled of pine trees. There was a small line for check-out. A middle-aged woman with raven dark hair stood waiting. In front of her at the desk was quite an old man talking with the attendant. Saul got in line and stood waiting and listening.

A few feet away, there was a coffee table and couch at which

RISE THE MOON

two girls sat. They both had long dark hair like the woman in line. One of the girls was bent over a notebook, writing. Her feet were tucked up underneath her, and she used her knees as a little table. But it was the other one that caught Saul's attention. The girl was leaning forward over the coffee table. There was a green candle burning there, giving off the pine scent. The girl's hair dangled out in front of her face some, hiding it as she leaned. Still, her nostrils flared, and Saul could even hear the wind as it passed into her nose.

Then the girl reached forward exposing an immaculate hand to the flame. She winced and snapped the fingers back to her chest. The girl beside her looked up from her work for a few moments before returning again to the paper.

The line moved and the dark-haired woman took to the front. The girl who had been writing on the sofa stood up. She ripped a leaf from the book and joined the woman at the desk.

"Can we mail this here?" Saul heard her ask.

"No, honey," said the woman.

"We have an outgoing box," the receptionist said. "Stamps are a quarter." He gave an envelope to the girl.

As he waited, Saul looked back and watched as the other girl reached again at the candle. A curious finger stretched out for the fire to surround. Once again, she winced and for a moment looked as though tears would fall from her tightly shut eyes.

Saul stirred, pointing his feet alternately at the poor girl and the presumptive mother. When for a third time the girl reached her hand out to the flame Saul dropped his bag and hurried over. He got there only in time to see the flame curl around the flesh of her thumb, turning it red and charred. "Hey there," he said. The sound of his dropping bag alerted everyone else.

Saul bent to a knee before the injured girl. The voice of the other, the one who wrote, was calling loudly, though Saul did not hear the words. The wounded one stayed entirely quiet. With his re-bandaged hand, Saul took her by the wrist to get a look at the burn. Just then there was a hand on his shoulder, and someone was trying to pull him away. But the girl's hand unfurled in his to show the purest, whitest, manikin tone Saul had ever laid eyes on. He touched the burned fingers with his own. They were soft and clean as the petals of a daisy. The hand pulled harder at his shoulder, and

JACOB KOCKEN

Saul would have given way if as he raised his eyes from the girl's immaculate hands he had not looked her in the eyes. The face was of porcelain. She was the moon without craters, and her eyes were made of glass. Saul looked deep into her stare. And in those fields of cold, intentionless space, Saul saw it. It was in the reflective sheen on the dumb, glazed pupil looking nowhere at all.

Then a second person pulled his shoulder and sent Saul tumbling sideways. From the ground, he saw a flurry of black hair and delicate hands swarming the girl, hurrying her out the door. Saul was slow to stand. When finally he rose to his feet, they were gone. The candle still burned, and the motel still smelled like pine.

He froze there for more than a minute. Finally, the attendant was tapping at his shoulder when Saul ripped himself away and ran out into the parking lot. At every car he stopped to check the windows. Then the rough grating of rubber and gravel sounded as a white Pinto pulled around the back of the building and shot into the street. It did not stop at the intersection and drove over the bending shoulder of the southbound road.

Saul ran to the Cavalier. His fingers fumbled at the keys, and soon he was spinning out into the parking lot. A small cloud of dust marked the disturbed gravel at the intersection beside the hotel. Saul followed it, pressing the gas nearly to the floor.

The sky was bright with morning daylight, but the road wound through trees and hills, and for a long time, all that was visible was the hundred yards of road ahead before another turn. The longer he drove without a sign of them the more his eyes swung and searched. When the way bent to the left Saul crossed the yellow lines to keep his speed and hoped with all his might that they were alone on the road. Trees passed with such speed they melded into a single wall on either side. A light flicked on the dashboard. The alarm he'd once fixed rang again. Saul slammed his fist on the steering column. Then again. The alarm continued at regular intervals and the light stayed bright and warning. Saul slammed it over and over and did not ease up on the gas. He breathed hard through his nose to calm himself. The smell of the forest was mixed with something like motor oil.

Soon, the road came to a steep hill, and as he began the climb, Saul could see the red flash of taillights at the top. His hands began

RISE THE MOON

to sweat, and he squeezed the wheel hard. For a few brief seconds, he closed his eyes and prayed. His breath was labored as he came near the crest.

Up at the top, his car leveled out. After fifty yards, the hill sloped down again. The sky opened up so one could see for miles. There it was. The white car was flying down the path. He continued to gain on them when all of a sudden there was a popping sound from the hood. Only seconds passed before it happened again, and a steady vibration rocked the floor.

He could see her face flashing in the back window. "Stop!" He screamed at the top of his lungs. They were so close now he could see her face if only she would turn around. The other girl looked out with fear.

Saul dropped the passenger side window and sped into the left lane. He crept steadily up beside them and yelled, shaping the words forcefully on his lips, "Stop! Pull over!" The woman driving looked at him. Her face was red and tense. The one he wanted was in the back seat. He could see the figure, but the other girl draped over her, clinging like a straight jacket. Then all of a sudden, there was the popping in the hood again. The vibration turned to a rattle, and his car shook back and forth. Saul pounded the dash with his fist. Metal screeched from below, and a trail of smoke leaked through the edge of the hood. And amidst the shaking, Saul could feel the loss of momentum. His foot stomped the gas up and down without a sound, and the blur of the world around him slowed. The trees promised to take solitary shape once again. His white knuckles left the wheel and he waved with both hands, ushering the woman to the shoulder of the road. But she did not obey, and her panicked eyes, locked on his, moved slowly back as her neck twisted to watch him fall behind. Then she was past him, and he came level with the backseat window. Saul shouted, begging to see the girl one more time. And as she too passed him up and the white car he'd chased pulled out in front threatening to fly beyond the edge of the world, he guided his front tires against their rear, yanking clockwise on the wheel until he displaced the trunk and drove himself off the road. Saul coasted for a moment as the dead car rolled over the grass and gravel. It reached the ditch and spun over the edge like a barrel. Things went black as Saul was thrown

JACOB KOCKEN

from side to side. His eyes were closed in prayer. His knees tucked up beneath his chin. Windows shattered under the turning weight of the car. The frame bent in, and every loose object except Saul himself was ejected from the wreck. But soon enough, the car came to an upside-down halt, and Saul opened his eyes.

He looked up at the floor while the world spun. For several moments, there were no thoughts in his head except the taste of blood. The back of his skull pounded. He touched the tender spot, and his hand came away dry. Then the sunlight touched his eyes and Saul wrestled the pain in his bones. He had to kick the door to pry it open, and when he crawled out Saul heard a scream.

Down the road, he saw the Pinto he'd chased, its front end wrapped around the base of a pine tree. The rear window was spider-webbed, and he could not see in. For a hundred yards, Saul limped toward the white car. When he finally reached his object he approached from the passenger side. The backseat door was open, and he called out to the women. All was silent except his breath and a plaintive, mechanical hissing. He entered the car halfway. There were two bodies; one still in the driver's seat and the other strewn across the floor. He shouted to them as if they were a mile away. He touched the girl on the floor with his palm and moved her face gently side to side. She did not stir, and he shouted to her again.

Then Saul received an answer; a hoarse and wandering call from somewhere far behind him. He caught the flash of her hair as she ran behind the trees. It swung over her face like a drape in the wind. She was a lost silhouette; starting, stopping, and searching all around.

"Hold still!" yelled Saul as he hustled off the road. He fought through a wall of branches and stumbled in the tall grass. She saw him coming and turned away, no longer running or skirting about. Her shoulders laid back and her steps relaxed, a fawn ambling through the wilderness. "Come back!" he called. Again, she faced him for a moment before drifting off through the woods. "Come here!" At last, a hundred yards from the road, she came to rest and stood there looking up at the sky.

Saul's feet slowed. He tried not to upset even the blades of grass as he stepped. "Are you alright?" he asked. A strange breathy sound issued from her mouth, and she covered her face with her

RISE THE MOON

hands. "Don't cry," said Saul. He turned to point back at the road where the smoke was rising. "I didn't mean it to happen."

But as he spoke, she stepped away, and the sound of her retreating footfall snapped his gaze back to her. "Don't run!" he pleaded, and Saul fell to one knee as he leaned out and grabbed the cloth of her dress. She stopped. Her hands came down over his, soft as satin and comforting as the rays of early spring. Her eyes fluttered all about; as if in wonder at the trees, and the ground, and the very air of the forest. The breathy sound came again through her smile. Two little syllables he understood as, "Papa."

The soothing scent of warm milk was all about her. Saul gripped the hands back and stared into her endless, shifting eyes. The harder he looked the deeper they went with no reflection of the Earth around her. "You?" he whispered. The girl's smile widened even brighter and from low down in her stomach, she laughed aloud. Her knees and shoulders bounced in delight. Saul squeezed the delicate hands hard and exhaled a deep, exhausted laugh of his own. Then her eyes came to him, and his stare was returned. She seemed really to see him for the first time. Her gaze stopped its flutter. Her smile dropped to a grimace, and she leaned in closer to his face. Her eyes were brown and wide, and in those dark pools Saul saw his kneeling body, his back to the haze as smoke filled the air. He felt something then, and the gauze loosened. The wrappings fell like an old snake skin, and he saw sanctitude on the palm of his hand.

Suddenly, the other hands pulled out of his grip. He looked up and the girl's face was contorted in pain. She clutched at herself, and the next moment, her palm struck the bridge of his nose with all her weight.

He bowed to the earth and blood came trickling down his lips and chin. She ran again, and Saul hollered, scrambling after her. His eyes watered. His head swam. For a moment, he thought he might be sick. He chased, but she galloped with the speed of fear, so Saul took up a stone from the ground and hurled it. It struck her leg, and she cried out. The sound was a long and droning whine, and as it receded there came in its place the sirens of a small fleet of emergency vehicles. Through the trees, Saul could see the red and blue lights streaming in toward the white car at the base of the broken tree.

JACOB KOCKEN

"Come back!" he yelled. And then, easy as a dandelion thistle blows, Saul forgot all the soreness and cramping in his legs and chased after the perfect, gallivanting shape. The girl sprang into the depths of the woods, and Saul ran like he never had before. "Come back!"

47.
Ira

IRA HAD SHUT HIMSELF AWAY. At first, he tried to think through all that had happened, but that soon overcame him. There were many black patches on his memory. Then he tried to simply sit and calm himself, but every object around triggered some uncomfortable upstream thought always flowing down through these most recent days.

The bottle he'd kept hidden underneath his bed was empty now. It had been for an hour or so. The smooth, round glass was warm with the heat of Ira's body. It lay next to him in the bed, transparent and nestled into the curve of his stomach beneath the blankets. It was hard to think clearly. His brain was dull and fuzzy. His father was gone. He knew the facts, but the story was in pieces. Few questions had been asked and fewer answers had been given.

Discharged from the hospital, his grandfather had come home with them. Last Ira saw, he was sleeping on the couch. They'd had to clear it for him. A large picture frame lay empty there like wide window. All across the floor there were pieces of the family. Ira didn't ask. He put something together in his head; something that had felt like a dream. His mother was quiet while she gathered the scattered leaves. She didn't seem surprised. Ira had tried to help her, but she quickly shooed him off. He'd picked up just one of the torn bits. It had his face on it, smiling brightly. Then Frank had dragged him to the kitchen to look for water.

Ira had not known his grandfather long but marked a decided change in the old man's demeanor since he'd woken from his tribulation. Frank's body was very weak. They'd offered a wheelchair

JACOB KOCKEN

though he ended up agreeing to a walker that announced his every move with dragging metal. They'd talked for a while alone at the hospital, but when Ira's mother returned things had gotten quiet again. Frank had gone back to sleep, and they waited there a long time in his room.

So, Ira lay face down in bed with a blanket cocooning him head to toe. He lay all day breathing the same hot, recycled air. It was Monday, and the time for school had come and gone, but still he laid there. Nor did his mother come in to urge him out. Now and then he could hear her in the hallway. She did not call out to him for lunch. He did not hear her voice at all, only a rogue set of footsteps that from time to time lingered at his door before passing on.

Then, breaking the internal silence of the day, someone struck the doorbell, and the ringing sounded throughout the house. Ira lay as still as ever, but his mother's footsteps moved out in the hall and down the stairs. Only moments later, there was a knock at his door. It was a soft and patient knock, but Ira did not want to see his mother. He'd been locking his door ever since they arrived home, but each time he caught a glimpse of the silver handle it had been unfastened again. Ira clenched the ends of the blanket tighter around his hidden body.

The door handle creaked, and very soon he felt the mattress beside him sink beneath the concentrated weight of another person.

"Ira, buddy," said Furke. "You sick?" The voice was soft and kind, but it sent a shadowy dread on Ira. His muscles tightened and his eyes shut tighter against the mattress. He was stiff as a corpse.

Then a column of light came peaking at the corner of his eye. Cool air moved in around his head and neck. His vision was blurry when at last he worked up the courage to look. Furke sat there patiently, the edge of the blanket lofted back in his hand.

"Did you puke?" said Furke. His teeth were showing with the tender froggish smile. There was something in his other hand, resting on his knee. "You look like you got a migraine. Want the blanket back?" Ira nodded slowly, and his friend lowered the shroud back down.

"I see you've got to sleep or something. That's okay. I'll go. I just came by to give you something since you weren't at school. I got one too. They both got mailed to my house in one envelope, but

RISE THE MOON

I didn't read yours. That's illegal or something. I'm putting a letter on your nightstand, okay?" A tender pat of the hand came down on Ira's shoulder. "Feel better, bud." Then the sounds of the past few minutes came back in reverse, and instead of a doorbell, there was a cheerful, "Goodbye Mrs. Foster."

Ira lay there for a long time.

When he finally emerged, the paper on his nightstand beckoned, bending slightly upwards at the fold. He took it up and saw there was no name anywhere except his own at the very top. He swung his leg off the edge of the bed. Then his head dropped between his knees. Underneath the bed frame, his eyes darted to the back corner. Ira took the empty bottle from where it lay on the bed and rolled it into the depths of the little cave. When he turned right-side up again his fingers were searching the paper's edges, lifting at the seams.

Ira,

We're on the move again. The middle of the country is flat, and I can hardly tell by the look of things if we have really gotten anywhere. I do not like moving. Getting used to a new place is hard, but it's the reason for moving that is constant trouble. I can't explain. You were there, so I hope you understand. I believe you were sorry. I believe you still are. When he fell, I hated you. Furke was very good to me. That's why I hated you. And I hated you the same way I've been hating her. But I love her too. Like a sister. Like a baby. And you were crying just the way she cries. But she always stops crying after a while, and I was afraid you never would. Because I knew the way you looked at us that everything would stick in your head forever. She's been stuck in one way all her life already, and I don't want any more of that. I don't want to be stuck, and I don't want to keep moving. When we reach another place to call home I'll write to you again. Goodbye for now.

Ira sat there on the edge of his bed. He read the note over again. That strange night replayed in his head. Everything was terribly vivid. He could see Anna Lee's face and the woman she had brought with her. There was something quite unsettling. Vague words in Anna Lee's letter corroborated an uneasy feeling that had tainted any inkling of relief since then. He kept seeing that strange woman, who next to Anna Lee seemed somehow awkward in her

JACOB KOCKEN

proportions yet perfect as the waning moon.

Downstairs, Ira found his grandfather on the living room couch. Though he slept, the old man looked anything but tranquil. He was rigid the way he laid there. His jaw was clenched, and his brow was furrowed as if someone had carved the tracts in marble. Miriam could be heard in the kitchen. The sink was running, and there was the slow, irregular sound of mindless work.

Ira exited through the garage door. The sky was dreary with clouds of every grey. He pedaled the maze of suburban streets with purpose. Graumont was quiet all around him. The only sounds were the whispering wind he cut through and the steel grind of gears endlessly turning.

Soon the blacktop and concrete turned to prairies and those grasslands turned to great forest trees. The road was long and singular. Where finally the old highway bent away toward the edge of town, Ira rolled into a narrow gravel drive. He kicked the bike up against the north wall of the house beside the cellar's bulkhead doors.

Mold that Ira had never smelled before permeated the descent. The air was damp. The dark room widened slowly into view as Ira approached the bottom of the stairs. Falling sunlight lit the landing; further into the cellar, the perimeter was draped in shadow's gloom. Miniscule, glittering refractions flashed at the base of one wall like crystalline stars. They called Ira that way as he took the last of the stairs.

Before his foot could hit the cement floor, Ira's crown was knocked back by the weight of the house. He stumbled and pressed both palms to the top of his head. Pain screamed through his scalp for a minute. He looked up at the low beam that had caught him. This Atlas of the house remained square and unperturbed. Ira rubbed at the bump forming beneath his hair and shuffled toward the cabinet. Glass popped and grated as he trod over twinkling stars.

Everything was black in the recesses of the hutch. Spirits showed their form only in vague glistenings. Ira grasped one at random. It swished low to the bottom. Ira threw his pounding head back until the stinging liquid dribbled down his chin. Then the ring of shattered glass filled the room, and Ira grabbed hold of a second bottle.

RISE THE MOON

He moved to sit down on the couch in the center of the room. As he moved out from the edges back toward the cellar stairs, Ira was struck by a spotlight. He climbed the creaking, ancient steps with a dangled, swilling jug in one hand. At the top, he squinted out at the world while his free hand groped around the edge of the opening. It found a hot iron handle, and Ira used all the weight of his body to swing the heavy basement door's rusted hinges shut.

IRA WOKE, BUT HIS OPEN eyes showed nothing. There was dust on his tongue. He could feel the sofa's dull scratch on one calf. The rest of his body was low and frigid. He pushed himself up, chill from the concrete seeping through his palm. He lay his cold bones down across the seat of the couch and looked up at a blankness that might have been the floor of a house or else the far celestial reaches. There was a vague thought he noticed. It rapped the side of his head as one knocks on a wooden door. And by the resident's silence, the solicitor was turned away, his plodding feet fading to white noise on the sidewalk.

Calmness pressed into him. It anchored his limbs to the sofa, and Ira began drifting toward sleep again. His body warmed itself with the comfort of the cushions. For a long time, he noticed nothing.

Then Ira jolted from his seat. The ground had begun to rumble beneath him, and the black walls were singing. He'd heard the voice some time before but did not know the speaker. It's ghostly hand grabbed hold of his spine and shook. Ira was on his feet in a moment. The world inside spun, and he crumpled quickly to his knees. His heart was beating fast with fear, vibrating to the beat of the song. Numbness left his kneecaps as they scraped the solid ground. Ira found the couch with his shoulder and crawled straight away off its line, groping with blind limbs until he found the set of old timber planks and clambered up the stairs.

Upon pressing the doors above, the light of late afternoon pierced through like a thousand sieging spears. He clamped his eyes in reflex and dropped the metal hatch. A great iron clap bounced through the basement as the door fell back onto its frame, melding with the music as a cymbal struck crescendo. Ira pushed at the lid again but could not raise the weight with clumsy hands, and again it

JACOB KOCKEN

came crashing down. Then the blaring tones ceased. The darkness held only a hazy quiet.

Ira climbed nearest he could to the level of ground above. With bent knees and flat back he heaved himself against the cover, breaking through a membrane of rust and dust at the edges until the door swung vertical and opened into the world.

Ambient woodland crickets squeaked another music here. Ira staggered out of his hole. His vision swam before him. Blue paint glistened on his bicycle's aluminum frame, waving him in. The ground and grass teetered side to side as he mounted the seat and set to pedaling. He went too slow, and the handles twisted ninety degrees, spilling his ribs over the front bar. Ira tried again, pushing faster. He held his arms out, bowed like rickets, and the front wheel wobbled. Soon enough, he was off the shaky gravel and rolling a winding path down the country road. He did not look back until a hundred yards were covered. By then, the house's roof peaked just over the tree line. A shiver went through him.

A pale sliver of moon was on the sky as twilight marched in. Most of it was hidden away where the moon runs to now and then. But it was hard to look up. When Ira raised his head it felt as though a soaking wool blanket lay stretched across his brain. So, he watched the little cobbled grey stones of the street blur by below. Then he was on his side. His shirt was torn at the shoulder where he'd fallen. Pink skin was scraped raw in a few square inches below. It would sting later on, but for the moment, Ira did not feel a thing. Still, he resolved to walk with the bike at his side, leading and being led like a bridled donkey.

The way was long, and the afternoon turned to evening. Hues changed in the sky from brilliant to somber, and Ira's head cleared slightly. There was still a distance between him and everything else when he found the house he lived in. He tucked his bike in the corner of the garage and was conscious enough of things to shade his face when he entered the building.

Lights were off in the kitchen and living room. He remembered then suddenly the old man he'd left lying on the couch. He stood next to it now. It was empty.

Ira moved toward his bedroom upstairs. He checked around the corners of every wall but found no one. At the bottom of the stairs,

RISE THE MOON

he could see the electric light shining down and hear the soft tones of quiet talking. He climbed slowly, trying not to creak the steps. Both hands gripped the railing for balance.

At the top of the staircase, he saw it was his light that lit the hall. He turned in toward his room and found his mother there. She was sitting on his bed with her feet on the floor and her hair dangling forward past her ears. There was a glass of milk in her hand. The image startled Ira. He jumped slightly and gasped. He could taste in that sharp intake of breath the sheen of liquor that lingered on his teeth. Her head tilted gradually his way.

"Baby," she said softly. "Come sit."

Ira stood as tall as he could. He felt loose bolts in his knees. Halfway there his rubber sole faltered against the carpet. He caught himself only barely and sat down quickly at the foot of the bed. He said nothing.

"Where have you been?"

"Biking."

"You seem to have fallen." She touched the spot where his shirt was torn. Ira tensed when her finger came down. His shoulder stung and retreated. "It's okay, dear. I'll fix you up. But baby, you ought to tell me when you're going out. If you're going out this long you have to tell me."

"I'm sorry."

His mother sighed. "Just the same, it's good you were out." She was silent for a moment. A bit more clarity had returned to Ira's head. He looked around the room. The walls were the same color as ever, but they shined a smidge more brightly. His collection of shoes was organized neatly at the base of the closet. His hamper was empty. Everything was clean.

"Where's Grandpa?"

"That's the thing, my sweet. Something's happened. Something important I'm not sure how to tell you." Her face contorted, and she tried to look him in the face. Then her neck swung back, and she stared at the eggshell wall. "You know what the doctor said? About why we all ended up in the hospital."

Ira nodded, trusting her vision was wide and watching the whole room all at once.

"It's a bad habit. Very bad. It ruins people's minds. You understand? Tell me you understand."

"I understand."

"I was cleaning today," said his mother. "I only got as far as your room." From the other side of the bed, she lifted back a blanket. When she took up the bottle she held it by the neck. The veins in her wrist showed round and blue. The glass bottom wagged back and forth, brandished like a bullish medieval club. "Your grandfather's been drinking again."

Ira found he had shut his eyes. Upon hearing these words, he twisted his whole body toward his mother. She still stared straight ahead with that benefacted chestnut river rolling down her cheeks.

"Your grandpa is an old man," she said. "He's done a lot of things in his life. You don't know him the way a lot of people do. The more time you spend around him the more you learn what I mean. I don't want you to learn anything from him."

"What?"

"He tried to lie about it when I confronted him today. And look." Her other, clutching hand emerged from her lap. Between the netted fingers was a silver statue. "It's a lighter," she said. "He's been smoking too. He hid it up here way in the back of your drawer where you'd never find it. He doesn't do the things good people do, baby. He does now and then, but he's got a bad nature, and there's nothing to do about that. He can't change it. Everyone's just stuck the way they are. You can get away with the little crimes. But there are things a person can do that last," she said, pointing to the nick on his neck, nearly flat and healed from the day his father taught him to shave. "A little cut like that, it will heal in a few days. But if someone went too deep, too wide, well, that's it." Her finger drew absently over his throat. The nails were painted white, and one of them scraped his skin. "We can think about how they should have been more careful every day of our lives, but there's nothing that can be done about it. That's what some people are like. Understand?"

Ira could not speak.

"So, I told him to leave," said his mother. "Do something for me. Will you? Put it out of your mind, dear." After some time, she seemed to take his silence for agreement. "You look tired, baby. Are you very tired?"

RISE THE MOON

He managed to nod, and the dizziness circled him up. His mother stood and threw back the comforter, making a place for him to lie. Ira removed his shoes where he sat. The rest of his clothes remained on as he turned horizontal and rested ear to pillow. He faced the wall.

Then there was a touch on his shoulder, and he looked back at her. She was holding the glass of milk out as she did every night. He sat up again and took it. The glass was warm like the touch of someone's hand. He raised it to his lips and took a shallow sip. Ira held it back out toward his mother, but the release of its weight did not come. When he looked up at her she was standing there looming over him. Her arms were at her sides, and she was staring at the milk. Then her eyes met his, and he took another sip. Still, she did not move until silent minutes passed and Ira's grudging sips drained the drink. Then he set it on the bedside table with a hollow clink.

His mother's voice hummed half muffled. "Goodnight my sweet, sweet baby." He heard her shifting steps move toward the door where a light switch clicked, and the color of everything stepped down a shade. Then her feet came to the room's far wall where plastic window blinds came clattering down. Little orange rays snuck through the slats to line the darkened wall. Ira kept very still. He was thinking of his grandfather when the mattress sunk at his knees. The depression pulled him in like gravity. All of Ira's muscles clenched tight and rigid. He remained that way for several minutes, staring at the wall and breathing slow and even, feigning a profound slumber.

The lines of light on the wall gradually faded. Finally, Ira tucked his chin and peered over his raised shoulder. Her form was pitch and vague, but he could still feel her weight pushing on the bed.

"Mom?" he mumbled.

She made a cooing with her throat and tongue. Ira locked up all over again. "Hush now," she said. "Get some rest. I could see how tired you are." Her hand patted him on the back where his heart beat heavily. Then the weight on the mattress shifted, and her long hair tickled his neck. She kissed the top of his head and combed through the length of his locks with her fingers. Then the sensation came again; nails lightly on his scalp and streaming down with the

JACOB KOCKEN

chestnut wave over his shoulders. Her petting continued in the silence. At long last, it slowed and stopped. But still she did not rise. When Ira tried to adjust his position, a great resistance pulled at his roots. His mother's curled hand anchored absently upon the loose hair behind him.

Ira did not sleep. It was more than an hour before he felt her weight and warmth rise and heard the door click shut behind her. He let his quivering breath escape and threw the thickest blanket over his head to mute the noise. He could not find respite or comfort of any kind. His eyes were wide; alert and static. Still more, he did not wish to move nor for the next day to come. His heart wrenched at the thought of seeing his mother's or grandfather's face again; at living alongside the emptiness his father left; at hearing the friendly voice of Furke. As time progressed into the depths of night, Ira hoped that God would forget the morning star and mistakenly rise the moon.

48.
Miriam

MIRIAM LAY IN BED. THE clouds were thick and blocked out the light of the moon and every star. It was late in the night, and several times already she'd woken from a restless sleep. The nightstand clock had ticked an hour since last she saw it. Her body was sore, and the nest of blankets and pillows did nothing to coax on comfort.

A small noise caught her attention. She was on the verge of that restive dozing when it sounded a second time; the quiet creak of a floorboard. In an instant, her eyes were open, peering into the darkness. A flash of heat went down her neck, and she removed herself from bed, all the while breathing slow and straining her ears for the noise. There was nothing for a moment, but the mother could not keep out the visions she'd fought these last several weeks. She slid open the wooden drawer of the nightstand she had shared with her husband. From the box, she withdrew a long, steel kitchen knife.

Miriam moved in the dark, gliding against the hallway wall in her nightgown. The blade she kept behind her, its cool steel grazing the skin of her thigh.

Her son's door was shut. Her heart began to pound, and the breath fell heavily from her mouth as she cranked the knob. In a motion, Miriam flipped his light and stepped inside. Her grip on the knife handle tightened, and her eyes darted from corner to corner around the room. Her son was nowhere to be seen. His bed in the center of the room was disturbed. The sheets and blankets were bunched between mattress and frame. His pillows were on the floor. To her horror, drops of red flecked the floor and fabric on the bed. She touched one of them with the tip of the knife, and it spread with a viscous fluidity. Her heart pounded in every inch of her. Miriam's hand was sweating, and her grip loosened for only a moment before she heard the shifting noise again. It was unmistakably below her.

She rushed to the stairs in silence. Small beams of light from her baby's half open door showed the hallway and the staircase like a tunnel descending into the ground. Her steps were light, trying not to call attention. With her right hand clutching the knife she did not use the railing, and instead leant her body against the wall toward the kitchen where the shuffling continued, louder and clearer in this open space. At the bottom of the stairs, the kitchen was cast in half shadow. The pantry door was cracked, and the sounds persisted. The light switch was beside the same door. Miriam moved with all the speed she could muster. The clammy soles of her feet slid over the kitchen tile, and she slipped momentarily on another small, red pool. Miriam prepared herself to scream as she pulled the pantry door by the edge of the wood. Her grip tightened again over the knife as she saw first the man's scalped head.

"Dad?" The word escaped her. Bald as a cue, filled all over that white orb with small lines of blood, a man was rummaging through the shelves. His pupils were dilated like one who is compelled to live in the dark. He stood hunched as if the weight of the air were a burden on his shoulders. And when the light sprung on he began instantly to cry.

The knife fell clattering to the floor between them. "Oh dear," she said, trying to bring him close and feeling at the skin on his head and neck. Miriam tried to embrace him. He did not resist, but the duffle bag slung over his shoulder hung between them, blocking their bodies. The zipper was undone, and the top flap was open. With one hand around her son, she dug into the bag; a jar of peanut butter, crackers, three apples, two pairs of pants, shirts, socks, underwear, a toothbrush, and a razorblade.

"What did you do?" she said, running her hands over his head. Traces of drying blood rubbed onto her hands from the nicks. "What did you do?"

Dark moons colored the wary eyes. Lines of weariness touched all over his cheeks and forehead like sullen crow's feet. Miriam pushed the duffle's strap off his shoulder, and he let it fall to the

RISE THE MOON

ground. It was then that she could embrace him in full, and he crumpled between her arms. His legs bent, and she buckled over to catch him. His lips distorted in some unseen agony, and when she pulled him back up it was off the ground entirely with her one arm around his back and the other in the crook of his knees. "What is it? What is it?" she asked. There was no intelligible response among his tears. "Baby," she said. "My sweet." She moved him back and forth in her arms, and her lips came down softly on the crown of his naked head. A lingering salty taste stayed with her. "I cannot hold you."

Under the weight of a grown man, her grip was failing. Her shoulders slacked. The muscles burned. With her son in her arms, Miriam climbed the stairs. All the time she kept asking what had happened. But he would not or could not speak. Up in her dark bedroom, she let him drop on the mattress. Miriam lay beside him whispering gently. Her hands consoled, caressing the hair on his arms and the skin on his head. His body matched too closely the impression long left by her husband. Some long time afterward his sounds of agony stopped, and Miriam could feel that the slow steady breath of sleep had found her baby boy.

49.
Ira

WHEN IRA WOKE UP IT was midday. Sunshine bled through the drawn curtains beside his parents' bed. His mother lay on her back beside him with her eyes closed. For a moment, he was far back in the past; back when as a small child he would stumble through the hall after dark dreams and crawl up between his parents as they slept. The reminiscence disappeared when he rubbed his bleary eyes. He could feel the air brushing over his scalp with every movement. His hand tracked over it all, activating little throbs of pain where the razor had split skin.

Beneath the blanket, he was fully clothed. Even his shoes were still tied in bows from the night before. He slid off the far end of the bed, trying not to disturb his mother. When his depression in the mattress lifted, one of Miriam's arms moved out to the warm spot where he'd lain. On his way to the door, he passed his mother's dresser. It was draped over with a set of his clothes, waiting for him.

In the bathroom, Ira found parts of his old self. His long brown hair was piled in the waste basket. Individual strands of all lengths lay scattered almost invisibly across the floor. Kneeling down, Ira swept the stray hairs together with his hands. As they gathered closer, their color began to congeal. The little pile in his hand was soft and weightless as the air itself and shined like silk in the light. Ira lifted the stuff to his head and watched his reflection in the mirror. No one hair went in the same direction as another, each one unbefitting his image. With a toss of the hand, the gathered hair joined the wastebasket where all the strands stacked up into a brown and

RISE THE MOON

matted mess.

There was a shuffle in the hall, and Ira saw his mother's shape moving in the corner of the mirror. She was calling his name, loud and anxious down the hall. In a moment, she appeared at the door. The blanket was wrapped around her shoulders, and she immediately engulfed him in that drape.

"Where are you going?" she said. Her arms were locked around each other behind his back. Her head tipped forward and her hair swung down onto his bald head. Its light touch on the new sensitive skin pricked like thistles. Ira squirmed, and she held tighter. "Don't leave."

"Where is Grandpa?"

"Oh baby," she said. "Say you aren't leaving."

Ira kept his head bowed. "I have to see him. And Furke."

"Baby, what's happened? Why did you cut your hair?"

Ira caught another glimpse of the mirror over the edge of the blanket. His eyes seemed wider now than they ever had before. They popped from his skull. "It has to go," said Ira. "Eventually."

"You cut it, honey. I can see the marks."

"Yes," said Ira.

"Oh dear," said Miriam. "You're not well, are you? Do you need to eat?"

"I want to see Furke."

"Why, honey? What's wrong?"

"I hurt him."

"No. He was happy when he came yesterday," said his mother.

"I hurt him, Mama. Bad."

"It can't have been bad."

"Bad."

"No honey, not bad."

"Bad, Mama," he said. "I want to see him."

"You don't want to go to school like this. No honey, you're not well. Why are you talking this way? You can't go. It's you who's hurt. There's blood on your head. We have to wash you. Please, honey. I know it's been a horrible few days. We all just want it to end; to be away from all of this. Is that why you had a bag? Were you going to run away?"

"Yes."

JACOB KOCKEN

"If you leave, you take me with you. I won't lose you. You're my baby. We'll run away together. Don't leave me." Her heart pounded against his ear. "You let me wash your head now," she said. "Your head is full of blood." Ira sat down with his mother on the bathtub wall. The floor rumbled with the rushing of the pipes. The water was warm. Her hands, wet from the faucet, massaged the dark lines of dried blood. He had cut himself several times. Under his mother's gentle touch, the wounds smoothed out, making tainted water that rolled in rivulets. First red, then pink, then colorless they dripped down his face from his eyes to his chin. She draped the blanket around his shoulders to catch the drops, and at the end, wiped his whole head dry.

"We'll go away, honey," said his mother. "Me and you. We'll go away from all of this forever. Pack your bag again. Wherever you want to go." She took him by the hand and stood. They went to his room, and before disappearing down the stairs, she told him to gather up his things. She returned a minute later with a dozen empty garbage bags. "Everything you can fit in the car," she said. "We'll run away together."

She pulled open his dresser drawers and emptied all his clothes into the plastic bags. The things he owned were swept across the room on the furious wind from her hands, each belonging caught up in bulging bindles by the doorside. Her eyes stared off somewhere beyond the task. Her jaw clenched. Then her hand reached for the bedside things and a flash of white pierced Ira's heart.

"Wait," said Ira. His mother seemed not to hear. Her hands wandered, searching, shoveling. Ira plunged a hand into the bag and found the edge of Anna Lee's letter.

"What is it?" his mother asked. He held the letter silently in his hand. Then it slid gently up from his grip, and his mother was reading. She shook her head and pursed her lips. "What is it?" she said again. "This doesn't make any sense, baby. Who wrote it?"

"A girl named Anna Lee."

"Why are you talking to a girl? Who is she? What does she want with you?"

"I have to see Furke," Ira insisted.

"Pack the rest of your things," she said sighing, "and then we'll go find him."

50.
Miriam

THE TRUNK AND BACK SEATS were piled on with white garbage bags and luggage. She'd packed clothes and food; the few necessary things that might fit in the back of a car. They stood like mountains in the rearview mirror. Maybe that's where she'd go; mountains, somewhere private in the mountains. Miriam's mind raced and her jaw worked over a long tasteless wad of gum. With her son out of sight, she'd grown nervous.

A long line of school busses idled behind her. An hour ago, she'd watched him walk up the lonely drive. Today, he did not wear his backpack. He did not wear anything on his head. Despite the clothes she'd laid out for him, her son had seemed nearly bare.

When the final bell rang the students streamed out from the doors and, like separate currents, drifted in bunches to one ride or another. She picked him out in an instant. The attention of the surrounding children seemed to converge every few seconds on the place where he walked. His head and shoulders still slouched beneath some weight. The hangdog walk was all too familiar, and Miriam anguished.

Then he changed course from her. The sea of students broke for him, and he approached a pair of boys. She recognized them vaguely as faces of the neighborhood. Their amber mops bounced as they walked together. In unison, they stopped and turned to face her son. His mouth was open, calling something she could not hear. A triangle was formed. The two others were taller than her son, and he had to look up a bit to speak to their faces.

Miriam started the car. She rolled down the front windows and

406

JACOB KOCKEN

leant an elbow out the open space while she waited. When her gaze turned back to the school she did not spot him immediately. The swarm of children was churning with great excitement. All heads were turned in the same direction. A ripple of exclamation pulsed out through the mass from where a fist cocked back. Miriam didn't have to see it land before she was out of the car and running up the hard concrete. Everyone's back was to her. Hooting imps blocked her way, and Miriam tore through their limbs and backpacks.

They stopped beating him when she screamed. The twins were huffing, and one of them had blood on his knuckles. When she stepped inside the ring of onlookers they dispersed like startled minnows. Even the two redheaded boys ran off. All around, people swirled on eddies in the wind. Her son was sitting on the ground, slouching forward into his hands. Miriam ushered him to his feet and beseeched him with hurried questions as they marched back toward the running car.

"Are you hurt?" she said. "Why would they hit you? Who were those awful boys? I've seen them before. Who are they? Baby, are you hurt?"

There was a rising color where he'd been struck on the jaw. He rubbed at it and was slow to talk but seemed to Miriam otherwise unperturbed, stoic.

"They live down by the water tower, don't they? That's where I've seen those faces. Their parents ought to know. What were you doing talking to miscreants? Should we go back? Should we find your principal? I'd like to have a word with your principal."

She stopped on one heel to turn course back to the school. Her son pulled gently from her grip.

"No," he said. "It's okay."

"It is not okay. People can't go punching for no reason. You. Punching *you*. Just because of your hair? Is that what it was? Men are atrocious. Just because you cut your hair? No. It won't end there."

"I don't want to talk to the principal."

"Yes, you do," she said. "That's how we sort this out. That's how bullies get punished. People can't go around punching you, baby. For what? Just because you cut your hair?"

"The Paulsen's aren't bullies."

RISE THE MOON

"Like hell they're not. They punched you for no reason. You tell me why that's okay or you tell the principal why it's not. He'll do what needs to be done. He'll suspend them. Or expel them. That's what we'll ask for, baby. Expulsion. Did you say Paulsen? That's why I know them. They're being questioned by the police. I heard the other day they burned that house down. They're criminals, baby. It's not expulsion for them. It's jail." Her son inched closer to the car, away from her. His face was to the concrete for a while, and all she could see were lesions running his bald head. When he met her eyes again it was for just a second.

Her son stared into his hands. The palms were up, and his twisting fingers locked into a motionless knot. "Really?" he asked.

"Yes," said Miriam. "That's how you deal with bad people. That's what they get; what they deserve. I'd turn the key on their cell doors myself. I'd never let them out."

And before she could reach out and stop him, Ira was running down the sidewalk. Miriam tried to chase, but he was far faster. Very soon, he had disappeared down the slate grey path that wrapped around the school.

Instead of following, Miriam ran back to the car. She whipped around and sped out to the road. She could see him at the turn, but he disappeared through someone's yard, running as if the Devil were clutching at his tail.

With the windows down, Miriam screamed his name. Now and then a flash of him would be seen through the shrubs and fences. She hardly saw the street as she drove, but a reluctant sense of direction took her as she went. The tires squealed against the curb. Her hands slipped with clammy sweat over the wheel. Her voice went hoarse with fearful calling every time he slipped away. The blocks went by. Now and then she slowed down or stopped entirely and quit the car to search and yell. Though he was fugitive most of the time, Miriam progressed after him down familiar roads until at last the suburbs passed and she came upon her own childhood home.

She parked on the road. Her head scanned all around her, watching for the twitch of a bush and listening for his hard, tired steps. There was another vehicle parked on the street before her. It was somehow familiar to the back of her mind.

JACOB KOCKEN

As soon as she was out of the car and near the driveway, the dreadful height of the house cast its shadow over her. "Baby!" she called out, pacing from end to end of the property. The road was clear of all movement. With the speed of the car she assumed to have outstripped him, but with every moment that passed, his presence called her toward the house. "Baby!"

She strode up the drive breathing furiously but stopped suddenly some feet from the porch. The façade of the house with its wood and windows stood strong and flat-faced like some giant, seamless wall. She would not go forward. "Baby!" she screamed. The great window loomed directly above. She was standing below it, and her legs began to tremble. Her face went hot, and she called for her son again.

A face appeared in the living room window, and Miriam's heart jumped at the sight of the bald head. It was not her boy, however, but rather the old hermit of the house. His face bobbed close to the glass and then away again. In a moment, the front door parted, and he came marching onto the porch.

"No!" She screamed now at her father instead of for her son. He stopped a dozen paces away on the porch.

"What is it, Mimi?"

"You hound," her voice was hoarse already.

"Mimi." Frank descended the porch step. Without a thought, Miriam bent down to the gravel. She came up with a stone pinched between her thumb and the club of her bad hand. Miriam went red with anger and flung the rock. It missed her father by inches and sailed into the face of the house. A loud wooden crack vibrated the air and Miriam came up with another stone. "Mimi," was all Frank had time to say as he retreated toward the door. She fired at him again and then again, denting the walls with pock holes.

"You stupid drunk!" she screamed. With each toss she stumbled aimlessly one way or the other, carried on by the force of her passion. She was surprised then and confused to see another form lurking in the quarters. Father David was at the front door, his head peering out into the commotion. But she did not relent on her father. She clawed up handfuls of gravel and threw again. The echo of the rocks clapped down the road. The sound of heavy breath redoubled.

409

RISE THE MOON

Miriam let fly another stone. In the torquing of her body, she saw only too late the flash of another body running obliquely through the yard. The brush from early autumn trees beside the house shook and crackled as her son burst through them. His lungs heaved, and his eyes, missing her as she had missed him, were bent solely on the house. Instead of the wooden crack, there was only a soft thud as the stone struck her boy across the side of his head. Both of Ira's hands shot halfway up to the temple before his legs went limp and he hit the ground with the full weight of his body.

Miriam stopped. Her clutching knuckles lost strength, and the remaining chunks of gravel fell like hail. She ran to him. "Baby!" she called. "Baby!" she screamed. He did not move. One arm hung outstretched toward the porch while the other lay pinned beneath his chest. One foot lay crossed atop the other leg. His bludgeoned head, streaming blood from an already darkening contusion, faced her, and he did not move. She squeezed his arms, imploring him to stand, or move, or blink. But her son only lay there with his mouth half open on the concrete. Saliva dripped and blood ran. It was on her hands now and on her knees as the dark red stream crawled slowly on the driveway. She tried to sweep him up in her arms. But his slouching, adult weight proved unwieldy, and she could not take him up.

Then the door of the house opened and shut with audible abandon, and there was a rush of feet and voices toward Miriam.

"Oh, God," someone said.

Miriam looked up through tears at her father followed closely by the priest. The collared man moved to kneel but rebounded quickly to his feet at the sight of the wound. Miriam's breath shortened. "Help him," she said, imploring the priest. Father David's eyes went wide searching over her and the boy. The smell of blood wove into their breath.

Then her father descended on her son. Pulling open the buttons of his over-shirt, Frank swept it off and compressed the mess of fabric to Ira's temple. "Car," he called out. The old man's arms flexed with forgotten strength, and he swept the boy up, his hand cradling the unconscious head. The priest seized Miriam by the hand and ushered her to his car at the end of the driveway. Frank came after them, holding his grandson to his chest.

JACOB KOCKEN

In a moment, they were off to the hospital. Father David drove, and Miriam sat in the backseat alongside her father and child. She whispered the whole time to her baby. His face was going pale. The shirt in turn grew red and heavy, and Frank held it ever tighter to the wound. The blood filled his hand and trickled down to stain his white cotton tank. Their two bald heads leaned together like coeval moons, a twilight's reflection on the rearview mirror.

When the car stopped they rushed in through the automatic doors of St. Michael's Emergency Room. A nurse ran for a gurney. Another nurse was asking questions. Miriam voiced her shame to everyone present in a short, disjointed confession. They wheeled her baby down the hall, and she ran after them. She followed them to another room where the doctor disposed of Frank's shirt and stopped the bleeding with gauze. The priest stood behind while Miriam leaned into her father's chest. Streaks of Ira's drying blood were on him, and she shut her eyes to it all for a moment.

The bleeding was stabilized, and the doctors transferred him to another room. Miriam, Frank, and Father David were shown to a waiting area.

"Your son is being treated by Dr. Zilich," a nurse told her. "He's a head trauma specialist; one of our best doctors. Ira is still unresponsive. I will come to you as soon as you can see him."

When the nurse left she took all the noise with her except the ticking of a clock. Miriam could not sit down. Her nerves were humming.

"I hit him with a rock," she said. It kept coming out of her mouth near a whisper. "I hit him with a rock." Her father took her by the shoulders. His hands were rough but warm and she melted into him. "I hit him with a rock. I hit him with a rock."

"Father," said Frank. "Say a prayer."

Miriam shut her eyes against her father's chest. The soft voice of the priest filled her head.

"Father, I pray You, hear Your children. Hear my supplication now, and hear the plight of these people. Her son, Your son, lies a blameless victim. We know all good things come from You. Heal Your son and the gift You grant will not go unheeded." The priest bowed his head.

"I hit him with a rock," she said again.

RISE THE MOON

Frank said nothing. Instead, he led her to a bench where they sat waiting side by side in half embrace. She leaned a cheek against his shoulder bone. His hand squeezed her arm in consolation, and through the thickness of her hair, she felt the lightest touch of lips on the top of her head.

THEY WAITED IN RELATIVE SILENCE. At first, they were alone; the three of them on a bench against the wall, surrounded only by the hospital's cold, florescent lights. It had been more than an hour. After such time alone, an elderly couple was ushered into the room. The man moved very slowly. His aluminum walker chafed over the hard tile floor in small, regular intervals. The woman, presumably his wife, walked at his side, her hands gently upturned as if ready to catch him at any moment. But she was thin and frail with hardly any more life in the bones than he. They sat at opposite benches as far away as the room allowed. There was a low and continuous groaning coming from the old man. His wife was at his ear, whispering something inaudible and rubbing one of her knuckly hands over his hunched and shaking back.

It wasn't more than a few minutes before the entrance doors swung open again and the room was joined by a man in an olive-green jacket, the collar of which he kept pulled up over his chin as he coughed. His fit was heavy and rasping, coloring the fabric with a sickly, phlegmatic humor. Now and then it sounded as though something had gone terribly wrong and his wheezing cut the air piteously. A woman following shortly behind him kept her distance. She led a small crying girl by the hand; no more than four years old. The little one tugged at the woman's wrist, asking to be picked up. But the woman tugged back, turning the girl straight and compelling her to walk on her own two feet. She kept trying to suppress her tears, but they choked on out anyway and joined the horrible chorus of coughing from the man beside them.

Miriam studied these people in silence, watching them wait alone in their corners. The sound of the ticking clock above was drowned in white noise then when near a dozen strangers shuffled in together. Each of them shared a familial shape of the eyes and nose. The somber group huddled in the middle of the room, keeping to their feet. A low chatter was amongst them. One of this

JACOB KOCKEN

bunch, a tall man with burly shoulders and a great hearth of a chest, stood out as the patriarch. The others gathered round him, some with maturity in their face but all a head shorter at least. Those others numbered seven, and their heads inclined toward the great man now and then. He showed a habit of touching them consolingly on the head or arms. When his great arms unfurled toward one or another of the clan, they seemed as wings, strong and broad as seraphim. He looked up after a while from beneath two brambled black brows and touched eyes with Miriam. He was utterly afraid.

They kept coming; now one, now two; grave strangers shuffling down the hospital corridor. What was once an empty room was turning tight for space as the bench seats filled with patients. The remaining souls stood, quiet and lonely as marble pillars. The children cried, and the elderly moaned. Then through the faces, Miriam saw one she recognized as their nurse, the one who'd taken Ira away. She, with her lower half concealed by the people, floated ghostly and slow. Miriam stood to await her. The women's eyes met, and the nurse cast her face to the ground though still she marched in. When the messenger was halfway there, just into the waiting room and sifting her way through the crowd, she was overtaken by another uniformed woman. Her hand caught the nurse swiftly from behind. Their lips moved, silent to Miriam, and the two women turned with brisk and powerful strides back in the direction they'd come. A call half escaped Miriam, and she nearly took pursuit. Their look of urgency caused her heart to sink. It weighed her all the way back down to her seat where she felt she may be sick and leaned backwards into her father's chest.

The priest on their bench sat in a daze. He looked not at her but at the multitude. There seemed as many people in the waiting room here as would have filled the sanctuary of St. Francis. His eyes scanned over each person as if he could see the demons on their backs. One of these, a middle-aged woman with disheveled brown hair trembled at the sight of the priest. She approached him and spoke in a low expectant tone.

"You're here for the rites?"

"Excuse me?"

"The rites. For my Joe? Joe Hadler."

"Oh," said David. "No, I wasn't."

RISE THE MOON

The woman's countenance fell, and she waited for a moment before them with her hands clasped tight together. Her head was bowed slightly with eyes closed. She was still as a statue and standing nearly on top of Miriam. When another bustling resident of the room knocked into her, she tipped over like an empty vase. Frank and Miriam caught her rigid body and set her right again, but she hardly seemed to notice.

"Are you alright?" asked Frank.

But the woman was a million miles away. All of them were. The whole town must have shown up in the emergency room that day. They were practically standing on top on each other, yet their miseries kept them.

"Tell me he will be alright, Father." Miriam said suddenly.

The priest looked at her with lost eyes. It was Frank who spoke.

"He'll be alright. Whether he wakes here or in the Kingdom. I know we don't want to think that. But it must be good and easy up there to account for all the mess there is on this end. This place can be an awful knot. That's what Emily used to say. So it must be good and easy up there. What's the Bible say of Heaven, Father?"

"Well," Father David started. "Not a lot of specifics."

"I figure that's because the trouble with doing things the right way is that there's only one right way in the end. Everywhere you look there's another path to take, and only one of them is right like how two plus two is four and only four. But considering all the other numbers you could choose from, getting any answer right is a shot in the dark; a shot at some blinking starlight somewhere off this world that you know is there because light is undeniable but the way to get there looks dark and unreachable. I've been bumping around in the dark for so long. For so long I had it going one way and knew it was wrong, but I couldn't see the right path because how could you when the whole Earth is a knot. And even if one path is more right than another it's only a matter of time before even a small angle drifts so far off into the dark you don't know where you are again. I don't know. So it must be good and easy up in Heaven."

Miriam was breathing hard. There were tears coming to her eyes as her imagination ran. Then, over the confusion of the crowd, she heard the even steps of their nurse marching dutifully down

JACOB KOCKEN

the corridor. The woman was looking down at something in her hands when she came into the waiting room. Blonde hair fell from the crook in her ear and hung like a tapered drape before her face. People ambled here and there, covering her from sight now and then until, in an instant, she was before them. It was a clipboard she was looking down at. Her eyes were large, dark, and soft as the night sky. When she turned them on Miriam they were filled with wonder.

"Is Emily here?"

"What?" said Miriam.

The nurse's eyes flicked down to the paper then back again. "Miriam? Ira's mother?"

"Yes! Is he alright? Tell me he's awake!"

"He's awake. The doctor says you can see him, though he's surely in a bit of a state."

"A state?"

"He said he came here with Emily."

Dr. Zilich was a tall, lean man with thin, silver rimmed spectacles that magnified grey eyes. He received Miriam, with Frank and Father David in tow, just outside the room that kept her boy.

"We'll go in to see him in just a moment," said the doctor. "But I wanted to impress some instructions on you quickly. First, do not touch his head. The wound is dressed properly, and we have him stabilized with a brace. There was a small amount of internal bleeding that we had to act on, and that site will be delicate for a while." Dr. Zilich had a deep, calm voice. He said such things as this with the equanimity of a man tossing bread crumbs to the birds. His hands were folded at his waist, and he stood strong and still as the foundation of the Earth.

Despite the composure of the doctor, Miriam could not help but notice the other eyes in the hallway, the heads flicking their way, and the whispers that ran along the walls. Two nurses standing some dozen feet off behind Dr. Zilich were bent close toward each other speaking in hushed, and for that, altogether more noticeable, tones.

"Second," said the doctor, "let us not overwhelm him. He's been through a lot today. He needs rest above all. Because of that,

RISE THE MOON

we will be keeping him overnight and monitoring the vitals. You will notice something of a lazy eye. Lazy eyes perhaps. There may have been some disturbance to the optic nerve, however, an MRI was taken and shows no obvious trauma. It will likely resolve itself with rest and convalescence."

"Is he blind?" Panic crept back into Miriam's voice.

"No. His depth perception may be off, but otherwise his vision seems clear." The doctor raised a patient finger. "Another thing, and this runs along similar lines as before, do not be distressed if he is not quite himself. Do not be distressed, but do take note. Certain memory problems and alterations in speech are common after head injuries and can be more or less serious. I would like you to look out for those irregularities and let me or the nurses know if you don't believe he's right."

Miriam nodded. She had heard every word, but her attention was now split again between the doctor and the passersby who were unmistakably glancing their direction. When she looked back up to Dr. Zilich he seemed to have noticed the phenomenon as well. He was shooting a mild glare at the two gossipers who had left their post behind him and were striding down the hall still with their heads bent together.

"Lastly," said the doctor. "I get the intuition that you may hear stories from someone if you're to stay here for his convalescence. I'd rather you not get the wrong idea." Miriam's head swung back to where the whispering nurses had walked. They were gone now, but Dr. Zilich nodded at her gesture.

"He spoke of Emily?" It was her father who entered the conversation. Frank controlled the volume of his voice, but its eager quality was irrepressible.

"Yes, what did he say?" asked Miriam.

"All I heard was the voice," said the doctor. "He may as well have been speaking in tongues. It was not words so much as a moan or a cry. Then the vitals began to climb back up."

"They told us he spoke of Emily," said Frank. "That's my late wife. His grandma."

"I'm afraid I cannot add a relevant opinion on the boy's soul or psyche. I can recommend some professionals for that type of inquiry. Or perhaps that's why you've brought a priest." The doctor

JACOB KOCKEN

gave an ironical smile and stretched his arm out to the door of the hospital room, saying, "Now, in you go."

Frank turned the steel handle and stood back for Miriam to enter. Her feet were fast and heavy. The room she rushed into was small. A single bed stretched across the center of the floor perpendicular to the door, so the patient was displayed in profile. A light linen blanket was tucked in at the foot of the bed and pulled up to his chest where a loose blue gown draped his upper body. Miriam pulled up before she reached the edge of the bed.

Her son was awake. He lay back with his wrapped head against a stack of two thin pillows. The bandage was white, clean, and thick enough to conceal the dome of his shaved head. His nose was pointed at the ceiling. But his left eye, the one nearest her, was trained so far to the side that it pierced her with attention even as she approached. It was a bright and dazzling blue that caught her movement from moment to moment as it flicked in staccato vibration upon each of the three trailing visitors. His head lay still on the pillow, his neck did not turn.

The air caught in Miriam's mouth and the worry of the hours' wait erupted. Her hand shook as she slipped her fingers through his. She bent against the side of the bed and closed her eyes with wailing. Her forehead pressed into the thin white sheets. In the darkness, Ira responded with a firm and gentle squeeze of the hand to which Miriam clutched with all her soul. Another hand, rough and leathery, moved back and forth in a quiet caress on the back of her neck.

When the tears dripped away and her sight returned, Miriam raised her head. She came eye to eye with him. His face was calm but severe. The lips did not move. The nostrils pulsed slow and smooth with his breath. His eye burned through everything. It was the left one, the one that had first seen her enter. It tracked Miriam with a strange vibrating stare. A thousand minute jumps showed the pupil in constant motion over every piece of her. She stared into it and felt, for the first time in the face of her son, afraid. Still, Miriam wished to hold his discerning watch and never look away. When she did for a moment it was to check the other eye whose direction was bent crosswise toward the foot of the bed where Frank now stood silent.

RISE THE MOON

Miriam's attention snapped back to the one that looked into her, the left eye. Then she returned to the right. It was not lazy as the doctor had said. It did not drift or waver. It saw.

Her father moved to the opposite side of the bed and took Ira's right hand as Miriam had done the left. She watched as the other eye followed Frank around the end of the mattress and sunk into the far corner of its socket so that he looked sidelong in either direction. She spoke words of guilt and love and care and when Ira's reply came it was steady and knowing from a throat aimed straight to the sky.

Frank began to speak and console him and ask after Emily. Miriam saw with what intensity her son's right eye latched onto the old man. She loosed herself from Ira's hand and hurried to the other side of the bed. The left eye followed her until she stood at Frank's hip. For the first time, the two lenses converged on one scene, and the boy's countenance recalled his old self. This relieved Miriam greatly for she feared if she had run the other way the strength in the sole eye that tracked her would have rent her son in two.

51.
David

"Forgive me Father for I have sinned. It has been three days since my last confession." The chapel was awash in candlelight, and the novitiate went on speaking his crimes. Early April sun glowed varicolored through stained glass scenes all along the eastern wall. Their counterparts to the west still hung dreary as the night's last fingers clutched weakly on the lattice. A touch of frost obscured the one side while the other thawed and dripped. The winter had come sudden and harsh that year. The temperature sunk to zero before Christmas and continued to fall so that even those hearty citizens experienced of the northern clime shunted the outdoors for several weeks. At the turn of the New Year, car batteries froze in driveways. Poorly insulated pipes iced through and burst while whistling wind found every open crack in the walls and roofs. Many remained in their own quiet homes. Some nested down on the sofas and guest beds of friends and relatives, but still the perennial mortality of terrible summer heat was reflected on this opposite season at Graumont's mausoleum as the earth froze too resolute for gravedigging. Funerals were small. People did not brave the blizzards for acquaintanceship. A single exposure to some of the days' frigid claws threatened injury of permanently purpled skin. There was only one man who found himself unlocking doors nearly every day. These doors led him

RISE THE MOON

out from his hole for a mile or so to where the day's mourners collected beside the wall of the dead. People tended to stand still even indoors, huddling against themselves for warmth while he spoke the ceremonies. Their heads, David thought, seemed frozen on their necks, staring always at the encasing marble where their parent's or child's or sibling's name was engraved in thin black letters. Only the Foster boy broke the pattern when the widowed Bess Garland came to final rest. He'd seen that family every week for some months at Mass. They were always together in their four generations, linked by some unfriendly love. They'd sat together in mixed chronology, waiting for the sign of peace with hands that tarried first in their own laps and then in each other's grasp.

Now, David sat hunchbacked in jeans and an old pinstriped t-shirt with the Milwaukee Brewers logo in fading print over the breast pocket. His robes still hung inside the small wooden wardrobe in the corner of his office. He'd known Frank was coming; he came two or three times a week now. But the weekend was on David's mind, and when he'd come in to prepare some kind of homily there was the old man standing patiently by the chapel doors.

"I remembered something further back," Frank was saying. The man was thinner now. Loose skin hung at the jowls where his weight had been. Not all of Frank's clothes had yet been replaced, and today he wore one of those old outfits that hung on his body like a cassock. "When I was real young I knocked some kid off a swing. It was after school. I was maybe six. He was just swinging, and I got in there behind him and shoved. He hit the ground all dazed and started crying. I didn't even take the swing. I don't know what compelled me to do it, but that's what happened. That's all for way back. The other thing was yesterday. I had that meeting you set up with Father Tim in Devinsville. He was kind. He is older than me by the way, only by a year. We talked about my training, and he put me on the path. Then he gave me a tour of the place. It's a beautiful church. Down below, though, where they keep the wine, I had the old thoughts. I didn't do anything about it, but I had the old thoughts about His blood. Forgive me, Father."

"Is that everything?"

"Yes."

They said the Lord's Prayer together, and David stood to leave.

JACOB KOCKEN

"Penance, Father?" said Frank.

"You're doing enough."

The morning newspaper was folded into Frank's pocket. The top half poked out from this hold and showed the front page in partial scope. Only a few words were visible. Only one was necessary. David's glance fell continually to it, and the older man took notice.

"I'm glad I'm not ordained yet," said Frank. "I don't know what I'd tell a parish this week. I know a man can repent. I'm my own proof of that. But being sorry is a private thing. There's hardly a good way to show it even if you're earnest. Words don't do justice. My Miriam and I have been talking about it. She didn't want me around, you know? She was going to leave that day; take the boy and leave."

"And now you're thick as thieves?"

"Thickening. It's strange. Sometimes we talk about the past. There's no getting away from it, yet when we talk it's as if those people we were are specters; haunts that decorate everything we do and say but don't weigh an ounce."

"She used to come see me almost as much as you do now," David said. His gaze touched the corner of the room where the flames smoked silent petitions. Many weeks had passed since Miriam's custom had burned to its base. The golden holder sat there still, caked over with hoary, half translucent wax.

"She's stopped?"

"Mhm."

"Was it Emily?"

The priest did not answer.

"Forgive me," said Frank. "That was inappropriate."

"It was."

"Forgive me."

"It was Emily," said David.

"It's between her and God," said Frank, ashamed. "Don't. If she came to you in confidence."

David did not look up. His face stayed directed toward the petition candles where another among them flickered and, throwing off a final flash, relinquished to a mess of ashen-black snuff. "She kept so much guilt. Early on, I was confused. Of course neglect is a sin, but she had been forgiven. I had said the words. Still, she

RISE THE MOON

kept coming. So I kept saying the words, and every time she came back I knew more and more I was doing something wrong. But I didn't know what else to give her except ritual absolution. There was something else to do; something her absence now tells me she's found."

The two men sat in silence a while.

"Ira's hair is back down to his ears. There's a scar under there where nothing grows, but you only see it if you go looking. He stays in Miriam's old room sometimes. It's odd, walking in there now. You can't shake the memories, the way things used to be. For moments I can still feel that little girl when I stand in there. There's a way the walls feel. I suppose all walls look very near the same, but so do all faces really, and yet, you know certain ones from anything in the world. So I can still feel that way in there even if he's asleep on the bed."

"His eyes are still like that."

"I can't quite imagine what it must be like in there. People are built for consonance; that's what feels good. But him; well, I can't tell if it's a blessing or a curse. The Kepling kid helps lead him around," said Frank. "You've never seen two young men so comfortable holding hands." David gave a passive nod as if he might say something about the affliction. Then his empty palms rolled out and, with this gesture, passed the moment back to his novitiate.

"When they stay over I still sleep in the living room. On the couch," Frank went on. "Oddly enough it's one part of the arrangement that doesn't feel strange at all. I go to bed late, so we always end up there in the evenings. Records spin always on the gramophone. I play them. They don't seem to mind. It is calming music. The other night we danced to it. Just me and Miriam in the living room. She got married on the coast. We never had our father-daughter dance. I'm sure she didn't care for it then. Miriam says she can hear the music from upstairs even in the middle of the night; that it's always coming through the floor and the walls. Like as though the wind sways the house and music comes straight from the rubbing boards."

David blew a long, pensive breath. He nodded but felt his head equivocate from shoulder to shoulder.

"Something on your mind, Father?" said Frank. He tugged at

the newspaper that stood halfway out his pocket. "Is it the verdict? I'll be damned if I haven't been thinking of it too. I guess we all saw it coming. Everyone's been saying for months they'd give him the chair."

"Yes, it's hardly a surprise." When the news of the trial broke, simultaneously through the town it seemed, David had entered the chapel and replaced all ninety-nine empty candle stands that had burned for Sophia Joy that day of her funeral service. He hoped to honor her short, beautiful life, but it was her death that still burned in him with the lighting of every wick. Death, in congruence with death, was the verdict on Yokoven. Now, as he sat listening to Frank, his eyes watched the candles. Even as they spoke, the wax pooled and melted, evaporating into nothing. Soon they would reach their ends; Yokoven would be dead and all the little girl will have gained is ninety-nine candles lost to flame.

"I sat in at the trial," said Frank. "Back in the public benches. It was hard to get a seat. It was a whole lot like that little girl's funeral. Sad and quiet. He was real quiet too. He didn't hardly talk at all. I'm sure you read about that."

"Yes, I read that," said Father David.

"At first, I thought he'd gone soft in the head. We were all looking around, everyone who was there, wondering if it was our imagination. I suppose there was nothing to say really; not for him. They brought him up three times. I guess there's something in that number that makes things seem more solid, and then they knew nothing was coming out of him on purpose. You could hear the dust settling on the floorboards he was so quiet. Then he would start fidgeting. Not with his hands but like some kind of tic. It was in his face, and you could see it for a second now and then. I'm sure something was tearing at him. It reminded me of an old buddy who lost his leg in the war. Sometimes we'd just be sitting around, and he'd howl something monstrous. It was the leg; the missing one. There wasn't any good reason as far as we could tell, but something was hurting him. That's what it reminded me of. I'll be damned if it means anything. What do you make of it all, Father?"

David cleared his throat.

"If a man truly repents..." David lost his tongue. He cleared his throat again.

RISE THE MOON

"That's a hard sell," said Frank. "Did I ever tell you he was a student of mine?"

"Is that so?"

"Ethics 222. I think that was the last class I had him. A classic course on Kant and Bentham, a few others."

"Could you tell? Back then?"

"He was different, yes," said Frank. "Articulate. His essays were penetrating. I remember that. He did tend to fixate though; always on about the same thing one way or another. Even outside the writing. He came to my office several times. Just to talk. It was academic at first, but before long I told him he ought to see a counselor too. That met some resistance. He was a sharp kid. He wanted to think his way out. It didn't seem to me like a problem for thinking."

"Did he go?"

"I don't know," Frank said. "I got fired then."

A BLEAK, GRAY OVERCAST WAS ON the sky when David pulled up to Lake Duval. The surface of the water had no shimmer today. Everything was still. There was a rock in David's pocket. He'd carried it every day in mimic of the girl he'd found it with. She'd told a story about rocks, and David hoped her wisdom would help.

As he walked, David tried to put his mind to Sunday's sermon. But a cardinal was singing in the trees. Every few minutes his mind would wander off to listen to the easy beauty of its song. He looked around for the red wings and found something else that out in the distance poked through the vision of branches, stretching toward the heavens like a thin and pointing compass needle. Then he would drag himself back to the jumbled thoughts of death, justice, and mercy.

In his decade of priesthood, David had stood at the lectern every week. The hundred faces in the crowd had at first been only a mass. He came to recognize them slowly. When his service was at an end and he proceeded with the deacon out of the sanctuary, David had always stood at the doors as the people filed out. Some of them stopped to talk or shake his hand or simply smile and nod. Others, he was sure he never saw more than once. But he did come to recognize the lot of them. By habit, they sat in regular pews, and Sundays took the shape of their attendance. The newcomers

JACOB KOCKEN

and the absent were conspicuous by such a pattern of form. When Mrs. Helman's seat remained empty for three weeks in a row, his notice turned to concern for that staunch disciple. An inquiry found she had been laid up in the hospital with pneumonia. Two weeks later, the Gospel readings told of Jesus' healing for the centurion at Capernaum. David shaped the words of his homily around the sick woman. Behind the theology and the rhetoric, his speech was about her; it was for her. But he did not mention her. He never mentioned them by name. Still, one of Mrs. Helman's relatives stopped to talk after Mass and praised his words for the inspiration of cherished love it gave her. Mrs. Helman passed away a week and a half later in the middle of the night.

When Calvin Deen, the funeral home director, told him in confession that the price of things inflated when a dead man's own estate covered all the proceedings, it was under real and urgent shame. He had been caught, and begged the priest outright for guidance, saying he would quit, run away and retire from all dealings with honest, trustworthy people should he not be able to restore his name. David did what he could to calm the man, to urge patience, introspection, and penance. Still, Mr. Deen left with an equivocal expression and David set to mulling over the meanings of theft. In a week's time he'd prepared a sermon around Ephesians 4:28. It had been some of his more insightful work, but when he failed to find Mr. Deen among the Sunday congregation, he had that reading postponed. A month down the road the man was present, and though David could say nothing explicit, he tried to speak to the funeral director. The message, whether or not in its full intention, was presumably received. That was the last time the man had come to St. Francis. Later on, David had written to Calvin Deen. A letter came back telling how he was picking up carpentry, making things of quality. It was a thank you note, though vague and sorrowful. He did not respond to David's further letters.

Gordan Yokoven had never shown up in the Sunday pews. The once radiant blonde hair would've stood out as memorable. David knew him only from that one preemptive confession half a year ago.

Duval Lake disappeared behind him as David wandered into the deeper parts of the wood, thinking back on triumphs and loss-

RISE THE MOON

es, the ambiguities of his task. But now, and for the past several months, each of these once unique and powerful memories was cast through a prism. He thought of and understood them only so far as they reflected some small light onto the one consuming failure. And as it seemed to pull all other thoughts into itself, David too became victim to a dragging gravity beyond the park boundaries.

The penitentiary watchtower poked up through the haze of trees and clouds. David broke from the dirt path and trudged toward the looming pillar. After a mile of unhewn forest, David heard the sounds of rubber and gravel. An old country highway ran through the wood, and he took to the shoulder of the road, following it for a long time until the way curved around and split off into the narrow prison drive.

The building was a fortress. Earth colored bricks stood tall and flat for a hundred yards. A twelve-foot fence ran the perimeter and intersected the drive with a gate and security station. As David approached, a uniformed guard waved him over.

"Someone expecting you?" said the guard.

"I'm here to give the rites." David inclined his chin, showing the collar he always wore.

"One moment." The guard turned and took up a phone. The window slid back to closed, and David watched the man's silent lips through the glass. He talked for a good long time. Then there was a sudden start of dragging metal as the gate retracted, and David walked on through. A short courtyard of splendidly green grass flanked the single sidewalk up to the main doors.

Inside, at the crossing of a threshold, all the color of the world was gone. Everything was gray and flat. Walls of concrete stood fifteen feet high, boxing the room into a tasteless rectangle. One woman sat occupied at the desk behind a pane of bulletproof glass.

"It's visiting hours?" said David through the speaking holes.

"Name of inmate."

"Yokoven."

"He's being seen," said the woman. "Wait here if you'd like."

David sat on an old wooden bench. It appeared familiar to him and stretched the length of one entire wall. David hung his head and waited. His forefinger absently traced lines in the seat where the termites had gotten. He wasn't long that way before the sound of sobbing leaked into the hall. A thick steel door opened on the opposite wall and out came a woman escorted, or rather trailed, by an officer. She led their way in a frantic rush. Her hands covered the expression of her face upon entering the lobby. She dressed in a suit, all black except the gleaming beads of pearl that ringed her neck. Before coming to the exit, her whole pitiful figure collapsed to the floor where her guard dropped away, and she wailed as if lost alone in the wilderness. David recognized her in an instant by the sound of her moaning as much as by the face.

"Gillian," he said as he came to her. She seemed in agony compared even with her pain some months ago at her daughter's funeral. He knelt beside her on one knee and tried to stop her writhing. The officer approached as well but stood by at the sight of David's familiarity.

When finally he caught hold of her shoulder he spoke again, "Gillian. Gillian, what is it? What has happened?"

Her eyes fixed on his, and her throat went dumb. She looked up and down at his face and collar in creeping disbelief. David could see their reflections lock on the sheen of her pupil. It started with a widening of the eyes. Then her mouth contorted. Lips undulated in loose, uneven lines as her jaw was cranked open by the scream. She shoved at him with the strength of fear, and a new agony overtook her.

"Oh God!" she cried. "No! No! No!"

"Gillian," said David. He moved to touch her face; to comfort her with a gentle hand. In the next instant, he was sitting back with the sting of welting skin. The base of her palm had struck his nose, and now it began to drip warm red blood slow and regular into his own open hands. It was on his lips and crawled inside when David opened his mouth.

The officer was bringing her to her feet, and she stood beside him looking down at the priest. When David moved to stand as well, she flinched. Her eyes narrowed and something escaped from her throat that sat him down again on the precinct floor. She hissed.

The officer removed his hands from the woman who was both fuming with rage and recoiling like a thing in fear. Her eyes never came off David as she slunk away from him. One drooping shoulder traced the wall as she headed for the door. She walked hunched

RISE THE MOON

and jerking like a coward or as if her spine had been broken. In a flash of sunlight, she disappeared, and the heavy door shut them in again.

David sat stunned. After some time, the officer was at his side handing him a towel. David pressed it to his nose and looked down to see the blood soaked into the front of his clothes. He was shown to a washroom where he did what he could to clean his face. Then he removed his shirt and ran it under the faucet. The blood stains spread and lightened at first but quickly reached a diminishing point. David scrubbed with his fingers. He turned the water piping hot and beat at the stains with soap. But the red did not leave the fabric, and when he returned the wet shirt to his torso it seemed only more apparently bloody. His pants too were streaked with color, and now at the sight of it all he was struck again with his reason for coming and rushed from the room.

"She was with him, wasn't she?" he said to the clerk. "He's available?"

"He is waiting for you."

The same guard who'd shown him to the washroom now showed David down a corridor to where the walls and ceiling converged to a box only large enough for a door with a window only large enough for the eyes. On the other side of this door there was an immediate and noticeable change in some ambient sensory quality. As they entered, David felt the sound of his own steps pounding like timpanis. It was not, however, as if the sound were any louder than natural. Rather, it was the sound alone. There was no hum of machinery or flowing air. No voices or passing traffic intruded through the bricks. And for the first time in his life, by its absence, David noticed the illusion conjured up by a complex of senses. There was something to hear here. It came out of the walls, and David was deeply saddened. He breathed a sigh, and the empty room was filled with rushing. He heard the wind pass away from him and back like a raptorous hunter with no branch to land.

The officer extended his hand toward a bare table in the middle of the room. "We can see and hear you, sir. If you need anything, just say so. Ten minutes." Then the officer receded back into the corridor and the door clicked shut.

He was sitting there already. His arms were crossed on the

JACOB KOCKEN

tabletop supporting his chin as he stared forward. His beard was shaved, revealing florid skin. There were marks about his face and neck that David had seen once before in person and many times since on television screens. They were rusted red craters; circular; a quarter inch wide each. They stretched down over his arms as well in a scattered manner. Their darkly crimson centers sunk deeply through his florid skin like voids on the surface of the sun, ancient pocks. At the same time, their rings gleamed with leaking blisters; pale transparent rosebuds. He fingered them, picking at the flaking skin. David stood by the door a while, but Yokoven's head did not twist to find him.

The same swell of noise as before came when David made his pace to the opposite end of the table. It startled him, and David checked over each shoulder. Then he came into the sitting man's line of sight and watched the light of recognition blink. The man's expression was just as David remembered from months ago. The mouth was a subtle downward curve. Despite the ugly marks, his features were juvenile. And when he looked up at David, one eye met him square while the other lazy one drifted down and out to the side.

"Father," he said. "You got blood on you."

"Mm."

A chair was waiting for David, and he sat, still looking down at the man who did not lift himself from rest.

"It feels trite. You, come to give my rites."

"Do you want them?" said David.

The man's head rose an inch. He remained slouching over the table while he looked into the priest's eyes. Then his chin nestled back into the notch of his crossed arms while he picked at one of the scabbing blisters in the middle of his hand.

"I do."

"Very well."

"I didn't see you at the sentencing. Free you entering here and now. Why? How?"

"Did you expect me?" asked David.

"I saw a lot of other people, but I didn't see you. True?"

"The law was swift and just. I wouldn't have made a difference."

RISE THE MOON

"Is that so though?"

"I wasn't called to testify. I wouldn't have been a favor to you."

"I mean about the law, Father. Does such a flaw bother you?"

"I did not say good. But just."

"Are you allowed to say so though?"

"Some things are clear enough."

"It wasn't clear last time? I'm lost."

"It can be a sin to think terrible things, Gordan, but it's not a crime. You came to me as a priest, and I acted as a priest." The other man's words echoed off the walls, and in the silences those windy spirits rose resurrected in David's ears. It all played again in a faint and grisly loop. He thought at first it was the concrete walls, but found them porously old and softened by the usual temporal entropy so that they embraced all of his own supplications.

"That's not what you said last time."

"What?"

"That it's a sin to think some things. Did God or you change the tune? Does it bother you too, Father?"

"Of course. Why was Gillian here?"

"I was surprised to see her. Hard to be her, yes? Alone too. Women are often softened, though I would have thought that kind of thing irrelevant here. Mothers are often different from women. Mothers are some of the only truly loving and hateful people. They're like priests who fall in love with God when they think He's the only thing they can love forever. Until they find Him undeserving. That's mothers. Everyone else is far too concerned with themselves. She's an awful lot like my own. They both wear a pearl necklace, you know? She had had one on a thin silver chain. She does too. An awful lot alike. I told her about that too; how she had had one. How she had had the same one as her except hers was filled all the way around and my mother's had just one between two silver wings. Something my father had given her when I was born. Before he left."

"Why did she come?"

"Did you see her leave, Father?"

"Yes."

"How was she?"

"That's unnecessary, Gordan."

JACOB KOCKEN

"I'm not making fun. Did you get a sure look at her?"

"Of course."

"Did you get a look back? Did you see her in the eyes?"

"She was understandably unwell."

"Yes."

"Anyone would be, Gordan."

"Everyone should be, Father."

"Did she come to scream at you?"

"She screamed, but she came for the same reason I think you have. She and you. She and you."

"What's that?"

The prisoner picked at the wound on his hand. The cracking, blistering ring broke at the edge and ran red with a little droplet of excretion.

"At the sentencing she requested I take the stand. Did you know?" David shook his head. "To explain myself. She'd spoken out of turn and really stirred up the court. Did you know? You didn't know."

"What did you say?"

"I declined, Father."

"It's her right to know."

"That's what she said. I said it wouldn't help. But then she came here. She came to beg and shout. It was burning her up. I didn't like to see it."

"What did you say?"

"When I came to you, Father, when I found you in the church that day, I had a bag of apples with me. You remember?"

"Yes."

"I used to walk to the west side when food ran low. That's where he lives. That's where my father ran off to. I knocked on his door one day; a few years ago. He looked just as I remembered him. I know he recognized me. Or that he just knew somehow. But he said my name did not ring a bell. He went as far as to say he was new in town, and that he was pleased to meet a new neighbor. I insisted. So did he; we were only neighbors. So I began to steal. After some time, they put a gate up, so I'd go at night when it was easier to sneak over. It's best that way. My mother used to operate in the dark. That's a courtesy people learn. So I generally slipped

RISE THE MOON

over there in the nights. Not on that day though. I went out early that day while the sun was still on the way up. I always ate one while I picked the others. They're quite a thing to mull, Father."

"What does it have to do with anything?"

"Well I was seen, Father. Out in the heat and light, lost in the sweet bite. I never really got lost except with one of those fruits. It's pleasant to be lost. At least, it is not unpleasant. And that can really be something. But someone saw me, and soon they were chasing me down. They cut me off at the near fence, so I had to run across the fields and hike myself over the other end. It's prairie country there, so when I took off for home it was around a different, longer way where the houses block the view. I was always wary of the suburbs. My mother said people weren't meant to live so bunched up. People are always looking in your windows without even trying. Now, there I was, and all the windows were staring down at me too. After a few yards and fences, I stopped running. No one was tailing. So I walked in relative peace. I wanted to eat as I walked. I remember breathing hard from the run and pulling an apple from my bag blind. I had to spit it out the moment I began to chew. It was dry and sour. It reminded me of things; lots of things from long ago. They're never sour nowadays. They're supposed to be full and sweet. They're the only things that were always sweet. And just then Father, I heard her from two blocks down. You can't mistake a baby's crying. Not even if you've never heard it before. She was screaming, Father. She was screaming, and it was right where I was walking up on, so I watched. They were out there on the porch. Her and the baby girl. She was smoking a cigarette. My mother smoked too. I can't recall her without a stick in her mouth. And that woman was sucking like a pacifier. I could smell it even across the road where I was. She was bouncing her in her arms, holding her, but the baby kept crying. I don't know what that girl had to make her wail like that. Except perhaps that the burning tobacco was too close. It has a hateful stench, Father. That woman didn't even notice when I stopped. I just stopped and watched. You should've seen that tired woman, Father. Her eyes were so weary dark it looked like they might fall right in. Then the husband came out with one of those little trinkets for a baby; something pink, plastic, and noisy. But she just cried. They tried a whole lot of things, and you could see in that

JACOB KOCKEN

man's slumping shoulders the same resignation that was all over the mother as she cooed and bounced and eventually just joined the girl in tears. She set her down in a little baby chair right there in the sun, and they both went on shaking and crying. She ran inside, shaking, and the man went in after her, calling out some fragile plea. And the little girl was there alone, crying on the porch. She had a little white bonnet on. But in her fit it fell back, and the strap of lace hung around her throat. The sun was all the way rose by then, and she was looking right up there. It was hot. Every day is hot. The whole time she never stopped crying, and there was not a cloud in the sky. Every moment I felt sure they were going to come back out, to come save her. I could've done it too. I could've gone up there and moved her to the shade. But what's one time matter? What's one leaf on a tree; one tree in a forest? The perfect skin turned pink. Then it turned red. She was getting blisters. I waited so long for them to come out that I burned too. When the sun bent down I squinted toward the horizon. My stomach rumbled. My forehead was burnt. My nose and cheeks and ears were burnt too and stinging. And she was still crying, and no one was bringing her inside. I'd been scorched before, but hers was fresh and shocking. They might as well have held hot iron to her. The second I took a step in that direction the screen door popped open, and that woman came bustling out the same way she'd gone in hours before. And even when the little girl was back in her mother's arms I could hear it in her crying voice that the fire was still on her; that she was alone and burning. It was on the trees in the distance, and the rooftops. The blacktop roads were waving with Hellish heat. And in that moment, Father? Some yoke lifted from my shoulders. I stopped hating the mother. Not because she saved the babe but because my burns hurt too, and I finally realized the sun was ubiquitous. What could she really do? Fix the baby's bonnet? What is a bonnet against an infinity of flame?" Gordan Yokoven sat up straight in his chair. "I couldn't help but remember the house afterward. That's when I came to the church. I hadn't even thought to do it until I came upon that old church; until right before I talked to you. The golden bells were ringing. That hollow echo is what did it, Father. And the lingering scent of smoke from your censer."

"Gordan," said David. The prisoner's fingers were vainly try-

RISE THE MOON

ing to quell the seepage from one of his blistering neck sores. "You make too much of things."

"No, Father," said the inmate. "I can see the future is all. I can see it behind me. Do you feel better now, Father?" David didn't answer. "She came; she begged. Does she feel better? I suppose you'll tell everyone now. I suppose you'll preach about it all on Sunday. I suppose you'll say how she left her daughter burning in the sun. You'll tell them how when she finally returned at day's end she snatched the baby up by the elbow. Or how the flaming sky would find her eventually. No? Then you'll lie to them. Or you won't touch it at all. Leave things in the dark. Then you can save yourself a lie and settle for neglect, Father."

"Stop that now, Gordan."

"Come on, Father. What will you tell them?"

"I'll pray on it."

"Will you pray for me as well? Please, Father."

"You've put me in a terrible position, Gordan. I can only pray my earnest feelings. Should I want to see you in Heaven?"

"Pray for God's wisdom, not your own. You said He is infinite. You said He'd understand."

"Then what do you need my prayer for?"

The inmate put heavy, wringing hands over the sores on his face. He rubbed them, and their excretion streaked across his skin. He spoke quietly, and the echo on his voice was redoubled. "I'll pray for you, Father. I'll pray for you."

There was a rushing of air as the iron door clicked open. The officer entered. "That's ten minutes." The chain locking Yokoven's wrists dragged across the surface of the table as he was made to stand. The officer took the killer's arm and addressed David where he sat. "Wait here. I'll be back in a moment." Gordan Yokoven was ushered away without a turn of the head. His lazy eye, long moored to its sunken place, did not budge. His feet dragged against the dusty concrete, whishing back and forth on the wind.

David exhaled a long resignation. He breathed only through his mouth now. Blood stopped up his nostrils. He looked down at the streaking red stains on his shirt before cutting off the world behind closed eyes.

David's seat tipped back on two legs. His head rested on the

JACOB KOCKEN

wall behind as the chair's frame leaned into the echo of whispering bricks.

DAVID WATCHED HIS FEET OVER the St. Francis lot. The steps were slow and moved along by that weak magnetic force of reluctant hearts. There was no one in the sanctuary. There was no one in the halls. On his desk there was a pen. Beside it lay the little pad he used for sermon writing. The pages were open, blank except for the date of Sunday next. David sat down. The chair creaked and he froze. He lifted the four wooden legs and brought his seat up toward the pen and pad, soundlessly as if together they constituted an animal that dare not be startled, dare not be woken. He took up the pen and stared. A ball was forming in his throat. The longer he looked at the pages the more of his vision they filled, stretching into fields of white, blank and blurring. He shook his head and cleared his throat as if to speak. A dull pain came against the bone of his finger where the motionless pen sat pressing down. "Ahem," he cleared. "Ahem."

The heat of frustration and even the smallest bead of prickling sweat touched his forehead. "Ahem. Ahem." The ball in his throat was stuck, and he went into a fit of forced coughing. He loosened the collar around his neck, and at once the knot began to settle, to fade into a more visceral place. He put pen to paper now, almost without thinking.

Parishioner,

The last few years have been an honor. I was lucky to have been placed in such a connected community; to have a role of repute accompanied by the trust of faithful people. That trust was placed in me dutifully, blindly. I can say I have always done my best to earn all that was given.

I came into the Church a distraught young man. Though I was hardly devout before, there is something about the cross that calls to the lonely, desperate, and lost. I entered quickly into the seminary where I read and thought all day in a quiet dorm room. The place was gray and bare, but love and faith were all about. It took me under its sheltering wing. Seminary soothed me and I made those granite walls my home. But just as with any home, the chick grows up, and being deemed by some earthly metric to have moved

RISE THE MOON

into maturity, it's sent from the coop to be something in the world. And so I found myself with you; at a podium with a hundred hungry faces looking up with all the trust and faith in the world.

You come and confess to me. You lay your failing before this conduit. But I must return the act and confess as well. Your conduit is no wiser than you. I am not a link halfway to Heaven. No doubt, there are some who are, real prophets and shepherds who have convened with God and carry an understanding more delicate and discerning. But my study is all in books. I have done all that I can in puzzling right from wrong. But I have no special convention with God. I don't possess what warrants authority; that which you assume when you address my title. I will write to the diocese and have you sent a leader more capable, more worthy of your faith.

David ripped the page from its binding. He left the letter on the main desk for a secretary to find, along with instructions to have it mailed to every address in the parish directory. It was dark outside. His car left two faint rubber marks on his turn out from the church's drive.

52.
Ira

IRA WOKE. IT WAS EARLY in the cycle of the day. The sky outside was a swirling grey with the dark light of dawn. He rose in his bed and saw at once two things. He saw the letter on his nightstand; a piece of notebook paper that had remained unmoved for many cold months. He saw simultaneously the picture frame resting atop his dresser on the opposite side of the room. Erected only days ago, it was of Ira himself looking down at the brother in his arms, a babe of so recent birth he could hardly see. As Ira turned from the bed, he noted in the background of the photo the mother watching over his shoulder. Her hair was still pink. Her vision was fixed on the child in Ira's arms.

He had to walk carefully. Within the confines of his room, Ira's feet knew what to do on their own. They knew the space from wall to wall, from bed to door. Most of the house, in fact, was ingrained in unconscious proprioception. But still, Ira had to move slowly. He'd already had countless falls and smashed toes against the legs of tables, the edges of dressers, door frames. He saw with a double sight and found it near impossible to control. The ease with which a person is accustomed to captaining his body was gone. Often it helped to close one eye and walk without mixed messages. Then even if his one lens was occupied by something tangential, Ira could navigate by

RISE THE MOON

context.

When the slow plod to the bathroom was complete, Ira washed himself. This he could do without the gift of focused sight and was pleased for it. He took his time, feeling the sensations all about him as running water shifted between hot and cool and washed away the dirt of the previous day. After drying off back in his bedroom, he found clothes for the day from deep inside his closet. It would be the first time in quite a while that he'd worn a suit jacket. He was much taller now than even just a year before, and they'd had to get him fitted again. The jacket was grey as were the pants. Beneath, he wore a white button down and held in his hand a black necktie. He still did not know how to tie the knot but was happy to hear the hallway and staircase sounds of his mother up and about the house.

"Mom," called Ira, venturing toward the stairs. He came down into the kitchen whereupon he saw the sun streaming in through the front door, and at the other side of the house, his mother sitting at the table with the morsels of picked over breakfast toast on a small plate before her. Ira's mood fell some when he saw she was still wearing her sleeping clothes.

"Mom?" he said again. Miriam looked up at his formal wear. She smiled weakly. He could see that clearly. His left eye did not break from her face for a long time.

"Would you like me to do it?"

"Please," said Ira. He lifted the necktie, and she came to him. She looped the fabric beneath his collar and adjusted it a few times until it hung to the gleam of his belt buckle. Ira's right eye watched how her hands did the knot, hoping to remember. At the same time, his left watched her face as she worked, contemplating something more tangled than the Windsor. When she finished, she stepped back to admire him. They stood in expectant silence until Miriam answered his unspoken question.

"I'm not coming, dear."

Ira nodded.

"I'll call Furke," he said.

WHEN FURKE ARRIVED HE WAS on his bike. Ira waited outside on the porch where the spring breeze swelled, ushering in the growth of the season. Leaves in the treetops had retaken their place. Rob-

JACOB KOCKEN

in nests and those of grey squirrels hidden high in the nooks of branches were laden with the weight of their young. One of Ira's eyes watched a mother bird as she returned to the clutch. The other eye took in Furke as he rolled up the driveway. He too was dressed in nice clothes. He did not wear a suit like Ira, but in his khaki pants and button down still appeared ready for a special Sunday.

Ira's eye wouldn't let go of the robin in the tree. When he stood up and greeted his friend the picture of little beaks peaking out over the nest's edge was half of what he saw. The mother held something in her mouth and dipped in quick, successive fashion.

Furke took Ira by the hand. He led him a few steps down the driveway to where the bike was parked. The one of Ira's eyes continued to observe the feeding robins. His other eye found the pegs of Furke's back tire. Ira climbed aboard and leaned in against his friend's back. He held Furke's shoulders tightly as they set off down the pavement.

Though they'd done it many times now, the ride still made Ira uncomfortable. Things passed by too quickly. He found his eyes lighting in different directions on house doors, addresses, passersby, darting animals, and a dozen other pieces of the changing environment. The same thing happened when he rode beside his mother in the car. With too much to pay attention to, Ira shut his eyes and focused on the feeling of the tire beneath him and leaning carefully into the momentum as Furke turned the bike down one street after another.

Before they arrived at St. Francis church, Ira heard the great metal bells calling ten o'clock. They rolled in to a parking lot full as always for Sunday Mass. People trickled in from each corner of the lot toward the tall wooden doors as Furke and Ira pulled up beside them. Ira stepped carefully off the back of the bike. Both his eyes found the faces of different parishioners as they approached the church. Many of the faces, he knew. All of them, it seemed, knew him. Some smiled in his direction, linking with the eye that met them and nodding or mouthing a pleasant salutation. Others darted away as soon as a roving eye found theirs watching him. Their heads dropped to the ground concealing private displeasures.

Furke took Ira's hand again after he'd leant the bike safely against the stone wall of the church. The two ambled inside through

RISE THE MOON

the gathering space like young lovers, or father and son, or infirm and guardian, and came to the piscina at the sanctuary's entrance. This, Ira needed no help to do, for his right eye found the water as soon as they stepped through the threshold. Ira dipped his free fingers into the water and made over himself the sign of the cross. There was a sharp coolness to his forehead where the holy water had touched. At the same time, the rest of his face went warm as his left eye peered up at the bloody crucifixion.

The earsplitting cry of an infant was cutting through the church. It was not uncommon. Children often cried during Mass. But now, in the preceding quiet, the cry was especially conspicuous. Furke ushered Ira forward and they made their way to the front pews of the church. There they stopped and looked down an ancient bench of yew wood without a single soul sitting upon it. Not a single soul, save for one. At the center of the pew was a woman. Her pink hair was modestly styled, and she wore a light blue blouse with a white collar. Her skirt flowed all the way to her ankles as she sat and was fashioned with the floral pattern of daisies and lace. And in her lap there lay a child no more than four weeks old. She rocked the baby slowly, staring always down upon his face, floating lost in the little world inside his squinted eyes. It was this child whose crying sliced through the sanctuary.

As Ira approached her, one of his eyes scanned the congregation. They were looking at him, and those who weren't were eyeing the pink head in the front pew. There was a hush upon the benches. It was a silence not of tranquility but of words spoken too softly to be heard by anyone but those nearest.

The woman's head rose as Ira stepped beside her. She looked startled for a moment. Then her expression softened when she recognized the boys.

"Ira," she said. "It's good to see you." Her voice was almost as quiet as those who whispered about her. She greeted Furke as well, and the boys sat beside her. Ira took a moment to admire the face of his baby brother. The child had no hair at all yet. He was dressed in a white ceremonial gown. His hands were small enough that they barely wrapped Ira's index finger on the few occasions he'd been to see him. The child's skin was usually a pearly white. Today, however, he was red with emotion. His little lips curled up

JACOB KOCKEN

and down like rolling waves, and he seemed nearly gasping for air between his countless shrieking breaths.

"How's Ben?" Ira asked.

"Oh," mumbled Darla. Her face was weary suddenly, a sallow color in her skin was brought out especially strong by the contrasting blue she wore. "He's alright. He's just been fussy since we got here."

"He must know it's a big day."

"Yes. Yes, that must be all."

The little boy's mouth wrinkled as his crying broke and renewed again second after second. Ira caught with his right eye two of the people behind them, one man and one woman, reaching inconspicuous hands to their ears. Then from the other side, the motion of a black suit came into view and Ira's left eye found a familiar face. He stood and embraced his grandfather. Frank had lost weight. His jacket hung away from his body like an awning and bunched up in the back beneath the pressure of Ira's arms. The size he'd lost in the horizontal plain seemed to have transferred to the vertical. He stood tall, and Ira had to tilt his head up for his gaze to connect with the old man's.

His grandfather went to greet the child. Frank held Darla by the shoulder as he cooed over the crying infant. "Thanks for coming, Frank," Darla said.

"I wouldn't miss a party for the world," said Frank. The old man sat down on the other side of Ira. His breath smelled of toothpaste mint.

Soon the bell high in the steeple began to chime again. The knells came four times with deep, vibrating waves that signaled the start of Mass. A few more people hurried in from the gathering space, and then two sets of the three sanctuary doors were closed. The middle one stayed open, awaiting the procession of priest, deacon, and acolytes. Sunlight poured through the ceiling windows and the stained glass; each beam bent toward the center of the dais. The cloud of white noise whispers dissipated as everyone took their seats and looked up toward the altar. For some time, the congregation looked up at the empty table, the Savior nailed to His post hung high in the background. And the only sound was little Ben's bawling.

RISE THE MOON

When several minutes had passed, Ira looked up from his contemplation. The pianist was sitting at her instrument, but her hands did not dance. Instead of playing the processional song, she was turned at ninety degrees, and her spine stretched tall so she could see the better over the congregation. Ira's other eye looked in the same direction as the musician. The entrance door at the back of the sanctuary was open. Two acolytes dressed in white robes stood at the threshold. Their faces in turn were also spun behind them to where the deacon stood in his dalmatic talking with another man. This second person was dressed plainly but wore one of the wooden crosses borne by all the St. Francis ushers. The two of them were speaking rapidly and went bustling in and out of sight. Most of the attention in the crowd abandoned Ben's wailing and turned on the little commotion at the door.

"Where is Father David?" said Ira as the deacon came swiftly into the sanctuary and disappeared into a side door that Ira knew to lead to their dressing rooms.

"I just saw him yesterday," said Frank. "He heard my confession. Let's have patience. There's a lot on his mind."

The echoing din of the steeple bells had long fallen away. Their place had been taken by a murmur. Ira turned back to face the dais and wait. The altar was empty save for its adorning fabrics. The lectern stood bare where its liturgical book should reside. Darla began to stir. Sunlight from the rising day pierced through the clear windows as well as the stained-glass saints landing strong and focused on these first pews. Little Ben went on crying as if a thorn were stuck somewhere into his fragile flesh.

Minutes passed slowly, and the murmur of the crowd began to ripple again. Then a rumble broke the silence as one of the pews behind Ira was pushed inadvertently back. A coterie of well-dressed parishioners had stood up and begun a walk down the center aisle to exit the church. They were followed by several others, and soon the congregation became a mountain range of sitters and standers. As the impatient line filed out, the deacon reentered the sanctuary. A look of surprise overcame his countenance, and he rushed to signal the pianist as he took his place between the acolytes.

Chords from the piano muddled together with the plodding sound of feet as some parishioners continued to exit, others stopped where they were, and the deacon led his partial procession down toward the dais. He carried the liturgical tome and set it in its place. Instead of taking his customary seat at the end of the dais, the deacon remained standing as the music faded, and those who remained in the pews peered up at him behind the altar.

"Brothers and sisters," he said. Whether it was the music that had played, the soft voice of the deacon, or the constant rocking from his mother, as the Mass began, little Ben's incessant tears came to a merciful halt. "Brothers and sisters, we thank you for joining us on this beautiful spring morning. And thank you for your patience as we begin an unusual Mass. Please excuse Father David as he has found himself unexpectedly indisposed."

"He's sick?"

The voice had called out from the crowd. It was a sonorous voice increased in volume by the hard echoing walls of the church. It seemed to shake the timber as well as the bones of parishioners all around. A deep hush followed in its wake. Ira looked back as did the rest of the crowd. Heads turned all about to see who had spoken. Very seldom did a voice rise up in question during a Mass. The only people wont to speak aloud besides those on the dais were children who could not yet recognize decorum.

"He is indisposed," said the deacon in answer. The long folds of the ecumenical gown swung behind him as the deacon turned to approach the lectern.

"Does that mean he's sick?" came the voice again. This time it was followed by a swell of voices. Those in the wake of the booming voice were mixed with tones of support and scorn. Shoulders turned, and several people stood up again. The attention in everyone's eyes was flitting back and forth between the holy assistant on the dais and one man in the middle of the crowd.

"I don't know," said the deacon. "It appears to be a personal matter, brother."

"Ha!" Then the man who'd spoken took to his feet. A hulking suit charcoal dark rose up from the pews. The man stood tall with shoulders so broad that from where Ira sat he blocked all of the multicolored light from one of the windowed saints. "I'm not your brother," said the man.

"Please be seated," said the deacon. "I will lead us in celebrat-

RISE THE MOON

ing the Mass today, and I expect a normal service again next week."

"You're not a priest." This time the voice issued not from the bellows of the giant man but from somewhere else in the crowd. Ira's right eye scanned over the congregation to see who'd spoken, but they all sat or stood with quite comparable expressions of concern, and the deacon was left to address, rather than any individual, the uneasy spirit of the crowd who felt to be congealing more and more strongly in the air.

"I have no authority to consecrate the Eucharist. But I'm capable of everything else called for in a Mass. Please be seated brothers and sisters. We have a baptism to get to as well."

"Ha!" The giant man's body aimed to face the front pew where Ira sat beside Darla and her child. Ben was once again tortured with screams, his wants invisible to the weary mother. Now everyone looked on as Darla tried to comfort her baby. Her face went red as the attention of the crowd settled solely on her bright pink hair. Ira saw her one by one meet the faces around her. They were fixed and knowing. Word of sins of course had spread. "Well," said the big man in the pews. His echoing voice melded with another rumbling as a turn of his broad body pushed the pew back even further. Long strides took him into the aisle. With his back turned, he said aloud to the congregation, "Perhaps our priest had good sense to absent himself today." And just as he neared the entrance to the gathering area, the giant man came to the piscina with its tranquil water blessed just the day before. Instead of dipping his fingers to the surface, the man walked by and with a powerful hip collided with the great stone bowl. It seemed hardly to faze him, and indeed, he did not turn back to see as the bowl moved off kilter on its stand. A grinding sound gasped through the air as the heavy marble tipped, and with no piping to keep the pieces aligned, they came plummeting to the floor of the church.

A chorus of hollers came up from the people, led in volume by little Ben whose fear had seemed renewed by the crash. The stone bowl had cracked down the center, spilling holy water into the grooves of the floor that ran like forsaken streams until the weight of them was exhausted and they came to crawling halts along the grout, waiting hopelessly to dry. The parishioners who had not been standing now were. A hurry captured the crowd as

JACOB KOCKEN

people moved toward the door in confusion, fear, and shame. The deacon's voice was speaking over them but could not be discerned through such commotion. Ira's right eye watched the giant man in the charcoal suit disappear out the door with a herd of sheep behind him. They poured toward the exit, and Ira caught with his left eye the swiftness with which Darla stood and set baby Ben down in his carrier. In a moment, the pink hair had merged into the sea of people between the pews.

"Follow her," Ira said urgently with an eye on both his friend and his grandfather. Frank and Furke each took him by one hand and led his blinded steps over the tile. Ira felt his feet splash as they hurried past the baptismal font. He did not catch sight of it though. Both his eyes were searching desperately for the mother of his brother.

Soon the world beyond the church opened up and they stepped into daylight. People blustered through the parking lot; all of their backs turned to St. Francis as they marched out to find their cars. The flow out the door continued, and everyone moved in the same direction. Then, like a salmon who climbs the rocks upstream, the face of one woman showed itself amongst the crowd of those leaving.

"Mom!" Ira called out. Miriam, who was climbing the steps up from the parking lot, found him with a look of consternation.

"What's happened?" she said to the three of them. "Church isn't out this early."

"Father David isn't here," said Frank.

"Where is he?"

"We don't know details. Have you seen Darla and Benjamin?"

Miriam's head turned away from them. Rather than out into the parking lot, her eyes pointed down the drive to where the sidewalk stretched. The form of a woman was receding into the distance. She moved hurriedly, and the color of her hair burst under the bright sunlight.

The four of them hurried down to Miriam's car. Frank took the front seat while Furke helped Ira into the back. They peeled out of their parking stall, but the line of cars had jammed up the drive with fleeing parishioners. For the space of two or three minutes, they waited and inched forward over the pavement. When at last the car

RISE THE MOON

was free of the church grounds Miriam turned off in the direction they'd seen Darla walking. But as far as the eye could see, there was no woman or child trodding the sidewalk.

"Do you see her?" said Miriam.

"No," Frank sighed. "She must've gone home. Her last name is Hoakenson, right? There's some of them toward the school. By the water tower. Are those her parents?"

"Maybe."

"She doesn't live there anymore," said Ira. "Her parents told her to leave when she got pregnant."

"They did?" his mother said.

"Well, do you know where she lives now?" asked Frank.

"Yes," said Ira. "It's in Old Graumont."

Miriam spun the car around, and the four of them headed east. Ira sat on the passenger side of the backseat and his right eye rolled itself tirelessly out among the passing houses, the yards, and fences for any sign of Darla. His other rogue was fixed in one spot. In the thin rectangular reflection of the rearview mirror, Ira could see his mother's stoic face. She was chewing something, and her eyes seemed glazed with thought as she drove by instinct and habit over conscious decision.

It was a short way to the old river that divided Graumont. Soon they were on Lennox Street and the prairie across the way opened up beneath the sky. They could see all the way to the forest and a mile in either direction. It was beside the bridge that the hanging pink head was spotted bobbing up and down on a labored gait. The baby carrier dangled in one hand, but the child was held in the other. Darla turned her back to West Graumont and began crossing the stony archway when they pulled up to the curb.

Frank was the first one out of the car and Ira heard his grandfather's voice calling out to the woman while he himself waited for Furke to come around to the passenger side. Then Ira's door was opened and Furke took him by the hand, helping to find ground underfoot as Ira's eyes fixed simultaneously on the chasm and the child. Darla's hair flashed as she turned countenance toward the call of her name. Then it swung back like a curtain in front of her face when she saw them, and her face fell to the earth. Ira saw between his visions a blurred silhouette of his grandfather running up

JACOB KOCKEN

to the bridge. Furke ushered Ira in the same direction. They stumbled twice in their hurry, but soon the squishing of grass under Ira's shoes became the stability of stone and Ira's left hand found one of the short bridge walls.

There was the sound of a plastic clatter when Ira saw Ben's carrier toppling on the ground. The baby was in his mother's arms, crying just as passionately now as he had between the walls of St. Francis. Darla was being released from an embrace with Frank. Her head stayed down, and when Ira came close enough to get a look at her face he saw her eyes, like the infant's, were as hot and red as the rising sun.

"Is he cursed?" blurted the tearing woman.

"What?" said Frank. "No. No, don't talk like that."

"He's cursed because of me. I know it. Everyone in church knew it. Even he knows it, doesn't he? That's why he won't stop. He just won't stop crying." Darla tilted the baby back away from her so that they looked face to face. Ira saw each one of them at once. Both were growing tired. Darla's arms were beginning to tremble, and in them, Ben was wobbling. Ira went dizzy. His visions crossed and uncrossed as their focal points on the faces of mother and son focused into androgyny. Darla's partial expression broke, and the same rippling moans that came from little Ben began to issue from her throat as well. The resonance of their song was a choral cry.

"Why is he doing this to me?" Darla groaned. "Why is he doing it?" The mother's grip had weakened so that she held her child on the precarious balance of her forearm. Ira feared he may soon fall if Darla continued to sob, and he pulled Furke forward by the hand so that his guide might take the direction and leave him to save the baby. But before Furke had the chance to reach out, another body stepped between them and with one skillful arm swept beneath the fussing infant to take him up into a steady cradle.

Miriam held the child and looked down at him with palpable pity. It shone through her focused eyes, and Ira could see her nostrils flaring as she took in the scent of the new one. For a moment, she was lost far away from them just as Ira had found Darla in her church pew. Then Miriam's gaze flicked up toward the pink-haired woman, and Ira noticed the involuntary flash full of anger and sad-

RISE THE MOON

ness. Her stare washed back to the child. Then it sparked again at Darla. So quickly did her pupils move that Ira could have sworn she too had found separate sights.

"He smells like Ira," said Miriam quietly. "Just like Ira used to."

Ira, touched by his mother's tenderness, stepped forward to be beside her. As he did so, he stumbled and found himself kicking the carrier that had fallen to the ground.

"Darla," said Ira, looking at Ben with one eye and the carrier with the other. "Did you walk all the way to St. Francis this morning?" The new mother nodded. She was still choking on tears of frustration and had no heart to answer aloud. Ira's head tilted back to see the sky. Sunrays warmed the skin of his cheeks. It was one of the first times since early the previous autumn that the sensation had really touched him. "We ought to cool him a bit." With that, Ira took his mother by the hand and instructed Furke to lead them down into the gorge where the trickling water ran. Frank followed Miriam and led the struggling Darla as the six of them moved in procession across the bridge.

One at a time, they descended the stony steps. Ira saw many things on the way down. He saw the sloping rock face, smooth in places and jagged in others. He saw the painted works of graffiti which told broken, convoluted stories. He saw the memory of his tumbling friend who now entered the pit again holding his hand. He saw his mother whose stolid face watched over a stranger's son. He saw his grandfather, thinning so that the muscle showed once again down his arms. He saw a woman whose bright pink coiffure had struck him as solemnly familiar only weeks ago on the day he met his new brother. He saw Ben whose face was turning as pink as if it were a gene passed down by his mother. He saw the flame in the sky that lit the world, and also the stream that washed across the ground.

Ira set foot to the floor of the gorge. Furke led him around the stones and cracks to where the water ran. It was still Miriam holding Ben when the rest of the party joined the spot. The palm of her broken, clutching hand opened as wide as possible to cushion his head. Ira bent a knee and dipped his palm into the shallow creek. It came up with only a miniscule pool collected atop his shining,

JACOB KOCKEN

wet fingers. He turned and pressed the palm over Ben's forehead. Immediately, the baby's cry redoubled. The shock of cold water had frightened him. Then, gradually, as the minutes passed and Ira continued to drip relief over the infant's head, Ben began to calm. His quavering lips stiffened, and the overflow of water in his eyes dried up. Darla let out a long exhale.

53.
David

DAVID'S FOOT FELL HEAVY ON the gas pedal. The houses went by in blurs. When the street came for David to turn home, he passed it, going on beyond the suburbs to where the corn grew. It was night, and those waifish stalks bent as David dragged the wind behind him. In time, the farm fields gave way to prairies, and the prairies to the brush and pine of the forest. He traveled north. David stared straight ahead, following nothing but the pavement beneath the tunnel shine of his high beams. He drove in silence. Only the hum of the flight accompanied him, and he sank into its lull. His shoulders relaxed. His white knuckles around the wheel slowly regained the hue of man.

He drove the tank dry and stopped for gas just as the first rays of sun began to light the sky.

"Fishing at the lake?" said the attendant when David went to pay.

"Sorry?"

"Saw you coming up from the south. The only thing out where you're headed is trees and lakes. Mostly it's folks going fishing. We have a bait section 'round the corner here. Live minnows and everything."

"You don't sell line and poles too, do you?"

"Only that for a serious outdoorsman. And you sir, you got the look of a man who's ready to spend a day on the lake."

JACOB KOCKEN

There were indeed several different poles, line of varied strengths, jigs, and lures of every kind. A set of hooks called *The Shepherd's Crook* caught his eye, and David returned to the car with a box of worms and a new pole fixed up for fishing. It had strong, hopeful line and a steel hook; sharp and bigger than David had ever used before.

"Take this too," said a voice. The attendant was coming out the door behind him holding a small brochure aloft. He approached and handed the thing to David. "It's a map of all the lakes and camp grounds up north. All the best spots are marked for fifty miles. Happy fishing."

"Thank you," said David. The man nodded and returned inside as David stowed the things away into his car.

The road turned east, and David chased the sun as it rose. He dropped the sun visor to cover the bulk of its shine across his windshield, and before long, a smile was escaping him at the sight of a new day. Brisk morning air came through his open windows. It blew his hair about and woke his face from the trance of the night. A ray of sun caught the smooth steel of the fishing hook nocked high in the pole's top eye across the back seat. It twinkled like a morning star. David laughed. The pedal came down again, this time with joy, and the engine revved with his laughter. His reflection in the rearview mirror was new. Younger, he thought. He flipped on the radio to find *Rocky Mountain High* flowing on the rich tones of Denver. He sang along. He sang loud into rolling wind while following small wooden road signs down to the edge of a lake that ran wide and shone with a diamond's brilliance.

He left the car parked off the edge of a dirt road and marched his new pole to the water's bank. There was a great, long-fallen tree which he made his seat. The box of worms he placed near his feet, beneath the rounded shade of the log, and taking one of them to the hook, pierced its body through and through. The hook was nearly as long as the fingers that held it, and one worm could not cover the whole gleaming thing. David pierced a second worm and together they wriggled over the length of the steel. He cast his rig out into the endless lake where steady hands waited for tension in the line. They did not plead for a catch; rather, they simply sat, feeling the delicate shifts in the wind and the waves. And so David

RISE THE MOON

sat too, facing west to put the risen sun behind him. The scent of forest pines was pleasing. He listened to the bullfrogs croak in their hiding among the tall lake grass. Now and then, a dash would catch the corner of his eye as the amphibians sprung, darts disappearing below the surface.

With the occupation, some of the spring chill left him. David dropped the end of his pole to the ground. Holding it up between both knees, he undid the collar about his neck. He set it on the log beside him and breathed a free, relaxing breath. The top button of his shirt had come undone with it, letting in the breeze.

As he sat there, he realized an uncomfortable strain in his left pants pocket. His hand dug in and pulled out the rock he'd saved from some months before at Lake Duval. Big enough to cover the best of his palm, it was gray and replete with little pieces of sediment that shined in the sunlight like a poor man's gem. It was oblong, round but slightly more so on one side. Perhaps it was the fossilized form left behind by some desperately brooding reptile as the age of the dinosaurs ended, for it was a perfect little egg.

David rolled it in his hand and thought of the little girl he'd met at the lake; Ira Foster's friend. He had not seen her again in any of the months between then and now, and he wondered if she still carried that stone of little crystals. If she did, he wondered if one of her legs was considerably weaker from constant lugging. His egg stone was heavy; it weighed on his belt when it was in his pocket and felt as though it were pushing a hole through his hand as he held it now. Perhaps the time had come already when that little girl turned to regard her burden as a jewel. He hoped it had. That would be very good for her.

Then David leaned back and put all his body weight behind the stone as it shot from his clenched fist into a long, teardrop arc over the water. It plummeted from the clouds to the bottom of the world in a second with little more disturbance to the scene than if a baby bass broke the surface for a whim. Ripples spread in quick, perfect circles for the space of a few seconds. Then the lake forgot them, and the water was as tranquil as ever.

A swift tug came at the end of the fishing pole, and David forgot all else. His hands scrambled to set the hook, and when he felt the thing pull back his blood rose. David took to his feet and

JACOB KOCKEN

reeled. He tried to peer past the water as his line approached, but the surface gleamed indistinctly, half window and half mirror. It came close enough to break the surface, to thrash at the air before loosing itself from the line and dissolving back into the lake. Its dark shadow swam off toward a little eastward bed of lily pads, and David hurried to cast in that direction. The line was loose, and in haste he forgot to flip the reeling barrel. In a moment, everything was tangled. The big hook swung back, cleaned now of its bait, and David fussed with his mess of a spool. With the line reined back in, it stuck out from the center in a dozen disorderly loops. He spun out yard after yard of string before locating the knot. He tried the coils with his fingers and teeth, but pulling one end only tightened another, and David resorted in the end to snapping the spun thread in Gordian resignation.

"Goddamn," he muttered. Just as David had retied the hook and began to restring the eyes of the pole, there was a slow rustling in the forest that lifted his head. She wore a long white garment; loose fitting and soft, such as a parent might dress their child for baptism. It was stained by dirt and long use. Frayed ends hung from tears in the fabric that when her body shifted through the brush, revealed naked skin.

Her head hung down from the shoulders. Long black hair veiled her face. Her blouse rippled in the wind and gave her a strange, ambiguous shape. Her steps pushed through the fallen yellow leaves, a slow and rhythmic sound like the coming tide. She was barefoot. Then the noise stopped abruptly. Her hand went to the trunk of a maple tree, and her head snapped in his direction. For a moment, she froze, fawnlike. Then her body leaned into the maple's towering shadow.

David dropped the pole and took two quick steps in her direction. She flinched, curling her back and retreating further behind the trunk of another tree. David stopped still.

"Hello?" he called.

There was no response. Only the ends of her hair and garment were visible where they fluttered in the wind. From this outline, David saw how she hunched under the canopy's broken shade. Her head darted from place to place, tucking furtively back when the bright, ubiquitous sun fingered her anxious expression.

RISE THE MOON

Again, David approached, this time more delicate. He stopped, startled in turn when her face peeked out from its dark, gnarled shield. She had large and searching eyes that took account of his every breath. He called again, softer.

"Hello?"

David crouched and took to a knee. Cold morning dew soaked through the leg of his pants. It chilled his bones, and he saw too how she shivered in place. He knelt like a statue for the space of a dozen breaths.

With guarded arms and bent knees, she emerged. The blue glow of frostbite stretched up from her soiled feet, and with every step, she seemed to stumble. But she came nearer. Her eyes didn't blink.

"What's your name?" David asked. She came within a foot of where he knelt. Still, she said nothing, and he worried the cold had done too much. He rose and took her by the shoulder. There was an immediate, furtive retreat, but her stone face cracked at the warmth of his hand, and she leaned cautiously to his chest. She was freezing to the touch, and only with her body up against his did David notice the bulge about her waist.

"Oh my," said David, hardly audible. With one hand he felt the budding arc. His eyes widened as he saw now how the cloth she wore traced a bump several months along. And in the short time his palm rested there, perhaps in response to the warmth of his touch, he felt the kick. It was soft and singular, but the woman felt it too, and her hand shot down to the spot. A whining noise crept from her throat as she looked down at her stomach and back up at the world. Her eyes darted all over the forest; at trees, rocks, and animals, coming always back to her bulging belly in between, attempting to find a link. David's mouth fell open, and he tried to usher her back toward the car. "You need to get inside. Both of you."

But her feet, stiff as blocks, moved no more. She became heavy against him as her knees gave way. David swung the woman up into his arms. He held her just as she might soon hold the spring flower. She was stained by the scent of evaporated sweat, that of soured milk. And as they marched through the chill of the forest, nearing the abandoned pole and collar, she flung her arms around his neck and quivered with tears.

Her throat shook with a whine. The sound rose and fell as she worked her delicate jaw against his shoulder. Two shattered syllables broke out. She said them again; then again as soon as they left her mouth. David sured his grip on her thin and bulging body. He hushed her, tender as he could manage. "What's your name?" he asked. When the woman answered him her lips quivered and met uncertainly, as if she were only now learning to speak.

"Papa," she said.

Then David's arms began to shake and give way under the weight of the woman. He let her fall slowly near the shore and helped her sit carefully down on the old tree trunk. She clutched at his clothes.

"Stay here," he said. "I have a map. I'll find a hospital." She whined again when David started to run. When he looked back she was staring after him. She was touching her stomach with one hand and wringing a long mess of black hair with the other. Her eyes were big and full of fear. But her feet were blue and her legs were stiff, and David did not believe she could run off even had she wanted to.

He ran some fifty feet up the forest path to where his car sat parked. The brochure of wild area lay in the back seat, and he flipped frantically from one page to another. It showed mostly the green hue of wilderness, but the winding country roads did eventually find a town thirty miles off from where he was. No hospital showed on the map, but there would at least be people. There would at least be warm places for the woman and her infant to rest.

He tossed the map onto his dashboard and turned back to bring the woman. The strength in his arms was recovered enough, and he felt sure he could carry her the length of the path if need be.

Speeding back toward the lake, his breath broke loudly over the tranquil scene. The water was flat. The wind was still. The great fallen tree where he'd sat her down was empty. His head swung from side to side as he approached the spot. She did not move fast. He had only been gone a minute. He looked out at the lake in momentary fear. But then she groaned. The sound came from the shoreline, and when David followed its call a dozen more steps revealed her form lying flat-backed against the ground. She lay near the great log, shielding her from sight on one side. What he saw first were her knees. They were pointed up toward the sky.

RISE THE MOON

From several feet away, the fishing pole, abandoned earlier by its new owner, jumped. It moved a foot, scraping across the shoreline stones. Rather than to the water, it came towards David, towards the woman. The line was nearly invisible, but it caught his eye with subtle vibrations as it went taut, then slack, then taut again. He followed it up between her feet where it disappeared beneath the long white fabric. One of her hands was hidden down there too. She groaned again. The other hand, the one not hidden under garments, felt around at her stomach, searching. Her eyes were closed; shut tight so that wrinkles made of strain covered her whole expression.

David stopped in surprise. Then he sprang forward in unison with the fishing pole as it jumped once again. The woman had groaned a third time, and now her body jerked in similar fashion. The volume of her voice had risen. Her knees bent and snapped, kicking the open air and dragging in the dirt. Then a spot of red appeared. It seeped over the once blank whiteness of her dress. It was heavy there, and the fabric hung down to rest against her flesh. Her fingers worked.

Then David was at her side. An iron smell found him. He tried to calm her, but she did not hear his words. He spoke them frantically, yet they seemed not to pierce her ears. Her free hand was wandering over the stomach still, and he caught it. She squeezed him with her frozen fingers. His own knuckles turned colorless as if she stole the blood away, and, slowly, her kicking legs began to ease. Her soles found steady earth again, and her crying fell to whimpers. The hand beneath her dress relaxed. The fishing line stopped jumping.

She winced when he put a hand to her arm. He tugged softly at the elbow until she relinquished grip on the hook. Her hand retracted from beneath the dress. The fingers were wet and red. David moved uncertainly toward her feet. He found the fishing line with his own fingers and lifted it with caution. He pulled as lightly as he could manage. The woman squealed. The anchor was set.

David dropped the line. Then he dropped his stomach to the ground. He looked as quickly as he could. The sun shined through her soiled dress. Blood soaked into the ground beneath her. The hook could not be seen.

JACOB KOCKEN

David went immediately to the fishing pole some feet away and unspooled several feet of string. Once it was slack, he wrapped two hands worth and pulled, breaking the line. Then he went again to the woman. She lay still; almost tranquil. The hand once on her stomach had fallen to her side.

She was even heavier this time when David lifted her body. But his arms did not give way the whole walk up to his car. Dots of blood fell onto the dirt and rocks with teardrop splashes, bursting at the edges like little suns. Some of them dried that way as the real sun looked down strong and bright. Others were smeared by the subtle, sweeping weight of the fishing line as it trailed on the ground across them.

Jacob Kocken was born in 1994. He attended the University of Wisconsin-Stevens Point and subsequently lived in myriad places around the Midwestern United States. His study and writing centers on the intersection between psychology, religion, and literature. He currently lives in Green Bay, Wisconsin.